PRAISE FOR THE NOVELS OF JANE PORTER

"Jane Porter has written her way into his reader's heart."
—Susan Wiggs, *New York Times* bestselling author
of *Snowfall in the City*

"Porter writes with genuine warmth and quiet grace about the everyday problems all women face."
—*Chicago Tribune*

"She understands the passion of grown-up love . . . smart, satisfying."
—Robyn Carr, #1 New York Times bestselling author
of *Return to Virgin River*

"[Porter's] musings on balancing work, life, and love ring true."
—*Entertainment Weekly*

"Once more Porter is able to write about painful life situations with dignity, grace, and authenticity. What might be heavy and depressing in other writers' hands is gentle and cathartic in Porter's."
—*Library Journal*

"Two stories of heartbreak and loss wrap into one, demonstrating the depth of emotion humans are capable of and how extensive the healing process can sometimes be."
—RT Book Reviews

"An extremely well-written, emotional, and resonating story of grief and with an ending that isn't traditionally happy and neat. . . . For fans of Porter's Brennan Sisters trilogy, you'll be delighted with a number of guest appearances."
—Chicklitplus.com

FLIRTING

with

FIFTY

JANE PORTER

JOVE
New York

A JOVE BOOK
Published by Berkley
An imprint of Penguin Random House LLC
penguinrandomhouse.com

A JOVE BOOK, BERKLEY, and the BERKLEY & B colophon
are registered trademarks of Penguin Random House LLC.

ISBN: 9780593438381

First Edition: May 2022

Printed in the United States of America
1   3   5   7   9   10   8   6   4   2

Book design by George Towne

For Ty
My forever love

$$Chapter\ 1$$

IT WAS HOT.

And Paige Newsome was angry. No, make that boiling, as she stared steadily at Dr. Zayed Nair, her department chair. She wasn't going to have a tantrum. She wasn't a little girl. At forty-nine, she was strong, disciplined, and professional to the core. But really. *Seriously?* Dr. Nair wanted her to teach another course now, two weeks before the semester started, a course where she'd team teach with a visiting instructor?

"This is a lot to take in," she said tightly, wishing Dr. Nair would just once, once, turn on his air conditioner when temperatures were in the nineties. His office felt like an oven, and normally she could just leave, but she couldn't just leave now. Dr. Nair claimed he thought better when he was warm, but she felt as if she'd melt. Or explode. "I don't know what to say."

Dr. Nair's hands lifted, gestured broadly. "'Yes' would be nice?"

They both knew that wasn't the answer she wanted to give. They both knew he'd promised not to put her in this position again, but here she was. Paige squared her shoulders, gave her right arm a faint shake, making the bangles on her wrist softly clink. "There's really no one else who can do this?"

"I've asked."

She could feel the scratchy weight of her ponytail against her neck and the bold cat-eye glasses she liked to wear slip down her nose. She wasn't glowing, but sweating, and if she'd known this was why Dr. Nair wanted to meet with her, she would have just stayed home. "No grad students who could take it on?"

"It's not appropriate for a grad student. We need some-one with experience, someone with an outstanding reputa-tion. You have both."

"I don't mean to be rude, Dr. Nair, but how hard did you try to find a replacement before you decided on me?"

"I put out a call via email to the entire department, there were no takers."

Paige had noticed that as well, but she hoped he'd done more than just send the one email. She hoped he'd actually reached out to individuals directly. "Am I the first one you approached?"

"Esther suggested you."

"And here I thought Esther was my friend," Paige mut-tered.

Dr. Nair gave her a patient smile. "She is. That's why she suggested you. You'll be teaching with the legendary Pro-fessor King."

Paige pictured an elderly man leaning heavily on a cane. "What makes him legendary?"

"He's one of the most respected teaching scientists in the world."

"And he's going to be teaching for Orange?" She couldn't mask her incredulity.

"It's a huge win for us. We've got him for a year, and we want to take advantage of this opportunity. The alumni are thrilled. Dr. Keller is thrilled. Jack King's a fantastic instructor—"

"*Jack* King?" she interrupted, skin prickling. She'd known a Jack King, thirty odd years ago, and he wasn't an elderly man leaning on a cane. He'd been a PhD candidate, participating in an international forum she'd attended in Paris. He'd also been sex on two legs. She was fairly certain they weren't one and the same, but *still*. Paige hadn't thought of him in years, and yet it was still so easy to picture him. Tall, broad shoulders, handsome.

A great kisser. Adventurous in bed.

Her cheeks heated at the last.

"He's one of the leading epidemiologists in the world, and he's going to bring the college a lot of publicity. It'll be good for Orange. Alumni are already writing checks."

Paige was still trying to figure out if the legendary Jack King was her Jack King—not that he was hers, that was stretching it. But she needed to know.

Dr. Nair was still talking, hands gesturing broadly. "Private universities depend on donations, and thanks to Professor King, we will see some significant funding for the Veneman College of Science and Technology."

Paige couldn't complain about that. The College of Science and Technology had been overlooked for years. It needed new technology, new laboratories, an upgrade to the building itself. "That's a win, then."

"It is." Dr. Nair gave her a sympathetic look. "So, we're all good? You'll take Esther's course?"

"I still don't know anything about it."

"You've taught statistics for years. It won't be a problem for you. You'll just be using a different book and syllabus."

"Which book?"

Dr. Nair shuffled through papers on his desk before shaking his head. "I don't have the details here. But Jack should be able to fill you in on everything. You'll be meeting him tomorrow. He flies in tonight from Delhi."

"Delhi?"

"He was speaking at a conference. He does that a lot."

"He won't be too jet-lagged?"

"Jack assured me he'll be fine."

Jack King couldn't be that elderly, then. Not unless he was Superman. "Where will we be meeting?"

"I'll text you the time and place. I'm trying to find something convenient for everyone."

"You'll attend?"

Dr. Nair nodded. "I'm looking forward to meeting Jack. And so are the alumni. We're hosting an event Friday night at President Keller's house. Make sure to save the date. You'll want to be there."

Paige stood, feeling more than a little queasy. "'Want to be there' as in, it's required to be there?"

He smiled, as if she'd made a joke. "Everyone from the College is attending. It's important we put on a good show."

As Paige left Dr. Nair's office, she got a sympathetic look from his secretary, Andi McDermott. "Sorry," Andi mouthed.

Paige nodded grimly, grateful for Andi in a department dominated by men. "Did you know?" she asked, aware that Andi had been an ally ever since Paige joined the Orange faculty.

"I tried to suggest a few others, but Dr. Nair was convinced you were the right one."

"Thank you for having my back."

"Always."

Paige continued down the hall to her office, a narrow shoebox of a space, but she loved the tall window that let in lots of light and gave her a view of the historic quad, surrounded by two- and three-story white plaster buildings topped by handcrafted red tiles. Located ten minutes from the mission in San Juan Capistrano and twenty minutes from the ocean, Orange University had been founded in 1896 as a university for men but shifted in the early thirties to include women.

Closing her door, she turned on the fan positioned on top of her filing cabinet and stood in front of the whirling blades, trying to cool down. She was hot and sticky and annoyed. As well as slightly panicked.

Someone else should have been tapped to teach the course. Someone else should have stepped up to teach with the legend. This was the second time in less than two years she'd been squeezed into a last-minute assignment. The second time Dr. Nair was in a bind, with no other options. It seemed rather ludicrous that she was the only option he ever had. Or was she the only one he could count on to say yes?

A light knock sounded on her door before it opened. Greg Hsu, an assistant professor in the Biological Science program, stuck his head around the door. "Hey," he said. "Bad time?"

"No," Paige said, adjusting the fan so that it could better circulate the air. "Come in." She gestured for him to take a seat across from her desk. Greg was one of her favorite people in the college. They'd both been hired the same year, although he was twenty years younger and ten times funnier. "You're back," she added.

"I am."

"Did you have a good summer?"

He dropped into the empty chair and folded his arms behind his head. "I did, but I'm exhausted. I think three kids is plenty. No more."

"I like my three," she agreed, sitting on a corner of her desk. "You guys did that national park road trip, didn't you? How did it go?"

"Eight parks in four weeks. Four thousand, six hundred, twenty-nine miles."

"That's a lot of driving."

"A lot of campgrounds. A lot of crying and fighting. A lot of dump stations. Glad to be home."

"I'd like to see the parks, but I'd do hotels, maybe those big lodges. Not a big fan of camping or cooking over an open fire."

"No open fires anymore, at least during summer."

"So how do you make s'mores?"

"Over a propane grill."

"Not the same."

"Kids didn't mind." Greg leaned forward. "And congrats. I just heard the news."

Her stomach did a flip. She felt like throwing up. "Who told you?"

"A school-wide email went out a moment ago."

Now she really felt like throwing up. "But I just left Dr. Nair's office."

"I think everyone knew it was pretty much a slam dunk. Let's face it, you make us look good. Smart, loyal, devoted to both students and faculty. You have an impeccable reputation."

"I sound like a well-trained Labrador."

He laughed. "And that's why I like you so much. That very dry sense of humor."

"Not so dry. You just happen to get me."

"I do. You're my favorite person in this department." Greg looked hopeful. "When do you meet him?"

"Tomorrow."

"Lucky dog—sorry, no pun intended."

She rolled her eyes. "None taken."

"You know, Jack King is one of the reasons I focused on ecology and epidemiology of infectious diseases."

"So, you know who he is?"

"I do."

She was dying to ask the questions hovering on the tip of her tongue. How old is Jack King? Is he hot? Is he Australian? Instead she forced the questions back and managed a careless shrug. "Too bad you can't teach the course with him."

"I don't teach math, you do."

"Math is part of what you do."

"Yes, but this is an interdisciplinary course between the science and math departments. You represent math. Dr. King represents science. I'm not needed." Greg's watch buzzed, and he glanced down. "It's the babysitter. Wife's working. I better take this. But I'll see you Friday night at President Keller's?"

"See you there." Paige forced a smile, but the moment the door closed, she wanted to scream. There were thirteen math instructors. Thirteen who could have taught the course. And as much as she appreciated Greg's vote of confidence, surely there was someone else on the faculty with a *more* stellar reputation?

Until two hours ago Paige had been looking forward to the start of the Fall semester. This summer had been unusually quiet, and she was excited about classes resuming. It hadn't been a typical summer. Summer was usually when she saw her girls, but this summer her daughters were busy with their own lives—working, traveling, auditioning—and instead of traveling to see them, Paige made frequent trips to Paso Robles to see her mom, as well as picking up tutoring jobs when she could. Paige wasn't good at relaxing. Life was just easier when one was busy.

But life wouldn't be easier if she was team teaching with a man, much less one she'd slept with thirty years ago. It was just one night, a crazy, hormone-fueled hookup that shouldn't have ever happened. She blamed Paris and the moonlight. Thank goodness she hadn't gotten pregnant. She'd gone on to earn multiple degrees and have a real life—

Her phone rang, interrupting the thought.

Paige reached across her desk, checking the number. It was Nichole, her middle daughter, a chemical engineer working in Chicago. Paige popped in her earbuds and took the call. "This is a nice surprise," she said, sitting down in her chair. Of her girls, Nichole was the most independent, and the one who reached out the least. "How are you?"

"Not so good," Nichole said flatly. "Andreas and I broke up."

"Oh, Nichole, no."

"We've been fighting a lot lately. I just got to the point I couldn't take it anymore. It didn't make sense to stay together if we weren't going to be happy."

"You broke up with him?"

"I didn't know what else to do."

Paige could tell Nichole was fighting tears, and she bit her lip, thinking of something wise or useful to say. "Are you regretting your decision?" she asked carefully, trying to feel her way. Nichole didn't like opening up, and she didn't like opinions, either.

"I miss him. I miss how we were, before everything was a hassle."

"When did things change?"

"A couple months ago, after I got the promotion."

Paige shook her head, finding it hard to keep up. "You got a promotion?"

"I was made manager of my department."

"You didn't tell me. That's wonderful, Nichole. Did the promotion come with a bump in salary?"

"A significant bump, and a lot more responsibility." Nichole's voice thickened with emotion. "That's why Andreas has been upset. He'd been up for the promotion, too. He thought he deserved it. I think he was sure he'd get it."

Oh dear. That explained a lot. But Paige wouldn't say that, not aloud, not now. "I'm sure he was also proud of you. There aren't many women working for your company, and certainly not many in management."

"He said he was happy for me, but ever since, he's been . . . just antagonistic. He picks fights over everything. It's like he resents me now."

"But Andreas doesn't report to you, does he?"

"No. We work similar jobs but answer to different directors."

"He hoped to come to your department, then?"

"I guess." Nichole drew a slow, shuddering breath. "Now we don't even talk. He's moved out—"

"You were living together?"

"For the past year, yeah."

"You never told me."

"I told you I got a roommate."

"Yes, but you never said Andreas was your roommate."

"Well, he isn't now, is he?"

Paige understood Nichole was hurt, and sensitive, and she let her daughter's frustration go. "This is rough," she said. "I'm really sorry you're having to go through this. Is there anything I can do?"

"No."

"I could come out for a weekend. I could come maybe next weekend?"

"No, that's okay. I'm fine. I just thought you should know."

Paige opened the calendar on her phone to check her schedule. "I'd love to see you, even for a quick visit. Twenty-four hours—"

"It's okay, Mom. I appreciate the offer, but I'd rather be alone."

Paige smashed the sting, refusing to let herself feel hurt. Nichole was struggling. Paige wouldn't make it about herself. "Call me anytime."

"Okay. Love you, Mom."

"Love you, too, sweetheart." Paige hung up the phone and sat for a moment, processing the call. It took her another moment to realize she wasn't alone. The university president, Dr. Keller, filled her doorway.

She rose from behind her desk. "Come in, Dr. Keller. I hope I didn't keep you waiting."

"Not at all. Am I interrupting?"

"No, of course not. It's good to see you." And suddenly Paige knew exactly why he was here. Dr. Keller had come to check on her, to make sure she was suitably enthusiastic about the new teaching assignment. It crossed her mind that this was her moment; she could let Dr. Keller know that she wasn't pleased to be adding a new course at such a late date. She could be honest and communicate her disappointment. She could stand up for herself—

"I understand you're meeting Dr. King tomorrow," Dr. Keller said, hands folding behind his back.

This was it. A chance to be an effective communicator. But the words of protest didn't come. She didn't like making waves. Her job in her marriage had been to solve problems, not create them. "Yes. Dr. Nair is setting up the meeting. I believe it's going to be in the afternoon."

"Dr. King's flying in from India."

Again, she wondered about the name, and the man. She needed to look him up. Get informed. "I heard. That's quite a long flight."

"Dr. King is one of the most respected ecology and evolutionary biologists in the world. You should see his curriculum vitae. If he's not in the classroom, he's either in the field or at a podium somewhere. Very impressive man."

"He's not English, is he?"

"Jack? No. Australian. Born and raised in Melbourne."

Her heart fell. Her stomach followed. Her Jack had been Australian, too.

"He's about your age," Dr. Keller added. "You're going to enjoy this semester. We all will. We're very lucky to have him here."

She struggled to answer his beaming smile with one of her own.

"You know about the party Friday night?" the university president asked.

"I do."

"You'll be there, won't you? We're expecting a nice turnout. I'd like to introduce you, along with Dr. King. You're one of our stars, you know. There will be some interviews and press later. Of course, in the beginning, everyone will want to talk to Dr. King, but some of that attention will extend to you. This will be something to put on your résumé—not that we want you to go anywhere. We love you here. We want you to be happy here. We all have your back."

"Thank you, Dr. Keller. I appreciate the support. And I do look forward to seeing you again Friday."

JACK YAWNED, AND YAWNED AGAIN, AS HE SHUFFLED forward in the line for customs. Immigration was never fun, but immigration and customs in Los Angeles was nothing short of a grind. At least he was on the ground, and since he never checked luggage, he hadn't had to claim any. Once he cleared customs, he'd be free.

Initially he'd wanted to just get a cab and head to his son's place, but Oliver had insisted on picking him up despite the later hour, and now that he'd arrived, Jack was looking forward to seeing Oliver. It had been almost eight months since he'd last seen him. They'd had a few days together late December, which was never enough, but they were both busy, working, traveling.

Oliver hadn't gone into science. Instead he'd studied film and at twenty-eight was making a name for himself as a talented young director. Oliver would be leaving to go on set soon, sometime this week, which is why he'd wanted to pick Jack up tonight.

The customs agent asked Jack all the usual questions— Where have you been? What were you doing there? What do you plan to be doing here?—and Jack answered honestly but briefly, knowing that too much small talk actually made one look more suspicious. He thought he was about to be waved through when the agent flipped through Jack's passport one last time.

"Will you be doing any more episodes for your show, Dr. King?" the agent asked in a flat, monotone voice, even as he continued to study the colorful stamps in the passport.

Jack shouldn't have been surprised that the agent recognized him, but he was. He tended to forget about the Discovery Channel program, forgetting that the show had made him familiar to millions. "There is discussion about doing another season. Just trying to figure out when we'd go on location."

"Do you write the script, or do they?"

Jack couldn't help a laugh. "I do me, and they film."

"I thought all shows like that were scripted."

"They try to give me a script, but I have a hard time sticking to it. I'm not an actor. I won't reshoot scenes just to get a line right."

"Maybe that's why I like your show so much." The agent slid Jack's passport across the counter, handing it back. "Take care. Enjoy Los Angeles."

Jack nodded his thanks and, shouldering his bags, headed toward the exit into the arrivals hall. As he stepped out of immigration into the terminal, his watch pinged with a text from Oliver. Here. Driving your car. Let me know where to find you.

Outside on the curb, Jack looked at the signs around him. Terminal X, Door X, he texted back. Look for Air India.

It was another long wait as just getting around the airport could take forever. Jack fought a yawn, and another. He looked forward to sleeping in a bed tonight. Oliver had a guest room, which was also his office, but the pullout sofa in there was comfortable and the air-conditioning and blackout blinds meant Jack would sleep better than he had in days.

Then Jack saw his old car, driven by his tall, curly-haired son, and Jack grinned and lifted a hand to wave.

Oliver spotted him immediately and pulled as close to the curb as he could before climbing out.

Oliver was wearing old Levi's and a faded Smokey Bear T-shirt emblazoned with the words *Only You Can Prevent Forest Fires*.

Jack felt a surge of emotion—love and pride—and his chest tightened. The bond he had with his son was still so strong. It had been just Oliver and him for most of Oliver's life, and they'd been a team. A very good team. "Hey," he said, wrapping his son in a bear hug. "You look good."

Oliver hugged him back. "You're really going gray, Dad."

"Not that gray."

Oliver stepped back, smiled. "Have you seen your beard?"

"Okay, that is gray, but I'm planning on shaving in the morning."

"Let's get you home." Oliver took the duffel bag from Jack's shoulder. "You must be beat."

"I did sleep for a couple hours on the plane," Jack said, climbing into the passenger seat. "You brought Gertie," he added as Oliver slammed the trunk closed and slid behind the steering wheel.

"She hadn't been driven all summer. I figured it was time to warm her up, get her ready for her new life in California."

"Did she start up without a problem?"

"She did." Oliver patted the dash, even as he shifted into drive. "She's not a power machine, but she is reliable as hell."

"Which is all I want or need in a car."

"How did the conference go?" Oliver asked, merging into the slow airport traffic. Even though it was almost eleven at night the airport was crowded, the wide road filled with red brake lights.

"Good." Jack rolled down his window and rested his arm on the car door.

Oliver shot his dad an amused glance. "That's it?"

"It was a good conference. But they always are."

"Anyone there you knew?"

"A few." Jack hesitated. "Camille was there. She asked me to say hello to you."

"Camille Ormond?"

"Yes."

"How is Dr. Ormond?"

Jack took a moment to answer. Camille was a complicated subject, and it had been uncomfortable seeing her. Too many memories, too much of a past between them. "Exactly the same."

Oliver shot his father a curious side glance. "Do you regret not marrying her?"

"No."

"You loved her."

Jack felt the fatigue of his flight, and he rubbed his dry, gritty eyes. "She wasn't mom material."

"I had you," Oliver said simply.

"And I wasn't a mom."

"I didn't need a mom. You were everything."

Jack felt a sharp pang. Oliver once had a mom, and she'd been amazing. The best of the best. But she'd died when Oliver was seven, and while Oliver didn't remember much about her, he looked just like her. Dark wavy hair, dark blue eyes, strong cheekbones, and a generous mouth. Jack had met Oliver's mom early in his career. Mara had been a graduate student—not his, thankfully—working on the same field project in Montana, and she'd been a passionate conservationist. They'd spent hours discussing biodiversity, land-use change, climate change, the future of water. His interest leaned toward international, not surprising since he'd been raised in Australia by two English parents, and she'd been raised outside of Jackson, Wyoming. Mara's dad had been a national park ranger. Her mom had been a high school English teacher. Mara was happiest outside, hiking, camping, exploring. They spent their honeymoon in the Serengeti, where he was in charge of a field study, and Jack was conceived there, under the African sky.

Mara finished her doctorate just before she gave birth to Oliver, and together they moved to the East Coast where Jack taught.

Mara was not a city girl. She didn't love New Jersey. She pined for her mountains, and so every chance she could, she'd take Oliver home with her, back to her beloved Grand Tetons.

Oliver was two when she was diagnosed with ovarian cancer. She fought hard and made it until his first week of second grade before she couldn't fight anymore.

Three years after Mara passed, Jack began dating casually. It had to be casual as he was still numb. Camille was the first woman who'd made him feel much of anything, and they'd had a passionate, physical relationship. Camille, a fellow scientist from Winnipeg, was beautiful, sophisticated, interesting, but she would never replace Mara. Nor was she meant to.

"Is she still single?" Oliver asked, changing lanes, navigating traffic on the way to his apartment in Santa Monica.

"Who?" Jack asked, pulled from his thoughts.

"Dr. Ormond."

"I don't know. I didn't ask."

"Was she wearing a ring?"

"I didn't look."

"Dad. Come on."

Jack shrugged. "I'm happy as I am."

"Playing the field."

"What's wrong with that? You're happy single."

"I'm twenty-eight, not fifty-six."

"Fifty-five," Jack corrected. "And only a month ago."

"The point is, you're not getting younger."

"Neither are you."

Oliver gave him a look of disbelief. "You really want to see me settled down before I'm thirty?"

"I was married and a dad at your age."

"Yes, but you'd met Mom. I haven't met anyone that makes me think, *this should be forever.*"

"You will one day. When it's right. And relationships are hard when you're on the road as much as you are."

"I take it you're speaking from experience, Dad?"

"Relationships take a lot of time and energy. Don't ever settle just so you can be with someone. That's no way to live. Or love."

"I had no idea you were such a romantic, Dad."

"Hardly. I just don't see the point expending time and energy into a relationship if it doesn't add exponentially to your life. We're only here on earth so long. Make every day matter."

Traffic was growing lighter. Oliver put on his signal and turned at the corner. They weren't far from his place. "Advice you've modeled every day of my life."

"Must be annoying sometimes."

"Sometimes," Oliver agreed, smiling wryly. "But the rest of the time, you're damn inspiring, Dad. I'm proud of you."

"Proud of you, too, Oliver."

JACK TOOK AN ADVIL PM TO MAKE SURE HE'D SLEEP through the night and didn't wake the next day until it was almost noon. He was groggy when he threw back the covers, but by the time he'd showered and shaved, his head was clear, and he wanted a strong cup of coffee.

Oliver was in the kitchen, sitting on a barstool at the counter typing away on his laptop. "You're awake," he said, adding a few more keystrokes before closing the laptop. "Coffee or tea this morning?"

"I think I'll do coffee."

Oliver started to rise. "I'll make you a fresh pot."

Jack waved him back down. "Don't. If that's from this morning, I'll just reheat what's left."

Oliver settled back onto his counter stool. "I was keeping it warm for a while, but you were sleeping like the dead."

"I took one of those pills to knock me out. I didn't want to be tossing and turning with jet lag." Jack crossed the kitchen floor, opened a cupboard, wrong cupboard, opened another and found the mugs. "What are you working on?"

"Studying the shoot schedule for the movie I'm directing in Vancouver next week."

Jack filled his cup and put it in the microwave, hitting the reheat button. "How many weeks will you be on set?"

"Almost four."

"And then?"

"I'll be home for a week or two and then I'm off again."

"Back to BC?"

"No, New Zealand."

Jack waited for the microwave to ping before removing his coffee. He needed the moment to smash his disappointment. He'd hoped to see more of Oliver. Lately it was hard to get on the same page with his son. "You like what you do."

Oliver nodded. "I do. Can't imagine doing anything else."

"Do you still write at all?"

"I have a couple screenplays I've been working on, but I prefer directing. The writing is more frustrating."

"Then write for yourself. Write something you like writing."

"You like writing all those papers?"

Jack shrugged, sipped his coffee. It was tepid, not hot, but he didn't have time to put it back in the microwave. Nor did he care about the coffee that much, either. He wasn't ready to say goodbye to Oliver, wasn't ready to leave the one person who meant most to him in the world. But he had a meeting this afternoon with the department chairs from Orange University in Mission Viejo, and he needed to get on the road soon. He didn't trust LA traffic. "It's part of my job. I don't mind it."

Oliver stood and came around the counter to open the refrigerator. "I can make you some eggs or avocado toast. I have yogurt and blueberries." He glanced at his dad. "You've got to be hungry. You never eat on planes."

"I could use some food," Jack agreed. "But no need to put yourself out—"

"Not putting myself out. I'm glad to do it. It's good to see you. I hate that I'm already leaving."

"It's never been about quantity, Ollie. It's quality time."

Oliver stared at his dad a long moment before adding quietly, "It really is good to see you. I don't see enough of you."

"I know. I'm sorry."

"I was the one who chose to move across the country."

"It's where your work is."

Jack leaned against the counter as Oliver scrambled some eggs and put a slice of hearty brown bread in the toaster. Oliver had come a long way with his cooking skills. In just minutes he was plating the scrambled eggs and avocado toast.

Jack ate standing up while Oliver washed the small skillet and spatula. "How long do you think it'll take me to reach Mission Viejo?" he asked between bites.

"If you leave in the next hour, an hour and twenty. But that's just an optimistic estimate. You know traffic here. It can be a nightmare."

Jack nodded and concentrated on eating. He was just finishing the last of his toast when Oliver asked, "You think you'll be happy here in Southern California, Dad? It's not really you."

Jack didn't immediately answer, hearing something in his son's voice that he couldn't completely identify. Concern? Tension? Guilt? Jack rinsed his plate off, and then gave it a scour with soap. "Why isn't it me?"

"You prefer more trees, fewer people. And ideally, a lot of rain, mud, insects, and if you're lucky, disease."

"You do know me so well. But it's just for a year. I'm sure I can tolerate sunshine and a temperate winter."

"If you're going to take a sabbatical, why not go somewhere you're dying to go? Orange County isn't your dream spot."

"No, but you're just an hour and a half from me, and that's pretty cool."

"These next few months I'm rarely going to be here."

"We'll just keep doing FaceTime."

"But that's not why you took this job. You took it to be closer to me."

Oliver was right. Jack did need more time with his son. Not just because Oliver was one of the best people he knew—smart, creative, honest, loving, and fair—but Jack missed him. He missed being part of his son's life. "And I am closer to you. I'm in your kitchen right now."

"You know what I mean."

"I'm not worried. We'll get together when you're in LA."

"I just don't want you lonely—"

"Oliver, I'm never lonely, and I've a lot to do before the semester begins in two weeks. I have a meeting this afternoon as a matter of fact. I still need to find a place to live."

"Do you want to come back here tonight? You're welcome to crash here."

Jack smiled crookedly. "I can afford a hotel room. But thanks for the invite."

"Should I load your boxes into the car, then? I've got everything in the garage."

"I can do that."

"I'll help you." Oliver reached into the cupboard and pulled out one of his insulated thermoses. He filled it with purified water from a pitcher inside the fridge. "What classes are you teaching?"

"My Chaos and Complexity course, Ecology and the African Savannas, and Biodiversity Conservation Policy."

Oliver handed him the filled thermos. "You're the coolest nerd I've ever met, Dad."

"Thank you," Jack said, giving Oliver a swift hug. "Thank you for breakfast. I'll strip the sheets and head out to the garage."

"No, just leave it. I'll deal with it later."

"I don't want you to have to deal with it—"

"Dad, I've got it. I'd honestly prefer we pack your car and get you on the road. You don't know where you're going, and you don't want to be late."

"I'm not a doddering senior."

Oliver flashed a smile that never failed to make Jack smile. "No, not yet, thank goodness."

Chapter 2

PAIGE DIDN'T SLEEP WELL, WAKING REPEATEDLY IN THE night to adjust her pillows, get water, check the time, check her phone, check the Internet, wondering each time if the Australian scientist Jack King would still look like the Jack she'd known, and yes, he did.

Which made the meeting today even more stressful.

Her only hope was that Jack wouldn't remember her. She went by a different name now, using her married name, not her maiden name. She'd changed her hair. It used to be shorter, darker, the early choppy Rachel style made popular by Jennifer Aniston on *Friends*. She'd been heavier, too. There was a very good possibility he wouldn't recognize her.

She sincerely hoped so, because thirty years ago, Jack had been a tan, muscular twentysomething with a sexy accent and long, shaggy hair. He'd known far more about sex than she did, and she'd faked an orgasm because she was afraid she was taking too long to come.

He'd asked her if she'd faked it, too, and, mortified, she'd denied it.

The memory still mortified her, and Paige grabbed a pillow and smashed it over her face, praying her new colleague wouldn't—*please, please, please*—be her one-night stand. *Please, God*.

Paige glanced at the bedside clock. It was too early to call her youngest in New York. Ashley would be sleeping in after working late last night.

She needed to relax. She needed to sleep. Finally, just before five she did, managing to snag two more hours before finally leaving bed with the sun pouring through the blinds on her window.

It was going to be okay, she told herself, pulling on her short pink kimono robe and knotting the sash. No matter how much she dreaded today's meeting with Dr. King and the department chairs, she'd survive it, just like she survived everything else. Paige could juggle a lot, and handle pressure, and do it with grace. She'd proven her strength more than once. At some level, it was gratifying to be the one others could depend on. She'd been that person in the family, so why shouldn't she be that person at work?

In the kitchen she made coffee and, while it was brewing, opened her laptop to do yet another Google search on her new colleague, feeling slightly obsessed at this point. Dozens and dozens of links popped up, along with photos, including a photo of Jack in the field, wearing the proverbial khakis, his skin bronzed, his brown hair still thick, still shaggy, although not quite as long as he'd worn it thirty years ago.

Heart racing, she clicked on the different links. His biography. His published articles. Photos. Awards. Speeches.

She scanned the Wikipedia page to get an overview of his career, and it was daunting. He'd earned his undergraduate degree in Melbourne, and earned his PhD from Oxford. The man had more postdoctoral fellows than anyone she'd ever met. She actually counted them—twenty-four—and the web page hadn't been updated since 2017. God knew how many more he'd received since.

He even had a TV show on the Discovery Channel.

Paige closed the laptop, unsettled all over again, and marched into the bathroom to look at herself in the mirror. Artfully highlighted blond hair, blue eyes, skin beginning to soften at her eyes, mouth, chin, but when she smiled the only lines she could see were at her eyes. She'd inherited her Scandinavian mother's strong cheekbones and chin. If she continued to use sunscreen she should age well. Or at least that's what she told herself every time she headed out for a walk, careful to wear sunglasses and her oversize, floppy straw hat.

Her phone rang and Paige returned to the kitchen. It was Michelle, her oldest, and Paige put her on speaker while she filled her coffee cup. "Morning, sunshine," she said to her daughter. "How are you?"

"Okay." But Michelle said it slowly, drawing the word out, so Paige knew things weren't good.

"What's going on?"

"Have you talked to Nichole lately?"

So, the call was about Nichole. Paige shouldn't have been surprised. Michelle and Nichole were tight. Michelle usually knew everything that was going on with her middle sister. "Yesterday," Paige answered, keeping her voice neutral. "She phoned me."

"You know about Andreas?"

"Which part? The fact that they broke up, or that he moved out? Or that he got passed up for a promotion and is taking it out on your sister?"

"So, you pretty much know everything now."

"How long have you known?"

"All along."

"Even the living-together part?"

"Yes."

Paige rolled her eyes, but bit her tongue so as not to step in it. Michelle was fiercely protective of Nichole. "What about you? Are you okay?"

"Why wouldn't I be?"

"I don't know. It's your first day of school. Not sure if you're nervous."

"I'm fine. Second year teaching sixth grade. Just glad to be in the same classroom. It should be a lot easier this year."

Paige poured a generous splash of creamer into her coffee. "How is the new place? Like it?"

"Belltown's fun. I can walk to everything. Except my school, which is good. I don't want to live where I teach. The last thing I want to do is bump into students outside of school. It was mortifying that time I saw some of my kids in the checkout line at QFC. All I had in my cart was wine and yogurt."

"I'm sure they didn't notice."

"Oh, but their mom did. I saw the way she looked at the bottles of wine and then at me, thinking, *lush*."

Paige laughed, sipped her coffee. "Do you ever think about teaching junior high, or high school? You'd be able to focus on teaching just math."

"I actually have thought about it. I've also looked into earning my master's."

"At University of Washington?"

"Seattle U. They've got an evening course for working professionals."

"You'd certainly earn more money with a master's degree."

"That would be nice. Hey, Mom, a question. Your birthday is just over a month away. Shouldn't we start making plans? It's tough getting everyone together at the last minute."

Paige sighed inwardly. It was going to be tough getting her girls together. Ashley didn't have the money to fly out from New York, and Nichole was buried with work in Chicago. "I don't think we're going to get everyone together this time," she said carefully, aware that Michelle would want to jump on the phone and put pressure on her younger sisters to "make an effort for Mom." Michelle took her job as the firstborn very seriously, and she did it well. "Maybe you and I could just do something," she added. "I haven't spent a weekend just with you in ages."

"I think we can certainly try to get together," Michelle answered. "I'll reach out to Nichole and Ashley."

"Michelle."

"Yes, Mom?"

"Don't—" Paige broke off and swallowed hard, battling with herself. She wanted everyone together. She hated having them all so spread out. But this was also her girls' time to spread their wings, develop resiliency and experience true independence. "Don't make them feel guilty, okay? Money is tight for everyone. And we can always do my birthday later—"

"It's your fiftieth, Mom. And you deserve to be treated like a queen. You're our queen."

Paige's eyes burned and she bit into her bottom lip to stifle the emotion. "I love you."

"I love you, too, Mom. Let me see what I can do."

Call ended, she took another sip of coffee, and another, even as she rubbed her eyes, drying them.

She loved teaching and her students, but she'd never loved anyone, or anything, as much as she loved being a mom.

And now her beautiful, smart, kind, loving, ambitious daughters were gone.

Just as they were meant to be.

But my God, it still hurt, letting them go.

A half hour later, still flustered, Paige turned on the TV and did a search for Jack's *Population Dynamics* show. She might as well go in prepared for this afternoon's meeting. She went to season one, episode one, thinking she'd watch a few minutes, maybe the one episode, but ended up watching the entire season.

It was lunchtime when she finished, and Paige turned off the TV and sat still on her couch. Wow.

He'd grown up. Nicely, too. She could see why his show was popular. Jack was engaging and charismatic. And still incredibly good-looking. As well as fit. Dr. Jack King was built—at least in season one. His muscles rippled as he hiked, dug, climbed, jumped, swam, splashed, and stripped down to shorts for a quick dip in a watering hole that may or may not have had a hippo in it. Adult Jack, fifty-year-old Jack, was fascinating, witty, appealing. His accent alone made her a little breathless. It shouldn't have.

She hadn't realized that population dynamics had traditionally been a branch of mathematical biology, a study dating back over two hundred years, but it only took Jack a few minutes explaining how population was affected by three dynamic rate functions, and she understood why math was so important to his science. Everything he did in his work was based on math and statistics.

So, why was she needed to team teach?

Why didn't he just teach the entire course—math and science—himself?

TWO HOURS LATER PAIGE WAS KICKING HERSELF AS SHE drove north from Dana Point to Mission Viejo. She shouldn't have watched Jack's show, never mind the entire season one. It was one thing to binge on a thriller, but not smart to watch episode after episode starring the scientist she was supposed to work with this semester.

She was nervous and she didn't like being nervous. She liked calm, control. But everything in her felt unsettled and undone. She was going to have to fake it today, but that wouldn't be hard. She'd faked her way through much of life to ensure those around her were happy, secure. She'd hidden her own unhappiness during the last ten years of her marriage so that her girls didn't have to worry, much less worry about her. Her job as the mother was to protect the girls, not the other way around. Her own mother had needed so much from her that Paige had vowed she'd be a different kind of mother, and she had been.

Paige arrived early at the Bean Box, their meeting spot just off campus. The Bean Box tended to be busy all the time, but she was lucky to discover an empty table inside by the tinted window. She set her lavender leather tote down in a chair and went to order an iced coffee. While in line she got a ping and, checking her phone, saw a text from Andi, Dr. Nair's secretary. Due to unforeseen circumstances, Dr. Nair wasn't going to be able to make the meeting this afternoon. He was very sorry and asked her to pass on his apologies to Dr. King.

Paige's heart sank. She texted Andi back. Please tell me he's not sitting in his office avoiding this meeting.

I don't know if he's avoiding the meeting, Andi texted back.

Paige glared at the phone. Which meant that Dr. Nair was in his office. She slipped her phone away. This was not how the day was supposed to go.

But it's fine, she told herself, smashing the wave of irritation. She'd be fine. Back at her table she checked email, scanned the news, and killed time until Jack King arrived. She also kept compulsively watching the door and glancing at the time, but no, Dr. King wasn't late yet. She was just anxious.

And then, the tinted glass door swung open and Jack King entered the Bean Box. He paused just inside the door to get his bearings, giving her a moment to study him. He carried a beat-up backpack and wore jeans and a white linen collared shirt, sleeves rolled up on his forearms. It was impossible not to recognize him. He looked exactly like he did on TV—only taller, more polished, more vital.

As he peeled off his sunglasses to glance around the coffeehouse, she rose from the table and lifted a hand.

His brow furrowed slightly as he approached. "Dr. Hagopian?"

"No, Dr. Newsome," she said, extending her hand. "Call me Paige."

"Paige?" he repeated, expression slightly puzzled as he took her hand, his fingers wrapping around hers, his grip strong, skin warm, his accent making her pulse quicken ever so slightly. Or was it that tingle in her hand where his palm touched hers?

She quickly pulled her hand away and forced a small smile. "Dr. Hagopian couldn't be here. I'm filling in for her."

"Good of you," he said with a quick smile.

Her insides felt wobbly. "I had expected Dr. Nair to be here, but he's cancelled on us at the last moment."

"What about Dr. Rakovski?" Jack asked, referencing the science department chair.

"I didn't know he was supposed to be here."

"Not a problem," Jack answered easily. "We'll get more done without them. Do you need a coffee or tea?"

She shook her head, self-consciously tucking a strand of hair behind her ear. "I got here a bit early, so I'm all set."

"Let me grab a drink and I'll be back."

Heart thumping, she watched him walk away. He didn't remember her. Wow. Okay. Paige should have been glad. It's what she'd wanted, and yet it stung.

She took a breath, trying to calm her racing pulse, but looking at Jack didn't help. But she couldn't stop looking. His shirtsleeves were rolled up on his forearms, revealing more tan skin. Her gaze slowly swept over him, shifting from his arms to his shoulders to his lean waist and then to his butt. He had a good butt. She could see it naked, the moonlight of Paris illuminating that magnificent body of his. She flushed, glanced away, trying to put the vision of a naked Jack from her mind.

She never ogled the men she taught with. She barely noticed them. At least, not physically. They were her colleagues. Her peers. That's it. But Jack . . .

He returned with a hot green tea and sat down across from her. He ran fingers through his thick hair, moving it off his high forehead. "I might need you to help me out here. I thought I was teaching with a Dr. Hagopian."

"You were." She glanced from his thick sun-streaked hair

to his eyes. They had gold in them as well. She'd forgotten that. Paige swallowed hard, forced herself to focus. "Dr. Hagopian had a sudden health issue come up and had to take an unexpected leave of absence this semester. I would have thought one of the department chairs would have told you."

"Dr. Rakovski did email that he wanted to discuss a few things with me, but I haven't had a chance to call him. But it's fine. I hope Dr. Hagopian is okay."

"Me too. And I'm sorry I had to break the bad news to you. I thought Dr. Nair would be here today, and he had an emergency pop up. This isn't the norm, though. Orange is a wonderful school."

"I'm not worried. Things happen, and Dr. Hagopian and I exchanged a few emails, but that was it." Jack paused, looking at her intently. "You remind me of someone."

"I hear that all the time."

Silence stretched for a long moment. Paige struggled not to wiggle.

"When did you find out you'd be taking over from Dr. Hagopian?" he asked, finally breaking the quiet.

"Yesterday."

"Just yesterday?"

"It was a little bit of a shock," she admitted.

"Did they take a class away from you?"

"No. But I'll be fine. I've had heavy loads before. One extra class won't kill me."

Jack gave her a sympathetic smile. "Do you know very much about the course we'll be teaching?"

"No."

"You are a good sport, aren't you?"

She felt that uncomfortable wobbly sensation in the pit of her stomach again. She ought to tell him who she was. She ought to come clean. But she didn't. She couldn't. He'd done such amazing things in his life. She wasn't embarrassed that she hadn't accomplished as much, and yet she did feel a wave of insecurity. "Not always, but Esther's a good friend and I'm always happy to help her out." She forced herself to meet his gaze. "Besides, everyone is really excited about you joining Orange this year. There are a lot of high expectations from what I understand."

"Oh?"

"Alumni, department chairs, the university president, the media . . ."

"That's a lot of pressure."

He said it lightly, though, and Paige could tell he wasn't worried. In fact, Jack looked incredibly relaxed and rested for a man who'd supposedly just flown in from Delhi. "Did you really just return from India?"

"Last night, yes."

"And you're not jet-lagged?"

"Not now, but I will be later. Hopefully by then I'll have found a place to stay."

"You don't have a place to live yet?"

"That's next on my to-do list."

She marveled at how untroubled he was. If the situation was reversed, she'd have been incredibly anxious about where she'd be living. In fact, before she moved from Durham, she flew out on an apartment hunting trip, and didn't return until she'd signed a lease. "I'm surprised the university didn't give you any help with that."

"Dr. Rakovski offered some assistance but I declined. I saw online that there is quite a lot available in the Mission Viejo–Irvine area, so I'm not worried."

"It sounds as if you don't worry about a lot of things."

"I worry about big things—climate change, species extinction, the rise of disease and poverty. But the rest of it is small stuff, and I've learned not to lose sleep over it."

"You must do yoga or meditate."

"No. That's been suggested to me more than once. I run, hike, swim. Work out. But all those things are a kind of meditation. We can't save the world if we can't save ourselves."

"You want to save the world?"

"Don't you?" he retorted.

Jack saw Paige's smile fade, her already guarded expression shuttering further. This was not the meeting he'd thought he'd be having this morning. First, there were no department heads. Second, there was no Dr. Hagopian. And then perhaps most importantly, this was Paige, the Paige he knew from Paris, and yet she didn't seem to remember him.

Odd.

More than odd.

She was no longer the fresh-faced coed of twenty, but she was even more beautiful now, her features mature, elegant, reminding him of Michelle Pfeiffer with her high, prominent cheekbones, wide blue eyes, and generous mouth. He'd always thought it was interesting how women became more beautiful as they aged, wisdom adding layers and mystery. The Paige he'd known in Paris was smart, articulate, confident, brilliant with her head for numbers. The Paige he'd known wouldn't have forgotten him. So why this pretense?

Could this Paige be a doppelgänger? Someone so much like Paige—even down to the same name—but not the same woman? Was it coincidental? Possible? He suspected not.

Regardless, he was intrigued. This would be an interesting semester. "Tell me a little bit about yourself," he asked. "Where are you from? Where did you go to school?"

Her shoulders twisted evasively. "I don't have a very interesting background. Grew up in a small town in California. Earned my PhD at Berkeley." Her lashes lifted, and she gave a wry smile. "I checked out your curriculum vitae. You've done a lot in your life. Pretty impressive."

It was her voice. Her mannerisms. Same education. Paige had attended Berkeley. He was silent a moment, processing.

Could she really not remember?

Had she perhaps been in an accident? Suffered some kind of trauma, something that would have hurt her memory?

His brow creased, but as much as he wanted to ask more

questions and press for clarification, he did the opposite. He'd let it ride for now. School started soon and there was a lot to get done. "I enjoy my work."

"You've earned hundreds of fellowships."

His lips quirked. "I thought you were supposed to be good with numbers."

"Okay, not hundreds of fellowships, but you've had hundreds of papers published. You must like writing."

"I don't dislike writing. It's part of the job."

"My least favorite part," she admitted. "I like my numbers. Equations are my friends. But sentences? Paragraphs? Essays explaining research? No, thank you."

"We all have our strengths. It's what makes the world interesting." He meant it, too.

Over the years many of Jack's colleagues had thought he was too zealous about his work, too passionate about his causes. But he believed his work mattered. He believed he could make a difference. It's why he woke up every day, put in the hours he did. Traditionally, professors tended to be risk averse. They liked the comfort of academia. One could bury himself in books, surround one's self with idealistic students, and feel optimistic about the future. Jack couldn't. He never had. He could only feel optimistic in the field, putting research into practice. Field work was essential—necessary and transformative. "What do you know about our class?" he asked.

"Just that it's one you created, and apparently so popular it's already full, with a waiting list of thirty-five." She lifted an eyebrow. "I don't normally get thirty-five students waiting for one of my math classes."

"But you have taught statistics before."

"Of course, many times, but usually in the Spring semester."

"That's good," he said. "You'll be comfortable as we'll be using statistics to teach research methodology."

"And then you'll be taking some students on an actual research trip end of semester?"

"That's the culmination of the semester work, yes." Jack looked at her curiously. "You're not coming?"

"I wasn't aware that I was supposed to go."

"We're team teaching. It'd be great to have the other half of the team in the field."

Her blue gaze revealed wariness. "It's not mandatory, though, is it? Dr. Nair said nothing about that part, and I have three other classes. I don't know how I'm supposed to leave them, and to be honest, I'm not sure I'd want to leave them."

"I don't think that has to be decided today, no." Jack opened his khaki knapsack and pulled out a thick spiral-bound book. "I'll email you the syllabus later today, but I also have a hard copy. I thought Dr. Hagopian might want it."

"I'd love it," Paige said. "Technology has its advantages, but there's nothing like a book." She reached for the syllabus. "This is massive."

"It's the entire course. That way you know what I'm covering, what you're covering, and when our lessons will overlap."

"You normally teach this course yourself, don't you?"

"At Princeton, yes. But when I'm visiting a school for a summer, or semester, I've found it beneficial to teach with someone on the faculty." He could feel her reluctance. "What's wrong?"

"This is just your course. It's like your baby—"

"Not my baby, not at all. It's an undergraduate course that teaches upper division students research methodology." He smiled, wanting to reassure her. "I promise I'm not going to be riding you, criticizing your instruction. When we start teaching, you're the statistics expert, and I'm the biology expert, and by the end, students will realize you can't have one without the other, not in science, and definitely not in field research." He stopped talking then, thinking he might be overwhelming her. "Sorry. I'm passionate about my work."

"I'd rather teach with someone excited to teach than someone who's counting down the days to retirement."

He grimaced. "There are plenty of those out there."

"You won't find many here at Orange. It's a fairly young faculty. Very friendly."

"Have you done a lot of team teaching?"

"Not very much, and not in years."

"We'll make this fun."

She lifted a quizzical brow. "Is that a challenge?"

He laughed. She was a little guarded, a little prickly, and refreshingly feisty. He tried to remember if the Paige he'd known in Paris had been the same. But there had been too many years. Three decades. "Any advice on where I should begin looking for an apartment? Any neighborhoods to stay away from?"

"I liked the complex I used to live at. It's walking distance to campus, and there are lots of Orange faculty there. If you mention you teach at Orange, you should get a better rate, and they'll waive some of the deposit." She reached for her phone. "What's your phone number? I'll send you a text with their info."

DRIVING BACK HOME, PAIGE WANTED TO PHONE ELIZABETH, her best friend since high school, and a fellow Orange professor, but what would she say? That she was panicked about teaching with Jack because she'd slept with him thirty years ago?

That, worse, she'd acted like she didn't know Jack, further complicating everything?

But obviously Jack didn't remember her, either. He'd merely said she looked familiar but couldn't place her. If he'd known her, wouldn't he have said so? And wasn't it better if they were strangers for the duration of the semester? It'd be easier to teach with someone who didn't remember that she'd had a mad crush on him.

Good lord, she'd had a crush on him.

So no, she couldn't call Elizabeth.

Back home, too restless to sit and too wound up to talk to anyone, Paige changed into shorts and a T-shirt, put on her walking shoes, filled her thermos with water, and drove to one of her favorite hiking trails high in the hills overlooking Dana Point and Laguna. It was hot, but she had her favorite floppy hat to shield her eyes from the sun, and the heat and exertion helped her work through her anxiety.

She ought to have come clean with Jack. She ought to have been casual and amused, remarking on coincidences, and how here they were, thirty years after Paris, teaching together. Instead, she felt like Peter denying Jesus. Okay, it wasn't that big, but still, it was stupid of her, creating complications where there didn't need to be any.

So what if she'd slept with him one time? It was so long ago; she'd been a different person then. How could that one night matter? It didn't. One brief sexual encounter when she was twenty was nothing in the scheme of things. Not even a blip on her radar. And yet, she was uncomfortable. Uncomfortable because she'd run away from him and their night together, because she'd felt so much, and she'd known he didn't feel the same way. He liked sex, and he'd liked her, and so it had been easy for him to sleep with her. But for her, it had been still such a new thing. She'd only had a couple of sexual experiences. Jack was her third. The first two times had been disappointments. Jack had not been a disappointment. But Jack was a free spirit, and she wasn't, and rather than get her heart bruised, she'd left Paris and returned home.

He'd never tried to track her down later, and she'd never reached back out to him. She'd put him firmly from her mind, and after a while it was as if it had never happened. But when she dated, she'd find herself comparing the lovemaking to Jack, comparing the pleasure to what she'd felt that night in Paris, and it was never the same, never as good.

Then finally, she told herself she'd made up the pleasure, that the experience hadn't been all that remarkable, that it was Paris that had seduced her, not the sexy, confident Australian. In fact, she added, correcting her memory, Jack wasn't that attractive, or sexy. He'd been confident. Cocky. Brash. And yes, he'd had an appealing accent, but honestly, he wasn't someone to put on a pedestal. He'd been good in bed because he'd slept with dozens of women, and the whole I'm-charming-Jack-King was part of his schtick.

After Paige met, and then married, Ted, she'd truly forgotten about Jack. Jack was part of the past, and there were new experiences, and more precious memories to cherish as she and Ted bought their first house and had their first baby, creating the family Paige loved more than anything.

Paige reached the top of the hill, the brush dry and sun-bleached, the sun hot. She faced west, her gaze drinking in the blue of the sea. It was a clear day and she could see Catalina, as well as a fleet of boats in the water, taking advantage of the weekend. She'd grown up on the West Coast, not far from the ocean, and she'd missed it while living in North Carolina, missed the expansiveness of the view, of a blue horizon that stretched as far as the eye could see.

She was happy being back in California, happy at Orange, happy with her daughters and her friends. Everything was good in her world. She was in a better place than she'd been for years. So why hadn't she acknowledged that she knew Jack? That they'd gone to the same international summer program together?

But on the other hand, Jack hadn't recognized her. He'd said she reminded him of someone, but there had been no immediate click, no *Oh, this is Paige from Paris.* So why should she bring any of that up when he'd clearly forgotten her? It was a relief actually. Since he didn't remember her, he wouldn't feel awkward about teaching with her, and since he wouldn't feel awkward, she didn't need to, either.

Paige took a quick swig from her water bottle before recapping the bottle and heading back down the mountain.

All was good. Everything would be fine. But on reaching the parking lot she checked her phone. She'd received texts from Michelle and Elizabeth, both asking about her meeting with Jack.

She bit her bottom lip for a moment before answering both with the same text: Went great. Should be an interesting semester.

Maybe too interesting, she added silently, starting the car.

Chapter 3

PAIGE HAD ATTENDED DOZENS OF DEPARTMENT PARTIES and big-donor-alumni events over the years, first at the University of North Carolina, then at Duke, and now at Orange. She understood how important the events are for securing donations and underwriting, and she knew her role—mingle, make nice, and impress. It was a dog and pony show, but she didn't mind doing her part, not if she could contribute to the university's financial bottom line.

The president's house was on a corner of the campus, a handsome 1920s Spanish Colonial Revival that had been built for the second university president at a time when Southern California was flush with money, with the wealthy Midwesterners all heading to California for the winter, wanting to escape the cold and snow.

She climbed the front steps of the stucco mansion, admiring the little white lights strung in the graceful, leafy green jacaranda trees scattered on the vast lawn. The trees were huge and handsome, planted decades ago. She was met at the front door by Rose Keller, President Keller's wife. "Good to see you, Paige," Rose said, giving her a quick hug. "Glad you could join us tonight."

"Wouldn't miss it for the world." Paige could hear voices from the living room and beyond. "I think I know where the party is."

"Most people are on the terrace right now. Bartender's back there, too."

"I think I'll wander that way."

"What do you think of our visiting professor, Dr. King?"

Paige glanced toward the living room doorway, praying Jack wouldn't materialize. "He seems . . . nice."

"You don't like him?"

"No, he's quite impressive. I'm looking forward to teaching with him." Paige forced a smile. "Is he here yet?"

"Yes. We had a light bite with him earlier. Walter invited some of our key benefactors to a private gathering before the party. It went very well. Everyone is so impressed by Dr. King."

The doorbell rang and Rose excused herself to answer it while Paige slipped away, passing through the living room with its gold-stenciled beams and out through the tall French doors lining one wall.

A couple dozen guests were outside on the terrace. Paige's gaze skimmed the well-heeled crowd, looking for friends. Greg wasn't here yet, but most of her department was. And yes, Jack, too. He was talking to an older couple who Paige knew were university benefactors. She struggled to remember their names. Mr. and Mrs. Goldsmith, maybe? Goldstein? Jack's gaze suddenly met hers and he gave a slight nod, the corner of his mouth lifting.

Paige felt a funny curl in her middle. She didn't understand it, uncertain if he made her nervous or unsettled, hard to say which. But she gave him a quick nod and headed toward the bartender at the edge of the terrace and asked for a glass of Pinot Gris.

As the bartender poured her wine, she glanced past the

terrace to the pool. It wasn't quite dark yet, but lights shone in the trees, and the pool glowed with light.

It was a beautiful night, a perfect seventy-two degrees, no humidity, not like North Carolina. She'd been born and raised in central California, in Paso Robles, thirty miles north of San Luis Obispo. When she was growing up, Paso Robles had been mainly a ranching community with some grapes. Today it was filled with vineyards, the grapes increasingly claiming the gently rolling hills, but it was still considered rural, unlike the sprawl of LA and Orange County.

She glanced up as Dr. Walter Keller, the university's president, approached with Jack and the Goldsmiths.

"And there's the other half of our dynamic duo," Walter said cheerfully. "Harry and Susan, you know Dr. Paige Newsome, one of our newer professors in the math department. As you might recall, we stole her from Duke. She's extremely popular with the students." Walter gestured to Jack. "And now Dr. Newsome and Dr. King will be teaching Dr. King's course—what's the name again? Chaos and change . . . ?"

"Chaos and Complexity for a Changing Planet," Jack said, extending his hand to Paige. "Good to see you again, Dr. Newsome."

She hesitated before taking his hand, remembering how it felt just a few days ago. Warm, strong, masculine. But she couldn't very well ignore his hand, either. Reluctantly she took it, giving a firm shake, but the heat in his palm was electric, and she felt uncomfortable little sparks shoot through her arm, a sensation that she could feel all the way through her.

She dropped his hand. "A lovely night, isn't it?" she said, speaking to the group.

"You must be excited about teaching with Dr. King," Susan answered.

"Yes," Paige said quickly. "Very excited." She saw Jack's right eyebrow rise a fraction but ignored it. "I'm looking forward to teaching something new. I hate getting too comfortable."

"Change is good," Harry agreed. "And it's quite a feat to have you here at Orange," he added, focusing on Jack. "How did we get so lucky?"

"I've met Andy Rakovski, your science department chair, at a couple of conferences and we hit it off. Last time I saw him he mentioned that he'd give his right arm to have me visit, and so here I am. Without him having to lose that right arm. Didn't seem fair to ask him to make such a sacrifice."

Everyone laughed, charmed. Paige smiled reluctantly. Everyone seemed to adore Jack. He was outgoing, positive, engaging. He also happened to be handsome, articulate, and charming, his charm helped immensely by his Australian accent. And then there was that dimple. Not fair, not cool.

Jack, the Goldsmiths, and President Keller moved on but then Jack somehow broke free and ended back up at her side.

"Do you enjoy this?" he asked, gesturing to the gathering on the terrace, a gathering that looked just like what it was: wealthy alumni and a gathering of math and science professors.

She looked up into his face, trying to read his expression, but he just looked relaxed. Affable. Relentlessly cheerful. "It's not as bad as the dentist—" She broke off as a shriek came from behind her, and she and Jack—everyone— turned to see a huge curly haired dog sprinting across the terrace.

Rose Keller was the one shrieking as she chased after the dog. Her high heels made little clicking sounds as she ran. "Taffy, no. No. Taffy, come!"

But Taffy did not come, and one of the caterers began chasing Taffy, and then another. Then Dr. Keller joined in, calling for the dog in his most commanding voice. But Taffy paid no heed, thoroughly enjoying her escape.

Taffy allowed Mrs. Keller to get close, but just as she reached for the big fluffy dog, Taffy bolted again, tail high, tongue lolling. Paige could almost hear the dog laughing. *She* was trying not to laugh. One of the young caterers got close to Taffy and then the dog did a Thelma and Louise move, bounding high, before sailing into the pool. Water surged out, huge splashes. The elegant floating candles were overturned and Taffy paddled around, delighted with herself.

Paige covered her mouth and looked at Jack.

He lifted a brow, his voice dry. "You do know what comes next."

Then it happened. Taffy climbed up the steps, dashed between guests and began vigorously shaking, drying herself, all over the Goldsmiths and the journalist from the *Los Angeles Times*.

Rose Keller let out a moan. Dr. Keller grimly marched on the dog, a dog that was not about to end her performance, a wet dog that was running again.

Jack crouched down, crooned Taffy's name, and held out his hand as if he held a treat. "Good dog, Taffy, good girl."

And Taffy, bless her heart, ran to Jack, sniffed his empty hand, and stood still for a pat. Everyone clapped as Jack took Taffy's collar and began walking the wet dog to the house. Paige stifled a laugh because as Jack walked the prancing Taffy, he was complimenting the dog's excellent listening skills.

Jack returned to her side a few minutes later. Guests were still laughing and reliving Taffy's great escape.

"That was impressive," Paige said. "You have skills."

"Chasing a dog never works," he answered, smiling, flashing white teeth. The fascinating dimple in his lean, tan cheek deepened. Paige's heart did a hard, mad pump and she quickly looked away, unnerved by her response.

She couldn't remember the last time she'd found a man attractive, and now here she was, consumed with thoughts of Jack with his earthy Indiana Jones swagger. But even that comparison didn't sit well with her as she'd had the worst crush on Harrison Ford when she was younger. She'd secretly wanted to be Mrs. Indiana Jones and share those adventures with him. Traveling the world, discovering hidden treasures, knowing interesting things. Indiana Jones, Professor Jones, made teaching look sexy, too, not that she'd ever had a teacher like him, or known a professor like him. At least, not until Paris.

And again, now.

Paige swallowed hard and turned her attention back to Jack. "Based on your knowledge of university socials, how would you rate this one?"

"A ten. Probably the most entertaining one I've ever attended."

"Thanks to Taffy?"

"And you."

She wasn't sure how she felt about being lumped together with a huge wet dog. "Do you have a dog?"

"I did when Oliver was young. It's too hard now that I live alone. What about you?"

"We did on the ranch growing up, but Ted was allergic to pet dander, so no." She hesitated. "Is Oliver your son?"

"Yes. He's twenty-eight, a filmmaker, based out of Los Angeles."

"Is that how you ended up here? You wanted to be closer to him?"

Jack's brow lifted. "You understand."

"Part of me would love to move in next to my girls, but they'd be horrified. They like their space, but they also like to come visit me here. They love the beach. And so, this summer, I moved to a new apartment, just north of Dana Point so we're close to the beach."

"Hoping to lure them back?"

"Absolutely. A mom's got to do what a mom's got to do." She laughed, feeling surprisingly relaxed. She'd forgotten how easy it was to talk to Jack. "Are you also divorced?"

"No. My wife, Mara, died when Oliver was seven. It's just been him and me ever since."

"I'm sorry."

"It's been twenty-one years. A lifetime ago."

"And you never remarried?"

"No. Tell me about your girls."

"Michelle is twenty-six, Nichole is twenty-five, and Ashley is twenty-three. They're all wonderful and pursuing their careers, scattered across the country."

"You miss them."

"I do." It was time to stop sharing, time to stop probing, even though there were suddenly a dozen different things she wanted to ask Jack, like, when did he marry, and how did he end up with a TV show? Why hadn't he remarried and how did he manage raising a son on his own with his extraordinary career? From the corner of her eye she spotted Greg Hsu but she didn't see his wife, Leigh, and wondered if Leigh was on call tonight. Paige lifted a hand, and he waved back and headed toward them.

"Have you two met yet?" she asked as Greg joined them, and when she saw Greg shake his head, she made the introductions. Greg knew an astonishing amount about Jack's work and they were soon discussing evolutionary biology, and the intrinsic and extrinsic impacts on population.

Paige let her mind wander. She wasn't a science fiend; she preferred math, preferred equations, preferred an orderly world ruled by numbers. Science wasn't orderly. Science was full of change and chaos . . . just like the name of the course she'd soon be co-teaching.

There was a lull in the conversation, and she felt a prickly sensation at her nape. Glancing up she discovered Jack watching her, and the prickly sensation turned into a blush, heat spreading over her cheeks, across her chest. She shifted self-consciously, wondering what he was thinking. Did he recognize her? Or was he just sizing her up? She should have worn something more business casual for tonight instead of a white embroidered dress and high strappy wedges. Her outfit was one younger girls would wear. In fact, her daughters borrowed both when they came to visit.

"Did I miss something?" she asked, body tingling uncomfortably.

"I just said that you're my favorite instructor in the math department." Greg smiled at her and then at Jack. "Students love Paige, especially the ones that struggle with math. She has an uncanny knack for making difficult subjects easy."

"You don't know that," she protested, embarrassed.

"You have an A on Rate My Professors. That's practically unheard of in our departments. Students fight to get into your classes."

She wrinkled her nose. "Math makes sense to me. I want it to make sense to my students, too."

"Why did you become a professor?" Jack asked.

"Education fascinates me. I enjoyed being a student, and then a grad student. Why not spend my entire life on a college campus?"

"It is a nice world," Jack agreed.

"Idealized," Greg said. "It's not the real world."

"Maybe that's what I like," Paige said, smiling, and yet feeling defiant. "Why not create the world we want to live in? I don't see anything wrong with that."

Jack looked at her, and their gazes locked. She couldn't read his expression and yet she had a feeling he didn't agree with her. In fact, she was quite sure he objected to what she'd just said, but she didn't care. Jack King might be the new king of the campus, but he wasn't her king and she wasn't about to change who she was, or what she thought, just to make nice with him.

LEAVING THE PARTY, PAIGE CHECKED HER PHONE, NOTing the missed call from Elizabeth. There was also a follow-up text. You'd better fill me in soon. I'm dying of curiosity. Please put me out of my misery.

Paige and Elizabeth had met their freshman year of high school in Paso Robles, and they'd become fast friends immediately, both in the same honors classes, both on the college track. Elizabeth went on to UC Santa Barbara where she eventually earned a PhD in English, while Paige had focused on math at UC Berkeley.

It was Elizabeth, a tenured professor at Orange specializing in Victorian literature and female writers of the nineteenth century, who'd alerted Paige to the opening at Orange University. She'd been encouraging Paige to move back to California ever since Paige's divorce six years ago, but Paige couldn't move until her girls were all out of school and onto the next thing, and they were most definitely onto the next thing now.

Paige used the Bluetooth in her car to call Elizabeth. Her friend answered right away. "Long time no talk, PG," Elizabeth said, the nickname for Paige when she'd still been Paige Gilbert. "I thought you dropped off the face of the Earth."

"I saw your messages," Paige said. "I'm sorry. It's been a crazy few days."

"I can only imagine. What's he like? Are you excited?"

"I don't know what I feel," Paige answered honestly. "Part of me is annoyed that Dr. Nair squeezed me into filling in for Esther. I suppose another part of me is flattered. Everyone seems so pleased for me, as if I've just won the lottery."

"So, tell me about Jack. I've looked him up a couple of times. Went to Hulu and watched an episode of his series. Is he as good-looking in real life as he is on TV?"

Her insides felt squirmy. She hesitated for a second. "Yes."

"Wow. Scale of one to ten?"

"Elizabeth."

"Come on. Humor me. A seven? An eight? Nine?"

"Nine point seven."

"Wow. From you that's . . . pretty much a ten."

"A ten is a ten. In fact, he's probably more of a nine point two. Maybe just a nine."

"I think we're going to go with your first assessment. Those first impressions are important."

"So says the one that still watches *The Bachelor*."

"I like the sense of possibility."

"Just don't tell me you like the dialogue."

Elizabeth laughed. "No. And it's fairly scripted, but it's better than shows that open with a violent murder."

Paige knew that was a jab at her. "Listen, you might love your Brontës and Jane Austen, but you're not going to manufacture a romance for me."

"No, of course not. And your Jack probably has a serious significant other. But that doesn't mean we can't appreciate his manly attributes."

"He's not my Jack." Paige winced inwardly because he kind of was. Once upon a time. Briefly.

"How did tonight's party go at Dr. Keller's?"

Paige pictured the evening, remembering the strands of white lights in the trees and the glimmering water of the pool and the jazz trio—students from Orange's music department—playing in the background, and then Taffy leaping into the pool, water drenching those standing near the edge.

She snorted. "The Kellers' Labradoodle made a surprise appearance at the party. Chaos ensued. It was hilarious, not that I'll ever say that to Dr. Keller."

"Oh dear. Knowing Dr. Keller, he must have been mortified."

"He was. Especially when Taffy shook out her coat on the VIPs." Paige remembered how Jack had saved the day. Tarzan and the Labradoodle. "Fortunately, Jack King was able to get the dog back in the house. Party saved. He was definitely the hero of the night."

"Why do you sound so grumpy about it? That's a good thing."

"It is." Paige hesitated, wishing she could confide in Elizabeth about her one night with Jack many years ago, but Elizabeth was a little too amped about Jack, romanticizing him a little too much. "I just can't help wondering what Jack's fatal flaw is."

"He might not have one. You know, Paige, you can't hate all men just because your ex was an ass."

Paige had spent twenty years being married to a man who seemed to think he was her boss, and she had no desire to ever end up in that situation again. She didn't need a man telling her what to do, or where to be, or what time to be home. She didn't want to ask for permission to meet friends, see a movie, or take a barre class. She was turning fifty at the end of September, and she was done asking. Done getting permission for anything. Done compromising. And relationships were just one compromise after another. "I don't hate men. I just don't need to spend a lot of one-on-one time with any of them."

"You'll change your mind one day. You're too young to be single for the rest of your life."

"Nope. I'm in menopause. Have no hormones left. It's not going to happen."

"You have plenty of hormones left. You just haven't met the right one."

"There's no right one."

"What about David Muir?" Elizabeth asked sweetly.

Paige sighed. It was so unfair that Elizabeth had gone straight to news anchor David Muir. "David Muir is not going to ask me out."

"He might."

"No, he won't. One, he doesn't know me. Two, he's in a relationship—"

"How do you know?"

"It's obvious. He's not on the market."

"We don't know that, and you might one day meet him and he *could* ask you out."

"Elizabeth, you're worse than my kids."

"They want you to date, too?"

"No. They don't care. They just want me happy—"

"I want you happy."

"Your idea of happy is my idea of hell. Fighting for the remote, doing his laundry, picking up after him—"

"Not all men are slobs. I seriously doubt David Muir is a slob. In fact, I bet he's very organized and tidy, just like you. You wouldn't have to share the remote, either. You'd both like the same shows."

Paige laughed, because she couldn't help it. "Fine, if David Muir asked me out, I'd consider it. But since I can safely say he's not going to, I can also safely assure you that I will never date again."

"At least we've established something important. You're not dead."

"Just close."

"Stop it. You're beautiful. And smart, and loving, and loyal—"

"And happy single."

"Do you really want to be alone for the rest of your life?"

"Yes."

"Why?"

"Because I refuse to wear rose-colored glasses any longer. Maybe when I was a little girl I believed in fairy tales, but I don't anymore. I haven't in a long, long time."

"I don't, either."

"Elizabeth, you read romance and I read true crime. You believe in happy endings. I believe no one's to be trusted."

"You're not that cynical."

"I'm getting there."

"Just tell me this, why is it such a bad thing to like Jack? No one is saying you have to date him. But you can be friends. You're friends with Greg."

"That's different. He's not single. Being overly friendly with single men leads to complications. Every time."

"Because men want to sleep with you, and you don't want to get naked with them."

"Ugh. Just the very idea of getting naked with an old guy. Yuck."

"You've plenty of younger men interested. Remember

that new art professor? The one from New York? He dug you big-time."

"I don't date colleagues."

"What you mean is, you don't date."

"Yes. That is what I mean." Paige signaled, taking the exit off the 5 for Dana Point. "Are we going to barre in the morning? You've bailed on me twice now."

"I can't tomorrow morning. But maybe Sunday?"

"You'll bail on me. You're going to go to church and then brunch somewhere."

"Maybe."

"Elizabeth."

"Love you."

"*Grr.* Love you, too. Good night."

Paige parked in her garage and walked up the stairs to her second-floor apartment. It was dark and warm when she unlocked the door but would cool quickly once she opened windows and let in the breeze coming in from the sea.

She'd spent her first three years at Orange in an apartment complex close to campus, thinking it would save money to walk instead of drive, but in the end, she'd rarely walked since so many of her classes ended late and she felt safer driving once it was dark. Every time one of her daughters would visit, they'd want to go to Laguna, and so she'd found a place close to Laguna without paying the high Laguna Beach rent.

Paige filled a glass with water from her refrigerator and carried it to the balcony. She had a sliver of a view of the ocean, but it was better than of a parking lot. She sat down in one of the folding chairs, took off her shoes and propped her bare feet on the railing, and thought about her weekend. She'd take an exercise class in the morning, read through the syllabus for Jack's class, check in with the two students she'd tutored all summer and see if they needed anything before they started school next week. Not a bad weekend. There'd be time to finish the book she was reading and maybe even watch a couple episodes of *Dead to Me*. Michelle had gotten her hooked on it but Paige didn't like to watch only one episode, so she'd saved them up so she could binge on two or three.

Little joys, she thought, smiling faintly.

A barre class.

A sliver of the ocean.

Two saved episodes of *Unsolved Mysteries* or *Dead to Me*.

It might not sound like much to someone else, but these things all represented freedom. Peace. Her little apartment was a haven of security and calm. She no longer had to play the game of the Emperor's New Clothes. There was no more ignoring the elephant in the room, no more pretending that she wasn't walking on eggshells, or pretending she had a satisfying marriage. She was free. Free of placating an alcoholic husband. Free of biting her tongue to keep from protesting just how angry she was at how her marriage, and life, had been hijacked, and her hijacker was none other than the man she'd once loved more than anything.

But a hard marriage squeezed the love out of you.

A hard marriage made love feel like torture.

So, no thank you. No dates. No men. She was good. Maybe not ecstatic, but content. And after the past twenty years, a tough twenty years, content was enough.

Chapter 4

JACK MOVED INTO HIS NEW APARTMENT ON FRIDAY, ONE week after the cocktail party at President Keller's house, and then spent the rest of his weekend finishing a paper he'd promised to have done weeks ago, at the beginning of summer, but things had kept popping up. Like this opportunity at Orange. Getting permission for the sabbatical. And then organizing the move to California so he could still get his speaking engagements in.

Fortunately, he'd found someone to sublet his house in Princeton, and then it had just been a matter of loading the things he wanted to take with him to California in Gertie and driving west.

On the way, he'd stopped in Jackson, Wyoming, to see Mara's parents, and then he'd made another stop in Montana to visit the wolf habitat run by one of his former students.

There were other visits on the way, with friends and colleagues, but there was also the peace that came with being on the open road, with no computer, phone, or other distractions. He drove, listened to classical music, and felt grateful to be alive.

He was one of the lucky ones. He had work he loved, friends he cared about, and a son who made him proud. Jack wasn't sure what he'd ever done to deserve Oliver, but Oliver was an incredible human being, and the best of the best. By the time he'd reached LA, he couldn't wait to see Oliver. They'd had one night to catch up before Oliver was on a plane to New York, and then Jack was off to Hilo, Paris, and Delhi.

He was done traveling now. A year ago, he'd made the decision to cut back on traveling during the school semester, finding the rigors of speaking, traveling, writing, and teaching were taking a toll. He could still push himself hard, but he didn't enjoy the juggling act, or the resulting fatigue. Jack had always prided himself on being able to accomplish a lot, but there was a price to be paid for missing sleep and having little, or no, downtime.

As it stood, Jack's next trip would be the field research in Costa Rica with the Orange University students. Thirteen weeks before his next trip. That seemed like an awfully long time to be in one place, but Jack would use every opportunity he could to see Oliver. This was the year of Oliver. Provided Oliver would be around.

And then he suddenly thought of Paige and how appealing she'd looked at the party in her flirty white dress with her long blond hair loose over her shoulders. That was the Paige he remembered from Paris, the one who loved white tank tops and short denim skirts, acid-wash denim in particular. It was rather maddening that she didn't remember him, or continued to pretend she didn't. He'd been a graduate student in the program, teaching two courses that summer—none of hers, though—but he'd see her during social events and on campus in passing. She was hard to miss, the quintessential California girl. He'd successfully avoided getting close to her, but then during the last week of the program, they'd been thrown together during an excursion, and all he could think about was how much he wanted her.

And then they'd gone to dinner with the group and after everyone else had left the brasserie for a night club, she'd remained at the table, and so had he. They'd drunk wine and talked, and talked, and he'd felt the tension between them, heady, sweet, seductive. The beautiful night contributed, as did the wine, but it was mostly her, and the sizzle of attraction. They ended up back at his room and it wasn't until she was beneath him, in his bed, that he'd realized she was still fairly inexperienced. She'd faked her orgasm, too, and when he'd wanted to go down on her to give her a real one, she'd stopped him.

Jack leaned back in his chair, away from his laptop. He didn't remember everything from that night, but he could see her, after, wrapped in his top sheet, blue gaze wary. He could see the wheels turning in her head, see her think, and the more she thought, the more distant she became.

He'd walked her back to her room. It had to be three, maybe four, in the morning, and he'd kissed her goodbye, and she'd kissed him back, and as warm as it had been, it also felt final.

He wasn't completely shocked to discover she'd returned to California the next day, but he had been disappointed.

There were things they should have said, things he should have said. He liked her. She was beautiful and bright. Fascinating, really. She had that very pretty face coupled with a sharp intellect, and he'd wanted more time with her, more time to discover who she was. But obviously she regretted the night together and he didn't pursue her. He let her escape and he moved on.

But seeing her again brought the Paris summer, and their night together, to life. She was still beautiful, still brilliant, still appealing.

Still as puzzling.

He didn't mind a puzzle. In fact, he was drawn to them. His career had been based on solving problems and puzzles. Problems and puzzles made the world interesting.

Jack reached for his phone and shot Paige a quick text, thanking her for the lead on his apartment, along with tips on shops he might like that sold high quality, organic food, as well as a popular vegetarian restaurant not far from the apartment complex.

His text was answered a minute later with a simple ☺

Jack studied the emoji for a moment before setting the phone down. Dr. Paige Newsome was definitely an intriguing human being.

THE NEXT WEEK PASSED TOO QUICKLY FOR PAIGE. SHE spent most of the work week preparing for her new class, as well as doing the admin that came with teaching. Students were emailing her asking if she'd waive the prerequisite for her advanced mathematical physics course, while others were hoping they could still get into a full course. She had department meetings and, of course, meetings with Jack, because he had a lot of opinions on how his course should be taught. She couldn't even be resentful, because every time they met, she was drawn into his enthusiasm and passion. The classwork, and the course assignments, all led to the hands-on field work, work students would be able to do toward the end of the semester, provided they had passing grades.

"Does anyone fail this course?" she asked him one day after an hour-long planning session. They were sitting at a table in the shade outside of the university's three coffeehouses, but there wasn't much respite from the heat as there was no breeze. Temperatures had been in the midnineties all week—a heat wave for Southern California—and yet it hadn't slowed Jack down. He claimed to still be acclimated to the high heat and humidity of Delhi, but she suspected weather just didn't bother him.

"Not often, but it happens," he said. "Usually we weed out those who aren't serious in the first week or two. There's a lot of reading right away, and a big paper due at the end of week three. If they can't get the paper in, or done well, they will usually drop the course then."

"A heavily weighted paper on week three isn't by accident, then."

"No. And I stress the paper quite a bit that first week, so don't be surprised to hear me mentioning it every day."

"Your version of *Scared Straight!*?"

"What's that?"

"It was an American television show where they'd take kids who were getting in trouble and show them what life was like behind bars. Inmates would talk to them, tell them it was rough in prison and they didn't want to end up there."

"I take it the inmates weren't always gentle."

"Or the corrections officers. It gave me nightmares when I was a girl. I *really* didn't want to end up in jail."

Jack grinned. "At least you had goals."

"I had so many goals it wasn't even funny. I wrote them all down, too, in this diary my mom gave me. I think she'd hoped I would use it to better express myself, but I'm not a writer. I do like lists, though."

"What was your first goal? Do you remember?"

"To go away for college, leave the ranch. I wanted to get out of Paso Robles. See something else. Do something else."

"Your family are ranchers?"

"Cattle ranch and crops. Although my brother has begun converting some of the acreage to grapes. Paso Robles has become a winery destination."

"Isn't the climate hot and dry there?"

She nodded. "Rob started growing grapes for Cabernet Sauvignon and Zinfandel. He's also experimenting with

Chardonnay. There's a lot of pushback with cattle ranching right now. Environmental issues."

"I'm well familiar with the argument against."

"Are you vegetarian?" she asked.

"I try to eat a plant-based diet whenever I can, but I'm not incredibly strict, it's impossible with my travel schedule. Interestingly, much of the world is plant based, so I can get by wherever I am."

"Did you travel anywhere else besides India this summer?"

"A week in Hilo, and almost ten days in Paris."

"You spoke at conferences in each place?"

He nodded.

"Is it all work, or do you manage some play?"

"I try to squeeze in play whenever possible. I want to enjoy life."

"Is it easy for you to do that? Enjoy life?"

"Yes." Jack grinned. "It's one of my strengths. What about you? Do you have zest, gusto?"

But Paige didn't answer, distracted by the sound of footsteps. She glanced up. It was Elizabeth. "Hey, you," Paige said. "Want to join us?"

"Am I interrupting?" Elizabeth asked.

Paige glanced at Jack. He shook his head and moved his computer to make room for her. "We were just making small talk," he said, rising, extending his hand. "I'm Jack King."

"Elizabeth Reynolds," Elizabeth answered, smiling broadly. "I teach in the English Department. I was the one who wooed Paige from North Carolina."

"Elizabeth and I have been best friends since high school," Paige said as Elizabeth pulled out a chair and sat down. Jack waited for Elizabeth to sit to take his seat again.

"Paige insists we met in English," Elizabeth said. "But I remember meeting her in math. I couldn't do math. I was constantly in a state of panic, especially because the Algebra One teacher loved to call on me, and I never knew the answer. Paige always knew the answer, and she began to feed me answers to save me from being embarrassed in front of the whole class."

"That's how you became friends?" Jack asked.

"No, it was how we met. I don't think we became really close friends until later, the Fall of our sophomore year." Elizabeth glanced at Paige. "My dad was killed in a car accident, and Paige's family took me under their wing, planned activities to keep me busy. Even took me on camping trips up and down the coast. I celebrated my sixteenth birthday with them."

"Sounds like Paige's parents are good people," Jack said.

"I had great parents," Paige agreed. "My dad's gone now, too, but my mom's still alive, and she and Elizabeth's mom have become friends over the years. They're part of the same birthday group so they see each other frequently."

Jack looked at Paige. "How many years were you in North Carolina?"

"Twenty. Moved there when Michelle was one and I was pregnant with Nichole. I didn't leave until they were all out of the house."

"Where did you teach?"

"I started at UNC and ended up at Duke."

"Two great schools."

Paige nodded. "But I missed California, missed being closer to my mom, and Elizabeth. Now I can drive up to Paso Robles on weekends, and I've been doing that every four to six weeks. It's a lot easier than jumping on planes and renting cars." She studied Jack from across the table. "Do you go home often? That's quite a flight."

"To Melbourne? No. My parents are both gone, and I was an only child so there aren't brothers or sisters missing me, which is maybe why I don't really think of it as home anymore."

"So, home is Princeton?"

"It's where I keep my stuff, and it's where I raised Oliver."

"You sound like a rolling stone," Elizabeth said.

"I am," he agreed. "I have a hard time staying in one place for a long time."

Paige couldn't imagine constantly traveling. She was a homebody. She liked having her own place in the world. "But you're a tenured professor at Princeton."

He grinned. "They tolerate me."

Elizabeth laughed. "I imagine they know field work is important to your work."

"I just keep publishing papers, which makes them happy."

"You make them look good," Elizabeth said.

He shrugged. "It's been a good relationship. I've been happy there."

"And now you're here," Elizabeth persisted.

"Orange reached out to me letting me know they had an opening this year in the science department, and as I haven't seen much of Oliver these past few years I thought it'd be nice to be closer. So here I am." He glanced at his watch, frowned. "Speaking of the science department, looks like I'm missing a department meeting now. Don't want to make a bad impression before school has even started." He collected his things, rose, and was off.

Paige watched him walk away, strides long, knapsack casually hanging from one broad shoulder. He was older than her, but he moved like a man in his thirties. Fit, strong, confident.

Paige turned back to Elizabeth and discovered Elizabeth was smiling at her, and it was that incredibly annoying, knowing kind of smile that only Elizabeth could do.

"What?" Paige demanded. "Why the smirk?"

"Not smirking."

"You're totally smirking."

Elizabeth gave her a knowing look. "You like him."

Paige wondered what Elizabeth would say if she knew that this was the guy Paige had met in Paris. The guy who was adventurous in bed but completely out of Paige's league. And realm of experience. "He's a colleague who's interesting, so yes, I like him in a professional sense, but I don't like him romantically."

"I disagree."

"Disagree all you want. It's the truth."

"You think he's attractive."

"Yes. He is attractive, but that doesn't mean anything. Michelle's boyfriend is attractive and I'm not interested in him."

"That's good because one, Michelle's boyfriend is Michelle's, and two, he's twenty-five years too young for you. If you're going to date, you want to date someone like . . . Jack. Someone mature, someone successful, someone who won't expect you to spend all your free time doing laundry and housework."

Paige knew Elizabeth was referencing Ted, her ex-husband, but she wouldn't acknowledge it. "I'm glad you've remarried. I'm glad you're happy, Elizabeth, but not everyone has to be married to be happy."

"I just worry about when you're older. I worry you'll be cut off from the world—"

"I'm still not fifty—"

"You have three weeks until then, yes."

"Please stop terrorizing me with visions of a sad, lonely, desperate future. My future isn't going to look like that. My future includes a really cute house somewhere on the coast, close to Mom, but not necessarily in her back pocket."

"So, that's your goal? To live alone in your house where you'll grow sunflowers, make sun tea, and have a vegetable garden?"

"You've forgotten the swing on the front porch," Paige said dryly.

"Can you possibly picture our Jack on that swing?"

"*No.* And he's not ours. Now please be my BFF and stop pushing me into the dating pool. I've been there. I didn't like it."

THE FIRST WEEK OF SCHOOL WENT OFF WITHOUT A hitch. Paige couldn't quite believe what a smooth first week it was. The normal problems didn't seem to materialize, and rather than dreading the course she was team teaching with Jack, Paige found herself looking forward to it every Monday, Wednesday, and Friday.

Jack was fun to watch in action. He had so much energy and warmth in his voice. The students smiled and laughed throughout much of his lecture. He wasn't slapstick funny but witty and insightful. Paige had always considered herself a good instructor, but Jack elevated teaching, taking it to another level. He could be very serious, too, and somber, making grave points in such a way that it seemed to have a profound impact on the class.

After class, he always had a gaggle of students waiting to speak to him, to discuss a point he'd made or ask further questions.

It was rare that they walked out the classroom door together, and today was no exception. He was surrounded again, and Paige flashed him a smile as she gathered her things and headed for the door. He caught her eye, gave her a faint, wry smile, and continued speaking to the students.

That private smile made her feel warm. Slightly breathless, slightly tingly. The breathless, tingly feeling was uncomfortable, as well as annoying. There was no reason to feel anything, and the last thing she wanted was to be aware of Jack as a man. It didn't help that Jack looked more like a man in his forties than his fifties. His hair was thick and sun-streaked. His frame was strong and muscular. Even his forearms had corded muscles. And even when talking, he had a challenging glint in his eye.

Outside, she skirted the quad, sticking to the shadows where it was cooler. She'd brought lunch today in a bright blue insulated bag she'd tucked into her lavender tote, and she looked for a bench somewhere in the shade where she could eat before returning to the math building for office hours.

She'd just sat down when she got a FaceTime call from Ashley, her youngest, who now called New York home, where she waitressed in between going to auditions. Ashley had grown up acting and dancing and singing, and it was her dream to be a star on Broadway. Paige knew it was a long shot, but she had vowed to never discourage her. There was no need to, either, when her ex, Ted, did that constantly, picking at the girls, tearing them down. It infuriated her the way he interacted with them. He hated that he had no relationship with them anymore, but it was his fault. If he couldn't be kind, if he couldn't encourage them, why would they want to stay in touch with him?

"Hi, honey," Paige said, answering the call and waiting for Ashley's beautiful face to appear on her screen. All her girls were beautiful, but Ashley had been told more than once that she looked just like a Disney princess. "How are you?"

But Ashley wasn't smiling. Tears shone in her dark blue eyes. "I didn't get the part," she said brokenly. "Three callbacks and then it went to someone else."

It had been a long year for Ashley without a lot of positive outcomes. "I'm sorry."

Ashley swiped away a tear. "I get so close but then . . . nothing."

"Three callbacks—that's so impressive. Think about all the girls who didn't even make it to one."

Ashley shook her head, fresh tears welling. "I really thought I had a chance this time."

"You did. And you're getting closer every time. Don't get discouraged."

"Mom, I want to be an actress, not a waitress."

"You could do temp work instead of waitressing."

"I make a lot more money waitressing."

"Then give yourself a day to feel bad, and start tomorrow focused and strong because you know you've chosen a hard road, but I believe in you. And I believe you can do whatever you set your mind to."

"And what if I never succeed?" Ashley demanded.

"Then you've had the adventure of a lifetime."

"Mom."

"What?"

"I don't want the adventure of a lifetime. I want a career on Broadway. I want to do this forever."

"Then don't give up."

Paige sat motionless for a long moment after Ashley had hung up. There were times she felt like a failure as a mom, and maybe it was unreasonable to think she would always know the right thing to say, but she tried. She wanted to be supportive. She wanted her daughters to feel empowered. She wanted them to believe they could do anything if they didn't give up.

Tenacity was essential in life.

As was hard work.

"You look deep in thought," Jack said, standing next to her bench.

She blinked and looked up. "I was."

"I shouldn't interrupt, then."

"No, please do. I'm ready to think of something else. Please distract me."

"I'll do my best." Jack gestured to the blue tote on her lap. "I brought my lunch, too. Can I join you?"

"Yes." She scooted down, giving him more room. "Class went well today."

"A lot of class participation," he agreed. "It's great to see them so engaged already. I think it's going to be a really good semester."

"I've enjoyed this first week."

"You didn't expect to?" he asked with a smile, pulling

his lunch from his knapsack. It looked like tahini and vegetables.

She grinned, shrugged. "You never know. You were an unknown entity."

"And you dislike chaos and change."

"And you don't?" she flashed.

"I like it better than conformity."

"I'm not a conformist."

"No?"

Her temper flared. "*No.*" She held up an arm, showing off her numerous gold bangles. "This is bohemian. I am bohemian."

His lips twitched. "I'm sorry, I didn't know."

"How could you not know? I wear fun clothes, and interesting jewelry—"

"And scary black glasses to hide the fact that you're incredibly pretty."

Heat rushed through her, and her cheeks suddenly burned hot. Paige glanced down at her pathetic turkey sandwich with its limp lettuce leaf, no longer hungry. "I'm not trying to hide anything," she said flatly. "I'm just being me."

"I wasn't criticizing you. I think you're smart to be careful. Smart to keep some armor around you. The world is a hard, unforgiving place."

That gave her pause, and she looked him over, seeing just possibly behind his charming, affable persona. "And here I thought you were such an optimist."

"Sorry to disappoint you. You're looking at a die-hard realist who naively—stubbornly?—clings to hope. Change is essential in life. If we can't grow, can't evolve, we won't survive."

"But it's not enough to survive," she said after a moment, feeling a peculiar tug on her heart. "Is it?"

He took a long moment to answer. "Not for me, no."

Chapter 5

PAIGE HAD FALLEN ASLEEP LISTENING TO AN ECONOMIC podcast, and then woke up slowly, happy it was the weekend. She snuggled back into her pillows and covers, wanting to linger in that lovely, relaxed, sleepy state, and maybe fall back asleep for another hour or so.

But somehow in her lovely, relaxed, sleepy state she pictured Jack, and her pulse quickened, and before she could dismiss him, her mind began to work. He'd done so much in the thirty years since they'd both been in Paris. His list of accomplishments was so impressive, it was almost too much. How did one do all that he'd done and have a personal life? A family life?

Maybe he'd sacrificed family for his professional life, much as she'd done the opposite. She'd avoided—declined—opportunities that would have earned her more money, given her a higher profile, because more work meant less time to be the mother she wanted to be, and the wife her husband had wanted her to be.

Turning over in bed, Paige fluffed her pillow and told

herself she didn't regret her choices—but she did feel some envy that there were others who could juggle responsibilities better, and had been able to pursue more opportunities, possibly more lucrative opportunities. Although, to be fair, her passions were her girls, and that wasn't something academics wanted to hear from colleagues. Passions were to be one's field, not the people at home.

She'd tried to have both, and do both, but from the beginning of motherhood she'd been aware that her daughters were only with her for a short time before they'd declare their own emancipation and move on in the world. She'd raised them to be strong and independent, and they were. Their careers were starting to absorb them, their adult relationships were taking up increasing amounts of time, and one day— not that far off—they'd start families of their own and Paige would be lucky to be included in birthdays and holidays.

This is why she worked hard now, saving for retirement, making plans for her own future. The little house in Cayucos or Avila Beach. The garden teeming with vegetables and sunflowers. The front porch with a chair facing the sea. She'd be close to her mom, but not on top of her. Close to her brother's family, but again, not in their back pocket.

She'd have time to read all those books that she hadn't been able to read, time to binge those interesting streaming shows, time for all the farmers markets, beach walks, and shell collecting her heart desired. She'd be outside as much as possible with the sun on her face and the smell of salt in the air.

But later, a little voice challenged her, whispering, *is that really enough?* Because she wasn't an introvert. She didn't enjoy farmers markets on her own. She liked to visit with her daughters. And then she left to go to lunch somewhere, sit outside on the patio and enjoy a meal with her girls or with Elizabeth. She enjoyed being with others, being surrounded by those she loved . . . and those who loved her.

There was a certain disquieting unease in the idea of

growing older alone, which is why she'd always pictured a life where she'd be a very involved grandmother, someone who'd come in and take care of the grandkids, plan fun weekend things with her extended family . . .

But what if Nichole didn't have kids? She said she wasn't sure. And what if Michelle didn't want or need her visiting too often, because as a firstborn, she was fiercely independent? Her youngest would probably always need her, which was a comfort, but again, that would probably change one day after she married. And Paige had to be realistic—even the best sons-in-law didn't want their mother-in-law always over, hovering. Interfering. Not that Paige would ever want to hover or interfere, but she'd learned from her marriage that men only had so much patience for one's mother-in-law before they simply didn't want another visit. Or at least not for a year. Once a year had been enough for Ted, but Paige couldn't imagine only seeing her girls, or grandchildren, so infrequently. It was one of the reasons she wanted a charming beach house filled with sunflowers. She wanted her girls to always feel welcome, to know she'd always be there for them, no matter what.

It struck her then just how often she framed her future in terms of being accessible for her daughters.

How decisions were made, or not made, so that she'd be available for them.

Even when they didn't ask it of her.

Elizabeth had challenged her before to say yes to more opportunities that had nothing to do with her girls— opportunities like dating and travel.

Paige had disagreed, rather fiercely. She wasn't hanging around just waiting for a call from one of the girls. Paige had a life.

In fact, she was doing something today, for herself, she thought, throwing back the covers and climbing from bed. She was going to take a barre class at nine, and then do some errands, maybe hit the farmers market and pick up fish and fresh produce. She was going to have a wonderful day, the kind of day she liked best.

Even if she was on her own.

WITH NO PAPERS TO WRITE AND OLIVER UNEXPECTEDLY home for the weekend, Jack offered to drive up to see him and take Oliver to lunch. Instead, Oliver suggested driving to Orange County Saturday morning, saying he'd like to see his dad's place, and maybe they could eat near the water somewhere before he returned home as he had an engagement for that evening.

"A date?" Jack asked.

"A premiere for a friend's film." Oliver paused. "But yes, I'm taking someone with me, so I'll need to make an effort."

"If today's not good—"

"Today's great. It looks like a beautiful morning, too, so perfect for a drive."

Less than two hours later, Oliver called to say he was exiting the freeway and should be to Jack's complex in less than five minutes. Jack headed down to the parking lot, eager to see his son.

Jack pointed to the visitor parking where there was still one spot open, and Oliver parked, exited the car. Jack gave his son a bear hug. Oliver smelled fresh, as if he'd just stepped from the shower. "How was the traffic?" Jack asked.

"Not bad at all. Got down here in just a little over an hour. Practically record time."

"Good. Are you hungry?"

"Not yet, but I will be."

"Anything special you want to do?"

"I want to see your apartment, and then I thought maybe we'd head to the coast. You know I love the water."

"There's not much to see in my apartment, Oliver. I have a bed, a table, a chair, and that's about it."

"I thought you were going to rent furniture?"

"I did. A bed, a table, and a chair."

"What about a couch?"

"If I want to lie down, I've got my bed."

"What if you want to watch TV?"

"I don't own a TV, and if I wanted to watch something on my laptop—"

"You have your bed. I got it." But Oliver was smiling. "You don't change."

Jack lifted a brow. "Do I need to?"

"No, Dad. I like you the way you are. Predictable."

"I'm not predictable."

"Oh, you are, but in a good way." Oliver laughed. "It's comforting."

"How am I predictable?"

"You don't need a lot of creature comforts. You don't need people—"

"That's not true."

"It is true. You love me, but you're quite happy on your own."

Jack shrugged, unable to argue Oliver's point.

"You have a sentimental attachment to a very old car. You have a lot of money, money you never spend."

"Money doesn't give me happiness."

Oliver gave his dark head a shake, expression amused. "I could have predicted every answer. You don't change, and I'm not complaining. I'm lucky to have been raised by someone who believes value comes from accomplishments, not from acquisitions."

"I wouldn't have a problem if you had hundreds of toys. I don't care what other people do. I just don't need a lot of things." Jack clapped his son's shoulder. "How about we hop in Gertie and go for a drive?"

After a very brief tour of Jack's apartment, they headed back downstairs and got into Gertie and drove south on Highway 5 to the harbor town of Dana Point. Traffic was picking up as those inland flocked to the beach for the day.

Jack parked in a lot down by the water and they left the car to watch the surfers. It was a surprisingly crowded point for how shallow it was, but because it was shallow, it looked like a good spot for beginners.

"Do you ever come south to surf?" Jack asked, glancing at Oliver.

Oliver shook his head. "There's good surf by me. No desire to fight traffic just to get in the water, not when there are great breaks in Los Angeles." He looked at his dad. "When is the last time you paddled out?"

"Too long," Jack answered. "Maybe Costa Rica with you?"

"Dad, that was years ago."

"I've been busy." He paused. His gaze narrowed on the lineup of surfers. "But maybe now that I'm here in Orange County I should think about picking up a board and heading out. I'll be pretty rusty, though."

"It's like riding a bike. Muscle memory. You don't forget. At least, that's what you used to tell me when I was a grommet." Oliver shifted his weight, arms folding over his broad chest. "I'll bring a board down to you before I leave for Auckland."

"Only if you'll bring one for yourself and we can paddle out together."

"That way I can make sure no one messes with you. You know how locals could be."

Jack laughed. "I can still handle myself, thanks, son."

"I'm just saying—"

"I know what you're saying. But I was the one who taught you to surf, and taught you self-defense. Your old man can still handle himself. If I didn't, I wouldn't still be traveling as much as I do."

They turned away from the water and started back for the parking lot when Oliver pointed out the farmers market. "Want to check it out?" he asked.

"Sure," Jack answered.

They walked for a moment in silence before Oliver asked about the semester. "Teaching going well? No surprises?"

"No surprises," Jack said, then hesitated when he pictured Paige with her long blond ponytail, colorful hoop earrings, and serious black cat-eye glasses. It almost seemed like Paige went out of her way to hide how pretty she was. "It's going well. I'm enjoying it. Living here feels like I'm on holiday. The climate and vegetation remind me of Greece."

"You love Greece."

"I do."

Oliver smiled at his dad. "So, you're good."

"I am," he agreed, even as Paige came to mind once more. He'd been drawn to her thirty years ago. He was just as intrigued by her now. Maybe it was time to figure out why she was pretending she didn't know him. Unless she truly didn't remember, but his gut told him that wasn't the case.

They entered the open-air market with the white tents and vendor tables piled high with colorful produce, jars of honey, and steaming tamales. Jack bought some fresh salmon and vegetables for dinner, and then examined the fruit, choosing a basket of fresh berries. Just as he finished paying for the berries, a woman in a short flared skirt, pink baseball cap, and heart-shaped sunglasses approached the register with a mango and an avocado. It was Paige. He was just about to greet her when her phone rang, and she juggled the fruit while retrieving her phone. "Michelle," she said, answering the phone, "hi, give me just one second, okay?"

Thinking Paige looked very young and pretty this morning, very much like the girl in Paris, Jack watched her put the fruit into the mesh bag she carried and continue on, still talking on the phone. Jack gave Paige one last look before joining Oliver, who stood at a distance to stay out of shoppers' way. He almost pointed Paige out to Oliver, but didn't. Oliver, being a filmmaker and storyteller, would ask questions, wanting to know more, but at this point, Jack had little he could say. Paige was a mystery, and for now, his mystery.

"Are you flying back up to Vancouver tomorrow?" he asked Oliver as they left the market to find a spot by the water for lunch.

Oliver nodded. "I am. And then I should be back in another week or two. Let's get together, as once I'm in New Zealand, I won't be home for a while."

"A month, you said."

"Could be longer."

"Then we'll definitely get together after you return from Vancouver."

IT WAS A GOOD WEEK, A PRODUCTIVE WEEK, AND PAIGE attended a department meeting where Jack had been asked to share a little bit about his work, what he was teaching this semester, and what he'd teach in the Spring. He charmed the faculty with his charisma and wit. Paige tried to suppress the warmth she felt, listening, watching. He was incredibly appealing with his strong jaw and quick smile that reflected in his clear, bright eyes.

He looked fit—virile—and a little too much like a movie star. At least, she felt rather dazzled. The attraction was still there. The pull to be near him. She wished it wasn't. It would be so much easier if all she felt was a polite, detached professional respect, and yes, she respected him, but she also felt more. The man had a brilliant mind, encased in a sexy, confident package—face, body, charm, athleticism. She'd find him less appealing if he was one of those intellectuals who took themselves too seriously and didn't know how to laugh at themselves, but Jack laughed at himself, and his humor made her smile, even if she kept her smile to herself.

She'd found him watching her on more than one occasion, a speculative gleam in his eyes.

Had he recognized her?

Or was he trying to place her?

Either way, she couldn't get close to him. She'd been close once, and it had almost done her in. True, she was older now. Experienced. But Paige didn't know if she could handle what he represented: Sex. And probably sex without commitments. Sex that would be just for the fun of it. The pleasure.

Uncomfortable, Paige crossed her legs, shifting in her seat. It had been a long time since sex sounded like fun. Since sex gave pleasure. By the end of her marriage, there had been no sex. The last few years she and Ted practically slept in separate bedrooms, or if the girls were all home, she'd take the couch. Ted would come looking for her, though, when he'd had too much to drink, and there was nothing she wanted less than sex with someone sloppy and drunk. Ted accused her of not caring for him, of not being a good wife, but if he wanted to save their marriage, maybe he could have given up the alcohol and tried to be present. A little bit kind. Maybe focusing on having a relationship—friendship—would have helped save their marriage, although Paige privately doubted it. If she were honest, she'd stopped feeling love years before, but she'd been taught that even if one didn't feel loving, one should still act on it, and so she tried to at least act loving: making dinners and coffee in the morning. She'd tried to be warm and cheerful, welcoming when he came home, but when he started coming home already drunk, everything inside of her iced over, hardening with distaste. Maybe some men could handle their alcohol, but Ted wasn't one of them. Inebriated, he became obnoxious, grabby, and demanding. Even now, remembering, she felt sick on the inside. Those had not been good years.

Faculty were asking Jack questions now, and she forced herself to focus. He answered one question, mentioning her by name, and he looked at her and smiled as he talked about the upcoming field work they'd be doing during the last part of the semester.

Mentally, she corrected, field work *he'd be doing*, even as Jack's smile did something to her, sending a ripple of energy.

The fact that she was still so drawn to him troubled her. Relationships were like ropes—entangling. Entrapping. She didn't ever want to feel trapped again. She never wanted to invest so much in someone only to have her heart thrown back at her face. Far better to be single, safe, unencumbered.

Jack sought her out as the meeting ended. "How did I do?" he asked. "Do you think the department heads were happy?"

"You did what you always do—charmed everyone."

"Really? I wouldn't have guessed by your expression. You looked . . . bored."

"No. Definitely wasn't bored. You just got me thinking, so I might have been lost in thought. I'm sorry if I gave the impression that I wasn't interested, because that's not how I felt." And then she flushed and gave her head a quick shake. "I'm always interested in your insights. You're not like anyone else I've ever taught with."

"It's okay. Not criticizing you," he said.

She grew warmer as his gaze settled on her face and then focused on her mouth.

SHE WAS ON DAY TWO OF MIGRAINES TRIGGERED BY THE Santa Ana winds. The worst of the Santa Ana's were still ahead, coming later in fall—usually October—but they'd hit hard early this year, and the combination of hot, dry wind, low moisture in the air, and her head did her in. Light sensitive, she'd spent the weekend living like a vampire: curtains closed, blinds drawn, sunglasses on.

Even now she couldn't handle the light from her phone or computer, making it impossible to get work done. It was maddening to fall behind but getting upset didn't help the situation. As soon as her head was better, and her eyes less sensitive, she'd get back to grading.

In the meantime, groceries were getting low, both produce and dairy virtually gone, but she was too frugal to use any of the popular shopping and delivery services. It made no sense to spend an extra twenty on tips and fees when she could do it herself as soon as she felt better. And she would soon feel better. She had to feel better tomorrow as it was Monday, and she wouldn't miss a day of work, not for a headache, no matter how bad. Sick days were for things like stomach bugs and transmittable viruses. For those she stayed home. The rest—she'd get through.

And yet, as she shuffled around her kitchen and eyed the contents of her refrigerator—egg whites, a little bit of feta cheese, a bag of baby carrots, a pitcher of unsweetened ice tea—she felt nauseous and closed the door again. She was hungry but she'd had an egg white omelet yesterday and had used up her spinach then. She didn't want more egg whites today.

This was one of those times when she wasn't a fan of living alone and wished one of her daughters was closer. But honestly, even if her girls were closer, would she bother them? It was unlikely. Paige hated to be dependent on anyone. She didn't like to ask favors. Far better to do it herself than to be beholden to someone.

She'd always been independent, self-sufficient, but in the last years of her marriage she became even more determined to manage on her own. Maybe it's because the marriage had taught her she had no other choice but to do it herself. Marriage taught her that there was no such thing as a true partnership, that at the end of the day, she was still ultimately responsible for virtually everything. Or at the very least, the things that mattered most to her, like love, patience, kindness, compassion.

Ashley had phoned yesterday, and Paige had chatted with her, hiding the fact that she felt terrible, focusing instead on encouraging her daughter before the next audition coming Monday morning. They discussed the role and how Ashley was preparing. Ashley was excited that she needed to be prepared to sing and possibly follow some choreography. It sounded as if the show was a musical, and Ashley loved musicals, even if dancing wasn't her strongest skill.

Paige had also briefly checked emails early that morning, and finding two from Jack about some of the students he was worried about in class, she answered his second message, letting him know she'd been off-line most of the weekend due to one of her Santa Ana–induced migraines, but that she'd try to catch up with emails and messages later in the day.

She'd logged off then and had taken a nap and was just now trying to rouse herself, when a knock sounded on her front door. Paige dragged her hat lower, adjusted her sunglasses, and headed for the door, peeking out the peephole. It was Jack on her doorstep, backpack on his shoulder, a paper bag in his hand.

She unlocked the door and opened it. "What are you doing here?" she asked huskily.

"Checking on you," he said, his gaze sweeping over her. "Migraines can be debilitating, and I wanted to make sure you were okay."

"I'm fine."

Jack didn't think she looked fine. She was wearing a dark blue baseball cap and oversize sunglasses in the house, the lights off behind her. He glanced past her, into the dark shadows of her apartment. "I wasn't sure you had anyone here helping you."

"No, but there's not much anyone can do. I just need to wait it out." She reached up and smoothed her long hair, as if trying to flatten it against her shoulder. "The good news is that I'm on day two, which means I should start feeling better soon and will be able to teach tomorrow. Elizabeth has promised to pick me up for school so that I won't have to drive."

"Don't you think you should take the day off?"

"I'll be fine. I'll probably wear sunglasses in class, but my students have seen it before. It won't be the first, or the last, time." She clutched the door to her as if it were armor. "How did you even know where I lived?"

"Elizabeth gave me your address when I told her I wanted to bring you lunch as I wasn't sure you were eating."

"You brought me lunch?"

He nodded. "Chicken salad on a croissant with a fruit cup. If it doesn't sound good, just stick it in the fridge."

Her expression wavered. "It actually sounds really good. Thank you." She hesitated. "Want to share the sandwich with me?"

"I already ate, but I'd be happy to keep you company while you eat. I promise not to talk too much. Or at least, not to make you talk too much."

She smiled grimly and stepped back into the shadowy hall. "Sounds like you're familiar with migraines."

"I don't get them, but a friend did." Jack entered the apartment, closing the door behind him before following her to her small living room where she took a seat on the couch, legs curling up under her. When Oliver was a boy he loved Peter Pan, and Jack had read him the novel *Peter Pan* over and over, and later he and Oliver had watched every movie version of Peter Pan and Captain Hook ever made; and at the moment, huddled into the corner of the couch, Paige reminded him of Tinker Bell with her light dimmed. "Do you want to eat now, or later?" he asked.

"I'll eat some now. That way I can take some more medicine."

"What are you drinking?"

"Iced tea."

"Need a refill?"

"There's a pitcher in the fridge."

He topped off her iced tea while she nibbled on half of the croissant sandwich. Her small kitchen was spotless, as well as bright and welcoming, with a big glazed jug filled with sunflowers on the counter. Dozens of photos, handwritten notes, and cards covered the refrigerator. One heart-shaped stickie said, *Love you, Mom, to the moon and back!* The photographs were mostly of her and her daughters, and the daughters looked so much like her, they could all be sisters. He recognized Elizabeth with Paige in another photo. It was most definitely a very personal refrigerator door, decorated with expressions of love.

Paige had finished eating, and he put the container with the other half of the sandwich in the refrigerator before sitting down in a chair close to where she sat. He was no expert, but she did look better, sitting a little taller. "Medicine now?" he asked.

"I'll take it in a bit. But thank you, you're a very attentive caregiver."

"I had years of practice."

Her expression faltered. "I'm sorry—"

"Nothing to be sorry about."

"I should have been more sensitive."

"It was years ago."

"And yet it had to have been awful."

"It was, but in hindsight, it was mostly unfair," he said. "Mara was so young, and Oliver needed a mom." Jack hesitated, picturing Paige's refrigerator and how it was a testament of love. "But it also taught me resiliency, and the importance of living in the moment. Until then, I'd always projected ahead, endless plans for the future. Mara's cancer taught me to embrace the now, because the present is the future, sometimes our only future."

Despite the oversize sunglasses hiding half her face, he could feel her scrutiny. "What?" he asked.

"Just trying to figure you out."

That piqued him. What was this? What game was she playing? Because even he was playing it now, pretending there was no past, pretending they hadn't ever known each other. He knew she hurt today, knew she wasn't feeling well, but his temper flared. He felt angry. Resentful. Jack didn't like pretense. He didn't like lies. Facades.

"You said a friend had migraines," Paige said. "So, it wasn't Mara?"

He bit back his frustration. "No, not Mara."

"A girlfriend?"

"She was my girlfriend." Normally he'd be amused, but he wasn't amused right now. He wanted answers. He wanted the truth. But at the same time, it wasn't fair to press her when she didn't feel well. He'd come over to help, not make things more difficult.

"Tell me about her," Paige said.

"Why?"

Her shoulders lifted, fell. "Just curious. But if it's not something you want to discuss . . ."

"Camille's a scientist, too, but we've never taught together. She's based in Canada, and we've worked on a number of research projects together, but it's been years since we were in a relationship." He gave her a long, considering look. "Does that satisfy your curiosity?"

"I just wonder how you do it all. Work, research, teaching, relationships." Her lips pursed. "You must be better at time management than me."

"It helped that Camille was a long-distance relationship. It freed up a lot of time."

Paige laughed, the sound muffled, husky. "You prefer long-distance relationships."

She said it as a statement, not a question, and he wasn't sure if he was amused or annoyed. "I do stay busy, and I probably prefer special moments over the day-to-day engagement."

"So, not getting married again," she guessed.

"I don't see a reason to marry. Not sure of the benefits."

Paige leaned deeper into the couch, arms crossing over her chest. "I agree with you."

"You do?"

She nodded. "Marriage might be a good thing for others, but I don't ever want to marry again. Relationships shouldn't be a trap, something that boxes you in, makes you smaller. Relationships shouldn't make you suffer."

For a long moment, her words just hung there in the air, and they sounded so bleak. He didn't immediately speak. "You can't escape pain in relationships," he finally said after another moment. "Love, even the best love, can hurt. Mara's cancer ravaged her. The pain when she was dying— it's hard to even go there. The confusion Oliver felt when his mom was finally gone. The questions he asked. It was years before he stopped asking for her."

"That would have killed me. My girls are my heart."

"I had to be strong for him. I had to be everything for him."

She pushed her sunglasses up on her nose. "I wish my girls had had a father like you. I thought Ted would be like my dad. My dad was amazing." She sighed softly. "Ted wasn't amazing. He was just hurtful. For years I tried to tell myself it was the alcohol that made him petty and unkind, but after a while, I couldn't keep making excuses, not when everyone was so miserable."

Jack leaned forward. "Why do you pretend you don't know me?" he asked bluntly. He hadn't meant to ask, not today, not when Paige wasn't well, but the question popped out. "We know each other. I know you. Do you really not remember me?"

Silence stretched for a long, uncomfortable moment, and then Paige's lips pursed. "Of course I remember you." Her voice had dropped, deepened. "How does one *not* remember you, Jack King?"

He didn't understand. His brow creased. "Then why pretend?"

"You didn't recognize me, either. Not at first."

"I knew who you were within minutes—seconds—of sitting down at the coffeehouse. But I was baffled by your response, or lack of response. I wondered if maybe you'd had an accident, suffered a memory loss."

Even in the shadowy light he could see her cheeks flush. "I was embarrassed," she confessed huskily.

"Embarrassed about what?"

"Everything. That night in Paris. Me. The differences between us, and our careers. You've accomplished so much, and in comparison—"

"That's rubbish."

Her shoulders lifted, fell. "I just panicked. It's awful to admit, but I felt insecure."

He was more confused than ever. "But *why*?"

"Jack, I never thought I'd see you again after that summer trip to Paris, and then suddenly I'm supposed to teach with you. I was embarrassed that I fell so easily into bed with you all those years ago. Embarrassed that you've had this huge career and in comparison—"

"Then stop comparing, Paige."

"You're right," she agreed. "I hate feeling ashamed, because I have nothing to feel ashamed about. I'm proud of everything I've accomplished, but—" She broke off, and she gave her head a slight shake. "I'm sorry."

He rose and walked to the kitchen, where he filled a glass with water. He took a long drink, buying time, even as he tried to calm down. He was disappointed. Angry. And he didn't know how to respond.

She entered the kitchen behind him. "Everyone was so excited about you coming to Orange. It was such a big deal."

He turned to face her. "You weren't pleased."

"I was . . . shocked." She leaned against the wall. "At first I thought it had to be a different Jack King. But no, it was you."

"I thought we had a good time in Paris."

Her laugh was low and mocking. "I didn't know what I was doing in Paris. You were totally out of my league."

Jack's chest grew tight, confusion warring with his temper. He didn't get angry often. He didn't like to feel angry. It was such a pointless, destructive emotion. "Did I take advantage of you?"

"No."

He wasn't convinced. He wasn't sure of anything right now. "I was an instructor that summer. You were a student. If I used my position to seduce you—"

"Oh, for God's sake, Jack, *no*. That's not what happened. I wasn't drunk. You didn't take advantage of me. There was no power imbalance. Okay?"

"You left Paris the next day."

"It was time for me to go home." Her chin lifted, expression defiant. "You did nothing wrong. If I'm uncomfortable, it's because I'm uncomfortable with me."

"I don't know why. You're beautiful. Brilliant—"

"Insecure."

"But why? Look at you. Look at what you've achieved."

"I'm also divorced. And I struggle with self-esteem. I take criticism hard. I work too hard to make others happy—"

"Probably at your own expense."

"Probably," she agreed. "I'm a perfectionist, Jack. Always have been." She crossed the kitchen, picked up her pill bottle from the counter, and popped the cap, easing one tablet from the bottle. "But that's my problem," she added, returning to the living room to retrieve her tea. "Not yours."

He followed her back to the living room, watched as she washed down her pill. His chest remained tight with emotion. He was still puzzled and frustrated. He didn't know how to talk to this Paige. He didn't know this Paige. But maybe he'd never known her. "I should go."

"I'll probably be able to sleep now that I have a full stomach. Thank you for the sandwich."

"My pleasure."

"Thank you for checking on me. I appreciate it."

He hesitated. "You don't have to keep up the brave face with me. You can just be you."

"I am me." She pushed a long tendril of hair back from her face, tucking it behind her ear. "I'm sorry I pretended not to know you. I should have come clean—"

"It's fine. You had your reasons."

"It's not fine. It was immature. I'm em—"

"—barrassed, I know, but don't be. We're friends. You can be yourself with me. Warts and all."

"I have no warts, thankfully."

He smiled reluctantly. He wasn't mad at her, not anymore. If anything, he felt empathy. It must be awful thinking you had to be perfect to be liked. Respected. "I saw that you don't have much in your fridge. Can I go do a quick shop for you? Milk, yogurt, veggies, anything?"

"That's nice of you, but I'm good. I think I have a couple cans of soup still in there and some bread in the freezer."

"Tinned soup? That sounds awful."

"I like soup."

"In that case, I'll be off. But if you change your mind, call or text. I'm just fifteen minutes away."

She walked him to the door. "We never talked about the students you're worried about. Is there a reason you wanted me to look over the papers?"

"I just wanted to keep you looped in."

"If that's the case, I'm good without looking at the papers; you know what you want to see. But once you've uploaded the grades, maybe we should see who is struggling. I have a few students who aren't doing well on statistics quizzes and exams, but they might not be the same who didn't do well on your paper."

"I can pull the low grades later tonight and then maybe tomorrow after class we can go through them, if you're up to it."

"I should be," she said. "On Mondays I have office hours right after class, so what about two thirty?"

"Sounds good. See you tomorrow," he said.

After locking the door behind him, Paige returned to the kitchen and then forgot why she was there. Her thoughts were scattered, and her emotions were mixed, but underlying everything was a sense of gratitude. Paige was used to doing everything herself, and accustomed to problem solving for everyone, and yet today she didn't have to figure it all out. Jack was her partner, a very capable partner.

She might actually like being on a team after all.

Chapter 6

PAIGE DIDN'T SLEEP WELL. THE MIGRAINES LEFT HER flattened and then guilt nibbled at her conscience, making it difficult to fall asleep and stay asleep. Deception was never a good plan. She regretted starting off with Jack as she had. She should have welcomed him as a long-lost friend instead of acting like she had no memory. So stupid.

She took a shower, an extra-long shower, and needed a second cup of coffee before she felt together enough to meet the day.

Elizabeth texted to let Paige know she was leaving her house to pick Paige up, and then texted again fifteen minutes later that she was outside. Paige gathered her briefcase, lunch bag, and keys. She hesitated on her doorstep, making sure she'd also brought pain killers. She had.

"How are you feeling?" Elizabeth asked as Paige slid into the passenger seat.

"Better."

"Head still sensitive?"

Paige nodded before buckling up and adjusting her sunglasses. "Not as bad as it was. Just the lingering aftermath. Just wish I'd gotten more done all weekend."

"Did Jack come by?"

"He brought me a sandwich."

"He is so nice. I really like him."

Paige pressed her lips together, not a fan of the subject. Jack's visit yesterday had been incredibly uncomfortable. It was mortifying to be called out. He'd been polite, but it had still been awkward, and after he'd left she couldn't think about anything else.

Elizabeth shot her a side glance as she shifted into drive. "You're quiet."

"Just relaxing."

"You don't have to work constantly. You can take time off. Take a sick day."

"But then I'll get behind."

"Not you. You're always so organized."

"I just like being on top of things." Paige was trying hard not to view it as a wasted weekend, but she did measure things in terms of accomplishments and success. The more she got done, the more satisfied she felt. Her work ethic had been an issue for Ted. He made good money himself. He didn't think she needed to work, but it was her choice, and maybe that was where the resentment came from. That she chose to work, which in his mind, meant she chose to put him second. It wasn't that way, but he'd been raised by a mom who didn't work, and for him, a working wife was almost a criticism of him as a man and a provider.

He'd never understood that she worked because it made her feel accomplished, that she thrived on challenge and loved feeling competent.

She sighed, and Elizabeth glanced at her again.

"Something happen? Is your mom okay? Girls okay?" Elizabeth asked.

"Nothing happened. Just thinking."

"About?"

"Ted."

"Oh, Paige. Why do that to yourself?"

"Good question. But speaking of the girls, Ashley has a big audition this morning. I keep checking my phone, looking for an update. I hope she gets at least a callback."

"She's so talented, she will," Elizabeth said firmly.

Paige smiled. She loved Elizabeth's faith. "How is everyone at your house?"

"My adult two are good, but the twins, that's a whole different ball game."

Paige's lips curved. Elizabeth's twins were hilarious. And a lot of work. Paige adored them but, at the same time, was grateful they weren't hers.

Elizabeth's smile turned wry. "I sometimes envy you, with your girls grown-up and self-sufficient. And then I also wonder if I'll ever be there. I'm still in the middle of homework hell, and emails from teachers regarding my inadequacy as a parent."

"That's only because you had a second set of babies who are gorgeous and gorgeously full of life."

"Oh, very full of life. And if only we could socialize our little animals, we'd be good. I dread the calls and emails letting me know that once again Justin has not kept his hands to himself, and Jason has been disrespectful at Mass, splashing holy water onto other kids instead of making the sign of the cross." Elizabeth grimaced. "What was I thinking, having more kids?"

"That you loved your new husband and wanted to grow your family." Paige patted Elizabeth's arm. "You're doing great. It's just the age. Fourth grade is a hard year."

"Last Thursday I got an email from their teacher asking if I read to my kids, because they were struggling with reading." She shook her head. "Do I read to them? My God, I'm an English professor. I've been reading them everything from Dr. Seuss to Dickens since birth."

"The boys can read. They're probably just not applying themselves, which is natural. They're energetic."

"That's a polite way of saying little beasts."

Paige laughed. "Your husband is full of life. Your kids are. They will be fine. And *I* think your boys are wonderful. Don't stress. Especially since we both know they won't be little forever."

Elizabeth nodded. "When are you going to head to Paso Robles again? I'm thinking of heading home in a few weeks to see Dad. Didn't know if you'd want to drive up together."

"That might be a good idea. I haven't been home for a while, and I know Mom would like to see me."

"Especially with your birthday coming up." Elizabeth gave her a meaningful look. "It being the big one."

Paige laughed, as she was meant to. "Fifty isn't the big one."

"That's probably true. I found thirty the hardest so far," Elizabeth answered. "It's such a shock. One day you're young, and then the next day, you're middle-aged."

"Thirty isn't middle-aged."

"No, but when you're a kid you think thirty is old."

"Fortunately, we haven't been kids for a long time." Paige fell silent for a moment, thinking, because it was true. She hadn't felt young in forever. She couldn't even remember very well what young felt like. "You know, I didn't mind turning thirty, but forty was tough. Everything about forty was hard. I'd never do that one again." Paige had still been married then, still trying to work and smile and act like she wasn't dead on the inside. It had taken so much energy just to keep the mask on, just to survive each day.

"Fortunately, a lot has changed for you since then," Elizabeth said. "You're here now. Settled. Successful. Free."

Free. That was maybe the most important thing. Paige turned her paper coffee cup in the holder. "What do you think sixty will be like?"

Elizabeth pursed her lips, considered the future. "Good.

As long as long as we have our health and our mental faculties intact, we should be fine." Her expression brightened. "And speaking of faculties, how is our favorite new faculty member?"

Paige rolled her eyes. "Oh, Elizabeth, that was a very bad pun. Even for you."

Elizabeth grinned. "Agreed, but that doesn't answer the question. Things going well with the sexiest scientist in all of Australia?"

"It's going well," Paige said, wondering if maybe it was time to mention the fact that she actually knew Jack a little bit better than she'd admitted, but she dreaded Elizabeth's reaction, because there would be a reaction. A big one. But if she wanted Elizabeth to stop matchmaking, then maybe she needed to bring Elizabeth up to speed.

Or not.

She took in Elizabeth's expression, still laughing, still full of happy mischief, and decided against it.

And Elizabeth wondered why her twins were so much trouble? Come on. Elizabeth was trouble. But that's also why Paige loved her.

CLASS WAS EASY. PAIGE LECTURED AND ANSWERED questions, and then she was back in her office, door open, going through emails, waiting for any student needing her help. One student had made an appointment, but he never showed. Her office hours ended with Jack knocking on the open door.

"Am I interrupting?" he asked, and then glanced at her desk, with the two open computers, and smiled. "Dumb question. Of course I'm interrupting."

"Just waiting for you," she answered, rolling back from her desk. "Want to close the door and we'll get started?"

He shut the door but before taking one of the chairs opposite her desk he walked around the small room, briefly glancing at her diplomas before studying a large framed poster titled Important Women of Math, with photos of sixteen women below, women from ancient Greece to famous American mathematicians of color. "I've never seen this poster before," he said.

"It was a slide I made to use in class. One of my former students said I should turn it into a poster, so I did."

He turned back to the poster and tapped the drawing of Hypatia, the first woman to ever study and teach mathematics and philosophy. "Now, she's a woman who suffered for her art."

"Stoned because she wasn't a Christian."

"But if she hadn't been famous, she wouldn't have drawn such attention."

"I suspect if she hadn't been a woman, she wouldn't have been pulled from her chariot and shredded by a bunch of zealots." She returned to her desk. "You better not get me started. I've been accused of carting around a feminist soapbox."

"Get on that soapbox. I love smart women with a point of view."

"Maybe one day. But it'd probably take a drink or two."

"I'll hold you to that," he answered, pulling out a chair opposite her. "How are you feeling now?"

"Better. By tomorrow I should be good as new."

He frowned as his gaze swept the room. "Your office is hot, and bright. Don't you have any blinds?"

"No. I don't think any of us have blinds."

"I do."

She was shocked. "What?"

He nodded. "No wonder you get a headache. What if we go to the Bean Box to work? It's darker and cooler than here. They also have food."

"I don't have wheels today. I'm relying on Elizabeth."

"I can take you, and then drop you off at home."

"That's out of your way."

"I have nothing pressing to do today."

"No research papers to write? No Zoom meetings to attend?"

He smiled. "I do have a Zoom tonight, but that's not for hours."

"What's your Zoom for?"

"The Nelson Mandela African Institution of Science and Technology in Arusha."

"Arusha?"

"Tanzania. It's one of the universities set up by Mandela and Jim Wolfensohn when Jim was head of the World Bank that was created to focus on the sciences that are vital for Africa—human and wildlife health, conservation and the environment, and food sciences."

"What do you do for them?"

"Consult. Teach. Research. Every year a number of my Princeton grad students head there for field work, teaming with students in Arusha."

She could hear the enthusiasm in his voice and see the light in his eyes. He was passionate about his work. He'd been passionate about his work thirty years ago, too. She was glad that hadn't changed. "Do you usually go with them?"

He nodded. "I have wonderful colleagues at the institute in Arusha. I like to return every chance I can." He paused. "So, can I give you that ride, or should we schedule for another day?"

"Let me send Elizabeth a text. I wouldn't mind getting out of here now."

After packing up, they left the building and headed to the faculty and staff parking structure on the edge of campus. Jack was parked on the second floor, and he walked her to an old four-door car. "This is Gertie," he said. "Not much to look at, but she's reliable and has served me well."

She arched an eyebrow. "You named your car?"

"You don't?"

"I don't form relationships with my vehicles, no."

"You're missing out, then." He opened the passenger door for her and closed it once she was inside.

As he started the car and backed out of the parking spot, he asked her about her migraines. "Yesterday you called them Santa Ana migraines. What does that mean?"

"The hot, dry winds that blow west, from over the mountains, seem to trigger my headaches. Something to do with the very dry air, I think. I never had migraines until I moved here, but I'm learning to cope."

"You have prescription medicine?"

"I don't have one I love. I should see the doctor again, ask if there's anything new on the market he'd recommend. In the meantime, I try to manage by using lavender and peppermint oils, ice compresses, dark rooms, humidifiers." She smiled. "It's a bit ridiculous, but if it helps, I'll do it."

There was little traffic and they made good time, reaching the Bean Box just minutes after leaving the university. The coffeehouse was half-empty, and they found a big table in a cool, shadowy corner. Paige chose a chair that put her back to the tinted windows. This was exactly what she needed.

"What do you want?" Jack asked. "I'll go order for us."

"Iced coffee with a splash of milk. No sugar."

"Anything to eat?"

She shook her head. While he was placing the order, she drew her laptop from her bag and opened it up, checking email while waiting for him to return.

Jack carried over the drinks and a small paper bag of miniature scones. "I couldn't resist," he said, opening the crisp bag and offering her one. "They're blueberry with a lemon glaze."

"Oh, temptation. How did you know I like those?" she asked, reaching for a scone.

"The barista told me. She recognized you." Jack settled

at the table and took his computer from his knapsack. "She also said you were the best math teacher she'd ever had."

Paige glanced over her shoulder at the blond girl working the register. "Avery. And that's very sweet of her. She's quite bright. Just lacks confidence."

"Like you, hmm?"

Her head jerked up and she looked at Jack. "You can't use my words against me."

"Fair enough," he agreed. "Should we discuss the students we're worried about? As it turns out, I only have four. The rest are doing well with you, which is helping their grade average."

Paige finished the miniature scone and clicked on the file, opening her gradebook. Earlier she'd highlighted two students who weren't doing well with her, but they'd received good scores on their papers. "Doesn't look like we're going to lose anyone, does it?"

"I haven't heard from any students wanting to drop."

"I did have a student reach out, and he had an appointment for my office hours, but didn't show. I'll let you know what comes of that," she answered.

They discussed the next two weeks of instruction and class expectations. A student from their course stopped by to say hello, but then only wanted to talk to Jack about his TV show and ask about how he'd begun working with the Discovery Channel in the first place. The student said he hoped to have his own show one day, something combining food and travel maybe, a little bit like the late Anthony Bourdain.

Paige listened to the two. Jack was exceptionally warm and encouraging, and the student soaked it all up. When the student finally moved on, she looked at Jack, feeling fresh admiration. "You were really patient with all of his questions."

"Happy to help."

"Do you hear that often? About students wanting to follow in your footsteps?"

"Students don't really want to do what I do—study the biology of bacteria, viruses, and parasites—they just think being on TV is glamorous and exciting."

"Isn't it?"

"There are certainly times it's been good fun. I love being outdoors, turning over rocks, studying fungi, protozoan, and anthropods. I like the adventure that comes with visiting far-off places, but there have been times when I wonder what I'm doing and why I'm risking so much for a TV show that not many people actually watch."

"They wouldn't have made a season two or three if you didn't have decent numbers." She felt her lips quiver as she fought a smile. "Although to be fair, I've read that many of your fans are female and they're not interested in the science, but in you."

"They'd be disappointed if they met me. I'm far less interesting in real life."

"That's not true. You're more interesting in real life. At least I think so, because when I watched your season one, I kept wondering how much was scripted, and how much was you, and I realize now, it was you, not the script, that made the show so fascinating."

The corner of his mouth tugged. "I thought you didn't like me."

She felt her face warm. "I never said that."

"You weren't happy about teaching with me."

"I didn't want to team teach."

"With *me*," he corrected.

"With anyone," she answered, before adding reluctantly, "And definitely not with you."

"Why?"

"Oh, come on, Jack, you know why."

"Because of something that happened thirty years ago?"

Her cheeks burned. "It wasn't something. It was quite specific."

"S-e-x."

"Yes. It's made everything awkward."

"It doesn't have to be. We were practically kids. The world has changed. We have changed. We now have kids older than we were then."

A very good point, she thought. Not that she'd tell him that. "A lot *has* happened since then," she agreed, hesitating. "I take it, then, you don't remember much of that night."

"Now, I didn't say that."

Her stomach did a somersault, her skin growing sensitive. She glanced over her shoulder. They were thankfully alone. "What do you remember from that night?" she asked, crossing one leg over the other, hands clasped in her lap, feeling the strangest rush of awareness. Him. Her. Who they were. Who they'd become.

"Enough," he answered, his lashes dropping as his gaze rested on her mouth. "You. Your hair. Your lips. The way you felt against me."

She exhaled hard, skin prickling, nerves stretched taut. He'd felt amazing, too. But then her brain turned on and wouldn't turn off. "I got shy."

"I didn't mind." His voice was low, and the deep husky note scraped her senses. "But then you were gone."

"The conference was over. It was time to go."

"Everyone else stayed on a couple days."

"I needed to get home."

He said nothing, and yet she could tell he didn't believe her. Not then, not now. "I felt ashamed," she admitted. "It was so out of character. I didn't do things like that."

"Sex?"

"I didn't know you."

"We'd spent two weeks together."

"In a program, attending classes." She pulled off her

sunglasses and set them on the table. "Did you sleep with anyone else that summer, during the program?" she asked abruptly, not even aware she was going to ask the question until it popped out. And yet, it was something she'd wondered then . . . and after. It had driven her somewhat crazy in the weeks after she'd returned to California following the course. How many people had Jack slept with besides her? Had she meant anything to him, or was she just another body . . . another conquest?

"Does it matter?" he asked.

Disappointment rushed through her. "I wasn't the only one."

"You are so fast to jump to conclusions. But no, I didn't sleep with anyone else in the program. Or during the program. But I had someone back in Melbourne. We'd broken off just before I left for Europe, and we got back together when I came home."

She'd wondered. She'd thought there had to be someone, somewhere. He was too smart, too attractive, too . . . sexy . . . not to have someone. "Was she the one you married? Oliver's mother?"

"No. I didn't meet Oliver's mother for another year." His gaze again rested intently on her face. "What about you? When did you marry?"

"During my last year of grad school. He was finishing his MBA, and I was finishing my PhD."

"And you were happy?"

"In the beginning, yes. He was smart. Ambitious. He liked to cut loose on the weekends and have fun. We made good friends in North Carolina and started our family. The rest is history."

"When did it stop being fun?"

"When he wanted alcohol more than he wanted me." Paige tapped her coffee cup. "For years we acted like everything was normal. At least, I acted like everything was normal, but things had deteriorated so much. Once

Ashley was a senior in high school, I began thinking about the future, *my* future, and Elizabeth told me about a position in the math department at Orange. And here I am."

"You're happy now?"

She nodded, smiling faintly. "Yes. And you?"

"Yes. Even happier to see you."

She didn't know what to say, nor did she want to misinterpret his words. But suddenly she felt sentimental, and a little bit emotional. An ache filled her chest, the heaviness making her long to be young again. Innocent, unscathed, unscarred. Imagine being able to see the world as it once had been—huge and full of opportunity.

"Ready to go?" Jack asked.

She nodded, and they packed up and headed outside. But sitting next to him in his car, the energy was different. He felt different. Or maybe it was her. Paige wasn't sure if it was something they'd said, or just the fact that they'd finally acknowledged the past, and what it had been—sex, intimacy—but it created a different awareness now. He wasn't twenty-five, and yet he still exuded the same energy and masculinity. She still found him attractive and appealing.

But as Jack drove south of the 5, she could remember how heartsick she'd been, leaving Jack's room to return to hers. She remembered how sad she'd felt flying home. It had been a long flight back to San Francisco. She'd cried into her travel pillow, hating herself and yet not even sure why she felt so upset.

Maybe it was because she wasn't good at casual sex. Or maybe it was because the sex hadn't felt casual to her. She'd had a crush on Jack and the crush ended up with her naked in his bed and then . . . nothing.

She couldn't relax and enjoy being together. She couldn't stop thinking that she could end up pregnant or hurt. She couldn't stop wondering what he thought of her, and her body. Were her breasts too small? Were her thighs too wide? Did he notice that her belly wasn't perfectly flat?

Was he comparing her to others?

Did she even matter to him?

No wonder she couldn't fully enjoy herself. In her twenties, Paige had liked her brain, but waged war on her body. She exercised relentlessly, all the way through grad school, trying to reshape parts that weren't perfect, thinking that once everything was perfect, she'd be . . . what?

Happy? Relaxed? Secure?

She shifted restlessly, thinking she'd put far too much pressure on herself for all the wrong reasons, and at the same time, she was glad she hadn't been raised in an era where social media influenced girls and young women so much.

Jack glanced at her. "You okay?"

She nodded. "Just thinking that there are advantages to getting older. I'm glad I'm not twenty anymore. I like being my age. I like having some perspective."

They arrived at her apartment complex soon after, and, climbing from the car, Paige thanked him for the ride. She watched as he did a U-turn and pulled out of her building's cul-de-sac. It was so strange being with Jack again. It had stirred up old memories, including memories she wasn't comfortable with.

Having been raised in a stable, loving home, she'd been naive about people and relationships. Neither of her parents drank very much, and they'd always worked hard, mom in the house, dad on the property. They each had their own area of responsibilities, but their work complemented each other. They complemented each other. Every time she dated someone, she'd wondered if this was the one. If he was the right one. She'd never dated just to date. She hadn't thought she'd been all that conservative, but looking back, she hadn't taken a lot of risks. Jack had probably been one of the biggest risks. Sex on a first date. How very daring.

Lips quirking, she unlocked her door and let herself into her apartment. It was dark, a little too dark. She moved around the living room, tilting the blinds on the windows, letting in soft afternoon light.

She'd liked Jack in Paris. She'd been almost dazzled by him. Heart-stoppingly handsome and impossibly interesting. He had more charisma than any man she'd ever met. She'd been flattered when he'd stayed at the brasserie to talk to her. She'd wanted him to kiss her. She'd wanted him to want her. But leaving his room in the early hours of the morning, she'd felt heartsick and confused, suspecting she liked him far more than he liked her. Suspecting she'd disappointed him. She wasn't a sophisticate in bed. She'd fumbled around but didn't know how to give a proper hand job, or blow job. Her lasting impression of their night had been one of incompetence. He was experienced. She was not. In bed, he was adventurous and playful. While she just . . . froze.

It's why she'd flown home. Better to lick her wounds in private.

Jump forward thirty years and she still found Jack handsome, and oh-so-interesting. He still gave her butterflies, too.

But she also still wanted to run away.

PAIGE AND ELIZABETH HEADED TO PASO ROBLES AFTER class Friday afternoon, leaving directly from school, hoping to make it through Los Angeles and into Ventura County before rush hour formally commenced, although to be fair, traffic was heavy nearly all day on Fridays, and it was a slog today, too.

They'd decided to take Paige's car, and Paige drove from Mission Viejo until they took a break in Ventura to get gas and stretch their legs. Elizabeth offered to drive the rest of the way, and Paige agreed, happy to be the passenger after three hours behind the wheel, including the hour where it was stop and start. At the gas station mini market, they bought a bag of nacho cheese Doritos and a bottle of iced tea for Paige and a Diet Coke for Elizabeth. This was their favorite snack of choice from road trips in the past—whether going to a concert at the state fair or Palm Springs for spring break.

When Elizabeth took the wheel, she also took control of the radio, choosing an eighties and nineties channel. She sang along with her favorite songs, happy to be on the road, as well as to escape her family for a few days.

As the sun dropped lower in the sky, they talked less, beginning to tire out. Paige was looking forward to seeing her mom. She enjoyed returning to the ranch, and she was lucky that her mom was still sharp mentally and in good shape physically. Her mom, Betsy, should be around for years to come, but who really knew what the future had in store? It's why Paige tried to head home every four to six weeks, but going home was always colored with worry. Fear.

"Does your mom know you're coming?" Paige asked Elizabeth.

Elizabeth shook her head. "No. I wanted to surprise her. Does your mom know?"

"Oh, yes. Mom isn't a fan of surprises. Better for her to know in advance and adjust her schedule. She's become quite the social butterfly. Golf, tennis, bridge club, book club, wine club, birthday club."

Elizabeth grinned. "Who would have ever thought your mom would take up golf?"

"Or want to attend a meeting every day of the week?"

"At least your mom's still driving."

"I almost wish she wouldn't. Have you seen her drive? She is so slow. People lose their minds. We get flipped off almost every time she drives us somewhere."

Elizabeth laughed. "What is she driving these days? Not your dad's old truck?"

"No. She has a new little wagon. Last May, Rob and I surprised her for her seventy-fifth birthday. We weren't sure she'd give up the truck, but she loves the new car."

"Who drives the truck now?"

"Rob is overhauling it for Anne for her twenty-first birthday," Paige said, referencing her brother Rob's youngest, who was studying veterinary science at UC Davis. "She's going to love it."

"I love that the family work truck is staying in the family."

"Me too." Paige paused, aware that she was lucky that Rob lived on the same property as their mom, allowing him and his family to see her daily. Mom benefitted from the company, and was clearly doing well, but that didn't keep Paige from feeling guilty she wasn't as involved in her mom's life.

They were almost to Paso Robles, and Elizabeth's mom lived in one of the older neighborhoods just a couple blocks from the historic downtown and all the restaurants and shops surrounding City Park. Elizabeth had grown up in a historic 1890s Victorian, but the tall narrow house with the steep central staircase was proving difficult for her mom to navigate, never mind take care of. One of the reasons Elizabeth had come home this weekend was to try to talk to her mom again about downsizing, or maybe looking into an assisted-living facility, but her mom loved the old house and the lifetime of memories she'd made there, and she didn't want to move.

Paige shot her friend a concerned glance. "The last time you talked to your mom about moving, you guys had a huge fight and she asked you to leave."

Elizabeth grimaced. "You mean, she told me to leave."

"I was trying to be nice."

"Yeah. Thinking I'll hold off on that conversation until the morning we're heading back."

"Could you hire someone to live in?"

"A nurse?"

"Or a home health aide. Someone who could help out, keep an eye on her."

"Mom would kill me. She's made it clear she doesn't want strangers in her house."

"What about in that apartment over the garage? Maybe rent it to someone who could just check in on her each day?"

"I've had all of these conversations with her. She said she'd feel 'spied on,' and that she's an adult and doesn't need babysitting."

Paige couldn't stifle a grin. Elizabeth's mom was a former English and drama teacher at the high school. Every student for thirty-five years had Mrs. Ortiz for at least one English class, if not two. And if you'd been interested in theatre, you auditioned for her twice-a-year shows—the Fall play and the Spring musical. Paige hadn't been a theatre geek, but Elizabeth had been in her fair share of shows and Paige had seen them all. "I love your mom," she said. "She's so feisty."

Elizabeth gave her a look. "I guess you know where I get it from."

A few minutes later, Elizabeth pulled in front of a tall, faded green Victorian and shifted into park. The house looked dark, but then, Mrs. Ortiz didn't know Elizabeth was coming and wouldn't have turned on the front porch light.

Paige climbed from the passenger seat, walked around, and gave Elizabeth a hug goodbye. "Call me if you need anything. Or if you want to meet for breakfast or lunch."

"You know I love Joe's Place for pancakes," Elizabeth answered, picking up her suitcase.

"Let me know and I'll scoop you up." Paige hesitated. "And don't give your mom a hard time."

"I don't. At the same time, I don't want her falling down the stairs again. I wouldn't forgive myself if anything happened to her."

Chapter 7

COMING HOME ALWAYS TURNED INTO LOTS OF MEALS and lots of cups of coffee and lots of conversations with Rob and his wife, Joy, and then a family dinner with Mom, and Rob, and Joy, and their daughter, Amy, who was newly married. Amy's husband traveled a lot for work and was gone that weekend so Amy, Joy, and Paige cooked dinner for Paige's last night home. Mom insisted on a game of Scrabble after dinner—a game Paige loathed but her mom loved because she usually won—and then finally everyone was gone, and Paige retired for the night.

She couldn't sleep, though, and texted the girls that Grandma and Uncle Rob and everyone sent their love. She then texted Elizabeth to check on her since she'd heard nothing from her since they'd arrived the night before.

Are you doing okay there?

Elizabeth answered immediately. Surviving. Drama city, though.

Paige smiled. What did you do now?

Nothing! Elizabeth responded. I just asked Mom if we should shift her bedroom to one of the downstairs rooms, like the dining room, or dad's old office. You would have thought I'd suggested she burn the house down.

I thought you were coming home to patch things up?

Elizabeth texted back furiously. I'm trying, but she's going to fall and break her neck.

Paige smiled crookedly. Maybe you need to think positive thoughts.

Elizabeth answered with an indignant emoji, adding, Maybe you need to pick me up for pancakes in the morning.

8? Paige answered.

Perfect.

Paige put the phone down and stretched and stared at the wall with the framed oil of a smiling cow. Her mom loved collecting farm-animal artwork now. The framed pieces were all over the house. Cows, horses, pigs, chickens. This was something new since her dad had died. When he was alive there had been no dancing pigs, no strutting roosters. No, it had been a rather masculine, practical house. Funny how things changed when older women were left alone.

Which reminded Paige, didn't she still have some of her things here? Paige went to her mom's sewing room next door and opened the closet. Boxes filled the shelves; boxes Paige had labeled with a fat purple Sharpie: *High School. UCB. Grad School.*

She pulled out the box marked *UCB* and set it on the floor. These were things from Berkeley—papers she'd saved, cards she'd gotten, even a sweet letter her brother, Rob, had written to her during her sophomore year at Berkeley, letting her know how proud Dad would have been of her, and how proud he was, too.

There were also old photos and photo albums, and there was one album in particular she was looking for now. She found it, too. The album from her summer in Paris, the adhesive pages not quite as sticky, the paper yellowing. She flipped through the books, sending photos sliding. Paige paused to study certain pictures. A group photo of all the American students at the airport in New York. Another photo of the first night at the hotel in Paris. Pictures of the sunset cruise the students took on the Seine River. Pictures of the friends she'd made, girls whose names she didn't even remember anymore. Pictures taken at the Louvre. Photos of the Notre-Dame and the Eiffel Tower. A pair of photos of her wearing all black, drinking wine, and smoking outside a café; Paige shook her head at those. The only time she'd ever tried to smoke was in Paris, and she'd hated it. But so many of the European students smoked, and they made it look chic. Cool. How she'd wanted to be cool, too, and not the girl from the sticks, raised surrounded by crops and cows.

Paige turned the page and looked at a photo of herself with her roommate, Genevieve. They were wearing lots of eyeliner, paired with dark lipstick. No highlighter in sight. Those were the days where makeup looked like makeup, a little heavy, a little savage. Twenty-year-old Paige was young, cheeks round, figure almost plump. She'd carried more weight then, "baby fat" her mother called it. Her hair was short, above her shoulders. She must have had a perm because it was a curly honey blond. The permanent looked dreadful. She didn't know how to style it well, and the big hair did nothing for her full face. But the twenty-year-old girl she'd been didn't seem to know or care. She looked happy. Exuberant.

Paige turned a few more pages, skimming through the photos of the field trip to Provence, before finding the picture she been looking for: Jack.

Jack.

Her heart did a painful little jump, making her chest squeeze.

Amazing how thirty years later, he still did a number on her heart.

AT BREAKFAST THE NEXT MORNING AFTER THEY'D BEEN seated, had ordered, and were savoring their coffee, Paige asked how Elizabeth's mom was doing that morning. "Is she feeling better? Or are things still strained?"

"In a better mood. We went through some of the old yearbooks and she talked about some of her favorite students and what they were doing now. Out of hundreds of students over thirty-five years, only one really made it big and is still acting."

"Who is that?"

"Nick Crawford."

"I don't know him."

"Yes, you do. He does all those insurance commercials. And he does a ton of voice-over work, including lots of cartoons."

"Is he really the only one?" Paige asked, thinking of Ashley and her odds of making it.

"There were others who worked in New York and LA, but most aren't pursuing acting as a career anymore. I think the one that disappoints Mom the most is Margot Hughes. Mom was sure Margot would succeed. She thinks she was one of her most talented students, as well as ambitious. Do you remember Margot?"

"No."

"She was a freshman when we were seniors. Light brown hair. Tall. Dramatic. Eccentric. She always wore cardigans draped over her shoulders. Ankle socks. Mary Janes. As if she were living in the fifties instead of the early nineties."

"Okay, that does sound vaguely familiar," Paige said.

"She used to hang out in Mom's classroom, and was always talking about leaving Paso Robles, going to New York, getting an agent, making it big."

"Did she?"

"She did go, after graduation, and Mom thought she had a real chance—" Elizabeth broke off as their breakfast was served: steaming eggs, pancakes, a side of crisp bacon. "I don't know how long she spent in New York, but apparently she's back in the area, working in Cambria for an escrow company. Mom wants me to reach out to Margot, but what am I supposed to say? I knew her because she was one of Mom's favorite students, but we weren't close."

"If she was one of your mom's favorites, why doesn't she reach out?" Paige asked, shaking hot sauce onto her eggs.

"I don't know. Mom seems to think she might need a friend."

"It's not as if you live in the area anymore."

"I know. But it made Mom happy to think I was being friendly and supportive, so I'll reach out to Margot next week at her office and give her my number and let her know that the next time I come home, it'd be fun to meet for coffee."

"Wouldn't Margot prefer to have coffee with your mom?"

"Mom thinks maybe Margot might feel . . . sensitive . . . since she isn't acting anymore."

"Or maybe Margot is really happy with her life," Paige answered. "A lot of us get to that point where we realize we just want a stable job, a decent income, and a comfortable life. Acting doesn't provide a lot of security. I see what Ashley's going through, and I would never want that for myself. To be honest, I wouldn't want it for anyone. You subject yourself to constant criticism and rejection. You put yourself out there over and over and you're lucky to get even a small part. At this point, Ashley would just be grateful to have any role in anything."

"Do you ever talk to Ashley about alternative careers? Does she have a backup plan?"

"No. She's waitressing, and going to auditions, and waiting for her big break." Paige sighed. "Or even a little break. I would be thrilled just to see her cast in *something* at this point."

"I wonder how many years Margot pursued her acting career before she gave it up."

"Well, if she's four years younger than us, she's about forty-six, and as we both know that's ancient by Hollywood standards. I would imagine she probably switched her career a long time ago."

"I'm lucky I had something I loved that I could be successful at," Elizabeth said, reaching for the syrup.

"Again, Margot might love what she's doing now. She might be making great money and proud of what she's accomplished. I hate that she might be viewed as a failure for giving up acting." Paige would be livid if anyone talked about Ashley this way. Just because something doesn't work out doesn't mean you're a failure. "I don't think your mom is being very fair. If Margot went to New York and pursued acting for five, ten years, then she is successful. She went after her dream, and she has every right to change her mind about what she wants to do. We're allowed to try different things."

"I'm not attacking her, Paige—"

"I know, but I hate how society judges people, especially women." She drew a deep breath and calmed herself. Ready to change the subject, Paige reached into her purse and pulled out the photo of Jack from Paris. She slid it across the table to Elizabeth, saying nothing, waiting for a reaction. It didn't take long.

Elizabeth looked at the photo, and then her head jerked up, brown eyes widening. "What? Is this who I think it is?"

"Yes." Paige leaned back in her chair, amused, thoroughly enjoying Elizabeth's reaction.

"Where did you get this from?"

"It was from my Paris trip. The one right after my senior year at Berkeley."

"He was there?"

"He was one of the grad students teaching in the program. Jack King, from Melbourne."

"Okay, wait. Wait, *wait*." Elizabeth put a hand to her

forehead, fingers pushing into her dark hair. "He's not the one . . . Is he?"

There was a reason best friends were your best friend. They remembered the important things. They remembered the secrets, the mistakes, and the things no one else knew. "He's the one I slept with, yes."

"Your one-night stand?"

"The one that made me run back home."

Elizabeth gave the photo a shake. "The one that messed with your head for almost the entire next year? The one that had you crying into your pillow—"

"Okay, wait. There was no crying into my pillow."

Elizabeth made a scoffing noise. "There was most definitely crying into your pillow. You were a wreck. A disaster. You were so hung up on him—"

"I was not."

"*Paige*. You liked him so much—"

"He was gorgeous, and he had this body—"

"He still has that body."

True, but Paige wasn't going to admit it. "He just knew what he was doing, and I was overwhelmed. I felt like a kid. I was completely unprepared for how it was . . . so I shut down." She met Elizabeth's incredulous gaze. "I wish I hadn't. I wish I could have enjoyed myself more, but my emotions were so intense, and being near him was intense, and . . ." She exhaled, pursed her lips, hating the ache in her chest. "In the end, it was nothing. We lived on different sides of the world. We were pursuing different things. Despite all that initial magic, in the end, we had nothing in common."

"Yet here you two are, years later, teaching together." Elizabeth's head slowly shook back and forth, her expression one that reminded Paige of a cat that had just finished licking a bowl of cream. "Oh, PG, this is good. I had no idea how interesting your life had become."

Chapter 8

PAIGE ENJOYED HER TRIP TO PASO ROBLES BUT WAS glad to be back home in her own place and in her own bed. She had missed calls from Ashley and Michelle, but she phoned Ashley first, wondering if Ashley had gotten a callback. Paige's call went to voice mail, so Paige left her youngest a message and then phoned Michelle. Michelle wasn't available, either, and so Paige showered and put on her comfiest pajamas and settled with her laptop to go over lesson plans for tomorrow.

She would see Jack tomorrow.

It was becoming increasingly difficult to feel nothing around him.

The next two weeks passed quickly. No headaches, no weekend trips, just teaching, grading, and her routine of staying healthy and keeping busy at home. With her birthday looming at the end of the month, her girls all called, worried that they wouldn't be with her, wondering if they shouldn't try to plan something, as something was better than nothing. Paige was touched by their concern, but trying to reassure her girls that she was honestly fine was a little exhausting. Because she was fine. Fifty didn't seem particularly scary, not when she liked herself, and her life. She was lucky to have work she loved, lucky to have children she adored, lucky to have good friends. She had everything she needed. Her life was complete.

Paige would have even described her life as peaceful if it weren't for Jack sharing a classroom with her three times a week, using Esther's office next door, walking across campus, usually with a gaggle of followers peppering him with questions. It wasn't Jack's fault that he radiated energy, vitality, charisma. But he certainly made things more complicated. When he was in his office next door, she found it hard to focus, hyperaware of him on the other side of the shared wall. She could hear his voice every now and then, too, when he was animated or laughing. His laugh was warm, and it often made her smile, and she wouldn't even realize she was smiling until she'd stopped working and was staring out the window, lost in thought. Daydreaming.

She didn't even know what she was daydreaming about. She just felt a pull toward Jack. Endless interest. It aggravated her that she was so drawn to him, but she wasn't the only one. Faculty frequently dropped by his office. His phone buzzed often. He even popped his head into her office now and then to check on something related to their class. They always kept the conversation professional, skirting the personal and any mention of the past, but she found herself wondering what he kissed like now and, God help her, what he'd be like in bed now.

Or what *she'd* be like in bed now.

She hadn't slept with anyone in years. Not since moving to California. Sex was so low on her radar, it wasn't even appealing. But then, she didn't feel appealing, not when that part of her—desire, need, whatever it was—was dead. Gone.

Paige left her desk and went to the window to look out over the quad. She drew in a deep breath and then exhaled, counting slowly, in and out, until some of the anxiety eased. The past was the past. She couldn't let it hold her hostage anymore. Maybe what she needed to do was remember the best parts of the marriage, remember how excited they'd been when she'd discovered she was pregnant with Michelle. It hadn't been all bad. There had been love, in the beginning.

Focusing on breathing helped, and her shoulders dropped, her nausea faded. It was midafternoon but cool and gray today, thanks to cloud cover. Now, if only it would rain. Poor California, almost constantly drought stricken.

A knock sounded on the door and then it opened. It was Jack. "I had a quick question. It looks like from the schedule, the university does two sets of midterms before the finals. Do you do that as well, or is it optional?"

She waved him in, glad for the distraction. "I like the two sets personally, because if students bomb one but do okay on another, they can still pass the class. It's a lot harder if someone has failed the midterm. It adds a lot of pressure to the final."

"I didn't have two sets of midterms planned. But we could change that if you want."

"But you also have the papers and the field study, so I'm not sure it's necessary."

"Have you thought any more about joining us for the trip to Costa Rica?"

She shook her head. "I don't know the first thing about tropical field biology. I'm far better here on campus."

"You'd probably have fun."

"I'd be stressed that the rest of my classes would suffer, and students might get neglected."

"You can do office hours by Zoom."

"It's not the same, especially for the students who struggle," she answered.

"We all made it work during the pandemic."

"That was the pandemic." She looked back out the window, watching students cross the quad. So many of her students had found learning remotely difficult. She'd never had so many students fail and drop out. She looked at Jack. "My job is to teach—"

"And you're not missing any teaching days. We fly out

of LAX Saturday of Thanksgiving weekend, and the next week is Dead Week. We return end of finals week. You hold office hours by Zoom, and someone else proctors your finals. It's easy."

For him, she thought. He was used to flitting all over the globe. She hadn't had a big international trip since . . . since . . . when? Paris? That couldn't be. She had traveled with Ted and the girls, but most of the trips had been to Florida, Hawaii, and twice to Cancún.

"Just keep thinking about it," he said.

"I am," she said.

Jack laughed. "No, you're not. You're thinking you can't do it. Try thinking you can."

PAIGE'S BIRTHDAY LOOMED, FALLING ON THURSDAY, BUT Thursday was a long day of classes, with her final class ending at six thirty, and she didn't want to do anything that night. Elizabeth suggested the two of them go out on Saturday; she'd make plans, and she assured Paige they'd do something fun.

Paige's daughters called, the night before her birthday and then again on Thursday morning, wishing her a happy birthday, and apologizing for not making it home to celebrate. Each time Paige reassured the daughter fretting that they would celebrate later, probably over the holidays, and she wasn't to worry because Paige was glad for a quiet birthday this year.

"But it's your fiftieth," Ashley protested, having called early, waking Paige up. "That's huge."

Still in bed, Paige yawned and then turned over on her side. "Does it help that I don't feel fifty?"

"You're beautiful. And the best mom in the whole world. Which is why we should be doing something."

"And we will." Paige suppressed another yawn. She hadn't slept well last night, waking up repeatedly to check the time. She didn't even know why, but she'd gone to bed antsy and her sleep had been restless, too. "What's your weekend like?"

"Just working. Hoping to take a dance class Saturday morning. I'm on the wait list."

"Hope you get in."

"Me too. It's all about being in the right place at the right time."

Since birth, Ashley had had a fear of missing out.

"You said you're going to do something with Elizabeth?" Ashley asked.

"Saturday. She's bought tickets for the Cabrillo Playhouse in San Clemente, and we're grabbing a bite of dinner beforehand."

"What are you going to see?"

"I don't remember. It's a play, not a musical."

"I like musicals better."

Paige smiled and flipped the covers back, ready for coffee. "Me too."

The phone calls continued to come, from Nichole in Chicago, Michelle in Seattle, and her brother, Rob, and her mom in Paso Robles. Elizabeth sent a birthday text, and then once on campus, Paige was showered with gifts all day: flowers from Elizabeth, more flowers from the department chair (which meant from his executive assistant, Andi). There were balloons from Nichole, including massive 5 and 0 balloons, screaming her age. There was even a small cake from her colleagues, and a handful of staff gathered in her open doorway to sing her a painfully off-key but very cheery "Happy Birthday." All in all, Paige felt celebrated and appreciated. It was just the kind of birthday she was most comfortable with—nothing fancy, nothing fussy.

After her last class wrapped up, she returned to her office and tried to figure out which flowers and balloons to take home tonight; she decided she'd just leave everything but the remaining slice of cake and get help tomorrow taking everything to her car.

Cake safely tucked behind the driver's seat, Paige was exiting the garage when her phone rang. Her Bluetooth identified Jack King as the caller. Just hearing his voice announced in her car made her insides flip-flop. The fluttery sensation exasperated her. She took a quick breath and answered the call. "Hi, Jack."

"Are you still on campus, or are you already on your way home?" he asked.

"Just leaving school now."

"Feel like getting dinner? I wasn't sure if you had plans for tonight or not."

Bittersweet emotion filled her. No, she didn't have plans. But did she want dinner with him?

Yes.

"Dinner sounds great," she answered quickly, before she could change her mind. "Do you have a place in mind?"

He named an Italian restaurant not very far from the campus, but one with a great menu and great reviews. It was a bit upscale but featured a lot of fresh fish and seafood on its menu, along with the usual pasta dishes. "They might be hard to get into," she said. "It can be quite a wait if you don't have a reservation."

"I have a reservation."

More fluttery, fizzy sensations in her middle. She gulped in a breath, flattered, nervous, excited. "What time?"

"Seven fifteen."

She glanced at her car dash. Twenty minutes from now. That was actually perfect. "I'll see you there."

Paige got to the restaurant with ten minutes to spare. She didn't see Jack's car, Gertie, and so she drew out her small makeup bag from her purse and freshened her lipstick and added a dab of pink color to the top of her cheeks. She took her hair out of the ponytail and fluffed it, trying to make it look fuller, before popping a mint into her mouth and stepping out of her car. As she closed the car door, she wondered, was this a date?

Were they meeting as colleagues and friends, or . . . ?

Again, that flutter. The butterflies were loose tonight.

She wasn't sure what she thought would happen, or worse, what she wanted to happen. Swallowing hard, Paige headed into the restaurant.

JACK SPOTTED PAIGE THE MOMENT SHE ENTERED THE restaurant. She was wearing the same fitted, wheat-colored skirt and matching jacket she'd worn today to teach in, with a wide leather belt cinched around her waist. Her hair was loose now, falling in long blond waves over her shoulders and down her back. He'd liked the feminine suit on her earlier, but now with her hair down, she looked downright sexy.

She saw him as he left the table and lifted a hand to acknowledge him, meeting him halfway across the restaurant. "It's crowded in here," she said, standing close enough that he could feel her warmth, smell the light fragrance she wore.

"That's why I sat down. Way too many people," he said. "You look beautiful," he added, leaning down to kiss her cheek. Her skin was warm, soft, and again he caught a whiff of something sweet and fresh, reminding him of lemon blossoms and sunshine.

"Thank you," she said, a hint of color staining her cheeks.

At the table, he drew her chair out for her. She murmured thanks as she sat down. "I didn't see Gertie outside," she said, reaching for her napkin.

Jack took a seat opposite her. Their table was against a window, giving them a view of artfully lit olive trees outside. "The lot was full when I arrived. I parked down the street."

"Ah, good. I worried that she was in the shop."

"Not Gertie. She's too reliable for that." Jack paused. "Thank you for being concerned about her. Not everyone is fond of her."

"Why ever not?"

"She's not a stylish car. Valet always looks askance when I pull up."

"Most valet is worked by young men who are easily impressed by an expensive sports car. I'm not." Her lips curved and her blue eyes warmed, creasing at the corners. "I'm too frugal to see the value of an expensive car."

"You approve of Gertie."

"I do."

He smiled back at her. "Did you have a good day?"

"I did. I felt very spoiled by everyone."

"I'm glad." Jack studied her, thinking she looked truly stunning in the candlelight, and finding her far more attractive now than she'd been thirty years ago. She was a smart woman. Poised. Passionate about her work. But there were also walls around her. She was always so careful, always rather guarded, which just made him more curious about her. "Have you heard from your daughters today?

She nodded. "I had calls this morning from all three. They were disappointed that we weren't able to get together, but I'm sure we'll celebrate later, probably around Christmas. It's hard for them to work out their schedules so we can all meet up."

"Especially when you're early in your career."

"Exactly."

"You are very much a family person," he said, taking the menu from the waiter.

"It's true. Love my girls. I love being a family with them. It's sometimes hard being so far apart." She smiled ruefully. "I think I did too good of a job getting them out of the nest. They're happy on their own, doing their own thing."

"But isn't that what we're supposed to do? Make them self-sufficient, independent? I imagine you miss them, as I miss Oliver, but I feel a lot of pride in who he's become, and what he's been able to do. I look forward to seeing what comes next."

"Do you think he'll get married one day?"

"I don't know. I haven't been a great example, but I do think he'll have kids, and if he does, he'll have at least two. He didn't like being an only child. He thought it was lonely."

"My middle one, Nichole, used to wish, quite loudly, that she was an only child."

Jack felt a tug in his chest. Paige's wry delivery amused him. She had a great sense of humor. "I'm sure that went over well with the others."

"Yeah, no."

He laughed, intrigued, thinking this Paige was more open and relaxed. He wasn't sure why, but he liked it. Liked her. The waiter returned to tell them the specials and Paige thanked him and watched the waiter walk away before turning her attention back to Jack.

Her lips pursed, and a furrow formed between her brows. "Why didn't you remarry? Especially since Oliver was so young when his mother died?"

"After Mara died, romance was the last thing on my mind. We were just trying to get by. I was in no shape to be dating or trying to find Oliver another mom."

"Did he want a new mom?"

"He never said he did."

"Did he want you to remarry?"

"Not when he was younger, but later, in high school, I think it was his senior year, he talked to me about a girlfriend of mine and said maybe I should settle down. He said I wasn't too old to get married again." Jack gave his head a shake. "I think he was just worried about going away to school and leaving me alone."

"He sounds like a wonderful person."

"He is. I don't know what I did to deserve him. He has a big heart."

"So, why didn't you marry the girlfriend?"

This wasn't what Jack had thought they'd talk about tonight, not during Paige's birthday dinner, but he didn't mind answering her questions. There were plenty of things he wanted to know about her. "I came close to proposing to her, but in the end, I'm glad I didn't. I can be gone for long stretches of time. When in the field, I get immersed in my work, and the rest of the world falls away. I'd make a lousy husband."

"The girlfriend said it? Or you just think that?"

He smiled crookedly. "We had enough conversations for me to know she wasn't always happy with me. She got lonely, and I hated how guilty I felt every time I packed to go on another trip. Or every time I headed in a different direction from where she was. I knew it bothered her. But I've always found it hard to turn down opportunities. I love teaching, speaking, research. But it's not a lifestyle that's conducive for relationships."

"I can see how too much time apart would be hard on the relationship. But at the same time, too much time together can be equally challenging. People need space."

"Some space," he said. "Too much creates resentment, and frustration. I hate angering someone I care about. It's never my intention."

"So, you're not Peter Pan, you're more of *The Absent-Minded Professor.*"

Jack made a face. "I don't think I like either comparison. I like to think of myself as Harrison Ford in Indiana Jones. Dedicated to teaching, enthralled with the world."

"Addicted to adventure," she added, smiling. "Yes, I can see that. You certainly embrace danger, at least on your show."

"There have been some unsettling moments. I'm never truly afraid for myself—what will happen will happen—but I never want to put the crew in danger."

"Animal attacks? Storms? Flooded rivers?"

"Corrupt border guards, unstable governments, encounters with heavily armed rebels. I'd rather deal with a snake or a charging rhino than unpredictable humans."

Her blue gaze lifted, her expression warm, admiring. "You've led the most interesting life," she said.

But there were negatives to it, he thought. He had no real home. He found it hard to relax when he wasn't traveling. And he did spend a lot of his life alone. There were times it was too much solitude. Times he wished he had someone to visit with in the evening or have coffee with before work in the morning. But it was impossible to have everything, and he couldn't imagine a woman like Paige would ever be good with a man who was rarely present. Camille certainly hadn't been happy with it.

The waiter returned to take their order, and Jack glanced at Paige. "Would you like a glass of wine with dinner? A cocktail? It is your birthday."

"Wine would be lovely."

He asked her preference and then ordered a bottle. Since it was late, they also ordered their entrées.

Jack waited until their wine had been poured to ask about a subject that had been on his mind. "Let's talk about us."

Paige frowned and lightly tapped the stem of her wine-glass with her finger. "You know, I didn't fall into bed with people. I've never understood why you were the exception."

"We had chemistry."

Paige looked away, and then down into her wine goblet, anywhere but into Jack's face. *It was chemistry*, she thought. It had been there thirty years ago and was still here humming between them. Chemistry. Law of attraction. Science.

Jack didn't just represent sex. He represented something else as well. Light. Energy.

Possibility.

"What are you doing Sunday?" he asked.

Light, energy, possibility, heartbreak. Paige silently kicked herself, hating that she went there. Hating that she was so fearful. "Not sure," she said. "Why?"

"I've heard about Crystal Cove and how there are some beautiful beach trails. Thought it'd be fun to go for a walk, or hike, whatever it is."

"Crystal Cove is gorgeous. There are a couple different trails, some easy, some requiring more effort."

"Feel like meeting me?"

"It would be a nice change from barre." She smiled at him. "Unless you'd like to join me for a barre class?"

"I'd rather stick with a hike."

"Can I give you a tentative yes?"

"Yes."

Chapter 9

FOR THE FIRST TIME IN A LONG TIME PAIGE WONDERED why she didn't do more things, why she didn't try more things.

For the first time maybe ever, she wondered why she gave her girls such unconditional support, and freedom to try things, without judgment. She wished she gave herself the same freedom, the same encouragement. Why couldn't she meet Jack for a hike tomorrow? Why couldn't they go for lunch after? Why couldn't they hang out and do things together? They were both single and living alone. Why couldn't she try different things without obsessing about the negatives, or the future?

She was constantly telling her daughters to take risks, to go after what they wanted. But it had been years since Paige thought she could. Since she thought she should. She didn't understand where the double standard came from, unless she was genuinely tired, fatigued by life, disappointed by what she discovered marriage and maturity was like.

But was maturity really about not experiencing anything new? Was maturity all about maintaining the status quo?

If Nichole came to her, and asked her advice about

changing jobs, moving to a new city, going on a trip with a friend or a boyfriend, Paige knew she would tell her to listen to her gut and rely on her instincts. If the new job, new city, or road trip sounded fun, why not do it? Why not want a little more?

Why not want a lot?

Paige felt as if her eyes were just being opened, and it wasn't entirely comfortable. It was almost as if she'd been asleep for a long, long time and she no longer really knew herself or her place in the world. But maybe that was a good thing. Maybe she could find her place then. Maybe she could explore the world, find herself, find new paths, new joy.

New love.

Although she wasn't so sure about that one. It was hard to let herself trust a man that much, let alone with her heart. It wasn't until recently that she'd realized how fragile she felt, how vulnerable. She might be confident as a teacher, a friend, and a mom, but she wasn't sure of herself as a woman. Her self-esteem in that regard was pretty damn low.

In her heart of hearts, she felt like a failure. She hated that. She hated being negative about anyone or anything, much less men, and relationships. Maybe she and Ted hadn't been happy, but that didn't mean she couldn't enjoy the company of an interesting man. It didn't mean she couldn't go to a movie or dinner.

She thought of her birthday dinner with Jack. She'd enjoyed his company. Immensely. She'd felt little sparks throughout the evening, sparks that made her feel pretty, and happy. Desirable. Whether or not that was real, she didn't know, but it had felt good to be sitting in a nice restaurant, having a delicious dinner by candlelight with a man who was undeniably handsome. Jack drew attention. Women liked looking at him. *She* liked looking at him. But then, she'd liked looking at him in Paris. She'd liked the way he walked, the way he used his hands, the way his features were so expressive. She'd liked the glimpse of humor in his eyes, and the curve of his mouth. He had a great mouth. He'd been a great kisser. That's how she'd ended up in his bed. Before she panicked that she wasn't good enough, attractive enough.

Paige had shared so much with Elizabeth over the years, but she'd never really shared how insecure she felt about her body, and about sex. Even when she was young, early in her marriage before everything went south with Ted, she'd needed a glass or two of something to help her relax. Not feel so self-conscious. She'd thought that once she found the right person, the self-consciousness would go away, and once she married, she did feel safer, and more secure, but it was hard to block out the little voices that wondered if Ted was happy. If he enjoyed their lovemaking. Or if he was ever disappointed. Did he ever compare her to anyone else?

Paige went to her closet, looked through her dresses and skirts and pretty tops. She was looking forward to tonight's play. She'd seen a lot of plays and musicals over the years with Ashley. One of their favorite things to do even now was for Paige to fly in for a long weekend and try to catch as many shows as they could. They loved Times Square. The theatres, the lights, the crowds. They'd dress up and go out and be two girls out on the town. Paige smiled, missing her youngest, her baby.

Paige's phone buzzed. She crossed to her nightstand where her phone was charging. It was Elizabeth. What are you wearing tonight?

I don't know, Paige texted in reply. I'm trying to decide.

Are we dressing up, or going casual? Elizabeth asked.

How about in between? Paige suggested. Cute clothes, fun earrings?

I'm not wearing heels.

Paige grinned. Elizabeth lived in flats. Paige loved shoes with height. You do you, Paige texted back.

Back at her closet, Paige flipped through her blouses once more and selected a navy, long-sleeve silk blouse, skinny white jeans, and her favorite espadrille wedges. Dressed, she put on makeup and ran a brush through her long hair. She loved her hair. Her girls had made her promise that she wouldn't cut it, and she had no desire to chop it off. Long hair made her feel young, and even though lots of women her age were embracing their gray, she wasn't ready to go natural. Blond was sunny and pretty, and she didn't color her hair for anyone else. She kept it blond for her. Her girls made her want to stay young. She liked being their fun mom.

Paige checked her watch, saw that Elizabeth would be arriving soon, and quickly added a bit more mascara before picking out a pair of sparkly silver chandelier earrings from her jewelry box. She put on the dangly earrings, slicked on a soft pink lipstick, looking forward to the night out. Elizabeth was the sister she'd never had, and Paige could always count on Elizabeth being fun, stress free. Unlike Ted, Elizabeth never embarrassed her in any way.

Paige grabbed a gauzy shawl and her purse, and stepped outside, locking the door behind her. As she waited on the curb for Elizabeth, she flashed back to Thursday night, and how dinner with Jack had not been comfortable. Dinner with Jack had been electric. She'd felt a rush of adrenaline walking into the restaurant and spotting him across the room. He'd been wearing a white linen shirt and dark trousers and he'd looked very male, and very appealing.

When he'd greeted her, kissing her cheek, she'd felt a frisson of energy, and awareness. The sparks continued all night, making her heart beat a little faster and her hands not quite steady. She'd forgotten how a man could make one feel a little giddy, a little shy. She'd told Elizabeth at the beginning of the school year that she had no hormones left, that on the inside she was essentially dead, but Paige hadn't felt dead Thursday night, and she didn't feel dead now. She still felt rather fizzy and hopeful.

Just thinking about Jack's invitation to go hiking tomorrow made her want to text him and say yes, and what time?

But would that be a mistake? Would spending more time together change things . . . ruin their friendship?

Maybe it was better to play it safe, and just focus on getting through this semester and finish team teaching with him and then, maybe in the new year, maybe once they weren't working closely together, she could think about having dinner with him again. Maybe then they could go out again, have a date. Maybe Jack wasn't completely out of her league.

They were almost to the Estrella exit in San Clemente when Elizabeth suddenly swore under her breath. "What's wrong?" Paige asked.

"I think I left the tickets at home."

"Are you sure?"

"They were on the kitchen counter. I don't remember picking them up."

"Maybe you did, and you just don't remember."

"Check my purse, would you? And my wallet? Just in case?"

Paige rummaged through Elizabeth's purse, which, typically, was like Elizabeth, full of everything impractical, with almost no essentials. "You have like eight pens in here, and three pairs of reading glasses."

"You can never have too many."

Paige pulled out a pair of little Lego men. "And these guys."

"They're everywhere thanks to the twins." She glanced worriedly at Paige. "Did you find them?"

"Nothing."

"Noooo."

Paige glanced at her watch. "We have time if we go back now."

"But we won't have time for the long, leisurely dinner I'd planned."

"That's okay. We can sit at the bar and have appetizers and that will be just as fun."

Elizabeth took the next exit and crossed the freeway to head north. "I'm so sorry about this. I was wrapping your gift and signing your card and I just spaced."

"It's okay. All I really wanted to do was spend time with you, so I'm happy."

But Elizabeth wasn't happy. "I can't believe I did that. I think dementia is setting in."

"It's not dementia. You were just multitasking."

"Maybe it's time I stopped and focused on one thing at a time."

Paige smiled sympathetically. "I tell myself that all the time now."

Elizabeth phoned home and asked her husband to look for the tickets, asking if he would bring them out to the car once they got there. He called back and said he couldn't find the tickets anywhere. Hanging up, Elizabeth shook her head. "So frustrating," she said.

"Don't get upset. It's okay. We're almost to your house, and then we'll find the tickets and be off. We still have time for a quick bite, and if we don't, we can always go get something after the play."

Elizabeth pulled into the driveway of her shingled house, the glossy white trim contrasting with the brown stain on the shingles. "I'll check the bedroom," Elizabeth said as they stepped from the car. "You search the kitchen. Men are terrible at finding things."

They headed inside, and Elizabeth turned on the hall light and suddenly there were shouts of "Surprise!" and "Happy birthday!" Elizabeth stepped out of the way, and Paige's gaze swept the living room. Dozens of pink, lavender, and navy balloons covered the living room ceiling, with long curling ribbon hanging down like colorful confetti. There was a birthday banner high on the wall, reading HAPPY BIRTHDAY PAIGE, featuring a photo of her as a one-year-old in a pink and silver party hat with a fistful of cake.

People streamed toward her, and Paige shook her head,

shocked to see all the different people from her department. Paige shot Elizabeth an incredulous look. "You didn't forget the tickets."

"There were no tickets," Elizabeth said, clearly proud of herself. "It's a party. For you."

"I had no idea."

"I know. I'm still a good actress."

Paige had never had a surprise party before and she felt off-balance, and yet these were her friends from the university. Greg and his wife, Leigh; Dr. Nair and his wife; beautiful Andi McDermott; and a dozen others. And then there was Jack, standing in the background, glass of wine in hand, watching. Her insides dropped, her pulse quickened. The way he was looking at her made her feel beautiful, hopeful, alive.

For a split second, she wondered yet again what her life would have been like with Jack. Would he have traveled as much? Would she have traveled with him? How different would her life be if she hadn't run away from him in Paris?

Andi approached, catching Paige in a warm, fierce hug. "Happy birthday, gorgeous," she said, giving Paige another quick squeeze. "So glad you joined us at Orange. You make the math department sexy."

Paige laughed, winked. "What do you mean? Math *is* sexy."

"And fifty is sexy, too."

They talked for a few minutes and then Greg and Leigh joined them; then Dr. Keller walked through the front door with his wife, and Elizabeth snuck behind Paige to whisper, "You're drawing the A-crowd."

"I have a feeling Dr. Keller showed to spend time with Jack," Paige answered. And it was true, Dr. Keller made a beeline for Jack and stayed glued to his side throughout dinner.

For the next couple of hours, they ate, drank—there were a number of lovely birthday toasts—and then there was cake. It was the most awesome cake Paige had ever seen—it was a math cake. The white icing was covered with math problems, mostly algebra, and in the center was an edible frosting photo of Paige in high school wearing serious glasses, clutching a trophy for the high school math team's win at the district level.

Tears pricked her eyes. It was the most ridiculous and wonderful cake.

Elizabeth stood at her side, cake cutter in hand. "President of the math club leads PR High to a first-place finish in the district championship."

"I didn't know you had that photo."

"You've always been a star." Elizabeth smiled affectionately at her. "What do you think of the cake?"

Paige blinked hard. "It's wonderful. I love it. I love you."

"I love you, too."

Then it was time to go, and people were saying goodbye. Paige hugged her colleagues as they left, grateful that they'd taken time to come celebrate her tonight. Paige glanced around, looking for Jack, wondering if he'd slipped out earlier when Dr. Keller and Dr. Nair left, but no, he was there in the kitchen, talking with Elizabeth's husband.

Paige began gathering discarded plates and glasses. Elizabeth stopped her. "No cleaning up. It's your party."

"I'm not going to leave you alone with this mess."

"I'm not alone. My cute hubby will help me. And what I don't do tonight, I can finish in the morning." Elizabeth moved toward the oversize kitchen island. "Jack, would you do me a favor and take Paige home?"

"Of course," he answered, looking at Paige. "Are you ready to go now?"

"That is not necessary," Paige answered, flustered. "I can call an Uber."

"Not on your birthday," Elizabeth said, scandalized. "Jack said he can take you. He's going that way anyway."

Paige shot her friend a dark look. Elizabeth ignored it. "Let me just send you with a to-go box. I know you'll love some of these leftovers tomorrow. Just give me a minute to wrap it up."

"That was so awkward," Paige said as Jack walked her down the street to where he'd parked his car. It was a beautiful night; the moon was out, high and full. In the distance, she could see the ripple of moonlight on water. "I feel like Elizabeth forced me on you."

"Not at all. I'm happy to drive you home. I didn't have a chance to talk to you at the party. But it looked as if you were having a good time."

"I did. It was fun." She flashed him a smile. "I've never had a surprise party before."

He opened the passenger door for her. "And were you surprised?"

She nodded and stepped into the car. "Elizabeth had me fooled. I thought we were going to a play and she'd forgotten the tickets."

He closed the door and came around to the driver's side. Once he was behind the wheel, she added, "I noticed you kept your distance tonight. Why didn't you talk to me?"

"I just had dinner with you. I thought I should give others a chance to visit with you." He glanced at her, gaze warm. "Besides, I knew I'd be taking you home and I'd have you all to myself then."

There was something in his eyes that made her breath catch. "This is all part of Elizabeth's plan?"

"Not hers. Mine."

The very air seemed charged with energy, and Paige's pulse quickened, a tiny shiver racing through her.

Jack drove her home on the Pacific Coast Highway, paralleling the water. Neither of them said much, and he turned on the stereo, jazz filling the car. Paige tried to relax against the worn leather seat, but couldn't focus on anything but Jack, and how aware she was of him, and his hand on the steering wheel, and how the moonlight illuminated his profile. He was tall, broad, a little weathered, and a whole lot of sexy. Being close to him made her skin prickle and heat coil in her middle.

He knew the way to her place, so there was no giving of

directions, no meaningless chatter, just an intense heady awareness of Jack, and how he made her feel things that she couldn't quite wrap her head around. The mournful saxophone didn't help, either. The notes stirred her, making her feel a little vulnerable, a little emotional. Everything felt different tonight. . . . She felt different tonight.

At her apartment, he parked, turned off the engine, and climbed from the car, walking her to the door of her apartment. Energy hummed around them, and her chest tightened with little electrical jolts. She wanted . . .

She didn't want.

She wanted . . .

She didn't want.

She stole a glance at him as she reached her front door. Time hadn't been kind to Ted, but Jack had just improved with age.

He wasn't just handsome, he was brilliant and generous and patient. She loved his spirit, and his passionate interest in the world around him.

"Thank you for the ride," she said huskily, fumbling in her purse for her key.

"Thank you for having a birthday. I enjoyed spending time with you this week."

She glanced up into his face and her pulse jumped. He looked a little rumpled, rather handsome, and very sure of himself. "You made this week special," she said. "I wasn't sure how I'd feel without my girls coming home, but it's been a really lovely week."

"Hopefully it's not over. Are we still going hiking tomorrow?"

She'd forgotten all about it. "As long as we don't have to wake up too early."

"Not an early riser?"

"Not if I don't have to be."

"How about I call you around ten? See if you're up for it."

"Sounds good." She looked up into his eyes, thinking

they were extraordinarily beautiful. It was too dark on her doorstep to see the flecks of gold and green, but she knew they were there, knew his lashes were dark, knew his mouth fascinated her, far more than it should.

And then, as if he could read her mind, his head dropped and his mouth covered hers, his lips firm and cool, the pressure just right.

Could you remember a kiss from thirty years ago?

Paige didn't think so, and yet there was an immediate spark of familiarity and pleasure. Her skin tingled, exquisitely sensitive, and her lips softened, yielding to his. To him.

She refused to think, not now, and gave herself over to sensation, because everything felt good. She felt good—better than good. Warm honey seemed to fill her veins and Paige felt like she was twenty again. She leaned against Jack, savoring the feel of him. She'd forgotten this, what it felt like being close to someone, had forgotten touch. Skin. A ripple of pleasure raced through her, and she lifted her arms, wrapping them around his neck.

Jack walked her back against the door, pinning her there, holding her captive while his mouth took hers, seeking, giving, stirring nerve endings she'd forgotten she had. Why had she thought she was dead? How could she have thought she didn't feel, because right now, every inch of her had come alive, the length of her body exquisitely stirred.

"If any of my neighbors are watching, we're putting on quite a show," she murmured against his mouth.

"Let them watch," he answered, kissing the side of her neck, just below her jaw.

She closed her eyes, sighing with pleasure. It felt amazing when he kissed her like that. She'd forgotten how sensitive she was on her neck, and nape, and collarbones. But the memory was coming back. Her body was reminding her.

Not dead, not dead, not even close.

"You're too good at this," she whispered, and it wasn't a criticism. Nor was it a complaint. More of an observation.

"I'd invite you in, but I'm afraid things might get out of hand."

"Like Paris?" His teeth scraped her earlobe.

She shuddered from head to toe, and her cheeks, already warm, tingled. Her mouth tingled. "You love to bring up Paris."

"Things would be different from Paris, though. I'd make sure you had a real orgasm this time."

Her eyes opened wide. "I did —"

He lifted his head, his eyes a golden sheen above her. "You did not. You faked it. We both know you faked it."

Paige pushed him back, feigning outrage. "You can't say that. You don't know that. You're not me, and you're not my body—"

"I was in your body."

"Oh my God." She pushed him on the chest once more, pushing him back a step. "I did not fake it," she choked, not sure whether to laugh or cry.

His expression was wicked. "I had a great time, even if you didn't come. I simply viewed it as an opportunity to do better next time."

"Whether I did, or didn't, have an O is none of your concern. And for you to remember that all these years later —"

"You don't remember? Has it truly slipped your mind?"

She pushed hair off her face, tucking it behind her ear. "Again, none of your business," she said primly.

"I have spent thirty years aware that I left you unsatisfied. I think that makes it my business."

Paige couldn't believe they were having this conversation. It was mortifying, and exasperating. And also rather funny. "I wasn't unsatisfied. I was very satisfied—"

"Without an orgasm? How can that be satisfying? I don't get it. Please explain." Then Jack paused, expression shifting, brow creasing. "Have you still never had one? Not a judgment, just—"

"Yes. I have. I'm perfectly familiar with an orgasm, but

I couldn't that night. I wasn't very experienced. I wasn't used to getting naked and climbing into bed with strange men on the first date."

"You were twenty."

"Yes, and cautious, and conservative."

"Why didn't you tell me?"

"That I was still practically a virgin? Oh, that's hot, isn't it?" She shook her head. "There was no way I was going to tell you I didn't know what I was doing."

"No wonder you ran away. You must have been disappointed with me."

"No. That's not what happened. You were amazing. I just froze. I got in my head and couldn't get out of it."

"Why am I not surprised?"

She gave him a little push on his chest again, but she left her hand on his chest. His body was hard and warm, and she very much liked the feel of it. "You're ruthless."

He covered her hand with his. "I suggest you let me rectify the disappointment of that night. I'm confident I can please you."

She laughed, nervous but intrigued. The idea of going to bed with Jack was there in the back of her mind, and yet it was also scary. She hadn't been naked with anyone in so long. She didn't think she even remembered how to have sex. "I think this is a good time to say good night." Paige stood up on tiptoe, kissed him quickly on the mouth. "Good night, Jack. Thank you for coming to my party. Thank you for bringing me home." She smiled up at him. "Thank you for the make-out session. I enjoyed it very much."

He laughed. "Anytime. I aim to please."

She arched her eyebrows. "I'll remember that."

Paige let herself into the house and no sooner had she closed and locked the front door than a pair of arms grabbed her.

"Oh my God, Mom, how long were you going to be out there? I've been waiting forever for you to come inside."

Paige turned to hug her middle daughter. "What are you doing here?"

"I got a great deal on a ticket and decided I would come surprise you for your birthday." She smiled into her mom's face. "Surprised?"

"Very." Paige gave Nichole another swift hug. "I'm shocked you're here, but also thrilled. How long will you stay?"

"I have to fly out tomorrow night, can't miss work Monday, but that gives us all day tomorrow."

"And tonight," Paige said, leading the way into the kitchen. "Hungry? Thirsty?"

"No. Just tired." Nichole smothered a yawn. "It's almost one in the morning my time. How about we go to bed soon and wake up early? I've got a lot of things planned for us tomorrow."

Paige wasn't surprised. Nichole loved to be busy. Back in high school, she'd played four sports a year. "Wake me up when you wake up, then. Don't let me oversleep if I only have one day with you."

"I will but, Mom, who was that guy? You two were all over each other—"

"We were not. It was just a kiss good night."

"It was more than a kiss good night. It was hands and tongue—"

"Nichole."

Her daughter shook her head. "I don't think I've ever seen you kiss anyone but dad. And that was so long ago. I was just a kid."

Paige made a face. "I didn't know you were here. Obviously, we wouldn't have spent that long . . . talking . . . outside." She swallowed and asked, "How much of our conversation did you hear?"

"A little bit. Something about Paris. And then when it sounded like you guys had old history"—she gave her mom a meaningful look—"I stepped back, not wanting to hear more about your sex life. That was, uh, weird. He's Australian?"

"Yes."

"From where?"

"Melbourne, but he's lived in the US for a long time. And before you go spreading rumors, he and I are just friends."

"Friends with tongues, right."

"Nichole."

Nichole lifted her hands in mock surrender. "You're just friends. You didn't hook up in Paris. And he doesn't want to rock your world. I got it."

Paige laughed. She couldn't help it. She planted a kiss on her daughter's forehead. "I'm just so happy you're here. What do you think you want to do tomorrow?"

"Breakfast, hike, and maybe some shopping?"

The mention of a hike reminded Paige that she and Jack had discussed going to Crystal Cove tomorrow. She'd need to text him and let him know she couldn't go. He'd understand, what with Nichole coming home. "I'll make up the sofa sleeper," Paige said.

"I can do it, Mom. I know where everything is."

"I just want to make it easier—"

"I'm an adult. I can make my own bed. You go to bed. Love you."

After taking off her makeup and brushing her teeth, Paige climbed in bed and stared into the darkness and replayed the passionate kiss in her head. She'd liked that he hadn't been tentative, liked how he'd pressed her to the door and closed the distance between them. He'd been all heat and muscle, hard and strong, and she'd loved it.

It had been an amazing kiss, too, the kind of kiss that made her melt, and feel, and imagine more. He'd left her wanting more, wondering what it would be like, now, to make love to him. It had been years since she'd been intimate, and sex wasn't on her need-to-do list, but Jack presented tantalizing possibilities.

Did she want casual sex?

Did she want a casual relationship?

Did she want a relationship?

She chewed her lip, still tender from the earlier kiss. What did Jack want?

She was still considering all the options when she drifted off to sleep.

IT WAS A BUSY DAY WITH NICHOLE. NICHOLE LOVED BE-ing active, and their morning started with a yoga class led by Nichole in Paige's living room, and then a quick shower, followed by a breakfast at one of Paige's favorite cafés, and then a long hike up into the foothills. The cool morning gave way to a very bright, sunny day. There were no clouds overhead, just a blazing sun and blue sky. Thankfully, they'd brought plenty of water in their thermoses and on reaching the peak, sat down side by side on a rock and gazed out toward the shimmering ocean, the color of teal.

"Andreas has moved back in," Nichole said, staring out over the horizon.

Paige glanced at her daughter's serene profile. "You're back together."

"He admitted he was jealous, and a jerk. He's sorry. Things are pretty good between us right now."

"Oh, Nichole, I'm glad. I know you cared a lot about him."

Nichole wiped a bead of perspiration from her upper lip. "It's not the same, though, not like before. I don't feel the same. Not sure I trust him like I did."

"Relationships are hard. A constant give and take."

"I've forgiven him, but I can't forget. I'm not sure I want to forget." She turned and met her mom's gaze. "If he was that upset about my career before, why wouldn't he be jealous again? I'm only going to get more successful, not less."

Paige felt a pang, a bittersweet mix of pride and pain. Pride, because Nichole was strong and fierce, but pain, because her daughter was right. Some men would be intimidated by her, some men would want to control her, marginalize her. "Are you happier with him than without him?"

Nichole hesitated, then nodded. "Right now."

"Then enjoy right now. There's no need to look too far down the road. We don't know the future, and there's no need to anticipate trouble. Deal with trouble if and when it comes."

Nichole stretched out her legs, rubbed at the muscle just above her right knee. She'd had a volleyball injury in high school and periodically her knee would bother her. "I didn't think you wanted to date again," she said after a moment, her gaze still locked on the horizon.

"It wasn't on my agenda, no."

Silence stretched. Nichole dug the toe of her sneaker into the dirt, kicking up a small cloud of dust. "I will never let anyone treat me the way Dad treated you."

Paige winced. "He wasn't always . . . that way."

"He was always an asshole. Even when I was little. He was always right. No one else could possibly be right."

Paige said nothing, uncomfortable, because Nichole's memory wasn't faulty. Ted had always blamed everyone else. He'd never tolerated dissention. Paige used to excuse him by saying that he'd grown up with a military father, but after a while, she found it harder and harder to make excuses for him. "His temper was exacerbated by the drinking."

"He hated that you were strong. He hated that you were determined to be happy." Nichole finally looked at Paige, jaw jutted. "He did his best to break you."

Paige's smile wasn't entirely steady. "But he didn't. Here I am. Not broken."

"He was lucky to have you."

Paige reached out and covered Nichole's hand with hers and gave it a quick squeeze before releasing it. "I wouldn't have you without him. We wouldn't have our family. I'm lucky to have my girls. You're my everything."

Nichole stood, took a long drink from her thermos, then

re-capped the bottle. "Should we head back down? I'm hoping we'll have time to swing by the farmers market. Remember that jewelry designer Michelle and I liked? I'm hoping the designer still has the earrings I liked on my last visit."

Paige glanced at her watch. "If we leave now, we might make it. They close at one."

It was a fast, relatively easy hike down. During the descent, Nichole told Paige about the work she was doing, and some of her department's interesting research, and the applications to medicine and technology. Paige checked her watch at the car. They'd gone five miles round-trip. Two of the three exercise rings on her watch had closed. Definitely a good day in terms of exercise goals.

They headed straight to Dana Point for the market. Many of the vendors were already beginning to close, but the jewelry designer still had her booth open. The earrings Nichole had liked were no longer available, but she found another pair she liked as much, if not better.

"Let me get them for you," Paige offered.

"It's your birthday, Mom. I should get you something."

"I don't want anything, Nichole. Spending today with you has been the best present."

Nichole hugged her mom. Nichole was fiercely independent and not always cuddly, which made the hug extra sweet. "It's been a great day, Mom. I'm so glad I flew out."

"I wish you didn't have to go tonight."

"I'll be back before you know it, and it's not as if you're going to be lonely," she added, shooting her mom a sly glance, "not when you have Mr. Melbourne to keep you company."

Paige gave her head a faint shake, even as she pressed her lips together. What could she say? How could she defend herself? And yet, just the mention of Jack made her feel slightly breathless. She quickly changed the subject. "What time do you want to leave for the airport?"

"Maybe five? That way we could go home, I can shower,

and we can have a bite to eat before we have to go. Would that work?"

"Absolutely."

That evening as Paige wiped down her kitchen counters and made sure everything was tidy before she turned off the lights for bed, she found herself humming and smiling. It'd been a great day, a great weekend. A great week. Turning fifty had been surprisingly painless. She honestly didn't mind getting older. She was calmer now than she'd been when she was younger, more sure of herself. She knew what she wanted, knew what she didn't want, and was finally learning how to stand up for herself.

Even better, she thought as she entered her bedroom, was that her daughters knew how to stand up for themselves. Her daughters were not doormats. They were strong, capable women and Paige couldn't wait to see where life took them.

Changing into her pajamas, Paige caught a glimpse of her body in the mirror. She was slender, but her skin showed age from all the suntanning she used to do, and her breasts were smaller, diminished from breastfeeding as well as staying lean. She didn't mind her breasts, or the wrinkles on her tummy, because no one but her saw them. But how would she feel if Jack saw more of her? Like all of her?

She stepped into her pajama shorts and pulled on the matching knit top, happier covered, not comfortable thinking of herself naked . . . with Jack.

But just thinking of Jack made her insides shift, and her pulse quicken. What was she going to do about Jack?

Chapter 10

PAIGE MET ELIZABETH MONDAY MORNING FOR COFFEE on campus before their first class. It was a gorgeous morning with the vivid blue sky overhead and the golden kiss of the sun on the red tiled roof of the campus. They ordered their coffee at the little coffeehouse in the main quad and carried their cups outside, finding a table by the tall fountain. "You said Nichole flew out Saturday night?" Elizabeth asked, picking up the thread of their conversation.

"She was there at my place when I arrived home, totally catching me off guard," Paige said, settling into her chair.

"It was a weekend of surprises," Elizabeth said.

Paige thought of Jack's kiss and how quickly things had gotten hot. "It was," she agreed, trying not to smile too broadly. "Thank you again for my party. It was so fun, and so unexpected."

"I'm glad you enjoyed it." Elizabeth blew on her hot coffee. "But what's different? You look rather glowy today."

Paige arched a brow. "Glowy? Is that a real word, professor?"

"'Giving off a steady light.' An adjective." Elizabeth grinned and sipped her coffee, attention fixed on Paige. "So, what's the secret?"

Paige shrugged. "Nothing. Same old, same old."

"But you don't look same old, same old. You look . . . happy."

"Hopefully, I look happy every day. I certainly feel happy every day."

"You look happy when you're with me, but you don't always look happy. You often look . . . worried."

"I do?"

"Or maybe just stressed."

Paige frowned. "I walk around looking stressed?"

"You just always seem to have a lot on your mind."

"Because I do have a lot on my mind, but I don't want that etched all over my face."

"You don't today, though. You look . . ."

"Glowy," Paige supplied, rolling her eyes. "Happy."

Elizabeth sat back. "Yes. Like a cat who's had a bowl of cream—" She broke off, eyes widening. "Did you and Jack . . . you know . . . ?"

"*No.*" Paige's brows flattened. "No," she repeated, reaching for her coffee. "Nichole was there waiting for me. Remember?"

"Oh, right." Elizabeth's face sagged with disappointment. "I just thought . . . Oh, never mind."

Paige lifted her coffee. "But we did kiss," she added under her breath.

"What?" Elizabeth cried, voice rising by a full octave.

Paige shushed her, aware that a number of the students studying at the outdoor café had glanced their way. "Be quiet," she hissed, "or I won't tell you anything."

"Lips sealed," Elizabeth answered, making a zipping motion over her mouth.

Paige fought a smile. "You're so ridiculous but you make me laugh." She lowered her voice, leaned forward. "But yes, he kissed me good night, we were outside on my door-step. It was a good kiss."

"What would you rate it? Seven out of ten? Eight?"

"Ten."

"Wow. No wonder you're glowing. You had a full endor-phin, dopamine-fueled experience."

"Can you try not to talk like a love scientist? It doesn't suit you."

Elizabeth grinned. "So, when do you two go out next?"

"I think we're trying to go for a hike this weekend, but it's not a date—"

"Says who?"

"Because it's a hike, not a make-out session in the back seat of his car."

"It could turn into one."

Paige considered this. "Hopefully not after a hike. I'd need a shower."

"He'd probably like your smell. Pheromones, and all that."

She grimaced. "I'm not into odor, but now that you men-tion it, I do like whatever it is Jack wears. I don't know if it's aftershave or cologne. He smells good."

"You really like him."

"I always liked him. That's never been the issue."

"What's the issue, then?"

"We're teaching together, we're colleagues—"

"Oh, stop. Live a little. Enjoy your life. *Please.*"

"I am enjoying my life. I'm sitting with my best friend, having coffee on a beautiful morning, on one of Califor-nia's beautiful campuses—"

"Yes, but I don't make you light up. I don't put that starry look in your eyes—"

"I don't have a starry look."

"You do. And that's good, because kissing is fun. You should kiss him again soon. Don't wait until December, that's months away. Kiss him this weekend. Or even better, kiss him this week." Elizabeth glanced at her phone and rose. "I have to go, but I'll be eagerly awaiting updates."

PAIGE DIDN'T SEE JACK UNTIL SHE REACHED THE LECTURE room later that morning. She paused on the platform, taking him in. He was wearing a white button-down shirt, the collar open, his throat tan, the cuffs rolled back on his muscular forearms. He was reading something on his phone, and he had a pair of glasses on, making him look like a very sexy professor.

He glanced up as she set her things on the front table. Warmth glimmered in his eyes. "And there is my favorite mathematician."

Her lips quivered, smiled. Her insides felt like fizzy candy and heat washed through her, making her nape, her face, her breasts sensitive. She hunched her shoulders at the jolt of adrenaline racing through her. "How many mathematicians have you dated?" she asked.

"You'd be the first." He stood close and his collar fell open, giving her a tantalizing glimpse of his broad chest.

More bronzed skin.

More firm muscles.

She could smell a hint of his aftershave and she inhaled deeply, thinking he smelled delicious, thinking she'd like to see him with his shirt off, thinking she'd very much like to touch his skin. Paige felt an ache low in her belly, an ache she could feel between her legs. Jack was turning her on, just standing there.

So weird to realize she wasn't dead, that a few hormones still flitted around, making her feel breathless and giddy.

She remembered the kiss Saturday night, as well as the conversation. He made her feel young again, as if she was a girl. It wasn't necessarily a bad way to feel. Just disconcerting.

"And you?" he asked, stepping away to arrange his lecture notes.

"No mathematicians for me, and no scientists except for you."

He glanced at her, a teasing light in his eye, and was just about to answer, when a student approached, mentioning some difficulty she'd had over the weekend, and she hadn't been able to do the reading for today's lecture.

The student went to find a seat, and Paige went to take her chair just off to the side. Jack placed his laptop and notes on the podium then crossed to her.

"Did you have a good time with Nichole?" he asked.

"Yes." She couldn't hide her happiness. "It was a shock seeing her. But I loved the spontaneity. We only had the day together, but we made the most of it."

"I'm glad."

"I still want to do the Crystal Cove hike with you, though. Maybe this weekend?"

"I'm hoping to see Oliver this weekend, but don't know his schedule yet. Once I do, I'll get back to you."

"Sounds good."

"I do have a proposition for you. I know you have office hours after class, but I wanted to fill you in, get your thoughts."

Jack's deep voice, coupled with the words, *I have a proposition for you*, made her think dirty thoughts. But then, she'd been thinking delightfully dirty things ever since Saturday night.

Jack taught the first half of the period, and Paige sat off to the side listening to the lecture. Or more accurately, listening to his voice, but not focusing too much on the actual words. Instead, she replayed Saturday night, the party, the drive home, and then the kiss.

She remembered how good it had felt to be pressed up against her front door, Jack's body leaning into hers, his broad chest against her breasts, his hips hard on hers. It had been intense and exciting, and she'd loved every moment of it.

It had been so long since she'd felt anything like that, so long since she'd been touched, and made to feel good.

Pleasure. It was a novelty concept at this point in her life, and yet just that small taste Saturday night made her want more.

Sleeping with Jack would be good. He'd kissed her as if he had all the time in the world. She suspected he made love that way, too. He'd be patient with her, and he'd make her come, if she let him.

She hadn't let him in Paris. She hadn't been able to relax, and she couldn't let go of control.

Control remained an issue for her, but at least she wasn't that inexperienced girl who didn't know her way around a man's body. She did now.

She looked at Jack standing at the podium, clicking through a PowerPoint on the regulation of single-species populations, long-sleeve shirt rolled back on muscular, tan forearms, buttons undone at the collar, hinting at the strong, broad planes of his chest. His legs were long, his hips narrow, his shoulders broad. He had an athlete's body. Fit. Sinewy. Appealing.

She wondered what he'd look like without clothes. Wondered where his tan lines were, and if he slept in pajamas, or naked. Probably naked, she guessed, biting back a smile.

Jack glanced at her, his warm gold-brown eyes meeting hers briefly before returning to the students. "Is anyone here getting excited about our field work?" he asked. "I know Dr. Newsome is." He looked at her once more. "And with that, I hand the class over to you."

She gathered her satchel with the books and notes and turned to whisper to Jack, "You play dirty, Dr. King."

He grinned, utterly unrepentant. "I play to win. You should, too."

Paige shook her head, but she was smiling, and as she opened her notes, she faced the class. "Good afternoon, everyone. It's nice to see you again."

Her hour flew by and then class was over, and students streamed out. A student approached Jack as she packed her books and notes up, but then the student was gone, and she and Jack climbed the stairs of the lecture hall together. "You're good at what you do," he said.

"Thank you. I really like what I do, and this school is a great fit. I enjoyed Duke, but I'm a California girl at heart. I love all the sunshine."

"Heard you went to a party Saturday night," he said.

She glanced up at him, feeling mischievous. "I did, and then this nice guy drove me home."

"Nice guy, was he?"

"Mmm. A scientist. From Australia."

"Sounds boring."

She laughed. "He's a little bit nerdy, but that's part of his charm."

Jack laughed, the sound a deep rumble. "You are hilarious."

"So I've been told."

He pushed open the door to the building, holding it for her. "I was wondering if you'd like to go to Yellowstone with me. Not this weekend, but next. October fifteenth, sixteenth, seventeenth."

They stepped out of the building into bright sunshine. Paige blinked at the light and reached into her bag for her sunglasses. "Yellowstone," she repeated.

"I've been asked to fill in for a speaker who had to cancel for this year's Yellowstone educator symposium. I've spoken at it before and it's a really good group of people. We stay right in the park."

She smiled as they passed two of her students from last year, even as she struggled to respond to Jack's invitation. He was asking her to go with him on a trip. To a conference. Where he was the guest speaker. She tried to sort through her thoughts and answer carefully. "I've been to enough symposiums and conferences to know that it's not necessarily the norm to bring a guest."

Jack shrugged. "It wouldn't be that strange. Others will be bringing spouses, partners."

She glanced up at him, brow furrowing. "Which I am neither."

"It's going to be a really relaxed weekend. I'm sure you can get someone to cover your Friday classes." He shrugged. "Or you could just cancel your Friday classes."

"Oh, it's that easy."

"It's not that hard, either."

"Won't people think it's odd that I'm coming with you? Won't they expect us to be in some kind of relationship?"

"I think you're overthinking this."

"I'm wondering if you've even thought this through."

They reached the math and science building, one of the most nondescript buildings on campus, and he opened the glass door, holding it for her. "What is your objection?" he asked.

"I just don't want to create gossip. Stir up speculation."

"You are such a chicken."

"I'm not a chicken. I'm cautious. I consider my reputation."

They climbed the stairs to the second floor. He glanced down at her, expression teasing. "No one is worrying about your reputation, Dr. Newsome."

"Well, certainly not you, Dr. King."

"Do you ever have any fun? Or are you always so incredibly uptight?"

Her mouth opened and closed. Part of her was offended, and another part of her thought, *Yes, I resemble that.* Annoyance won out. "You do you, and I'll do me."

"I'd like to do you—"

"*Ssssh.* Someone might hear you."

"The walls?"

They'd reached the end of the hall where their offices were, and she gazed up at him. He looked especially handsome today—rakish—with that bright glint in his eyes. She was drawn to him, and when he was charming and playful, she found him rather irresistible. "We're very much opposites—"

"They say opposites attract."

"Opposites also get on each other's nerves. They can

even grow to hate each other—" She broke off, wishing she hadn't added that part. It was a little too personal, a little too telling. "Not that I know from experience," she added quickly, drawing out the keys and unlocking her office door. "Reading and data and so forth."

"You remind me of my former headmaster at the boarding school I attended as a boy. He was very proper, too, and took everything very seriously."

"I'm not always proper and uptight. I have fun with my girls, and Elizabeth. We go to movies, and dinner, we go see shows, and have weekend road trips—"

"Then come to Yellowstone. I realize I'm not one of your girls or Elizabeth, but I can be good company, too. And we're talking about Yellowstone. Staying in historic cabins inside the park. Great food. Smart people. Interesting topics."

She spotted one of her students approaching. "I'll think about it," she said, because it did sound appealing. Very appealing. But then she remembered his kiss and how he'd made her feel so many things. But she couldn't handle another Paris. Couldn't handle disappointing him—or herself—again.

"When was the last time you visited Yellowstone?" he asked.

"I've never been," she admitted before seeing his incredulous expression. "But it *is* on my bucket list," she added defensively.

"Then join me. Check it off your list."

AFTER HER OFFICE HOURS, PAIGE HAD ONE MORE CLASS, and then she returned to her building to gather her things and check her mailbox in the math department. The math department office was empty. Andi wasn't at her desk but since the office door was unlocked Paige suspected she'd just stepped out for a moment. Paige headed to the small staff room with the faculty mailboxes, and as she reached into her mailbox, she heard a soft hiccuping sound. Paige froze, listening. She heard it again. A soft, muffled cry.

Paige stepped from the staff room and glanced down the hall toward Dr. Nair's office. Dr. Nair was out today, but in the shadows outside his door stood Andi, his executive assistant, head bent, a tissue pressed to her mouth.

"Andi, are you okay?" Paige asked, concerned.

Andi's head nodded, making her long dark curls bounce. Paige walked to her. "Did something happen?" she asked, putting a hand on Andi's back. Andi was such a sweetheart. Paige couldn't stand to see her upset.

"No, nothing," Andi said, using the crumpled tissue to blot her eyes and then dab her nose. "It's just a hard day. I thought maybe this year it would be different, but I guess not."

Then it hit Paige. "Is this the day Kevin died?" she asked carefully.

Andi had been widowed at fifty-four, just months before Paige joined Orange University. Greg Hsu told Paige that Andi had taken the job at Orange just months after her husband died, needing to feel needed since she'd never had kids of her own. Andi was very much the heart of the department, and Paige looked forward to seeing her smile every day.

Andi drew a shuddering breath. "It would have been our thirty-sixth anniversary today."

"I'm so sorry, Andi."

"I thought the grieving was behind me. I thought this year would be different."

"I don't think grief has a timeline," Paige said, hugging Andi.

Andi hugged her back and then eased away. "We didn't have a perfect marriage, but we were happy. I was happy. He was my best friend."

"You were lucky."

"I know. And with him gone, everything is just . . . empty. I hate living alone. I hate going home to an empty house every day."

"What are you doing after work? Do you want to get a drink or dinner?"

Andi managed a small, watery smile. "Can I have a raincheck? Because I've planned to take flowers to Kevin's grave site after work. It's over in Corona del Mar and I imagine there will be traffic—"

"Why don't you take the rest of the day off? Go early?"

"No, I have an inbox full of paperwork to do, and Dr. Nair needs me to coordinate some travel for a January conference. I promised him I'd get it done before I left, but, Paige, I'd love to get drinks sometime. Thank you for that."

Paige squashed the twinge of guilt that she'd never thought to invite Andi out before. They were both single women, relatively close in age, but Paige was always so busy it hadn't crossed her mind that others around her might have too much time on their hands. "Let's plan something soon."

"I'd enjoy that." Andi drew a slow, deep breath, scrubbed her face dry, and squared her shoulders. "Better? I don't want anyone to know I've been in here crying."

"I won't tell anyone."

"Good, because my job is to make things easier for everyone, not harder."

PAIGE DROVE HOME THINKING ABOUT ANDI, AND LOVE, and marriage. She wished she'd had the kind of marriage Andi and Kevin had known, marriage where two people were best friends and treated each other with love and kindness. Respect.

Paige hadn't felt respected in her marriage. Ted had always come first. His career, his goals, his needs. She and the girls were there to accommodate him, fit around his schedule, yield to his wants and dreams. No one else was as important. No one had the right to make demands on him, or on his time.

Paige thought of her dad and how he'd adored her mom. They'd been childhood sweethearts, too. Well, they'd met when Mom was a senior in high school and Dad was attending the community college. Mom had been working as a waitress at the local diner and Dad had come in with friends for lunch and left with Mom's number. They had a first date and he'd proposed a year to the day later. Her parents didn't always see eye to eye but when they'd had disagreements, the disagreements weren't ugly. Hateful words weren't said. No one went days without speaking.

What made some marriages work?

Why hadn't she succeeded in hers?

Paige stopped at her favorite barre studio for the five o'clock class. She arrived later than she liked; the big room was crowded but she found a spot on the barre and slid in. The fifty-minute class challenged her, making her squeeze and burn. Muscles quivering, she returned to her car, glad she'd gone. The focus and discipline had been exactly what she needed after today. Today had been long. It felt like three days rolled into one.

Home, she showered, put on pajamas, and sautéed a small chicken breast with vegetables. Dishing her dinner, she carried her plate to the couch and ate as she watched David Muir's evening news. David made her feel safe, and she'd always thought he was really good-looking, but it crossed her mind tonight that Jack King was actually more handsome. And every bit as smart. If not smarter.

Her phone rang just as the news ended. It was her oldest. Paige hadn't talked to her in over a week and was happy to hear her voice. They chatted for a few minutes about Michelle's weekend, and how she'd had a date with someone she really liked, a man Paige only remembered as being divorced and a single father. Paige had bit her tongue when Michelle told her last month that the man's divorce had been acrimonious, and that he and his ex-wife only communicated through a family member.

She had to bite her tongue tonight when Michelle shared that her new boyfriend said his ex-wife was self-centered and not very loving, not with him or with the kids. Paige knew there were always two sides to a story, and she knew people didn't marry to get divorced, but part of her longed to shake Michelle and ask her if this was really the man she wanted to spend time with. He certainly wasn't the man Paige wanted for her daughter, but Paige didn't say any of that.

Instead, she introduced the subject of Yellowstone, asking what Michelle thought of her going for a weekend. "I've been invited by a colleague," Paige added. "We're not dating, so I think it would be weird to go to Yellowstone for the symposium, but I've never been, and it sounds intriguing—"

"Is this with the Australian guy?" Michelle interrupted. "The one you were having a mad make-out session with?"

"It wasn't a mad make-out session," Paige answered crisply.

"That's not what Nichole said."

Warmth rushed to her cheeks. Paige muted the TV. "Tell me you haven't told Ashley."

"I haven't, and Nichole and Ashley had a fight so they're not talking."

"Why are they fighting?"

"I think Ashley was upset that Nichole came home and surprised you for your birthday. Ashley felt left out." Michelle sounded exasperated. "Anyway, I'm staying out of that one. But about Yellowstone. Go."

"I shouldn't. We're colleagues and we teach together—"

"Is that written in your contract? Or are these your rules?"

"My rules, but I'm certain Dr. Keller wouldn't want us getting too close. We have to think of the university."

"Next, you'll be saying you have to think of God and your country. It's okay to do something for you. It's time you put yourself first."

Paige's stomach did a somersault. "What if I'm supposed to share a room with him? I'm not ready for that."

"Why are you being a ninny? You're not a fifteen-year-old virgin. Ask him about the accommodations and then you'll know."

"If I ask him, he'll think I'm interested."

"Just because you divorced Dad doesn't mean you've taken a vow of celibacy. I never thought it was good that you decided to swear off men. But ultimately, it's your call. Do what feels right, and, Mom, sorry to cut the call short, but I need to go. Love you tons. You're the best."

Hanging up, Paige was even more conflicted than before. If she was this torn, she shouldn't go.

But she didn't like that answer. It didn't sit right with her.

And yet, what was the point of dating at her age? It would be different if she were young and wanted children, or needed another paycheck to help cover the rent. Or, if she really craved sex, but she didn't. Which was why she was good being single. Happy solo. It didn't feel like anything was missing, and just because Elizabeth loved being married didn't mean it was the right thing for every woman.

Paige went to the window over her kitchen sink, looked out at the metal roof over the parking lot. She wished she had a different view from her kitchen window, but at least she had that sliver of ocean from her balcony. It was better to have a little bit of ocean somewhere. She appreciated it. She was lucky to have—

Paige straightened abruptly, temper flaring.

This was such bullshit. She suddenly felt angry. Why did she go through life pretending to be grateful for slivers and morsels? Telling herself she was blessed, fortunate, but honestly, there were times her slivers and morsels weren't enough. Sometimes she longed to be greedy and want more. More adventure. More fun. More change. More new, fresh, interesting.

She would be a fool not to go to Yellowstone. She would be a fool to turn things down without even getting all the information first. For someone who loved facts, data, she hadn't tried very hard to get the whole picture. No, she was like that timid English major, terrified of algebra, closing her mind to what one could do, certain that math and numbers were beyond her. But numbers weren't terrifying.

Math wasn't the enemy. Fear and self-doubt were the enemy and she shouldn't be afraid of asking questions and getting the details. A trip to Yellowstone could be really cool. A trip anywhere right now would be really cool. She hadn't traveled over the summer. She'd worked hard, and made regular trips home to see Mom, but that was it.

Paige picked up her phone and texted Jack. When would you leave, and when would you come back?

She put her phone down and poured herself a glass of tea. She'd just added ice when her phone buzzed.

If we're talking about Yellowstone, he replied, I would fly out Thursday night and be back Monday, in time for our afternoon class.

Our class.

Ours.

For some reason that sent a shiver of sensation through her. She told herself to knock it off and forced herself to think about practicalities. There would only be two classes she'd need to cancel or reschedule, just the classes on Friday. Her long teaching days were Tuesday and Thursday, and it didn't sound like she'd miss any of those.

How are you getting there? she texted. How much is the airfare?

Flying into Bozeman from Orange County, with a connection in Salt Lake City.

She studied his reply. How much is it?

It's covered by my stipend. And if you want to go, yours would be, too.

Her heart did a little jump, matching the hum of excitement inside of her. Jack made it seem so easy. Just jump on a plane, fly into Montana, where he'd probably be met and whisked into the park. If he was filling in as the speaker, everyone would be falling all over themselves to accommodate him.

The idea of just tagging along and not having to do anything was incredibly appealing. Paige had always been in charge of making the arrangements, finding the best deals, handling all the reservations. In the last two years her daughters had begun to take over some of the trip planning, all three having inherited her thrifty nature. They avoided checking bags, refused to pay for assigned seats, accepted that connecting flights would often be a better deal.

She'd taught them well.

Mustering up her courage, Paige typed. And accommodations? What would the sleeping arrangements be like?

He didn't answer. She kept watching her phone, waiting to see those little blinking dots indicating that he was working on an answer, crafting a reply. But there were no blinking dots. Anxious, annoyed, she pushed off the counter and marched to her sink and reached for the damp sponge to wipe down the already pristine surface.

Her phone rang. Her insides lurched. She knew it was Jack. She returned to her phone, and saw she was right. "Hello?" she answered.

"Afraid you have to sleep with me?" he asked, laughter in his voice.

Her face heated. "Yes," she said stiffly. "It's crossed my mind."

"Sleeping with me?"

Her cheeks burned. She was glad he wasn't there to see her blush. "You're making me nervous."

"I owe you an orgasm."

"Oh my God, *Jack*."

"It's true. I've felt bad all these years—"

"Obviously, this isn't going to work. I don't know why I even asked—"

"You would have your own room. It's a small conference and there are extra cabins that aren't being used."

"I'd really have my own cabin?"

"If that's what you wanted."

She could feel him smiling over the phone. So annoying. "Tell me this, if I'd wanted to sleep with you, you would?"

"But of course."

She laughed and hung up. Then followed with a text.

RSVPing yes. But have not agreed to any hanky-panky.

What about rooting, or snogging? Jack replied.

No idea what that means.

No worries, mate. I'll show you.

Paige bit her lip, unable to stop smiling.

Chapter 11

JACK WAS UP LATE FINISHING AN ARTICLE HE'D OWED *The Scientist* for a couple weeks; he'd vowed he wouldn't go to bed until it was finally done and off to the editor. Jack didn't usually mind writing papers and articles, but lately he'd wanted less time at his desk, and more time socializing, with Paige to be specific.

It's one of the reasons he invited her to Yellowstone. He'd been happy to fill in for the missing speaker, but his immediate thought had been, *What about Paige?*

He missed her on weekends. The stretch between Friday's class and Monday's class felt too long, too empty. He'd always been quite happy with his own company, but lately he didn't enjoy his company. He wanted hers.

Already he was dreading December. He had a tightly packed schedule, one that would keep him away from California for at least four weeks, maybe six, depending on how filming went. Right after Costa Rica he was scheduled to fly to Tanzania for a conference in Arusha, and once that wrapped up on Sunday, he'd remain in Arusha for production meetings for his show, which was back on and slated to begin filming the third week of December. They usually filmed over four weeks, but with Christmas and New Year's in the middle, he wasn't sure how that would go.

This week, he and the producers had been on numerous Zoom calls, discussing setting and episodes, mapping out the schedule; but he'd felt distracted, and his heart wasn't completely in it.

The idea of filming in Tanzania was less appealing every day, and yet he loved Arusha, it was like a second—third?—home. He'd love Paige to come to Tanzania for her holidays, but he doubted she'd leave her girls, and if Yellowstone seemed far to her, he could only imagine how impossible Tanzania would be.

But he could try. Jack had never been afraid of going for it, not even when he failed. What was the point of going through life afraid? Far better to see opportunity and possibilities than disappointment.

Thinking of Paige in Tanzania reminded him that Camille would be in Tanzania at the December conference, where he was speaking. He wasn't looking forward to seeing her there. She'd been in touch with him to say it wasn't long now, and casually mentioned she was single again. He shared that he wasn't, that there was someone he was seeing, but he wasn't sure if that would discourage Camille. Camille had always been far more invested in him than he was in her.

PAIGE HADN'T WANTED TO OVERPACK FOR YELLOW-stone. This was her chance to show Jack that she could be relaxed, easygoing. She packed two nice blouses and a pair of crisp dark jeans in case she needed to dress for something, but otherwise, she chose her favorite weekend clothes: soft, faded denims, comfy T-shirts, oversize hoodies. She added a lightweight down coat for cold evenings, as well as three pairs of different shoes—sneakers, ankle boots, and a pair of leather loafers. At the last second, she tucked in a knit cap, scarf, and mittens just in case it snowed.

With the Friday classes cancelled, and her late Thursday class covered by a teaching assistant, Paige and Jack were able to head to the airport Thursday afternoon. Paige had caught a ride to school with Elizabeth on Thursday, and then she drove with Jack straight to the airport. They'd fly to Salt Lake City and connect to Bozeman, arriving at ten in Montana, where someone would be there to pick them up and drive them the hour to the education center in Yellowstone.

It was a lot of traveling, but Paige had a lot of work to do and she'd deliberately left the mystery she was reading at home so she wouldn't be tempted to read instead of grade. There were no hitches at the airport, nor were there any issues boarding. They were in the air, halfway to Salt Lake City, when Paige gave up pretending that she was actually working. Instead, she watched Jack, who was immersed in reading on his laptop.

He was so handsome.

Very, very, very hot.

Very, very, very appealing.

She wanted to be close to him. Wanted to hold his hand, and to kiss him. Wanted to lean against him, have his arms around her, feel his mouth against her lips, her cheek, her neck. It was hard to think in terms of sex—she'd felt sexless for so long—and yet she'd begun to crave touch, his touch. She just wished she didn't find sex so terrifying. There were still so many negative memories attached to it—not with him—but those last, final years with Ted where she'd gone numb and felt nothing as he climbed into bed intoxicated, demanding.

She closed her eyes now, hating the old shame and discomfort. The memories were hard. Lovemaking was a natural part of relationships, or at least it was supposed to be, but she didn't know how to let down her guard, let someone close. She had friends who could enjoy sex without strings, but she'd never been one of them.

Jack's hand touched her arm. "You okay?"

She opened her eyes, nodded, wondering what he'd seen in her face to make him ask. "I am, thank you." Her gaze swept from his golden-brown eyes to his firm, very kissable mouth. "I'm excited we're doing this."

"I love traveling, glad you do, too."

She looked again into his eyes. He had such beautiful eyes, in a beautiful face, but that's not what held her attention. It was the warmth in his gaze. The kindness. She admired his brilliant mind but loved his kindness. His inherent goodness. Paige reached for his hand and wrapped her fingers around his. "Thank you for inviting me."

His hand shifted, his fingers curling around hers before lifting her hand to his mouth. He kissed the base of her palm, sending a tingling ripple of sensation through her. "Thank you for coming." And then he winked. "Well, not yet, but we'll get that sorted soon."

"Jack!" she choked, heat rushing to her face. She tried to pull her hand away, but he wouldn't let her. Instead, he leaned forward and kissed her, and the kiss made her forget everything. Time stopped. She melted, yielding to the pressure and the pleasure. By the time he lifted his head, she was mindless and boneless. Paige just blinked at him, wanting more, wishing he hadn't stopped, wishing she always felt so good.

"Now what are you thinking?" he asked, deep voice husky.

She gave her head a slight shake, not about to tell him that she was falling for him.

Hard.

THE DRIVER MEETING THEM AT THE BOZEMAN AIRPORT was Zach Stevens, one of Jack's longtime friends and a professor at the University of Wyoming. While he drove to Yellowstone, he filled Jack in on who was coming, and a few last-minute changes to the schedule. Paige listened, but also gazed out the window at the sky. It was so dark, and the sky was so clear. Every star glimmered, a wash of white diamonds.

It was nearing eleven thirty when they reached the education center. Check-in was fast and easy since everyone else had already gone to bed. Zach handed over the keys to their cabins, apologizing that the cabins weren't next door, but they shared the same gravel path.

Jack sent Zach to bed and carried Paige's suitcase to her cabin. He unlocked the door, turned on the light, and inspected it, making sure she'd be comfortable. "Sleep in tomorrow. There's no need to get up early. They'll have a continental breakfast for everyone, and I can get you a yogurt, or whatever you want."

"Yogurt and a banana," she said, kissing him good night. "And coffee—"

"I've brought a thermos. I'll fill it for us."

She kissed him again. "Thank you," she whispered at the door. "Good night."

"Sweet dreams."

She watched him continue down the path to his cabin, which seemed to be three cabins down from hers. Closing her door, she locked it and turned to face the small space. It was chilly without the heater on, but snug. The furniture and bedding were on the practical side but there were two pillows and an extra blanket folded at the foot of the bed. More than adequate for the weekend. After a fast shower, she climbed into bed, turned out the light, and was asleep almost the moment her head hit the pillow.

Jack was busy almost all day Friday, but he sought her out at lunch and sat with her outside on one of the logs flanking the empty firepit where they ate their deli-style sandwiches. Most people were eating lunch inside, and Paige was glad to have Jack to herself.

"They've got me pretty busy today," he said, "but tomorrow should be better."

"I'm not worried. I'm just loving being here."

"What did you do this morning?"

"Walked around a little bit, checked out where everything was, and mostly worked. The good thing is I'm almost caught up. I might end up taking a nap this afternoon."

"I wish I could."

"Just cancel your meetings," she teased.

"Don't tempt me." He opened his bag of potato chips. "We should be done midafternoon, and then there's a group trip to Mammoth Hot Springs," he said. "It's just a walk, not a true hike, but it'll take about an hour."

"Will you go?" she asked, stealing one of his chips since she hadn't taken any for herself.

"I hope to."

"Good. Come get me when it's time."

THE TRIP TO MAMMOTH HOT SPRINGS TOOK TWO HOURS: a twenty-minute drive there, lots of walking around the boardwalks on the Upper and Lower Terraces with Jack at her side, explaining what she was seeing. Limestone, gasses, heat, moisture, new travertine formations. To be honest, she was more interested in having Jack's attention than in the volcanic activity beneath them. Then they were heading back to the education center for appetizers, dinner, and a guest presentation from one of the park's rangers.

Everyone drifted off by nine, ready to go to bed. Paige and Jack remained outside by the fire, and it reminded her of Paris, and how in the end, it was just the two of them talking.

The night was cold, but the sky was clear and stars glittered overhead. They sat bundled up, feet propped on the edge of the firepit, nursing their port, talking about the day. Between sips of wine, they watched the flames dance and listened to the crack and pop of the fire, as well as the not-so-distant howl of coyotes.

"How do you know those aren't wolves?" she asked.

"Because I know what wolves sound like."

"They don't sound the same?"

"Wolves have a deeper howl, their pitch is low and drawn

out, while coyotes have a higher howl, it's shorter, and rises and falls. One of my students once said coyotes sound like a pack of junior high girls shrieking at the sight of a ghost."

She laughed. "That's quite specific."

"Yes, but it helps differentiate the two howls. Coyotes sound more haunting, while wolves sound more like mournful dogs."

Paige tipped her head back and looked up into the purple-black sky. "I do love it here."

"You'll have to come back."

She nodded.

"With me," he added.

She turned her head and looked at him, gaze locking with his. "Or, you could come with me."

He smiled slowly, appreciation in his eyes. "If we come back together, when would you want to?"

"Whenever we could do this again." She gestured to the starry sky and the surrounding hills. "We're here in the park, virtually alone. This is magic."

"I think you're magic," he said, bringing her closer, tilting her chin up for a kiss.

The kiss was warm, sweet. It was a kiss of tenderness, and it sent delicious ripples through her. She leaned in, pressing close. He felt strong and steady, and she felt happier than she could remember. It had been a long time since she'd felt so good in her skin. It had been forever since she'd wanted to be held.

Paige broke off the kiss and looked up into Jack's face. She studied his features, her fingertip lightly tracing his cheekbone, his jaw, his warm, firm mouth. He hadn't shaved for the past few days and she liked him with scruff. She liked him.

More than liked him.

Emotion bubbled up and her eyes burned. Was it possible she had loved him all these years? Was it possible to have quietly carried a torch for someone she'd only known one night? "Why do you kiss so good?" she whispered.

"I just kiss you good."

Another warm bubble of emotion, larger, fuller, making her chest impossibly tender. "Why?"

"Because I'm meant to kiss you."

"You think?"

"I do." His gaze met hers, held, his golden irises dark. "From the very first time I laid eyes on you, I've wanted you. You feel like you're mine, as if you're meant to be with me."

"You never told me that."

"You never gave me a chance."

Her heart ached, even as a jolt of adrenaline raced through her. Something significant was happening. Some of the thick ice around her heart was cracking. Falling. She felt vulnerable and open, but it also felt good. "You didn't try to find me after I left."

"You left without leaving a number. You left without saying goodbye. I took that as a no-thank-you-not-interested sign."

She understood why he hadn't come after her, but it didn't change that she wished he had. She wished he'd fought for her, but that was also a childish wish, one that little girls read about in storybooks.

Paige captured his face between her hands and kissed him firmly, deeply, even as an electric sensation raced up and down her spine. Drawing back, she stroked her thumbs lightly over his high, hard cheekbones, and the bristle of a beard on his jaw. "I was scared," she admitted. "Scared you'd break my heart. I wasn't as worldly as you. Wasn't as experienced. And then there was that thing that happened—" She broke off as he lifted a brow. "Yes, I faked it. I panicked. I was taking too long to climax."

He laughed quietly, then kissed her. "Is that what you were worried about?"

She nodded.

He kissed her again, and then turned her in his arms, shifting her so that she rested against him, his arms around her waist. "I wasn't grading you. Wasn't comparing you."

"How was I to know? We barely knew each other."

"I had no idea you were so shy. But there was no reason to feel insecure. You were never just sex. I could have gotten laid a hundred times that summer but didn't. You were the one I wanted to know, but I had to keep my distance." He grimaced. "I was supposed to keep my distance. You were supposed to be off-limits."

"I wondered."

"I broke rules by taking you back to my place. But it was worth it. That night with you was special."

She turned her head, tried to see his expression. "Really?"

He nodded. "It just felt right. You felt like you belonged there, with me."

She said nothing, her chest tender, her heart racing.

"I feel that way now," he added. "You feel right in my arms. You fit. I felt this in Paris. I still feel it."

Her eyes stung and a lump filled her throat. She held tight to his arms, holding him, holding on. "What would have happened if I hadn't panicked and run away?"

"I've thought about that a lot."

"Have you?" she asked, unable to mask her surprise.

"I dug you." He kissed the side of her cheek, and then just beneath her earlobe. "You were beautiful. Smart. Sexy."

"Sexy?" She turned in his arms to look at him properly. "I was not sexy. I was chubby and nerdy and—"

"Smart. So smart, and gorgeous, and funny. You were this sun-kissed California girl with blond hair, big blue eyes, and the softest-looking mouth I've ever seen. You made me hard. I fantasized about you all the time."

"You did?"

"Yes. And your legs. I loved your legs. I loved your short skirts. Little denim skirts, tight little tank tops, some that I could see your nipples through—"

She punched him in the chest. "That's not true."

"It was true. And I spent a lot of time thinking about how I wanted to suck your nipples—"

She punched him again. "Stop it."

"And lick them."

Paige squirmed, embarrassed, aroused. "Okay, great. That was then, this is now."

"And I still am obsessed with your legs and your breasts, and everything in between."

She closed her eyes, pressed her knees together, feeling heat and a coil of maddening, distracting tension.

Who would have thought that just a little dirty talk would turn her on?

"I had no idea you even knew I existed," she said unsteadily.

His teeth caught her earlobe, scraping the tender skin. "That's not true. You watched me, just as I watched you. There was a lot of eye contact, and I knew you were as curious about me as I was about you."

She didn't know if it was the rasp in his voice, or the warmth of his mouth on her ear, but she was breathless. Her pulse thudded and she was sensitive all over. She'd begun to hum from the top of her head to the tips of her toes. "I was curious." Paige lightly dragged her nails across his forearm wrapped around her waist. "I wanted to know everything about you. That night at the restaurant, I could have talked to you forever."

"You should have." He kissed the side of her neck, and again lower. "I wish you'd stayed and we could have figured out this thing between us, because there is something. It was there from the beginning. It's there now. I suspect this connection will always be there."

She pressed his arms even closer, making him hold her tighter. "I'm glad you invited me here, Jack."

"I'm glad you joined me."

The wind blew, cold, biting, and she shivered. "It's getting late," she said regretfully.

"It is, and we have an early morning."

"Do we?"

"We have a morning drive planned. Thought we'd get out of here and watch the sun rise."

"Who all is going?"

"Just you and me. I've got keys and Zach's car. What do you think?"

Montana was already an hour ahead in terms of time zones. She dreaded waking up even earlier. "How early?"

"You'll survive."

"That early?"

He rose, pulled her to her feet. "I'll bring coffee, how's that?"

"You know all the right things to say."

He kissed her again on the doorstep of her small cabin. The kiss was even better than earlier, full of heat and hunger, and she pressed herself to him, savoring the feel of his hard body against hers. Kissing was waking her up, reminding her body how it felt to be touched, and how seductive touch could be. Somehow, she'd forgotten that her skin had nerve endings and that her body was good for more than carrying things and exercising. Her body could give her pleasure. Imagine.

Inside her cabin, Paige locked the door and listened to Jack's footsteps retreat.

Smiling, she bit her lip. She'd see him in just hours, and she couldn't wait. A few minutes later, tucked into her bed, Paige squeezed her pillow to her chest, reliving the kisses and the conversation.

She liked it all . . . him, his mind, his mouth, his body. Every time he touched her, she felt . . . beautiful. Alive. She'd forgotten what it felt like to be held, and her body still tingled, sensitive from head to toe. She'd forgotten the ache of desire, heat humming in her veins, everything warm, wanting. Paige suspected not everyone would make her feel this way.

After returning from Paris, Paige had immersed herself in her graduate studies. She hadn't dated seriously, or extensively, before she'd met Ted her final year at UC Berkeley. He was finishing his MBA and she was finishing her PhD. He'd taken six years off between earning his undergraduate degree and his master's. Ted had a plan for his life, a vision, and she admired people with plans. She admired Ted's plans.

She just hadn't realized that after marrying her, he wouldn't spend much energy or time focusing on their young family. Paige had tried to tell herself he was busy and stressed. He had a lot of pressure on him, and because he was the breadwinner at that point, she had to respect his schedule and demands. She didn't view herself as old-fashioned, but committed. She took her vows seriously, looked at no other men, refused to imagine any other life. She was determined to make her marriage work.

It wasn't that easy. Why had it been so hard? Her parents had made it work. Both of her grandparents had made marriage work. Even Ted's parents were still together.

Looking back, she'd put up with things she shouldn't have had to put up with because she wasn't a quitter. She didn't accept defeat. She wasn't going to have her girls come from a broken home. She wanted to be a couple, wanted to grow old with her husband, going from parents to grandparents, from Mom and Dad to Grandma and Grandpa. She'd needed to be that ideal family, that traditional family. Hardworking, practical, no excuses.

Paige tossed aside her pillow and reached for the water bottle next to her bed. She took a long drink, and then another.

If she just wanted sex with Jack, things would be easy. He was easy. But her interest was deeper, her feelings more complicated.

Feeling again, much less desiring again, was terrifying. It made her realize her walls weren't that strong. Her armor wasn't impenetrable. If she could feel so much kissing Jack, she could also be hurt. She didn't want to hurt.

Paige shivered and lay back down, pulling the covers higher. Her cabin was cold. She was chilled. But Jack wouldn't hurt her, she told herself, curling into a ball to get warm. That's not who Jack was.

But another little voice whispered, *He's fifty-five and single, which means he's not that interested in settling down.*

Chapter 12

JACK WOKE, CHECKED HIS PHONE. A FEW MINUTES AFTER four. He scrolled through the news and the weather, specifically news and weather coming from Costa Rica.

Another hurricane was on the way.

The country was being battered. There would be no field trip to Costa Rica next month. He'd had a feeling it was going to get cancelled, and with the unrelenting rain, even Monteverde would be flooding.

He hated disappointing people, and he knew his students were really looking forward to the trip coming up at the end of the semester. The easy thing would be to just cancel the field trip entirely, but Jack had never done the easy thing. There was no point in taking the easy way out, unless it was truly the smartest solution, and to his mind, that wasn't a solution for his Orange students.

He needed to get to work and find an alternative trip the Orange students could do. Almost immediately, Arusha came to mind. He was already heading there for the conference the second weekend of December, and then his show was slated to begin filming in Tanzania just before Christmas, wrapping mid-to-late January so he could return to Southern California for Orange's Spring semester. Months ago, he'd booked everything back to back, making choices that cut down on flights and expenses. A field trip to Arusha would be better for him, but what about his students?

It would be a much longer flight, and the time difference was substantial, but his students could easily be accommodated at one of Arusha's campus dorms, or even a hotel. But it was a huge change, and not everyone would be on board with it.

Paige, for example. He suspected she wouldn't be thrilled. She liked things safe and predictable. How interesting that his world was always about change, and hers was a fight for stability. But maybe that was the attraction, and the pull.

He opened his laptop, sent a few emails, before dressing and going in search of coffee. He had a cup of coffee before checking the time. It was almost five. Time to wake up Sleeping Beauty.

Jack left the pair of coffee thermoses on the hood of the car he'd borrowed from Zach, and then went to Paige's cabin and knocked on her door, wondering how loud he'd need to knock to get her attention. But she opened the door moments later, fully dressed, blond hair in a loose side braid, a baseball cap on her head.

"I thought I'd have to drag you from bed," he said.

She made a face. "I know how to set an alarm."

"Good girl. Coffee's waiting at the car."

"That's all you needed to say." She stepped out, locked her door, and slid the old-fashioned key ring into her purse before following him to the car.

PAIGE HAD GRUMBLED WHEN HER ALARM WENT OFF AT four in the morning, which was three at home. But as she got into the passenger seat of Zach's car, she was glad they were going for a morning drive, and appreciative that Jack was finding time to be with her.

Jack handed her a thermos of coffee. "I added a little milk and sugar, but it's hot, and caffeinated."

"Perfect."

He quietly backed out of the parking area, going slow over the gravel to not wake anyone in the nearby cabins. Once they were on the main road, he turned on the car's headlights. "The early morning is the best time to see the wildlife," he said. "We're going to drive east through Lamar Valley, forty-five minutes each way. With any luck we'll see some of the wolves we heard last night. A couple years ago, I did this drive and saw wolves, bison, black bears, and grizzly bears."

"I'd be happy to see them all from a distance."

"This probably isn't the best time to take a hike in an unpopulated area."

The sun slowly rose as they drove, the golden light illuminating the top of the mountains and then gradually lifting the lavender shadows in the valley. It had been hard to wake up, but it was a gorgeous morning, the meadow a burnished copper, while green still covered the higher elevation. "I'm glad you made me do this," she said, glancing at Jack.

"I didn't make you. You wanted to do it." Creases fanned from the corners of his eyes. "I just don't think you were as excited about an early morning drive as I was."

She smiled a lopsided smile. "Your enthusiasm was a ten, and mine was a three."

He grinned. "I love how good you are with numbers."

When he smiled at her, she had to smile back. "Is there anything you're hoping we'll see?"

"There's no checklist. I just love the park before it's filled with cars and people, but I'm hoping later we can sneak away for another drive, or maybe a hike to Tower Fall."

She pictured being chased by one of the grizzlies he'd mentioned. It wasn't very appealing. She was fairly fit but not a fast runner. Were you even supposed to run if confronted by a grizzly? "Do you have bear spray if we go on a hike?"

"I don't think we'll need it."

"So says the foolhardy man before he became dinner."

He laughed. "Fine, I'll get bear spray."

"Thank you." Paige adjusted her cap. "Is it going to be a long day for you today?"

"I'm speaking at eleven, and then on a panel this afternoon. Tomorrow is my keynote, just after breakfast, and then early Monday we'll drive back to Bozeman and make our flights home in time for the afternoon class."

She put her hand on Jack's leg. He reached down to cover her hand with his. The sun continued to rise, the sky lightening until it was a lovely, fragile blue. Paige saw an enormous herd of bison, and then a few miles east, another great herd, with a couple stragglers walking alongside the road. Jack slowed to a crawl, not wanting to scare the animals as they passed close by. Paige was delighted when one of the massive males turned his head and looked right at her, his large brown eyes soulful. "Look at the size of him," she whispered. "He's huge."

"Beautiful, aren't they?"

"It's amazing to see so many together. Can you imagine prairies once filled with them?"

"There were forty million across the US at one point, and then nearly all were gone. Yellowstone had lost most of theirs, too. In the early 1900s only fifty remained. The park has worked hard to bring their population back."

"We never appreciate what we have until it's gone," she said, glancing at his profile. She would miss him when he was gone. She'd miss him a lot.

They'd turned around at the edge of Lamar Valley and were heading back when Jack pointed out a moose on the distant hillside, with a leggy calf trailing behind. He pulled to the side of the road and they watched until the moose and its calf disappeared into a thicket of trees, and then Jack shifted into drive and they continued in companionable silence until they reached the education center.

Breakfast, like dinner last night, was served in the main cabin with the vaulted ceiling and thick exposed beams. A river-rock fireplace anchored one side of the main cabin, and round tables and a podium filled the other. Park staff were just starting to break down breakfast when Paige and Jack arrived. Starving, Paige quickly grabbed a plate, and Jack followed. They piled the ceramic plates with what remained of the scrambled eggs, bacon, sausage, and pancakes. Jack poured himself a juice. She snagged a container of Greek yogurt, intending to save it for later, before adding a couple spears of cantaloupe to her plate.

They took seats at a nearly empty round table in the back. Jack nodded and smiled at the two already seated at the table and Paige focused on her breakfast, not wanting to be eating when the first speaker took the podium. Fortunately, there was a welcome from one of the organizers of the symposium and then some general announcements, including a mention that a park shuttle bus had been made available to take the spouses to see Old Faithful as well as several other scenic spots. Paige hadn't intended to go but Jack leaned over and encouraged her to get out and see more of the park.

"You're not missing anything," he whispered.

"I wanted to hear you," she protested, matching his whisper.

"You hear me every day. I'm not that interesting."

"I think you're fascinating."

He kissed her. "Thank you."

She blushed and glanced around the room. No one was paying them any attention, but it was clear from the equipment being rolled in that this room would be used for today's symposium sessions. The idea of being cooped up in here all day wasn't as appealing as getting out and exploring further.

"I don't want you to feel unsupported," she said.

"I'm not breasts in need of a bra."

"Or balls in need of a jockstrap?"

He choked on a muffled laugh, eyes glinting with humor. "Please go. I promise to tell you if something riveting happens."

"Alright. But I'll want a full report later." She collected their plates, took them to the kitchen, and returned with a mug of tea for Jack.

He flashed her a smile that was as hot and sexy as they came. Paige's heart thumped hard and she quietly slipped away.

It was a wonderful morning. The conference had arranged a park ranger to accompany the shuttle and Paige loved all the information on the history of the park, as well as the facts about Yellowstone itself, from Yellowstone stretching over three states with the majority in Wyoming, to the park being viewed as the greatest megafauna in the country. There was discussion on how Yellowstone was the site of the largest ancient volcano in North America, and that the volcano is still active today. Eventually the discussion turned to humans, and how people had lived in Yellowstone for eleven thousand years, and that Native Americans were inhabiting the area when President Ulysses Grant named Yellowstone as the world's first national park.

Paige listened, riveted, glad to have the chance to see different geysers and hot springs. She noted the facts on the herds of bison, and how in 1902, fewer than fifty bison were left in Yellowstone, but today the number was above four thousand.

There was an easy walk along the boardwalk, and then a wait to see Old Faithful before lunch at a cafeteria adjacent to the historic lodge. A woman named Sheila sat down next to Paige. She'd introduced herself earlier as the wife of one of the visiting professors, her husband on the faculty of University of Georgia.

"We all wondered who he'd bring this year," Sheila said,

lifting the bun of her hamburger to squeeze on some ketchup. "We discussed taking bets but that seemed a little crass."

Paige didn't feel much like smiling. She glanced down at her chicken caesar salad, appetite gone as well. "How wonderful that you've been able to attend for so many years."

"Yes, and Camille was at many of them, and then she wasn't." Sheila shrugged. "It's been a bit of a revolving door ever since."

"Hundreds of women," Paige said, unable to hide her sarcasm.

"Oh no, a half dozen, maybe. It's just that we liked Dr. Ormond so much. She'd become one of us."

Paige counted to five, and then to ten, fighting her annoyance. Clearly Camille had been a big part of Jack's life, but they weren't together anymore and Paige really didn't feel like hearing about her. Nor did she want to spend the rest of lunch, never mind the day, talking to Sheila. "I think I'm going to call home and check in with everybody," Paige said, rising and picking up her lunch tray. She nearly threw it out, but then thought better of it, and carried her tray outside, finding a spot on a bench in the sun.

She shouldn't let Sheila get to her, but the woman had gotten under her skin, stirring those whispers of self-doubt. Why had Paige come? What made her think she belonged here? She wasn't a spouse, wasn't a significant other. Why did she think she belonged?

Paige stabbed her salad and tried to eat a few bites. It was hard to chew, harder to swallow, but she forced herself to eat at least half of the salad, aware that it'd be a long time until dinner. As she ate, she pictured Jack—broad shoulders, lean torso, muscular frame. She could see his smile and his eyes, and that flare of heat he'd get in his eyes when he looked at her, but she wondered if that was how he smiled at all the women who'd accompanied him here. Did he make every woman he dated feel special? The way he made her feel special?

Picturing him at this symposium with lots of different

women made her queasy. She closed the lid on her salad and walked it to a garbage can, throwing it away.

Paige avoided the gift shop after lunch, choosing instead to wander through the education center. She wished she'd come with her girls. She'd be far more comfortable with her daughters. When with her daughters, she had a purpose. She felt valued and needed. Paige didn't feel either at the moment. No wonder Elizabeth had more children after re-marrying. Motherhood kept one busy and shifted the focus onto the needs of others.

Finally, it was time to board the shuttle. Paige was quiet during the drive back to their conference, and once off the shuttle, headed straight for her cabin, where she shut herself inside and tackled work. She was still sitting on her bed entering grades when she heard a knock on her door.

She could tell just from the knock that it was Jack. Jack did everything with confidence and energy. Paige opened the door. "How did it go?" she asked, forcing warmth into her voice.

"Well. Did you doubt it?"

She smiled despite herself. "No. I've seen you in action. I'm sure everyone was enthralled."

His gaze swept over her, a quick glance from head to toe before returning to her face. "What happened? You've lost your sparkle."

"I don't sparkle," she answered grumpily.

"You do. It's one of my favorite things about you."

Paige started to deny that there was anything wrong before changing her mind. She was upset. She felt embarrassed. She dreaded dinner. "I was informed during today's excursion that Camille used to come with you every year." Trying not to fidget, Paige slid her hands into her jean pockets. "You've mentioned her to me before, but I hadn't realized she played such a significant role in your life." She saw his expression and hastened to add, "I'm not complaining. I was just caught off guard."

He gestured to her half-closed door. "Can I come in so we could talk?"

She nodded and stepped back. Jack entered her cabin, closed the door behind him. She saw him glance around her cabin. Full-size bed with rustic headboard. Two nightstands. Two lamps. Rustic dresser. Yellow plaid curtains hanging at the windows. Rocking chair in the corner. "Is your room the same?" she asked.

He sat down in the rocking chair. "I have green check curtains, and a green blanket."

Paige closed her laptop and sat down on the foot of her bed. "I don't want to put you on the spot. In fact, I don't want to know all the details of your personal life—that's your life—but it was awkward today, when Sheila—"

"Sheila, was it?"

Paige nodded. "She said you came with Camille for years, and then with others."

"Camille is a microbiologist, and I first met her in Quebec when I'd been invited to speak to the Wildlife Disease Association. She was visiting from Winnipeg. We connected on many levels, and I later introduced her to the organizers of this symposium. Over the years, she became a frequent speaker here and made numerous friends." Jack regarded her steadily. "As you know, we were also in a relationship for a long time. It was an on-again, off-again thing that lasted six or seven years, but we're just friends now, and we get along well. There are no hard feelings between us, and no reason you should feel awkward."

Paige grimaced. "I'm not sure if the mention of Camille made me uncomfortable, or the fact that Sheila said that with Camille no longer in the picture, it's been a 'revolving door.' You apparently bring a lot of women here." She'd expected him to laugh it off, but instead his jaw firmed, expression hardening.

"Doesn't paint me in a very flattering light."

"No." Paige shifted on the foot of the bed, wishing he'd

say more about the other women he'd brought here. She hadn't thought she wanted to know, but now her curiosity had been piqued. Worse, she craved reassurance. She wanted to believe that she was special, that she wasn't just another woman in his parade of weekend companions, because it wasn't a good look for him, nor was it a good look for her.

His phone vibrated with a text, and he glanced at it. "I'm supposed to do a quick video for the website and they're ready for me now. It shouldn't take long, fifteen minutes, twenty at the most. Can we finish talking when I'm done?"

"There's probably nothing to talk about—"

"I don't like seeing you rattled," he said. "Promise me you won't go away."

She laughed and glanced around the cabin. "Not sure where I'd go."

"Okay. See you in a few."

Paige showered and changed into clean jeans and an ivory sweater and went outside to sit on the front step of her cabin's porch. The sun was setting, casting long streaks of golden light across the mountains while dark lavender shadows pooled below.

In the distant meadow, Paige could see a small herd of buffalo. They were enormous, and striking against the gold and green backdrop, the sun silhouetting a massive bull as he ambled slowly over the road.

Jack appeared with two beers. "All I could find," he said, handing her an open bottle.

Paige wasn't much of a beer drinker, but she welcomed the beer, and the company. She'd felt troubled all afternoon, as well as confused. She didn't know what she wanted from Jack. But at the same time, she didn't not want Jack in her life. She liked him—more than liked him—and sitting with him by the fire last night had felt good. She'd felt right with him, content and secure, and then today to have Sheila make those comments . . .

It had been genuinely upsetting. She still felt strange. Disconnected.

"It's going to be a pretty sunset," he said, sitting on the porch railing.

"I love the sky here." She took a swig from her bottle, scrunching her nose at the taste. Maybe it'd improve as she drank it. "I'm not mad at you," she said after a moment. "I'm just trying to figure things out." She glanced at him. "It takes me a while."

"Sheila Hutchinson is a pain in the arse. She always has been, and always will be. But her husband, Walter, is a really decent man, a good friend, and a passionate educator, and so I try to ignore Sheila's negative qualities. Not always easy, I know."

"I was just caught off guard. Last night by the fire with you was so fun. I felt . . . close . . . to you, and then at lunch to have her hit me with details of your love life. I hadn't expected to be lumped with a parade of women—"

"There has been no parade. Have I brought guests? Yes. But they're brilliant women like you, women I respect."

Jack wasn't helping his case, she thought, taking another sip of beer, hoping the taste had improved. It had not.

She hadn't come with expectations. This trip hadn't been a romantic getaway. She didn't see Jack as a partner, but a friend.

Maybe more than a friend.

A possibility.

And kissing by the fire had been sexy and playful and fun. Last night had been fun, but she didn't like how she felt now. It was the same insecurity she'd felt in Paris, the same awareness that Jack was handsome and charming. A man who loved women.

A man who left women.

A man who wouldn't, couldn't, be tied down.

Her eyes stung as she lifted the bottle back to her mouth,

pressing the cold glass to her lips. At least she'd had her eyes opened before she'd slept with him—again.

"What are you thinking?" he asked, his deep voice pitched low.

She glanced to where he sat on the railing, bathed in golden light. He looked rugged and appealing, and very sure of who he was. She liked that about him. She liked *him*. And let's be real, she wasn't looking for a husband, or a lifetime partner. She didn't want to marry again. She wasn't trying to settle down, either. She had her girls, her friends, her life. Why couldn't she just enjoy Jack's company for what it was? Good company.

And if one day she wanted to sleep with him, why couldn't she do that, too?

There was no reason they couldn't kiss, or touch, or go to bed with each other. There was no reason she needed to feel insecure. She wasn't Jack's wife, girlfriend, or significant other. But she was his friend, and as his friend she wasn't going to continue this freak-out. There was no reason for it. Sheila may have caught her by surprise, but Paige was determined to pull herself together. "I'm thinking Sheila is annoying but she's not going to ruin my weekend," she said. "I'm in Montana, sitting on the steps of a sixty-five-year-old cabin, drinking a cold beer, talking to a hot guy, watching buffalo roam. How could I not love this?"

His expression warmed. "I like your attitude."

"I don't know why I let her rattle me in the first place."

"Because she was being petty and unkind, and you didn't like it. Nor did you deserve it."

"She's probably not a happy person."

"Which is a shame, because Leonard tries so hard to please her. I sometimes want him to stand up to her, and tell her to knock it off, but he's too much the Southern gentleman. Personally, I find it maddening. But I only see them here, and it's just a weekend, so I try not to get caught up in their drama."

The breeze blew and Paige shivered a little. "I'm going to need a coat tonight."

"Dinner will be inside, as will the presentation. You don't have to stick around for it, but at the same time, you might find it interesting."

"I'd like to stay," she said.

"Good." He rose from the railing. "I'm going to go shower before dinner, but, Paige, I will never lie to you. You can always ask me anything, and I'll always tell you the truth."

DINNER WAS ANOTHER BUFFET, WITH TWO DIFFERENT pastas and various vegetables for sides. Paige thought the eggplant parmigiana was excellent, as was the red wine served. She was also grateful Jack sat close. Under the table, he held her hand, and then later, rested his hand on her thigh. His warmth eased some of the coldness in her chest. She didn't want to be afraid, didn't want ice around her heart. Fear wasn't good. Fear was destructive. If they had been eating alone, she would have leaned over and kissed him, kissing away the anxiety. She liked Jack. The more time she spent with him, the more time she wanted to spend with him. He was incredibly interesting, incredibly good company.

She glanced at him and he met her gaze, his lips curving faintly. "After the presentation ends, maybe you and I could just sneak away," he said.

"I'd like that," she whispered.

His eyes never left hers. "So would I."

She grew warm, cheeks flushing. "I don't want to get you in trouble."

A spark heated his eyes. "I wish you would."

She captured his hand beneath the table, lacing her fingers with his. "I think you enjoy trouble more than I do."

"Probably," he agreed.

Thirty minutes later, he was steering her out of the dining room, leading her to his cabin, which sat toward the back, at the end of the gravel path.

Inside his cabin he flipped the lock, then walked her back against the door, his hands up on either side of her head, his big body pressing against her, holding her captive. The kiss was hot, possessive, demanding. Paige felt Jack's hunger, his desire barely leashed as he reduced her to a quivering mass.

"The things I want to do to you," he growled, dragging his fingers through her hair, moving it off her face to nip at her neck, making her breath catch in her throat. "I could eat you." He corrected. "I will eat you."

She closed her eyes, shy, but also turned on. Ted hadn't been a fan of oral sex—at least, not when it came to giving her pleasure. She couldn't even remember when she'd last done that . . . gone there. "I haven't had sex in years."

He lifted his head to study her, his eyes dark with passion. His thumb caressed her mouth, making her lower lip throb and tingle. "After Mara's diagnosis, we didn't make love, but I still loved her. She was my wife, my friend, my partner, my son's mother. Sex didn't make us a couple. Love made us a couple."

"Sex is confusing," she said.

"It is," he agreed, just before his head dropped and he pressed her lower lip down, so that his tongue could flick the inside, tormenting nerve endings, making her whimper. The kiss deepened, and he sucked on that soft, throbbing lower lip, and then bit at it, sending a shock of heat through her, making her warmer, wetter. Her head was spinning. Her body felt boneless. She wrapped her arms around his neck. "You make me want things I never thought I'd want again."

"Good. But I'd rather leave you wanting than push you into bed and lose what we've gained. I want you to trust me. I want you to feel safe—"

"I'm getting there," she whispered, eyes widening as his

palm slid down her body, over her breast, her ribs, her stomach to cover the apex of her thighs. He did nothing else, nothing invasive, and yet just having his hand there made everything in her ache and burn. "I think you know your way around women's bodies."

His mouth kissed the corner of her mouth. Such a fleeting kiss that her belly clenched, and she pressed her nails into his nape.

"I have a thing for your body," he said. "I have a thing for you. In case you haven't noticed."

He kissed the same spot on her lips again, and then caught her upper lip in his teeth. A sharp bite that had her gasping. His hand was still against her, pressed to her, and he ground his palm to her mound, and she shuddered and clutched his shoulders. "We can't," she said.

"No, you're right," he agreed, taking her mouth, his tongue teasing, seeking, before drawing her tongue into his mouth. He sucked on the tip and she whimpered again.

She could feel his hand against her, the sensation exquisite, the pressure building. She couldn't believe he could make her feel so much, and she should stop him, she should. But her body wasn't interested in what her brain had to say. Her body wasn't even hers now, but his. The rhythmic sucking on her tongue matched the pressure between her legs and she wanted him, wanted relief from this. It had been forever since she'd felt anything so intense.

Paige stopped fighting with herself, stopped fighting the pleasure. Her legs quivered as he pushed his hand between her legs, pressing, stroking. She couldn't hang on, couldn't hold back. Paige let out a cry. Helplessly, she arched against him, stiffening, shattering, tiny sparklers of light exploding behind her closed eyes.

The orgasm went on and on—an intense shuddering that rocked her from head to toe.

By the time she opened her eyes, she felt as if she'd crossed into a different universe.

Jack still stood close, his hand on her hip, his other arm braced over her head. He said nothing, just looked into her eyes. She could barely focus. She certainly couldn't think.

"Wow," she murmured.

"Now, that wasn't so bad, was it?" he teased, drawing her into his arms and hugging her close.

"No." She leaned against him as her legs weren't functioning. "But it wasn't supposed to happen. That wasn't on the agenda."

He laughed softly. "Sometimes the best things aren't scheduled." His lips brushed her forehead. "So, a question. Do you want to stay here with me tonight? Or would you be happier in your cabin?"

She stared up into his face, her gaze boring into his. He felt familiar in the best sort of way, as if being in his arms was a coming home, a return to herself. "Can I stay with you tonight?"

"Absolutely."

"But can we just . . . sleep?"

"Agreed." He pulled her toward the bed. "We'll know when we're ready. We're not ready."

She arched a brow. "I think you're ready."

"Not if it means I could possibly lose you. You mean too much to me."

Chapter 13

PAIGE SLEPT CURLED AGAINST HIM, AND HE HELD HER, his arm around her waist. He didn't sleep deeply, too aware of her there at his side. He felt so many different emotions, too. He felt protective of Paige, wanting the best for her, wanting her happiness, wanting to shield her from hurt and harm. And yet, at the same time, he also felt deeply calm, as if everything had clicked into place. Jack couldn't remember when he'd last felt this way—if ever.

His life had been a quest—find answers, find truth, educate, create change, save species, protect the environment, save the world—it was an endless quest, at times exhausting as the work was never done, and there was never a point he could stop, truly rest. But having Paige close, he felt a peace that usually escaped him. It was almost as if she was a reward for a life well lived. She was a blessing . . . a gift. He wasn't going to lose her. Not over sex. Not over careers. Not over a miscommunication.

He'd never come between her and her daughters, but he could give her something her daughters couldn't: he could hold her through the night, kiss her good morning, laugh with her—or grieve with her—through challenges and changes.

They weren't old, but they weren't kids, either. They didn't have seventy-five years ahead of them. There might be forty. There might be fewer. That wasn't the point. The point was they were meant to live, and embrace the changes ahead, good as well as bad.

Jack knew he wasn't perfect. He could be a self-absorbed, self-centered SOB, but he was tough, and determined, and he was good for Paige. He believed that. But did she?

PAIGE STRUGGLED THE NEXT DAY TO GET WORK DONE. She was busy filling out information for the university on her classes for the Spring semester. She wasn't ready to think about next semester, knowing she wouldn't be teaching with Jack, knowing they'd have very different schedules, knowing she wouldn't see him at school as often. She ought to ask him what his semester looked like, what days he thought he'd be on campus. Not that she could change her schedule any, but just so she knew.

Thinking of Jack took her back to last night, sleeping with him. Kissing him. Having that amazing O fully dressed. Jack was a man of many skills. And how she loved the way he kissed. Kissing him was intoxicating. Addictive. He made her feel delicious. Every part of her shivered with delight.

She missed him when he wasn't with her. Like today, she felt empty without him. Bereft. She knew she'd see him in a couple hours, but that still seemed so far away.

What she felt for him was pretty big. Pretty intense. Bordering on consuming. She feared what she felt, though, as falling in love could potentially change everything and she wasn't sure she was ready for change. Big change. She liked her life the way it was. She liked her world, and the routine, and the safety. And yet, love was important. As a mom, Paige knew that. But it'd been a very long time since she'd felt any desire to love anyone else. Family was family, but to love a man . . . ? To put her heart out there?

To open her heart?

To allow significant change into her life?

But holding Jack's hand, and seeing his smile, having him tease her, and sharing moments like the early morning drive in Yellowstone yesterday where they watched the sun rise, and then slowed for the big buffalo walking slowly along the side of the road . . . those moments created other moments, new moments that made her feel new.

Made her feel young.

Made her want to open her arms wide to the future and say, *Hello life, I'm coming for you.*

But then she thought of her girls, and the small, safe world they'd created together. She'd promised to always be there for them, devoted to them, and she'd keep that promise. But she didn't know where that left Jack. She didn't know if Jack fit in with them.

After lunch, Paige gave up trying to work, or enter grades, or answer the emails still sitting in her inbox demanding attention.

Instead, she sat outside on the edge of the stone firepit soaking up the sunshine and watching a white-striped chipmunk chase another. It was cool enough she needed a sweatshirt over a long sleeve T-shirt. The chipmunks had tiny stripes on their faces, making them look like bandits, and they seemed to be having the best time.

Paige loved the feel of the sun on her back, and the smell of the grass and trees, the air fresh, clean. She rarely just sat still. She was almost always moving, thinking, doing things. In her world, there was always something to be done. Bills to be paid, estimates to be gotten, questions her daughters had about insurance, car concerns, healthcare. If they'd had a good relationship with their dad, they could have gone to him for things, but instead they came to her, and she was good with that. But it was unusual not to have at least one frantic text a day, and so far, she'd had none. Maybe the girls were good, maybe there were no problems. Or maybe they were respecting her weekend and once she returned home, she'd be hit with everything all at once.

In that case, she'd enjoy the quiet and calm now, as it felt good to have no dramas, no heartbreaks, no problems. It had been a long time since she'd simply sat. Rested.

Paige continued to sit and listen to the chatter of birds, as well as the wind rustling the grass in the meadow across from the cabins. The afternoon sunlight stretched across the cabin roofs. The sun would disappear in the next hour, but the late afternoon's golden light was magical. She closed her eyes, lifted her face, and focused on her breathing. It was like a yoga class, but better, because there were no uncomfortable poses or stretching. Opening her eyes, she blinked and looked around, wondering where her chipmunks had gone, when she saw a big brown shape appear around a not-so-distant cabin.

Paige's heart jumped. Was that a—?

Yes.

Yes. It was a bear.

A *very* large bear with a cub. Paige had no idea if it was a grizzly or black bear. She tried to think of the proper exit strategy, if there was one.

Should she shout? Jump up on the table and wave her arms? Close her eyes and pretend she was dead? Where was the bear spray when she needed it?

Hand shaking, she reached into her pocket and slid her phone out. She texted Jack. Outside. Bear. Help.

She hit send, said a prayer. Paige wasn't sure Jack would even have his phone handy, nor was she sure he'd pay any attention to a text, should he have it handy.

Seconds later, the sturdy brown door of the cabin closest to her flew open with a bang. Sheila stepped out, talking on the phone, voice loud.

The bear stopped, stiffened, stared at Paige, then looked

toward Sheila for a long moment, before turning and disappearing back behind the cabins, the cub chasing after.

Jack and another man dashed from the main cabin. Paige struggled to her feet, legs a quivering mess, but she couldn't stand, and she sat back down.

She couldn't believe what had happened.

Sheila had saved her from a bear.

Paige was able to laugh about the bear after Jack joined her. It had been scary, but it was also a great story, and would be a great story to share with her girls when she returned home. However, when one of the park rangers arrived to talk to Paige about the bear, she learned that in the past year several black bears had begun entering tents looking for food, and had bitten one woman, resulting in the bear's death.

After the ranger departed, Jack remained with Paige for a bit, asking her if she'd like to join him inside. "They're wrapping up the symposium. I'll need to say a few words and then some will leave, and the rest of us will have dinner before calling it a night."

"You go finish up," she said. "I'll be fine."

"You're going to stay here?"

"*No.* I'm going to sit on the steps of the dining hall. That way you'll just be steps away should I need backup."

The symposium ended, and as Jack said, half of the visiting scientists and professors left, while those with early morning flights remained. Dinner was a Hungarian goulash, and then there was a huckleberry crisp for dessert. Paige spent their last night in Jack's cabin again, sharing his bed. Tonight, they talked a lot, with Jack telling her about his childhood in Melbourne and the moment he knew he wanted to be a scientist. "I think I imagined one day I'd work with Steve Irwin. We'd go save animals together," he said, smiling wryly. "I'd be on his show."

"Instead you have your own show."

He hesitated. "We're going to be filming the fourth season soon, over the winter break."

Paige rolled onto her side, so she could better see him. He was lying on his back, arms behind his head, his soft thermal shirt stretched over his chest. "Is that a new development?"

"It was on the books, and then off the books. There's been such back-and-forth with budget, and planning, but it was finally green-lit. We'll have production meetings for a few days, and then we begin filming Christmas week."

Her heart fell. "You'll be gone for Christmas?"

He lifted a strand of her hair, curled it around his finger. "I don't really celebrate Christmas."

"Why not?"

"It's usually just me."

"What about Oliver?"

"We don't make a fuss about Christmas. We get together when we can. Like this year, we're together for Thanksgiving but Christmas we'll each be doing our own thing."

She frowned. She thought it sounded awful. Thanksgiving wasn't Paige's favorite holiday, but she loved Christmas, loved having her girls all home. "Where will you be filming?"

"Tanzania."

She blinked at him. "Africa."

"Yes."

"And you'll be gone all winter break?"

"Depends on how long filming takes. The goal is four weeks, but it depends on weather and on the environment, and whether we've gotten the film we need." He lifted his head, kissed her. "I'll be back before the start of Spring semester."

When the kiss ended, she snuggled closer, lying across his chest. He smelled amazing. Felt amazing. "I'll miss you."

"You could come with me."

She sat back up. "Over Christmas?"

He shrugged. "Or after."

"Just get on a plane and go to Africa?"

"Why not?"

She had no answer for that. It just wasn't a possibility and she wasn't sure she'd ever make him understand. Instead, she burrowed in against his side, her hand flat on his chest, feeling the steady, reassuring beat of his heart. And yet, there was so much she didn't know about him, a whole life he'd lived in the years since they'd met in Paris. "Why did you marry Mara?"

He was silent a moment. His hand slowly stroked her back, down to the small of her spine, and then over her hip. "She was smart. She was pretty. She was passionate about the environment." He hesitated. "She was pregnant with Oliver."

Paige was glad he couldn't see her expression.

"Mara's parents don't live far from here," he added after a moment. "One day I'd like you to meet them. They're good people. They helped me a lot with Oliver, especially when I had to travel and couldn't take him with me."

Silence stretched, but it was comfortable, soothing. She felt a little bit sleepy, as well as happy. "I found it hard to relax with Ted," she said after a beat. "I could never just be still. To relax, we always had to have a drink, or two. In the beginning, it was fun, like we were on vacation. It wasn't until I was pregnant with Michelle, and not drinking, that I realized Ted had to drink, and not just one or two drinks, but a lot." She rolled over, slipped her hand into Jack's. "The worst thing in the world is counting someone's drinks, aware that you've got to get in a car with him, aware that he shouldn't be driving but he won't let anyone else drive because he can't accept he's had too much. I think that's when I went from disappointed to angry, because it was stupid and dangerous getting in a car with him, letting him drive the girls places, but he wouldn't listen, and he'd get ugly. I should have stood up to him more. I shouldn't have put the girls in danger."

"Did he ever hit you?"

"No. He just said mean things." Paige reached up, rubbed

at her eyes, suddenly feeling very tired. "Toward the end of my marriage, I felt like I couldn't breathe. I woke up every day anxious, a lead weight on my chest, fighting anxiety, fighting anger. I don't remember having anxiety before that. Maybe I did, maybe it just wasn't as intense, but the anxiety twisted me in knots. But even miserable, I wasn't going to leave him. I wasn't a quitter. I would make this work . . . and that was my plan, until the day came where I couldn't make it work."

He drew her back into the crook of his arm. "What was the breaking point?"

"I couldn't get out of bed. I couldn't teach. I couldn't talk to my friends, my mom, my girls. I was in trouble, and yet I couldn't see a way out."

"But you got out."

"Elizabeth came to see me." Paige's eyes burned. Her vision grew blurry. "She made me realize I was valuable. I mattered. I didn't leave Ted for another six months, but I finally realized I had to do something or I'd die." She knocked away a tear sliding down into her hair. "It sounds awfully dramatic put like that, but it's how I felt. I dreaded telling the girls that I was leaving their dad, but when I did, they cheered. They'd had a difficult relationship with him. I had always been the buffer, and it was exhausting. When I moved out, everything changed. I had energy again, hope again, and the girls and I grew even closer."

"How is their relationship with their dad now?"

"Not great. He doesn't make an effort, and they've given up trying. When Ted and I lived together, I was constantly trying to smooth things over, solve problems, be the peacemaker, but when we divorced, I stopped doing it. The girls were young adults and Ted was an adult, and they had to figure out the relationship they wanted without me in the middle." Paige exhaled. "My mom guilted me in the beginning, reminding me that he was their father, but he has a responsibility to them, too. He's their father. Doesn't he want to have a relationship with them? Not because it's a duty, but a privilege? A joy?"

"So, no regrets about the divorce," he said, drying the dampness on her cheek.

She looked over at him. "None at all. If anything, I just wish I'd done it sooner."

"You're happy," he said, expression somber.

"Yes," she said, snuggling into his arms, holding him tightly. "Very." Even as she thought that she was even happier now, being with him. She hadn't thought she wanted anyone, and she certainly hadn't thought she needed anyone, but somehow being with Jack made her feel really good.

No, better than good.

Perfect, actually.

AT THE BOZEMAN AIRPORT, JACK BROKE THE NEWS TO Paige that the end of semester field trip to Costa Rica wasn't going to happen, explaining that the Caribbean and eastern Costa Rica had been slammed by three hurricanes in a row, each one adding to the flooding and devastation.

She listened without interruption, her blue gaze focused on him, expression intent.

"You didn't say anything last night," she said when he'd finished speaking.

"That was our time. I thought this could wait."

"The center in Monteverde cancelled our stay?" she asked.

"They haven't officially cancelled, but I'm expecting a call or email any day, letting me know that the center is under water. It's happened before with hurricanes and heavy rains, and it'll happen again. The good news is that we have time to shift the field studies to another location."

"Jack, we're five weeks away."

"Plenty of time to make alternate arrangements. If it was one week, or two, I'd be concerned."

"You're talking airfare, accommodations, meals for over twenty people."

"Planes seat hundreds of people."

She rolled her eyes. "I know that. I'm just saying these are daunting logistics."

"You don't have to worry about the logistics. Leave that part to me."

She could tell he had a plan already percolating in his mind. "What are you thinking?"

"You know how I'm supposed to film my show in Tanzania?" He waited for her nod before he continued. "I go to Arusha several times a year, taking my Princeton grad students for field studies. I've got a conference there the weekend right after our Costa Rica trip, and then I stay for filming."

"Okay," she said slowly, still not seeing where this was going.

"Why don't we take our students to Arusha? I'm sure I can put the trip together, and we'd have a wonderful experience."

"And I thought Monteverde was far," she said under her breath.

"What part about going to Tanzania worries you?"

"Um, everything?" She looked at him, gave her head a slight shake. "I am not a world traveler like you. Going to Africa is a big deal. I imagine we'll have to get some shots—"

"—and take malaria medicine."

"See? Malaria medicine. That sounds scary."

"It's not. It's a very simple thing. Easy to get a prescription, all the students would take it, not a big deal."

"Unless you get malaria."

He smiled wryly even as he tugged on one of her silky strands of blond hair. "The point of taking the medicine is that you don't get malaria."

She continued to study him. "And you're comfortable taking all these kids so far from home?"

"I do this all the time." He hesitated before adding, "Although generally they are my grad students, so a bit older, a little more independent, but I'm not worried about our students. We don't have anyone in that class who isn't pulling their weight. They're a really good group of kids, very responsible, and I think everyone should go." He frowned. "But I do think we could lose a few students simply because some parents might be concerned about the distance, and the change of plans."

"How do you get to Arusha?"

"Fly to Europe and then I usually go to Zanzibar, and then hop over to Arusha. It's not that complicated."

"Three different flights?"

He nodded. "I can reach out to my colleagues in Arusha, and check on rooms and meals. I've gone so many times I know what needs to be done, and who to go to."

She sat back, shoulders slumping. "This is a huge endeavor."

"It's not Hawaii, no."

"Maybe we should go to Hawaii."

He gave her a look. "This field work was never designed as a vacation. Our studies contribute to real research. Our work is needed and appreciated."

Her silence spoke volumes.

"Are you opposed to Tanzania?" he asked.

She opened her mouth, then closed it, getting to her feet and pacing back and forth in front of their seats before slowing and facing him. "I'm not set against it. I'm just not . . ."

"Comfortable."

She nodded, anxious. "This is definitely out of my comfort zone."

"But it's not out of mine," he said, trying to reassure her. "Arusha is like a second home."

"Would the schedule differ greatly from Costa Rica?"

"The biggest difference would be the additional travel

days at the end. After I wrap up the coursework in Arusha, my Princeton students typically spend the last few days in Tanzania doing an escorted, guided safari before their return home. I would try to arrange the same thing for our students, with a three-day safari ending on Sunday afternoon, and then the flight to Zanzibar Sunday evening. Monday morning we'd fly from Zanzibar to Amsterdam and then connect to Los Angeles."

Her eyes got wider with every word. He checked his smile. "Since you like numbers, yes, there are six flights total and we'd tack on an additional three or four days to the trip."

"You've been thinking about this."

"I have. If we're going to fly thirty-five hours, we might as well pack the schedule."

"What day would you suggest we return?" she asked.

"The thirteenth instead of the ninth."

"Not everyone will be able to make the new travel dates work."

"True. And there will also be parents, and students, who might not support the idea of field work in Tanzania—"

He was silenced by the overhead speaker announcing a flight arrival from Seattle. Jack waited for the announcement to end before continuing. "We don't even know if Dr. Keller would approve even if I could get the pieces in place."

"Or which students would still go," she added, sitting down again.

"I don't think we're going to lose that many, but you're right, we need those numbers, and we need Dr. Keller's approval." He stretched. "And we need your participation if we're going to convince him. He knows you better than me. He'd want you there making sure everything goes well." His gaze met hers and held. "What do you say?"

Paige held her breath even as she held Jack's green-gold gaze. He was not like anyone else she'd ever known, and ever since he'd reentered her world, he'd filled it with activity and chaos and change.

Just like his course.

The corner of her mouth lifted, amused despite herself. "For a woman with no international travel experience, this is a rather daunting trip."

"You liked Yellowstone."

"I did."

"You'll like Arusha, too."

She stared into his eyes, as if trying to find truth, trying to find security and safety. Jack said he made this trip a number of times every year. Jack said Arusha was like his second home.

She supposed the question was: Did she trust him?

Could she depend on him?

She narrowed her eyes and then thought, *Yes*. Yes, to both. Jack was calm, dependable, and an experienced traveler. If she was going to go to Africa with anyone, Jack would be a safe bet.

Did she want to go to Africa?

Yes.

Her heart gave a little thump. After so many years saying no to things, it felt strange to say yes, but yes, Paige wanted to travel. Yes, she wanted adventure. Yes, she wanted to go with Jack to Tanzania. "I think we should go talk to Dr. Keller," she said. "Because if we're going to pull this off, we've got to be united."

She saw the slow smile start in his eyes, creases deepening at the corners, before shaping his mouth. "A team," he agreed, extending his hand to her.

She took his hand, but then leaned forward and sealed the deal with a kiss, on the mouth, in public, as if he was hers.

Was he hers?

Chapter 14

THEIR SALT LAKE FLIGHT TO ORANGE COUNTY WAS SIG-nificantly delayed, which meant that Paige had to cancel her afternoon class. She sent out the email and Jack phoned Dr. Keller, wanting to set up a meeting with the university president for tomorrow, if possible. Jack walked away from her while he was on the phone, so Paige missed the conversation, but when Jack returned he gave her a thumbs-up.

"We'll see him tomorrow," Jack said, dropping into the empty seat next to hers and opening his laptop to scroll through emails. "I think it's going to work out."

She glanced at him, half smiling. "You are always so positive."

"I've found that things just work out better that way."

She searched his eyes, amazed and awed at his conviction, and yet his confidence was appealing. She felt calm despite all the changes happening. "Anything I should do to prepare for the meeting with Dr. Keller?"

"Nope. Just show up and be you."

It was mid-afternoon when they arrived in Orange County. Jack walked Paige to the curb, where they said goodbye, parting with a kiss. He'd offered her a ride home, but she'd declined, wanting time to think and process the weekend before her phone began to ring with calls from Elizabeth and her daughters. She'd just settled into her Uber when her phone rang. It was Elizabeth. Incredible.

"Have you been tracking my flight? How did you know I landed?" Paige asked, shifting her carry-on bag into a different position on the seat.

"You gave me your schedule, so yes, I've been tracking your flight. So, talk to me, PG. How did it go?"

"It went great." Paige paused, remembering the weekend that had gone by far too fast. It felt like she'd only just left, but it had been a wonderful weekend. She just wished it had been longer. "I saw lots of bison, a moose, as well as a mama and baby bear up close."

"A grizzly bear?"

"No, a black bear. But I wasn't sure at first."

"What did you do?"

"I froze." Paige laughed. "Fortunately, it got scared away by Sheila, and then Jack appeared, and everything was fine."

"You feel good about Jack?"

"I do." She'd returned to Southern California even more infatuated. Jack made everything just a little bit better. More humor, more laughter, more understanding. More fun. "I can't wait to go back to Yellowstone. And now there's a whole list of parks I must see." *Hopefully with Jack*, she silently added.

"Were people nice?"

"Everyone was really nice, except for Sheila—"

"The same Sheila who scared the bear?"

"The same. Sweet Sheila couldn't not talk about Camille Ormond, Jack's former love." Paige sighed. "It wasn't the first time I've heard about her. Jack has mentioned her. They were together for a long time. I don't know all the details, just that she's a scientist, she does work similar to Jack, is French Canadian, very likable, and a Sheila favorite."

"But why would this Sheila bring her up?"

"That's a good question. It didn't sit well with me. It's not that I'm completely insecure, but hearing Jack described as a dating whore hit me wrong."

Elizabeth gasped. "She did not call Jack a dating whore, did she?"

"No. That's me. That's what it felt like. And I get it, Jack has a right to date who he wants, when he wants. But it was upsetting. I felt . . . weird."

"Dating is hard," Elizabeth said.

"It is. It brings up all kinds of fears, and honestly, at our age, there is some serious baggage. I've a whole lifetime of mistakes and hurts. There are times I've let others down, times people have let me down. It's almost as if you have to be mentally fit to date. And I'm not there yet, but at least I have an idea of what I need to do if I'm going to continue spending time with Jack."

"You're going to keep seeing him."

"I'd like to."

"This is huge."

"It's not that big of a deal. All I'm saying is that I'm open to more dates, but a lot can go wrong." Paige glanced out the window, saw that they were approaching a traffic slowdown. They were definitely back in Southern California. "Speaking of Jack, it looks like our field program has hit some snafus. Mainly weather. Our program in Monteverde is a washout. Literally. Jack's working on an alternative, and it's totally out of my comfort zone, but I've told him I'll leave it in his hands and see what happens."

There was silence on the other end of the line. Paige gave Elizabeth a moment to answer, but she didn't. "Are you there?" Paige asked.

"I'm just thinking about what you said." Elizabeth's voice hinted at laughter. "Paige Newsome is leaving it up to Jack? You're loosening the reins on control?"

Paige rolled her eyes. "I simply said that I'm leaving it to Jack to figure out options for *his* course. It has been *his* course from the beginning. I'm second fiddle here, and I've always been second fiddle. I know the role I'm supposed to play, and I'm playing it."

"I'm impressed, that's all. I commend you for being positive and open to change."

"You can be so exhausting, Elizabeth."

"You've been saying that since we were fifteen."

The Uber had stopped moving. Traffic was at a virtual standstill. Paige groaned inwardly. It wasn't a long drive from the Orange County airport to her house, thirty minutes without traffic, but today, who knew. "I'm going to check my emails, make sure there's nothing I need to do. Tomorrow is going to be hectic, but maybe we can meet for coffee Wednesday?"

"Absolutely. Just let me know."

JACK DROVE FROM THE AIRPORT TO HIS MISSION VIEJO apartment lost in thought. Traffic was heavy going south, but he was able to take different roads to get home, avoiding all the red brake lights.

It had been a really good weekend. He'd enjoyed getting away, and he was glad Paige had gone with him. The weather had been ideal. October could be unpredictable, but they'd had warm, clear days and cold, clear nights. He'd enjoyed seeing the park through Paige's eyes, and she been a really good travel companion. Undemanding, cheerful, curious, fun. He just wished Sheila had kept her mouth shut, but that was Sheila: always talking more than she should.

At least Paige had told him what Sheila had said so they could talk about it. He wasn't without a history. He'd always got along well with women. He appreciated them. He liked the physical as well as the mental stimulus. Yes, there had been a number of women in his life, but there hadn't been many serious relationships. He didn't do serious, choosing not to invest in long-term.

Jack didn't enjoy hurting people, and he didn't like to disappoint, either. It was better to be up front with those he dated. Fortunately, there were plenty of women who preferred things casual, and they, like him, appreciated the pleasures of a physical relationship without lots of complications or commitments.

He wasn't sure Paige fit into that category. He wasn't sure she fit into a category. But was that good, or bad? He wished he knew.

TUESDAY AFTER CLASS AND OFFICE HOURS, PAIGE MET Jack outside the door of Dr. Keller's office. Paige was nervous. Jack didn't seem to be worried at all. "Are you really this calm?" she whispered.

"Should I not be?"

"What if he doesn't approve?"

"He'll approve."

"He might not."

Jack shrugged. "Then we'll think of something else."

"I imagine he's going to have an issue with the logistics—twenty-four students, six flights, thirty-five hours travel. I'm not trying to be negative, but I've been trying to imagine all of his objections, and I expect he'll have many. Who's going to handle the bookings? Who will get the visas organized? I'm assuming we need visas?"

"Once we get Dr. Keller's approval, the rest will be easy. It's just a matter of making the air reservations, securing the space in Arusha, and making sure we—" He broke off as the door opened and Dr. Keller appeared in the doorway and gestured them in.

Paige drew a quick breath and followed Jack in. They took chairs opposite Dr. Keller's broad desk, covered with tidy piles of books and folders. "I understand from Jack there's a hitch in the field study," Dr. Keller said without preamble.

"The university's science center in Costa Rica is under water," Jack answered. "They're in a state of disaster."

Dr. Keller looked tired, and troubled. "What is your plan, then? You said you had one."

"I do," Jack said. "I propose we shift the field study to Arusha, Tanzania. I have a strong relationship with the African Institution of Science and Technology. My students from Princeton go three times a year, and have for over a decade. The biggest challenge is getting there, but once we're there, it's going to be an outstanding experience."

"Wouldn't the airfare be considerably more?" Dr. Keller asked.

"Maybe a hundred more per person."

Dr. Keller frowned. "We can't tack that on to the student costs. They've already paid in full."

"Could the university absorb it?" Jack asked. "If so, we could make this work, and I think the students would have the experience of a lifetime."

The university president was quiet for a long moment, a finger pressed to the side of his nose. "What about your coursework? I understand the class has been focusing on the biodiversity of Costa Rica. Science isn't my field, but somehow I doubt that Tanzania will be the same."

"I'm not worried about it," Jack answered. "We have over a month before we go. I can shift some of the research now. They'll be prepared."

Dr. Keller looked at Paige. "What are your thoughts? How do you feel about the change?"

"I was surprised," she said truthfully, "and worried about parents' reactions. Not everyone is comfortable with the idea of traveling so far. Americans don't really understand African politics, economics, or culture, which is why I think this trip would be good for our students."

"You're not apprehensive about taking twenty-four students to Tanzania?" Dr. Keller persisted.

Paige glanced at Jack. His gaze was warm, his expression patient. She envied his ability to go through life so at ease. She longed to be more like him. She craved that optimism and peace of mind. Her focus returned to the university president. "I wouldn't be comfortable if Jack weren't so comfortable, but this is his area of expertise, and he's spent years studying the savannah's biosphere."

Dr. Keller's brow knit, and his fingers steepled together. "There isn't any place closer? Easier? What about Yellowstone? What about the wolf habitat program? The bison studies? Isn't there anything you could do there?"

"Montana in early December is cold," Jack answered. "The park closes most of its programs for the winter. We could maybe get lodging, but we wouldn't have meals. I don't think we'd want to spend five days there let alone ten. If that was our only option, I'd suggest canceling the field program rather than trying to pull off something there."

Dr. Keller's gaze was fixed on a spot on his desk. His fingers bent, then straightened, then bent again. "What about Argentina, haven't you done things there?" he asked. "Patagonia, I think it was? Or Brazil?"

"Why does Tanzania scare you so much?" Jack asked.

Dr. Keller shrugged. "It's the distance and, to be honest, probably my ignorance. I know we've had students study abroad in Africa, but that's always been handled by our study programs, programs that have been in operation for decades."

"We will be working with a program that has been in operation for almost twenty years. Princeton, Harvard, Yale, Stanford, USC all work with them, as does the University of Dresden, University of Milan, Hanyang University, Beijing Institute of Technology." Jack paused. "I forwarded you the Center's educational programs and partners. There are forty-six universities around the world working with the Nelson Mandela African Institution of Science and Technology; it's a highly respected program pairing East African students and academics with international peers. There are a number of different dorms and lodging options, and we were lucky to find space at my favorite. They're holding space for us now. If we don't intend to go, I'd like to let them know sooner than later."

Dr. Keller leaned back. "Perhaps this could be the start of a relationship with Orange and the institute in Arusha."

"I would think so," Jack agreed.

Dr. Keller's expression turned wistful. "I confess, I'm envious. I wish I could go. All of my travels are centered around meetings and panels in vast hotel ballrooms. Bland conference rooms. Weak coffee setups at the back. Nothing so exciting as a trip to East Africa."

"Perhaps we can get you there in the future. Check out the program and form a relationship with the directors," Jack said.

"You've convinced me. I'm on board. So, how can my office help?" Dr. Keller asked. "What can my staff do to assist?"

Jack rose. "I'll send an email today with the checklist." He extended his hand to Dr. Keller. "Thank you."

IT WAS HAPPENING.

They were going to be heading to Tanzania for a little over two weeks, in just over five weeks' time. Staff in the president's office were assisting with booking flights and applying for visas. Apparently if they traveled through Istanbul instead of Amsterdam, flights to Arusha would actually be less than the original flight to Costa Rica. Jack had not yet broken the news to the students, but that would happen tomorrow in class. By the time she drove home that evening, she was exhausted. Part of her knew she'd benefit from a barre class, but she couldn't stomach being around more people. Nothing was wrong, but after the weekend in Yellowstone and the many conversations and meetings about adjusting the field studies program, Paige just needed some space. Solitude.

She couldn't even cope with meeting Elizabeth for coffee yet.

For years, Paige's life had been organized, structured, and reassuringly predictable.

Her life was anything but structured and predictable now. Jack King had turned her world inside out. She wasn't sure how she felt about it—her adrenaline was tempered with anxiety. Just because she wanted change didn't mean she knew how to process so much excitement. But at least she knew how she felt about Jack. She liked him. She wanted more time with him. And maybe she shouldn't think of the trip to Tanzania as a chance to spend more time with him, but she did.

Home, Paige changed into her favorite soft pajamas, reheated her vegetable stir-fry from last night, and sat down on the couch to eat and watch the news she always recorded. The news was depressing but David Muir almost made it palatable. At least every night's show ended with a warm fuzzy. After all the tragic stories, a warm fuzzy was needed.

News over, she went through the mail she'd picked up on her way in. Bills, advertisements, a copy of the UC Berkeley alumni association's magazine. Paige tossed the ads into the recycling, put the bills in her caddy, set the magazine in a basket with others she would one day read, and washed her plate from dinner, still feeling out of sorts.

Why was she out of sorts?

Was it the looming trip, or something else?

Had she not had enough alone time, or did she want more Jack time?

It was confusing. She felt unanchored. Maybe she and Jack could have dinner tomorrow night, or maybe Thursday if he didn't mind eating late. Thinking of him settled her. He was so positive and optimistic, and his optimism lifted her.

Paige brushed her teeth and headed to her bedroom, planning on texting Jack from bed, but no sooner had she climbed between the covers than her phone rang with a call from Ashley.

Paige hadn't heard from her in over a week. "Hi, honey," she said, answering. "How are you?"

"Good. I've got news."

"Oh? Tell me."

"I'm heading your way." Ashley paused. "I have a big audition in LA."

"That's exciting. Is it a movie, or play?"

"A movie," Ashley said quickly. "If I get the part, I might be in the area for a while. What do you think of that?"

"I think it'd be awesome. I'd be able to see a lot more of you."

"Maybe I could live with you."

Paige gulped, not sure she was ready to have a roommate. She liked her space, liked having a home of her own. "If you get the part, we could definitely talk about it."

"No one is using your second bedroom."

"No. It's there for you girls, or Grandma, if she wanted to come visit."

"Which she doesn't," Ashley said.

"It's been awhile," Paige agreed. "So, when is the audition?"

"Thursday. I fly out tomorrow. Would you mind coming and picking me up?"

"Which airport?" Paige asked, knowing full well it would be LAX and already dreading the drive. Getting in and out of LAX was a nightmare.

"LAX," Ashley said. "But I arrive late, after rush hour is over. There was no way I was going to make you deal with that."

Thank God for small mercies. "What time do you land?"

"Just before eleven, but I'll have a checked bag. I'll text you my flight info."

"I'll see you tomorrow."

"Can't wait, Mom."

But after hanging up, Paige couldn't sleep. Something seemed off about the call. Something seemed off with Ashley. She sounded too perky, as if her enthusiasm was forced.

Or was Paige reading into it? Projecting because she was tired?

She sent Jack a text. Wish I was in Yellowstone.

He answered right away. I wish I was there with you.

She pressed her phone to her chest and blinked back the sting in her eyes. If she were in Yellowstone, she knew where she'd be sleeping. She'd be in Jack's bed.

ELIZABETH APPEARED IN PAIGE'S OFFICE THE NEXT morning with two coffees in hand. "You're avoiding me," she said, bumping the door closed with her hip. "We were supposed to meet for coffee."

Paige leaned back in her chair, grumpy. "I think I'm avoiding myself." Paige rubbed the back of her neck, feeling all the little knots. "I'm out of sorts, and Ashley is coming in tonight, needs me to pick her up at the airport—"

"Which one?"

"You know which one."

"I'm sorry."

Paige smiled crookedly, her first smile of the day. "I do hope one of those coffees is for me."

"Of course. Best friend and all that." Elizabeth handed her the cup and sat down in one of chairs facing Paige's desk. "You'll be glad when Ashley's here. You always have fun with her. You'll dress up and go out, head to a movie and shop. It'll be a nonstop whirlwind of activity and then she'll be off again, and you'll cry on the way home from the airport because you miss her already."

"I will never confide in you again."

Elizabeth grinned. "Yes, you will." She popped the lid off her coffee and sniffed it. "Did they get our orders mixed up? Do you have a caramel macchiato?"

"No. It's vanilla."

"Hmph." Elizabeth put the lid back on her coffee. "Mom called me this morning. I think she wants to come for Thanksgiving."

"Would you go get her?"

"Michael offered to pick her up," Elizabeth said, referring to her husband, "but I thought I'd check the Amtrak schedule, too."

"It's a long trip by train. Seven hours, I think, and putting her on a train when she has balance issues? Not a good idea. She'll break her hip for sure." Paige wrapped her hands around her cup, savoring the warmth. "I don't know what we'll do for Thanksgiving. I don't think any of the girls will be coming home."

"You'll come to my house, just like last year."

Paige remembered the very crowded house, with people everywhere. And then there was the cleanup. Hours of cleanup. Thanksgiving was just too much work.

"You had a good time," Elizabeth insisted. "You know you did."

"I did," Paige conceded. Elizabeth was a great cook and the food had been wonderful, and there was lots of wine, and lots of dessert—four different kinds of pie and two kinds of cheesecake, plus a huge bowl of homemade whipped cream. Paige had picked at her dinner and then had three desserts. "If I'm alone, without my girls, I'll come, and I expect to be alone because we're supposed to leave for the field program on Saturday." Paige huffed a sigh. "Have I told you where we're going now?"

"It's not in Central America?"

"No." Paige paused, building the suspense. "Tanzania." Elizabeth's dark brows arched high. "Seriously?"

"The trip is now longer, and more involved."

"Won't you need shots?"

"I'm not worried about vaccines, I'm nervous we're going so far. What if something happens to one of the girls? What if there's an emergency?"

"Then Ted would have to step in and be a dad."

"And he would, if there was a true emergency." Paige hesitated. "I'm trying to be chill about the trip, but when I think about it, and all the unknowns, I get scared."

"You spent a summer in Paris when you were twenty. You're already a world traveler."

"But that was a straight shot. Los Angeles to Paris. Done. We're going to have three different flights, we'll be traveling for thirty-something hours, and I have this fear that we're going to plunge into the sea—"

"No wonder you're anxious. That's a terrible thought."

"But I think it."

"What does Jack say?"

"I haven't told him any of that." Paige gave Elizabeth a desperate glance. "He doesn't know about my anxiety. So far I've done a good job hiding it."

"You don't get that anxious. You just like control."

"But I won't have any control over the plane, or the mosquitos, or the being squeezed to death by a cobra."

"I don't think there are cobras in Africa."

"What about the snake in *Jungle Book*?"

"That's Rudyard Kipling's story set in India." Elizabeth reached for her phone, did a quick Google search. "Oh," she said, expression falling. "No, you're right. There are quite a few poisonous snakes in Africa." She read on, expression pained. "Lots of vipers, mambas, and cobras. The Cape cobra and then Mozambique spitting cobra—"

"Okay, that's enough. I don't need to hear any more. A spitting cobra? No, thank you."

There was a rap on her door. Elizabeth glanced at Paige, and Paige nodded. Elizabeth opened the door, revealing Jack.

He looked rested and handsome, and his beard was coming in nicely. He'd stopped shaving when they flew to Bozeman, and Paige thought she wouldn't like him with a beard, but it actually made him look more rugged. Sexy. And just like that she remembered him against her, so warm, so hard, so comfortable in his skin.

She flushed, squirming a little, praying no one could read her thoughts.

"Hello, Elizabeth," he said. "Good morning, Paige."

"Come in," Elizabeth said cheerfully. "We were just discussing the poisonous snakes of Africa."

Jack leaned against the doorframe. "Is that what you girls talk about when you're alone?"

"Snakes, spiders, you know," Elizabeth said airily.

"All an important part of our ecosystem," he said.

"Right?" Elizabeth smiled at him. "I was just saying that to Paige."

"You've heard about our trip?" Jack asked her.

She nodded, giving him another sunny smile. "I'm very envious. I would love to go. Are you sure you don't need someone who teaches Victorian literature?"

"Not this time, but we'll keep you in mind."

Elizabeth picked up her leather backpack, and then her cup. "I've class, but I can't wait to hear more about the trip. Paige is very excited. She's hoping she'll be sleeping under one of those mosquito nets. They're very romantic."

"As well as practical," Jack said.

Paige grimaced. "I did not say that. But I wouldn't mind mosquito nets. Not a fan of mosquitos, or bugs."

"Or lizards," Elizabeth said, heading into the hall. "Or snakes," she called back over her shoulder.

Paige turned to Jack, exasperated. "I sometimes don't know why we're even friends."

Jack flashed a quick smile, his straight teeth white against his tan. "Are you sure you're not sisters?"

"We should be." She gestured to a chair. "Want to sit?"

"I've got some grading to do, but I wondered if you'd want to get dinner sometime this week, or even this weekend?"

Some of the tension within her eased. "I'd love to."

"Good. Think about what works best for you. I'm pretty open."

"I'm picking up Ashley from the airport tonight, and I'll find out her schedule and then let you know."

"Sounds like a plan." He paused. "You're good to share

the news with our class today that we've got a change of plans?"

"If you're good to do the sharing. I have your pdf on the program in Arusha, but I assume you'll break the news, then send the pdf after?"

"Dr. Keller's office will be sending all parents and guardians the same pdf today, along with a letter from him."

"I'm glad he's being so supportive," she said.

"He's a good administrator, and he'll be talking up the program to all the media, so there's that. See you in class?"

"I will be there."

Paige watched him walk out, admiring his broad shoulders, the long muscular legs, his thick tousled hair. Her insides did a fluttery flip. He was hot. She loved looking at him. Loved kissing him. Would she love making love? That she didn't know.

TWO HOURS LATER THEY WERE WRAPPING UP THE Wednesday class they taught together when Jack looked at Paige, eyebrow lifted, and she knew what he was asking. Was it time to break the news? She thought so and nodded yes.

Paige stepped aside so Jack could take over. He didn't waste time, letting the students know that due to the recent hurricanes battering the Caribbean and eastern Central America, Monteverde, like much of Costa Rica, was under water, and that they were unable to host the students for the field program. However, Jack had been in touch with one of the programs he worked with when teaching at Princeton and they were happy to accommodate the students from Orange.

"We'll be working with Tanzanian partners at the Center for Wildlife Management Studies," Jack said, "focusing on natural resource conservation, human-wildlife conflict, and climate change, using the Arusha National Park and neighboring migratory corridors for the basis of our studies. Instead of studying the behavioral ecology of the Costa Rican forests, we will work with the Arushan community to study, and tackle, some of their environmental conservation challenges.

"Some of my Princeton students spend a semester in Tanzania, others are there for four weeks. We only have two weeks, so we're going to make every day count," Jack added. "The cost for the field studies remains the same, though, and the university is working with a travel agency to handle the shift in arrangements. We already have copies of your passports and will be applying for the necessary visas to Tanzania. Vaccines will be necessary, and student services here on campus will take care of necessary shots and antimalarial prescriptions. It's your job to make an appointment with student health. Do not procrastinate."

He glanced at Paige. "What am I forgetting?"

"The description of our Arusha campus. I'm sure everyone would like to know more about where we're staying."

"Good point, yes." He turned back to the class. "There are a number of different centers that house students on international study programs. We'll be staying at the Center for Wildlife Management Studies—hereafter referenced as the Center—which sits on the outskirts of Arusha, and just a few kilometers from the entrance to Arusha National Park, making it the ideal base for our studies as well as visits to the national parks—and there are many within a short drive. Our campus is a former hotel, with extensive grounds and a pool. You'll be two to a room. We'll have classes on the second floor in the conference rooms."

"Dr. King will be sending out a pdf after class with all the information he just shared along with a packing list," Paige said. "The packing list is not a suggestion; it's important you adhere to it. Tanzania is predominantly Muslim, and conservative, so, girls, no leggings and no skimpy outfits allowed, and that includes shorts and skirts above the knee, no midriffs, bare backs, low necklines."

"Thighs covered always," Jack added, "for both men and women except for swimming at the Center's pool, and then before you leave the pool area and go back to your room, cover up. For packing purposes, short-sleeved shirts are fine, but no halter tops, tank tops, as your shoulders should be covered. We do not want to give offense."

He glanced down at his notes before continuing. "I have some notes on cultural differences in the pdf, but we'll be discussing in-depth at the airport, as we'll have several hours between checking in and departure, but obviously wardrobe needs to be sorted soon. Pack lightly, though. The Cessna Caravans have a weight limit and you don't want to be the one with the heavy bag that gets left behind. Your backpack and suitcase combined can't weigh more than twenty kilograms, which is forty-four pounds for you Americans." He smiled as he looked around the lecture hall. "As much as we love the convenience of roller bags, you'll need a soft duffel bag as once we're in Zanzibar we'll be transferring to smaller aircraft, and their cargo holds can't accommodate larger luggage."

"Read through Dr. King's packet carefully," Paige said. "We'll answer questions Friday. See you then." She turned to Jack as the students began talking animatedly among themselves. "That went well," she said.

"How many emails do you think we're going to get between now and Friday?"

"Oh, maybe fifteen, twenty?"

"I say twelve," he said, packing his things up.

"I'm going to go with nineteen as my final answer," she replied. "Whoever is closer wins. Whoever loses pays for dinner."

"Deal."

Chapter 15

PAIGE WAS ON TIME FOR ASHLEY'S FLIGHT. UNFORTU-
nately, the flight wasn't on time, and she ended up parking at
an airport hotel to wait for Ashley's text that she'd landed and
was heading to baggage claim. In the car, Paige tipped her
seat back and listened to a podcast on politics and economics. One of the economists was making dire predictions.
Paige hoped it wasn't true. She had a large chunk of her retirement money invested in the stock market. Maybe she
needed to shift to something safer for the next few years.

She switched to an audio book, hoping that would keep
her awake. It was a relief when Ashley finally called, saying
she was on the ground.

Paige checked the time. Midnight. They weren't going
to get home until at least one thirty, and tomorrow was
Thursday, another long day. But next semester should be
easier. Esther was coming back and Paige would have a
normal course load again. Thank goodness.

And then come May, Jack would be gone.

She exhaled hard, not wanting to think of that. May was

still months away. Who knew if she'd even like him after Tanzania? She might get to Arusha and discover he was annoying, petty, controlling, unbearable.

Although she doubted it.

Or, she could sleep with him and realize she'd built him up in her mind too much, that he was actually very pedestrian, and completely ordinary.

She also doubted that.

Paige's phone vibrated. She glanced down at the text, started the car. Ashley was heading to the curb.

During the drive home Ashley said she wouldn't need Paige's car, that she could just ride-share to LA. "That's ridiculous," Paige answered, glancing at her stunning daughter. Ashley had inherited her father's height but took after Paige in terms of features and coloring. "That would cost a fortune," Paige added. "Take my car. Elizabeth had already offered to pick me up, and Jack could drop me off."

Ashley looked at her mom, brow creasing. "Who is Jack?"

"A colleague," she answered, and then, feeling guilty, added, "And someone I'm seeing."

Ashley's silence was deafening.

Paige shot her a swift glance. "What's wrong?"

Ashley made a faint choking sound. "You're seeing someone?"

"Michelle knows," Paige said, trying not to feel defensive.

It was the wrong thing to say. Ashley's mouth dropped open in outrage. "She didn't tell me. And you didn't tell me. Why not? Does Nichole know?"

"I haven't said anything to Nichole—" Paige broke off, grimacing inwardly as Nichole had been there during the protracted good-night kiss on the night of Paige's surprise birthday. "Actually, Nichole might know, too."

"What?"

Paige's shoulders lifted and fell. "She saw him kissing me good night the night of my surprise birthday party."

"So why didn't you tell me?"

"I don't know. It didn't seem important."

"Is he someone serious?"

"I . . ." Paige frowned, not sure how to answer. "That's a good question," she hedged. "I think it's still in the early stages."

"But could it be serious?"

Paige didn't want to create drama, but at the same time, she cared for Jack, and she wanted him in her life. "I don't know how to answer you, Ash. I like him. But we've only just started seeing each other—"

"So you don't really know him. He could be dangerous. He could be married—"

"He's not married."

"That's what they all say."

"His wife died twenty years ago."

"And you believe him?"

"*Yes*." Paige wasn't sure if she was amused or annoyed by Ashley's line of attack. "For your information, I didn't just meet him at the beginning of the semester. I've known Jack a long time. We went out thirty years ago, when we were both part of a study program in Paris."

Ashley didn't answer. She turned her head away, stared out the window.

"Ash—"

"Can we change the subject, Mom?" Ashley's voice cracked. "I don't really want to hear about you dating."

Paige flinched. Ashley's curtness stung. She opened her mouth, wanting to fire back, but at the last second, she closed it, swallowed the response. It was late. They were both tired.

Reaching the apartment, Paige helped Ashley carry her bags in. It was only then that Paige processed the amount of luggage Ashley had brought with her. Two checked bags, plus her carry-on. "What did you pack?" Paige teased, hauling one of the big cases into the second bedroom. "Your entire closet?"

Ashley managed a tight smile. "Pretty much." She

crossed to her mom, kissed her on the cheek, and then gave her a fierce hug. "Thank you for picking me up, Mom. I appreciate it."

Paige patted her back. Ashley, always lean, felt skinny, almost bony. "I'll leave my keys on the kitchen counter. Just drive yourself tomorrow—"

"My audition has been pushed back. Take your car. I'm just going to hang here tomorrow and get some rest." Ashley had shadows under her eyes, shadows almost the same color as her lavender-blue irises. "How about we have a girls' night tomorrow night? Dinner, a movie . . . ?"

"Thursday is one of my late nights. But we could do a dinner and movie this weekend."

"Should I order something for us for dinner?"

"That sounds great. Order whatever you want," Paige answered, glancing around the small bedroom with the suitcases and carry-on bags. Four pieces of luggage in all, for a simple audition. Something wasn't adding up, but Paige wasn't going to press Ashley now. "I won't wake you in the morning. I'm just going to slip out."

All day Paige fretted about Ashley. Her daughter wasn't usually evasive. Paige knew something was wrong, but she didn't know what. She was determined to get the truth out tonight when she got home. Paige phoned from the car to let Ashley know she was on her way.

"Can you pick up something for dinner?" Ashley asked. "I didn't get around to it."

"Yes," Paige said, not wanting to stop somewhere. She hadn't gotten enough sleep last night and she was tired. But she called in an order to one of her favorite Mediterranean restaurants, then stopped and picked up the kebabs and Greek salad on her way home.

Paige was starving. She ate almost everything, even the rice, which she normally tried not to do. Ashley picked at her food, more interested in the dating reality show she'd been watching than talking to her mom.

Paige finally reached over, took the remote, paused the show. "Okay, what's up? Something's going on."

Ashley reached for her ponytail and let it run through her hand. When anxious she played with her hair. Paige tried to stay calm and quiet, giving Ashley time to form her thoughts. But when she didn't speak, Paige broke the quiet. "Can we start with the audition? What happened with that?"

Ashley looked away, jaw tight. "I don't actually have an audition."

"What?"

Ashley looked at her mom and then away again, tears filling her eyes. "I'm having a hard time." Her voice cracked. "I needed to come home."

"Did something happen?"

"It's not one thing; it's everything. I've had so much anxiety and every audition makes it worse. I don't know what's happened to my confidence, but it's gone. I used to look around the room and think I was pretty and talented and had a shot, but now when I look around the room, I just feel terrible about myself because not even my best is good enough. I've gone to auditions and I've done so well but I still don't get the part. It just seems so pointless. I think that's the biggest thing right now. It all just seems really pointless."

Paige listened without interrupting. When Ashley was a little girl, she'd struggled with body image, and she still had some body dysmorphia. She was incredibly slender, exercising all the time, but in Ashley's mind she was a big girl. "How long are you going to be here? We could do some fun things while you're home. Maybe we could have a girls' getaway. Go to Palm Springs, maybe Ojai."

"Not planning on going back." Ashley drew her knees up to her chest. But restless, she dragged her long hair into a messy knot on top of her head. "I sublet my apartment. Brought everything I needed home with me."

Paige thought of all the furniture they'd bought for her studio. The dishes, the linens, the artwork. Her bike. She drew a deep breath to keep from saying anything too quickly. This wasn't the time to bring up money, even though money was always in the back of her mind. "You didn't bring much home."

"I have those two large suitcases. Trust me, they're packed, and heavy. I had to pay a surcharge for one of them."

Paige sucked in her lower lip, not knowing what to say.

"You're mad," Ashley said flatly, tugging on the ponytail, letting it fall.

"I'm not. I'm concerned."

"You think I gave up too soon."

"I didn't say that. I would never say that. I couldn't do what you do. I couldn't put myself out there like that. I couldn't handle the rejection."

"I tried so hard."

"I know, Ash, and I respect you for that. I'm proud of you."

"Even though I don't know what I'm going to do now? There's nothing else I want to do."

"That's the beauty of part-time jobs, and temp jobs. You could even waitress here while you figure out your next step."

Ashley covered her face, fists pressed to her eyes. "Do I have to start working right away? Can't I just relax for a while?"

"Of course."

She dropped her hands, tears darkening her lashes. "You really don't mind my being here?"

"It's going to be fun to have you here, and I wasn't trying to put any pressure on you. I just didn't know what you were thinking."

"I'm not thinking. I'm just . . . numb. Everything seems pointless. I seem pointless. I had this dream and it turns out half of America had the same dream. New York is filled with beautiful girls wanting to be on Broadway."

Paige held her breath, fighting her own anxiety. It scared her when her girls struggled. It made her worry that she hadn't been a good enough parent, that she hadn't given them the skills they needed to be successful adults. "There is no hurry. The most important thing right now is for you to get some rest, and get some healthy food into you, and things will work out. They always do."

"If I don't pursue acting, I don't know what I'm going to do. It's all I've ever wanted."

Paige stood, crossed to Ashley, and put a hand on top of her head. "You don't have to figure that out today. You've only just returned home. We can discuss this more next week."

She leaned over, kissed Ashley's cheek. "I've got to get to bed, but you're welcome to come in, sleep with me if you're lonely. You used to do that when you were a little girl."

Ashley caught her mom's hand and held it tightly. "I'm better in my own room, but thanks, Mom."

In bed, Paige stared at the ceiling and then turned on her side and looked to the window. She'd drawn the curtains but moonlight spilled between the two halves, a bright slice of light. Paige understood Ashley's anxiety as she had her own, although usually her anxiety was triggered by someone . . . or something. Like divorcing Ted. Moving out. Moving across the country. Her daughters hurting, struggling.

The first three were all behind her—but she'd always be sensitive to her girls, and their hopes and fears. Their future was her future. Or was it the other way around? She just knew that for her to be happy, they had to be happy. At least, that's how it had been, but suddenly, she realized she'd begun to develop a life of her own, a life apart from her girls.

Jack was part of that life.

No, Jack was that life.

She wasn't sure how that made her feel, because if Jack created that life, Jack could also take it away from her.

Paige's eyes burned and she grabbed a pillow, pressed her face into it, even as she fought her fear. *Don't start worrying. Don't panic. There's no reason to panic yet.*

* * *

PAIGE WENT TO FIND JACK IN HIS OFFICE THE NEXT morning. They'd begun walking together to their class each day, but she was a half hour early and she wasn't sure if he'd be in a meeting. He was. Instead of returning straight to her office she went to check her mailbox—although she'd done that earlier when she first arrived on campus—hoping Andi would be free, but Andi was with Dr. Nair, taking copious notes about something.

Paige was disappointed. She felt unsettled. She wanted a diversion, a distraction, anything but time alone, trapped with her thoughts.

"You came looking for me?" Jack asked, entering the mail room.

She turned, smiled, even as tears came to her eyes. She turned her face away, blinked hard, not wanting him to see. She didn't like to cry and being caught crying was a fate worse than death.

"I, uh," she cleared her throat, forced a smile, and faced him. "Ashley isn't in a good place at the moment. I don't think we're going to be able to do dinner soon. I'm sorry." And she was, she realized. There was nothing more she'd rather do today than escape school, escape her responsibilities, and just sit with Jack somewhere under the stars. Just the two of them.

"Come to my office," he said, taking her hand and tugging her out of the mail room and down the hall.

In his office he closed the door, locked it, and hugged her close. Paige leaned against him, her cheek on his chest, thinking she'd needed this more than she knew. He was strong, and warm, and she felt safe. Loved. "I get overwhelmed," she whispered. "I'm sorry."

His arms tightened around her. He kissed the top of her head much like she'd kissed Ashley's the night before. "Stop apologizing," he said, his deep voice pitched low. "We're supposed to have emotions."

"I just worry I'm starting to depend on you." She laughed and tried to make it a joke, but it sounded pathetic to her own ears.

He drew back, sat on the edge of his desk, and brought her forward so she was standing between his knees. "Is that such a bad thing?" he asked, holding her hands.

She looked into his eyes, saw kindness, concern, and her throat ached, a lump there. "In just a month we won't be teaching together anymore."

A shadow flickered in his eyes. "I'll miss it."

"I will, too."

"But I'm still going to be here. I've another semester here."

And what then? she wondered. What would happen then? But she didn't ask. Instead she stepped even closer and she kissed him, a deep lingering kiss. When she ended the kiss, she felt as if her heart were there in her throat, and her eyes. All she wanted was to burrow back into his arms and stay there. "If we can't do dinner, maybe we can have lunch here on campus next week?"

He ran a hand over her braid, smoothing it down her back. "Or just make out here in my office."

Paige laughed, as he'd meant her to. Still laughing, she stepped away. "I suppose we should get ready for class."

He winked at her. "Always the grown-up, aren't you?"

She made a face. "You are, too, Dr. King. You can't fool me."

THERE WAS NO LUNCH THE NEXT WEEK; JACK'S AND Paige's schedules didn't mesh. But there were brief kisses behind closed doors, and conversation to and from class. It wasn't enough for Paige, but she didn't know how to make Ashley happy and herself happy at the same time. Jack was heading to San Diego for the weekend as friends of his were in town for a few days. Sunday was Halloween and Elizabeth asked if Paige and Ashley would want to join them for a pre-trick-or-treating dinner. Paige declined, knowing already that Ashley wanted to just watch movies at home.

They stayed in that evening, having lined up two scary movies to watch. Ashley had made sure they had the appropriate snacks for a Halloween movie fest. There was popcorn and a box of Red Vines. However, during the first movie, Ashley seemed more interested in her phone, scrolling almost constantly through Instagram, mentioning parties her friends in New York were attending, showing Paige elaborate costumes, and talking about how fun New York was on Halloween. Paige never knew what she was supposed to say and tried to sound pleasant but also noncommittal.

Ashley had been home ten days now but hadn't done much of anything but watch TV, do workouts in front of the TV, worry she was gaining weight, worry she was breaking out, worry that she didn't have a dream anymore.

"Why don't you see if anyone is hiring a barre instructor here?" Paige suggested in between scary movie one and scary movie two. "You're certified. You could get a part-time job—"

"Nobody wants someone for just a month or two. There's really no point in that."

Paige digested this. Apparently, her daughter was planning on staying through Thanksgiving, possibly Christmas. That might not be a bad thing since Paige would be away from the end of November through the first two weeks of December. At least she'd have someone to water her plants and pick up her mail. "Have I mentioned that Elizabeth has invited us to her house for Thanksgiving?"

Ashley closed her eyes. "I love Elizabeth but I don't want to go. It's too loud, too many people, too much fuss." She opened her eyes, looked at Paige. "Can't we just make a res and go out somewhere, the two of us?"

Normally it's what Paige would do with Ashley, but Jack

had been invited to Elizabeth's for Thanksgiving, which made Elizabeth's the place Paige wanted to be this year. "You could meet Jack."

"Even more reason why I don't want to go."

Paige struggled with her disappointment, and hurt. "That's not very nice, Ash."

"I'm sorry, Mom, but you've taught us to be honest, and I don't think Jack is right for you. He doesn't live here. He's not going to stick around. You're just going to get your heart broken again. I would think after Dad, you'd want to avoid men."

Paige wanted to protest that Jack was different, but was he? Every now and then Sheila's words came back to her, and Paige pictured the revolving door of women. And then there was Camille, always looming in the background. The fact that Jack had spent seven years with her was pretty significant.

But Paige was looking forward to meeting Oliver and getting to know him a little bit. She'd wondered what kind of dad Jack was. It'd be interesting to see Jack and Oliver together. She wished she'd thought of inviting Oliver to dinner, but of course clever Elizabeth thought of it first.

THE FIRST WEEK OF NOVEMBER WAS GORGEOUS, THE weather glorious all week long. Bright blue sky, a perfect seventy degrees, not a cloud in sight. Paige was spending more time on campus now that Ashley was home. She found it harder to get work done with the TV always on in the living room. But there were positives to being in her office at Orange. Andi was always just down the hall, good for a quick chat, Greg for a laugh, and Jack . . . well, Jack for hugs, kisses, and inspiration because just looking at him, being near him, did her heart good.

"When are we going hiking?" he asked, standing in her door Thursday afternoon, before her last two classes. She really hoped next semester she wouldn't have such long

Tuesdays and Thursdays. She felt numb by the time she wrapped up the day.

She took off her glasses and rubbed the bridge of her nose. "This weekend?" she suggested because she was ready to escape her apartment and Ashley's unhappiness. "I need a good hike. I haven't exercised in forever."

"Let's go Saturday. I'll pick you up at eight."

Paige groaned. "Not that early."

Jack grinned, flashing white teeth. "That's not early, babe."

"But it's the weekend. *My* weekend."

"Fine. Eight thirty."

"Jack."

He wasn't the least bit sympathetic. "Drink some coffee. You'll be fine."

SHE WAS FINE, TOO, AND JUST WAKING UP, KNOWING she'd spend the morning with Jack made it easy to get out of bed and dress. It had been a long time since she'd had him all to herself, and Paige was looking forward to his company at Crystal Cove, a stunning stretch of coastline as well as a historic spot, with beach rentals that dated back to the 1920s. Crystal Cove, south of Newport Beach, was originally part of the Irvine Ranch, owned and managed by the Irvine family for almost a century. The beach cottages could be rented, but it was hard to find one available.

Paige hadn't appreciated California's history until she was living in North Carolina, and now that she was back, she wanted to take advantage of every hike, every opportunity, every view. This morning's hike was exactly what she needed. Jack was in a good mood, but neither of them felt inclined to talk a lot, both eager to get on the trail. They decided to do one of the longer, more challenging hikes, which meant some serious elevation gains, but the challenging hike was made easier with the water bottles and snacks Jack had brought. They stopped twice on the way up, and then at the peak, had a light lunch and savored the view. On the top of the mountain the air was cool and crisp, the sun shimmered on the water. Paige breathed in, letting the air expand her lungs and ribs, and then slowly exhaled, feeling two weeks' worth of stress start to dissipate.

"I needed this," she said, still gazing out over the ocean with the white-crested waves. "I hadn't realized how wound up I've been, and how much I've been holding it all in."

"You have a lot on your mind," he said, and it wasn't a question but a statement.

She nodded and, resting her chin on her forearm, looked at him. His thick brown hair was a bit damp at his nape and curling in different places. His beard defined his strong jawline. "I like your beard," she said. "I didn't think I would."

"I just have that kind of face."

She shook her head, but she couldn't hide her smile. "What am I going to do with you?"

"I have a few ideas if you're open to them," he said.

Paige smothered her laugh. Jack was good for her. He had a way of easing her worries, giving her much needed perspective. "Ashley's a lot for me sometimes," she said after a moment. "She's beautiful, brilliant, sensitive, but very intense. I feel like a bad mom for wanting her to return to New York, but I miss my quiet, and the freedom I had before she arrived."

"She won't stay forever. She just needs a safe place to rest and figure out her next step."

"I wish she'd give up acting all together and just get a real job."

"Acting is a real job."

"I didn't mean it that way. I guess I would prefer her to have more security, a job with paid sick days and holidays and vacations. A job that paid into a 401(k) plan. It's really important that women don't rely on men and marriage to be the answer—" Paige broke off, pressed her lips together, aware that Jack probably wasn't interested in any of this. "I like stability. I think it's important, and important for the girls."

"We don't all need the same thing."

She studied his profile, with the high forehead, the straight nose, lovely jaw and chin. When he smiled, he had these grooves on either side of his mouth and her fingers itched to trace them. "Do you worry about Oliver?"

"All the time."

"Really?"

"Well, less than I used to, but he'll always be my boy. I want him happy. I hope he marries one day and gives me grandkids. I'd love grandkids. I'd love to spoil them rotten."

Paige sat up. "You like kids?"

"Love them." He laughed, a slightly husky laugh, and then his laugh faded. "I didn't spend enough time with Oliver when he was small. I wish I could do that over. But I'm determined to be there when he has children."

"I haven't thought about grandkids, to be honest. That still seems so far away."

"Until one of the girls surprises you with news."

"Oh, no. I hope not. They're not ready—"

"Or, you're not ready."

"I'm *definitely* not ready. But neither are they. Babies are wonderful, but they change one's life forever and I want my daughters to live a little, well, a lot, before they have to start taking care of others. Despite all the strides we've made as a society, it's still not an equal society. Women still have way too much responsibility, at least in terms of hearth and home."

"You're not passionate about that at all," he teased.

"I don't want my girls to make the same mistakes I did." Paige stood, brushed off her backside. "Let's finish this hike. And no more talk of babies and grandkids. You're making me feel old."

DR. KELLER'S ADMINISTRATIVE ASSISTANT SENT OUT AN email the following week, letting Paige and Jack know that the visas had all come in, and they were good there. The director of the university's wellness program reached out letting them know that over half the students had been in for the shots needed for Africa, but at least ten students hadn't been seen yet, and they also needed to pick up their doxycycline prescriptions.

Jack had done a deep dive into Tanzanian conservation, teaching the difference between nature tourism and ecotourism, and the impact on the communities. Paige continued with her statistics, leaving program changes to Jack. Once a week, usually on Fridays, they'd devote the last fifteen minutes of class to discussing the trip.

Jack reminded students that the cutoff for getting their shots and picking up their antimalarial prescription was approaching. He expected it done by the sixteenth. "I need to know before we break for Thanksgiving week that it's been handled. Otherwise, let me know if you're not planning on going."

"I know a lot of you have early exams due to the trip," Paige added. "It's hard to juggle everything, especially when you're feeling overwhelmed by tests and final papers for your other classes, but making an appointment with Student Health and then getting the shots and malaria medicine should take less than an hour. Make the appointment, show up, get it over with."

Jack looked out over the class. "We leave fifteen days from today. You'll start the doxycycline thirteen days from today. Our trip will be here before you know it. It's going to be a great experience, I promise you."

WEEK THIRTEEN OF THE SEMESTER WAS FLYING BY. PAIGE couldn't believe Thanksgiving was next week. She'd had a call about Thanksgiving from Michelle, who wasn't going to be coming home as she'd be spending it with her boyfriend, Garrett, and his kids. "It's his year to have the kids," Michelle explained. "He wants me there. I've never done a turkey before. It'll be my first time."

"Are you making Thanksgiving dinner, or is he?"

"I offered. He was delighted. He's not very comfortable in the kitchen."

Paige bit the inside of her cheek, thinking unkind thoughts about this man who was so eager to turn Michelle into kitchen help. She wished he didn't want Michelle to cook. She wished he didn't need Michelle there while he spent time with his kids. She wished he didn't have these huge holes in his life that he needed her daughter to fill. But what did she know? She'd never met him, and maybe he was a wonderful man. Maybe he was the perfect person for her beautiful, intelligent, kind, compassionate daughter.

"Oh, and Dad's going to be in Los Angeles for Thanksgiving," Michelle added. "I guess he's going to take Ashley to dinner? At least that's what he told me."

"When did you talk to him?"

"Last week. He called about Gram's eightieth birthday. He's hoping we'll get together and surprise her in Orlando."

"He's taking Gram to Disney World?"

"No. Maybe it's not Orlando, but it's somewhere in Florida. He wants to rent some condos and make it a big family get-together. He said I could bring Garrett, but I don't think Gram would approve."

"Probably not. But she would love to see you all."

They said their goodbyes and hung up, and Paige forgot the conversation until she was home with Ashley that evening. "Have you talked to your dad about Thanksgiving?" Paige asked, turning down the heat under the chicken. She was making fajitas with a new low-carb tortilla, hoping it would taste good.

Ashley leaned against the counter. "Why would I have talked to him about it?"

"I thought he was going to be in LA for the weekend. I wondered if he had made plans to see you."

She shrugged. "He'd texted something about being in LA, but we've made no plans. He's coming out here to see a woman he met at on a plane a couple months ago. He calls her his girlfriend, but she's like thirty years younger than him. It's gross."

"How do you know that?"

"Because he sent me pictures." Ashley shuddered. "He looks like her dad. She's Michelle's age, I think. Just two months older. Doesn't that seem weird to him?"

It seemed weird to Paige, but she wouldn't say it aloud. Instead she counted to five, and only spoke when she was certain she could keep her tone neutral. "I think your dad does want to see you. He wouldn't have texted if he didn't."

"Then why doesn't he come here to see me in Orange County? Why do I have to drive to LA?"

"You can use my car."

"That's not the point, Mom."

Paige knew that, too. She knew what Ashley was objecting to was that her father had not made any effort to see her, not in New York, and not in California, at least not until now, when he had another reason to come to Southern California.

"He's probably convinced his new girlfriend that he's this great guy, and a wonderful dad—" Ashley broke off, compressed her lips, unable to finish the sentence. "It's part of his act. He should have been the actor, not me."

"Dad's not a happy person," Paige said, wanting to smooth things over.

"If that's truly the case, he should do something about it. Like take a hard look at himself. Maybe go to an AA meeting. Ask his family why no one wants a relationship with him."

Paige gave her a look. "That's a little harsh."

"It's the truth, and you know it."

Paige didn't say anything, uncomfortable with the past.

Ashley's chin lifted. "Dad always took out his frustration on us. He was always in a bad mood and he hated that we were happy. It wasn't okay. And it wasn't okay that he blamed you—"

"You're right," Paige interrupted, in part because Ashley was right, but also because Paige didn't want to do this now. She hated making excuses for Ted. She'd spent years making excuses for her ex-husband, and yet at the same time, she didn't want to live in the past, didn't want to examine it over and over. The past was the past. She needed to move forward. She wanted to move forward. "Obviously, I'd like for you to see your dad. He is your dad. But at the same time, it's your relationship, and you're an adult, and I refuse to get in the middle."

Ashley huffed a breath. "I didn't say I wouldn't go see him. But I don't want to have dinner with him and Lila, or whatever her name is. That would be weird. What would we talk about anyway? How great he is in bed?"

"Ashley!"

"They are sleeping together. One of the pictures was of them in bed."

Oh my God. Paige felt faint. "It wasn't."

"They were wrapped up in sheets. Shoulders were bare. Dad looked really happy."

Paige closed her eyes, trying—unsuccessfully—to block the picture from her mind, but Ted had a hairy arm and that's all she could see. "Can you spare me the details? We're not married anymore. What he does is his business."

"Exactly," Ashley crowed triumphantly. "And it's not going to be my business."

Chapter 16

ON SATURDAY MORNING, PAIGE BEGAN TO PACK IN EAR-
nest for the trip, since it was now only a week away. She'd
bought a large, lightweight duffel bag that met the dimen-
sions required. She'd never been in a really small plane, and
she was curious what a Cessna Caravan looked like. Paige
got online and started reading about them, and then reading about their use in Africa, and then reading about the
accidents.

It didn't take long for Paige to wish she'd never gone down
this rabbit hole of research. There had been eight small plane
accidents since 1980, and in most cases, everyone onboard
died. In virtually every case the plane was filled with tourists,
international travelers like her and the Orange students. She
shot Elizabeth a text with a screen shot of the statistics. This is
not good, Paige typed.

She didn't hear back from Elizabeth right away and tried to
distract herself by repacking the lime-green duffel, lightening
it up. She didn't need three pairs of walking shoes, or two
swimsuits. Her long, soft cotton skirts were thin and took up

little space. She re-counted her tops and T-shirts: she had three of each. She needed something for the evenings if it grew cold. Long sleeves to protect from mosquitos. Long pants for the same reason. Something if it rained. A pair of hiking pants. Another pair, just in case. Socks, underwear, a belt, a small pack for hikes and exploration. It didn't look like enough clothes, but she was sure Jack would think she had way too much. Paige reassured herself that there would be a place to do laundry. She'd ask Jack, just to be on the safe side, as she hadn't seen anything about it on the Center's website.

Paige's phone rang. It was Elizabeth. "You saw my text?" she demanded.

"You'll be fine," Elizabeth soothed.

"Those little planes crash all the time," Paige protested, pushing the duffel over so she could lie down, stretch out. "And when they crash, everybody dies. What if we don't make it? What if we all die? I keep trying to stay positive, but this trip is dangerous."

"Life is dangerous. Walking across the street is dangerous. Taking a flight to San Francisco is dangerous. Going to the mall is dangerous. Driving in your car is dangerous, especially here in Southern California. Road rage—"

"I hear you, and road rage is real. But I've never deliberately sought out danger, stared it in the face."

"I looked up those statistics you sent me. There hasn't been an aircraft fatality in years. Five years, I think—"

"Exactly. Every five years there seems to be an accident and everyone dies."

"You really need to run the numbers, Paige. You're a data girl. Look at the data. Millions and millions of people fly through Tanzania every year. There are very few accidents, and even fewer fatalities. From what I gathered, you're safer flying there than here with our overcrowded airports and overworked air traffic controllers. If you need me to do some research for you, I can."

"No." Paige closed her eyes. "I should probably avoid reading about accidents and air travel. It's making me panic."

"You are going far away, but you're going to be okay, and the students will be okay. Then, before you know it, you'll be back with amazing stories. I can't wait to see your pictures; I can't wait to hear about your adventures. You might have to even start using your Instagram again and post photos so I don't have to wait weeks for updates."

"I'm going to email you all the time. The Wi-Fi is free."

"Paige, even if you went nowhere, life is still out of our control. You know that. We just like to think we're in control. But all it takes is one of our moms taking a fall, or one of our kids getting hurt, and we realize control is an illusion."

"You're the only one who knows how anxious I get. Or how much I struggle."

"It's our secret. You make me look good, and I make you look good, and we'll do that until the day we die—" Elizabeth broke off, snorted. "Sorry, didn't mean to mention death again. Anyway, you know what I mean."

Paige smiled grimly. She did. "I wish you were going. It would be a lot more fun if you were on this trip. I'd have a friend."

"You have Jack. He's your friend, and he's more. He'll do things with you I won't do."

"That's the signal it's time to change the subject. What can I bring for Thanksgiving? Haven't heard you agonizing over your menu yet this year."

"Bite your tongue! I do not agonize. I'm a planner, and doing the family favorites, and maybe a different sweet potato casserole. Last year's was just too sweet, even cutting the sugar in half."

Paige hadn't had any so she couldn't comment on that. "Is your mom still coming?"

"Yes, Margot Hughes is driving her. Do you remember her?"

"The girl who was a couple years younger than us? The one your mom swore would be a Broadway star?"

Elizabeth sighed. "Yes. But don't bring that up. Margot's left New York behind and is still sensitive about it, I think."

"I get it. I have a Margot at home. Can we also agree not to mention musicals, theatre, or Lin-Manuel?"

"It will be hard, but I'll do my best," Elizabeth teased. "Oh, and Andi McDermott, she accepted my invitation."

"Oh, I'm glad. I had no idea she spent Thanksgiving alone the past few years until she mentioned it last week. I always thought she spent it with her stepson."

"I've also told your Jack to bring his son. Have you met Oliver yet?"

"*My* Jack?"

Elizabeth cleared her throat. "Is he yours now?"

Paige went warm, cheeks suddenly hot. "I just meant, the Jack I teach with."

"And sleep with."

"We don't sleep together—" Paige broke off, pursed her lips, corrected. "Well, we've slept together, but we haven't done it."

"Why not?"

Paige didn't answer. Besides, Elizabeth already knew.

"Paige, freak out about jets crashing and mambas dropping from trees. Don't freak out about sex. Sex is fun."

"Not for me."

"You are gorgeous. I would kill for your body. The things I would do if I had your body!"

"Good thing you don't have my body, then."

"Jack isn't Ted. Jack will not be Ted in bed. It won't be awful. Jack isn't that guy, and let's face it, you're not the same woman. You're stronger. Happier. Just be confident."

Paige's eyes stung, tears prickling. "What if I really am frigid?"

"You're not frigid, but it is time you ventured out of your ice castle."

"I think that's my cue to hang up. Goodbye, Elizabeth."

"Goodbye, Elsa."

Paige hung up and laughed under her breath. Elsa. *Good one, Elizabeth*. And then it hit her. She'd be meeting Oliver. Now, that would be interesting.

Page quickly texted Elizabeth. You never told me what to bring. And what time should we be there?

Elizabeth replied: Bring 2–3 bottles of wine, a green salad, and your gorgeous smile. Everyone's been invited for noon but come earlier if you want. xo

ELIZABETH ALWAYS SET THE MOST BEAUTIFUL THANKS-giving table, and this year was no exception. She had all those grown-up things Paige had given up years ago—elegant linens, crystal, fine China, sterling silver flatware. This year, the cloth covering the long table was an ivory linen with a thick band of burgundy and rust. The flowers were from a florist, and expensive. There wasn't a single daisy or baby's breath in sight. Paige and Ashley walked around the table, admiring the flowers and small gilded pumpkins before Ashley disappeared to go speak to Mrs. Ortiz.

Elizabeth managed to make entertaining look easy, and with Ashley having decided to come after all, Paige suddenly felt emotional, and grateful, that Elizabeth was still her best friend and still including her in holidays and celebrations all these years later. While Paige liked the ease of going to a restaurant on Thanksgiving, there was something to be said for sitting down with people who knew you well, people who made you feel most like yourself. In short, Paige was deeply thankful for Elizabeth.

At Elizabeth's request, Paige lit the candles on the table, added a second pitcher of water, and checked on the bottles of red wine breathing on the corner of the sideboard.

Elizabeth was bustling in and out of the kitchen, adding platters to the antique sideboard. She returned with Paige's green salad, sliding it between the vegetables and the warm rolls.

Elizabeth stepped back to survey the dining room. "Is there anything missing?"

Paige studied the buffet. Turkey, ham, mashed potatoes, sweet potatoes, two kinds of stuffing, two vegetables, salad, rolls, gravy. "The only thing we're missing are the cranberries," she said, turning to look at the table, just in case they were there.

"Good catch." Elizabeth gave Paige a swift hug. "I am so glad you're here."

Paige hugged her back, feeling a sting of bittersweet emotion. They were getting older, they were looking older, and yet Paige had been so blessed to have a friend like Elizabeth in her life. "I'm glad we're together again," Paige said. "I missed you when we were in North Carolina. I made friends, but there's no one like you."

"We've been through so much together."

"I don't know how I would have survived the divorce without you."

"That's what friends are for." Elizabeth gave her another quick squeeze. "Now I'm going to get the cranberries. Will you invite everyone to come to the table?"

Dinner was delicious. Candlelight flickered. The dining room hummed with conversation. Paige glanced across the table to where Jack sat next to Andi. He'd been very attentive to Andi throughout the meal, and he'd just made her laugh. Paige was glad. Andi deserved more happiness.

Paige then glanced at Oliver, who was tall like his dad, but darker and leaner. He had his dad's smile, though, and he was talking to Elizabeth's twins, making them laugh. It was a very animated discussion and Oliver seemed to enjoy entertaining them. Not all men Oliver's age would be so good with boys. Paige's heart felt full.

She couldn't remember when she'd last felt this way. Deeply content. Peaceful.

Her daughters were healthy and relatively happy. Her mom was well. Paige loved her work. Saturday she'd be leaving for an extended trip with a man who made her feel young and hopeful. Optimistic about the future.

She hadn't thought she'd ever feel this way about a man again, but Jack had somehow done the impossible.

The improbable.

She was falling in love and she wasn't even scared— well, not terribly scared—anymore.

JACK HAD EATEN FAR MORE THAN HE SHOULD HAVE, BUT it was all so good, and it had been years since he'd enjoyed a traditional Thanksgiving dinner. Elizabeth had outdone herself, too, and she sat at the end of the table, sipping her wine, beaming with pleasure.

He could see why she and Paige were best friends. They complemented each other, brought out the best in each other. He didn't have a best friend, but rather, many good friends, fellow scientists scattered across the globe, and he'd always thought he was fine with it, but seeing Paige and Elizabeth together made him wish he had that deep bond with someone else.

"Should we wait for pie?" Elizabeth asked the table.

There was a resounding yes, and Elizabeth smiled. "You're all excused, then. Relax, visit, go watch the game; it's on in the family room. I'm going to clear the table but no one is allowed to help."

People pushed away from the table, with Michael and the twins heading to the family room to check on the football game. Jack saw Oliver wander that way, even though he knew Oliver wasn't a big fan of American football. Oliver liked soccer, or European football, as well as rugby, which was Jack's favorite sport, but he hadn't played it since he'd left university.

Jack had heard Elizabeth's instructions, but he wasn't about to walk away from the table, not when it was covered in dirty dishes, and he began stacking plates and carrying crystal and china into the kitchen. Paige was already at the sink filling it with hot sudsy water.

Elizabeth appeared with crystal goblets and scolded them for not following directions. Paige grinned. "You're not the boss of me," she said with a wink.

"It's my house," Elizabeth grumbled.

"And you've just spent two days prepping and cooking. I'm not leaving you in here alone."

"Why don't you go sit with your guests and let Paige and me tackle dishes for a bit?" Jack suggested. "I'm sure Margot and your mom would enjoy having some time with you. Or, maybe you'd like to watch the game?"

"Ugh, no football for me," Elizabeth said. "But I'll go check on Mom and then I'll be back and I will kick you out."

Jack was comfortable in the kitchen and he quickly located storage containers and packed up food. Paige hand-washed the china and crystal while he dried. Next came the platters and silverware. By the time Elizabeth returned, they'd made a serious dent on the dishes.

Elizabeth paused, shocked, as she took in the almost-tidy kitchen. "Look at my kitchen fairies. This is incredible."

"It's our pleasure," Jack said.

"Mine, too," Elizabeth joked even as she took the damp dish towel from Jack and nudged Paige away from the sink. "Thank you, really, but now, do get out. Go enjoy yourselves a little."

"We are," Paige protested.

"Not buying it," Elizabeth said, pushing them both to the door. "Scram. See you later."

PAIGE LED JACK THROUGH THE HOUSE AND OUT ONTO the deck overlooking the ocean. It had been foggy earlier, but the clouds had lifted slightly, giving them a glimpse of the dark blue ocean. Paige drew in a deep breath and exhaled. "You can smell the salt in the air today."

"I like it," he said, slipping an arm around her waist, his palm resting in the small of her back. "I've been wanting to do this all day."

"What?" she asked, looking up into his face.

His head dipped, and his lips covered hers in a kiss. "This."

"Oh, well." She felt her cheeks warm. Her mouth felt extra sensitive. "Thank you."

"You look beautiful."

She didn't know what to say. She reached up to lightly scrape her fingers across his beard. "I like your beard."

"Not everyone does."

"Well, I do. You look very sexy."

"I always grow a beard when I go to Arusha."

"Is there a cultural reason?"

"No. Just an excuse to stop shaving."

She ran her fingers over his jaw. He was so very appealing. If they weren't here, she'd kiss him properly. But they were here, and his son was here, and her daughter was here, and the last thing she wanted was drama. "Are you enjoying yourself?" she asked, voice husky.

"Immensely."

She was conscious of the heat of his hand against her lower back, his touch firing nerve endings, making her wish his hand would just slide lower, cup her butt. Obviously not something he could, or would, do here, but still, she could fantasize. "Do you fit in wherever you go?"

"I try."

She smiled, expression teasing. "You *like people*," she said, quoting back words he'd told her early in the semester.

He recognized her words. "You listen."

"I do, especially if it's to you."

"Elizabeth outdid herself," he said, even as Elizabeth appeared on the deck with bottles of red and white wine.

Paige nodded, glad she'd put down her wineglass an hour ago, but Elizabeth was moving around the deck, topping off glasses, beginning with Ashley's.

Ashley smiled prettily and thanked Elizabeth before turning her attention back to Oliver. They'd been talking for the past half hour in outdoor chairs in the corner; Ashley seemed to be doing most of the talking, her expression earnest. Paige wondered if Ashley was telling him about her acting ambitions, and how she'd left New York crushed, but then thought, *No, Ashley wouldn't reveal anything negative.* She understood the importance of first impressions, and the value of networking.

"Do we need to rescue your son?" she asked, glancing at Jack.

"Why would we do that? I'm sure Oliver is very flattered by the attention." Jack lifted her hair from her shoulder, allowing the strands to slide through his fingers. "Are you ready for our flight? Everything packed?"

"I'll probably take everything out of the duffel bag and repack a half dozen more times before we leave. I'm a bit obsessive that way, but otherwise, yes, I'm ready. How about you?"

"I live with a bag always packed." He wrapped the strand of gleaming hair around his finger. "Have you started your doxycycline?"

"First dose this morning." She lifted her face to his. "I want to kiss you."

"Why don't you?"

"Ashley would have a fit."

"She doesn't approve of me?"

"She doesn't approve of me getting romantically involved with anyone. But to be fair, this is the first time I ever wanted to be romantically involved with anyone . . . since Ted."

His hand pressed against her spine, drawing her closer. "She'd really have a hard time if she knew all the things I intend to do to you very soon."

A shiver coursed through her. His voice had a rasp that made her feel tingly. "Will we get alone time in Arusha?"

"Yes."

She felt warm and off-balance. Her hand went to his chest. "This might not be the time, but I thought you should know, I'm not seeing anyone else. Or kissing anyone else."

"Nor I," he answered.

"And as long as I'm kissing you, I won't kiss anyone else." Her pulse sped up a little, realizing this was dangerous, and revealing, territory. She hadn't planned on saying anything, but the words were tumbling out of their own volition.

"As long as I'm kissing you, I can promise you, there will be no one else," he answered gravely.

She held his gaze, and his golden-brown eyes seemed to be able to see all the way through her, boring right to her very heart, and it was both wonderful and terrifying. She really cared for him, cared deeply, and for the first time in forever, she wanted to believe that maybe, just maybe, fairy tales came true.

Was she too old to have a happy ending of her own?

"I think we have something special," he said, his hand slowly sliding up her back, stirring nerve endings all the way. "I'm certainly not going to do anything to mess that up."

Her breath caught, and she managed a tremulous smile. Things had certainly gotten very serious, very quickly, but maybe it was good they were having this conversation now, before they left Saturday for Arusha. They'd be in very close quarters for the next two weeks and the last thing either of them needed were hurtful misunderstandings.

"So we're exclusive," she said carefully, trying to ignore the wild hammering of her heart.

He kissed the curve of her cheek, close to her ear. "Yes, I think that's exactly what it means."

WHILE EVERYONE WAS VISITING, ELIZABETH SET UP A dessert bar on the sideboard featuring four kinds of pies, two kinds of cheesecake, and a coffee bar with lots of accoutrements.

Jack hung back with Oliver while Elizabeth's twins and the women went ahead. Paige sat down at the empty dining table with Andi and Margot, and after taking slices of berry pie, Jack and Oliver headed back outside where it was cooler and quieter.

Being raised in Australia, Jack didn't have an affinity with Thanksgiving, but today had been special. It had been rather humbling seeing Oliver and Paige, his two favorite people, at the same table. "You haven't had a chance to talk to Paige very much, have you?" he asked his son.

"No, but I'm sure I will. If not today, then another time." Oliver's dark blue eyes glimmered with warmth and humor. "I think she's going to be around awhile."

"What are you? A fortune-teller?"

"When it comes to you, Dad, yes. You like her." Oliver paused, considered Jack. "I've never seen you like this with anyone."

Jack felt like a schoolboy. It wasn't comfortable. "Like what?"

"Don't be obtuse."

Jack rolled his eyes. "Now you sound like your grandad."

Oliver smiled patiently. "I like her, too. Probably not as much as you do—"

"—Which is probably a good thing."

His blue eyes glinted, his smile infectious. "Agreed. But seriously, the way you are with her, it's different. It's like you've met your person. Finally. I'm happy, Dad." Oliver's voice dropped, gentled. "Really happy."

Jack shifted restlessly. He'd stood practically in this same spot with Paige an hour ago. Time passed too quickly when he was with her. It was maddening but exhilarating. "I do like her," he admitted. "And she is different. But she's not interested in anything long-term or permanent. She had a bad first marriage and I think it's done a number on her. So, I'm just enjoying the now, and I think that's okay."

"Have you told her how you feel?"

Jack shook his head. "No." But that wasn't the only thing he hadn't told her. He hadn't said anything to Paige yet about Camille being in Arusha for the conference. He didn't want to worry her, nor was he planning on getting the two women together. Camille would be staying at one of the new hotels next to the big convention center. Paige would be off with the students on their end-of-program safari. It was always a highlight of the trip for his Princeton students and he'd worked it out so that the Orange students could do the same thing.

Should he drop Camille into a conversation with Paige? Give her a heads-up that Camille would be at his conference?

Imagining that conversation filled him with dread. He didn't know why Camille made Paige feel insecure, but Paige didn't need to feel that way. Camille meant nothing to him. She was part of his past. She also wasn't staying where the students were staying. She'd be on the other side of town. Maybe it was better if he didn't bring her up. Why upset Paige? She was just starting to feel safe with him.

"I don't know what I have to offer her," Jack said. "I travel all the time. I'm a workaholic. Even if we wanted to be together, I don't know how that would work." Jack fell silent, seeing the objections and obstacles stack up. There were so many things in the way.

"You're here for another semester, it's not as if you have to have all the answers now."

"For someone who avoids commitment, you're awfully good at giving relationship advice."

"I think she's wonderful, and you deserve someone wonderful. That's all."

Jack raised his eyebrows, but then, Oliver had been trying to marry him off for years now. Oliver hated the idea of his dad growing old on his own. "I think you said the same thing about Camille."

"I never did. I said I wanted you happy, and you could get married, and I'd be okay with it, but this is different. We both know it's different."

Jack *did* feel differently about Paige, but he hadn't realized it was so obvious. "What gave me away?"

"Besides you smiling all the time? The way you hold her, the way you look at her. You look at her as if she's something wonderful."

Because she was.

Jack had never been very big on public displays of affection, but Paige made him want to keep her close. After a few days of not seeing her, he missed her, missed the contact. He felt connected to her, and the attraction was more than physical. He cared about her well-being, cared about her future, cared about her health, her safety, her girls, her happiness.

Did he want her? Absolutely. She was gorgeous, and when she laughed, he wanted to pull her into his arms and kiss her. When she was worried, he wanted to pull her into his arms and kiss her. The fact was, he just wanted her in his arms, because when she was close, he felt pretty damn complete.

"I'm looking forward to going on this trip with her," he said. "I think it will tell us a lot about how we are together. If we work together. Because I can't imagine giving up international programs and studies. I can't imagine not traveling, not working. For all I know, Paige may get to Arusha and hate it. She might be incredibly uncomfortable, and not like the climate or the food, or the pace of it, and it would change things. I hate to say it would change everything, but my heart is in East Africa. I just don't know that I could give it up for anyone."

"I don't know why you're even going there yet." Oliver's expression firmed. "Give her a chance. She told me earlier that she'd been to Paris and Cancún, and that was it. Don't assume she won't like Tanzania. Maybe she will. Maybe she'll fall in love with it like you did."

Jack turned and looked at Paige where she was sitting inside at the table with Andi and Elizabeth's friend— Martha? Margaret? They were having dessert and coffee and talking nonstop. Paige looked comfortable, relaxed.

As if feeling his gaze, she suddenly turned her head and looked at him. Their eyes met and held. She gave him a small, private smile that made his chest grow tight and his body ache.

He desired her, there was no question about that. In fact, he wanted her more every day, but the wanting wasn't just a physical need. He craved time with her, wanting her thoughts, wanting her smile, wanting her company. He'd spent years on his own, and yes there had been women, but no one was like Paige. He didn't even know what it was about Paige that set her apart, but he was comfortable with her, as well as more hopeful.

She made him feel young. She made him want more out of life. She was good for him.

He glanced at her again, thinking she looked beautiful in her crisp navy linen dress with the sparkly bracelets on her wrist, her long hair loose, hanging in a gold curtain down her back. She was sophisticated and stylish. But as beautiful as she was now, she'd been perfect at Yellowstone in jeans, T-shirts, and sweatshirts. He loved her Converse shoes and the oversize hoodie. She looked like the California girl she was, and it had blown him away.

Mara had been intelligent.

Camille was intelligent.

Paige was intelligent, too. But Paige had something else,

a magic something that just worked . . . resonating within him. He wished he could articulate it, because he'd felt the same connection in Paris, even before they'd ever spoken. He'd watched her from afar, intrigued, drawn by her energy. As the weeks passed, he'd grown increasingly determined to meet her, and then when they'd finally talked, at the end of the program, the real-life connection had been better than his imagination.

Kismet.

Fate.

But then she'd left.

Sometimes he wondered if she hadn't run away, if she'd stayed in Paris with him, would they have stayed together? Could they have made it work?

He didn't know, but the fact that he was just as attracted to her now, thirty years later, said something. The fact that just kissing her made him want so much more time told him he was invested, and yes, just possibly in it for the long haul.

"I THINK YOU BETTER BRING ME UP TO SPEED," ANDI SAID between bites of pecan pie, a pie she'd brought since it wasn't Thanksgiving without it. "I had no idea you and Jack were together."

Paige's fork hovered in the air. It took every bit of restraint not to turn and look at him again. "It's a very new thing," she said carefully. She trusted Andi not to talk to anyone in the math department about Paige seeing Jack. Getting romantically close to colleagues wasn't forbidden, but Paige was private, and she didn't want her peers, or students, to know she'd gotten close to Jack.

"He's only been here a couple months," Andi answered.

"I actually had a date with him thirty years ago." Paige blurted the words and then mentally kicked herself when both Andi and Margot looked at her with avid interest. "In Paris," she added self-consciously.

"It just gets more intriguing all the time." Andi cut into the flakey crust. "You were what? A teenager?"

"No. I was twenty. Almost twenty-one."

"How old was Jack?"

Paige flushed. "Twenty-five."

"And you had a romance?"

Margot was looking back and forth as if watching a tennis match. Paige felt slightly queasy. Was it a mistake to share that she'd known Jack before? Again, Andi wouldn't say anything to anyone, but still, it'd been a secret until now. "It was just one night." Paige managed a smile, and then her smile faded when she realized how that sounded. "All pretty innocent."

Andi smiled, a very knowing smile. Margot continued to silently follow along.

Paige wished Elizabeth would sit down and save her, but Elizabeth was nowhere in sight.

"You told me last year you weren't interested in dating again," Andi added, taking a ladylike bite. "But I'm glad you changed your mind. You didn't have a happy marriage. You deserve to know what a good one is like."

Paige almost choked on her sip of tea. "We're not getting married. We're dating."

"Why wouldn't you get married?"

"Why should we get married?" Paige countered just as quickly. "Marriage is not the end all, be all."

"I wanted to get married," Margot interjected quietly. "Badly. It never happened."

Relieved to be off the hook, Paige turned to Margot. "Was there never anyone special?"

"No, there was. We met in New York, fell head over heels. We lived together for ten years, we were engaged for the last five years, and then, nothing." She stared across the table, lost in thought. After a moment she shook her head and pushed a lock of faded brown hair behind her ear. "He just changed his mind."

"I'm sorry," Andi said quietly. "That's heartbreaking."

Margot looked at Andi, expression pained. "He married someone else within a year. I shouldn't have hung on so long, hoping for the wedding, hoping for the family and the children. I should have realized he wasn't ever going to marry me. But he was a screenwriter, really talented, at least, I thought so, and I never wanted to put any pressure on him."

Andi clasped Margot's hand. "That's rotten. And most unfair. But you're young, you still have time."

"I'm in my forties."

"Just a baby," Andi replied with a wink. "Don't get discouraged. You'll meet your Prince Charming one day."

"I don't think I want a prince," Margot answered grimly, "just a nice boy next door would do. Someone kind, honest, dependable."

Those words, *someone kind, honest, dependable* stayed with Paige even as she finished dessert and then went looking for her daughter so they could say their goodbyes.

Yes, that's what Paige wanted, too. Kind, honest, dependable. But also, someone smart. Someone funny. Someone really comfortable, as well as good in bed.

Was that asking for too much?

"What did you think of Oliver?" Ashley asked as soon as they had gotten into Paige's car. But before Paige could say a word, Ashley answered her own question. "I really liked him. He's a director. He works all over the world. He's worked with some seriously famous people."

Paige checked her smile as she buckled up and started the car. "I thought he was a really nice person."

Ashley wrinkled her nose. "That's it? A nice person? He's smart. Funny. A cool, creative guy. Successful, too."

"I like that he and his dad have such a good relationship. That made me happy to see."

"He's not what you would call handsome, but he's not unattractive."

Startled, Paige shot Ashley a curious glance. "What are

you talking about? He's very handsome. He has that Orlando Bloom look."

"Orlando is prettier. Oliver is more . . . rugged? Masculine? That's not the point, though. The point is he's doing what he wants to do, and he's obviously good at it. Just this fall he's worked in New Zealand, Vancouver, LA." Ashley tipped her head against the seat, closed her eyes. "That's what I want. I want to do really interesting things. I don't want to work at some desk, for some company, and not be alive." She opened her eyes, looked at her mom. "For example, I would hate what you do. It's almost always the same old, same old. I think that's awful. I'd be miserable."

Paige adjusted the air. "My life is not same old, same old. I do different things every day. I've different students—"

"Same subjects."

"Not this year. Look at me. On Saturday, two days from now, I'm going to Africa. How is that same old, same old?"

"That's because Jack put it together. You would've never done a trip like that on your own."

That was true, Paige silently acknowledged. She wouldn't have thought of anything so far away, so foreign to what she knew, so risky. A hundred things could go wrong. She didn't have the faintest idea how she'd fix any of the problems, either. She would be relying heavily on Jack, and strangers. It wasn't her nature to rely on others, but this time she'd have to.

Paige thought of Yellowstone last month, and how she'd relied on Jack there, and everything had worked out. The trip had been smooth, details were handled, there had been no headaches, other than Sheila, and Paige couldn't even resent Sheila, not after Sheila had scared away the bear. The trip to Arusha would work out, too. Jack would see them through. She could count on Jack, she knew that.

"I'm excited about the trip," she said, "and yes, I wouldn't have thought of it, but I'm going, and I'm looking forward to seeing new things and learning new things." She looked over at Ashley. "Sometimes adventure is right there, waiting for us. Sometimes we don't even see it because we're so busy assuming we know everything."

Ashley laughed and reached out to pat her mom's arm. "Listen to the family philosopher. So much wisdom, Mom."

Paige glanced out toward the ocean on her right. The earlier tendrils of fog were growing thicker, obscuring the sky and water. November was so unpredictable. Her first Thanksgiving in California had been hot and sunny. Her second one had been cool and gray, but not cold. Her third had been sunny, but chilly, and now her fourth, soupy with fog.

"Do you think you and Jack are going to stay together?" Ashley asked, breaking the silence. "I mean, do you see this as serious?"

Paige didn't answer immediately. She wasn't sure how to. "Mom?"

Paige drew a deep breath, trying to ignore the quickening of her pulse. Thinking about Jack made her feel so many things. Always nerves, always excitement, and now this constant fluttery feeling in her middle. Butterflies, out-of-control butterflies. "Oh, Ashley. I don't know. Maybe that's why this is so hard for me. He has one more semester here and then he's back to Princeton. He travels constantly, speaking at conferences all over the world, teaching for different universities all over the world. That's not me. I'm a homebody. My life is you girls. I'm happy with you girls."

Ashley reached out, took her mom's hand, gave it a squeeze. "I'm glad. I like having you to myself. I'd hate to have to share you permanently with someone else. It's better just us girls, isn't it?"

Paige nodded, and yet her chest tightened, and her heart plummeted. Was it better? Would she be happier once Jack was gone?

No. She'd miss him. She'd miss him a lot. Her life would be quieter, emptier. Her heart would be emptier. She'd be sad.

Paige wasn't looking forward to that. She hadn't asked for

change, hadn't thought she wanted change, but then Jack entered her life, and everything felt different. Good different. Exciting different. She hadn't thought she was lonely. Hadn't thought she was missing anything, but life was different with Jack in it. She was different with Jack in it. She felt like she had a friend, a partner in crime, someone she could hang out with, someone who wanted to hang out with her. Elizabeth always had a family to return to. Jack had no one at home waiting for him. And she—well, until Ashley arrived—had no one waiting for her. It felt as if they'd carved out a little world for themselves, a space they belonged in, but once he left . . . ?

Once he was back in New Jersey?

She shook her head, not liking the thought, not comfortable thinking that far ahead, because she couldn't see how it would work. She wasn't about to move, and he wasn't going to leave his very sweet position at Princeton. Neither of them was cut out for a long-distance relationship. And quite frankly, Jack didn't strike her as the type to want a serious relationship. She imagined he was happy with things as they were.

Which meant this was probably all it would be. The rest of this semester. And then Spring semester, and . . .

Her eyes burned and her throat ached. She swallowed around the lump. Why even go there right now? Why anticipate the goodbye? It wasn't for months. She ought to be like Jack and just live in the moment. He said it worked for him. He said it made him happy. Could it possibly work for her? Paige didn't know, but she'd have to try.

Chapter 17

PAIGE COULDN'T SLEEP FRIDAY NIGHT. SHE TOSSED AND turned, aware that she'd be leaving for Tanzania the next day, meeting up with Jack and the students on the campus tomorrow. It wasn't an early departure; the flight was at six in the evening, and she had all morning to handle last minute details, but she couldn't turn her brain off. She wasn't worried or scared, just amped.

Mentally, she went through everything she'd meant to do, bills she'd wanted to pay, calls she'd wanted to make. She'd talked to her mother for an hour yesterday. She'd also spoken to her brother, Rob. She'd had numerous calls with Nichole and Michelle, and even a big group Zoom yesterday with all three girls and her.

She wanted to sleep because tomorrow night would not be restful. It was a red-eye flight and Paige found it hard to sleep on planes.

She scrolled through the news apps on her phone. All the headline news was about the same thing, a huge bushfire in Australia. Paige read the news with trepidation. It sounded devastating. Even though it was late, she texted Jack. The news coming from Australia is terrible.

It gets worse every year, he answered.

I'm so sorry, Paige responded.

Me too.

She felt the heaviness in his words and knew how much he worried about climate change. So much of his work addressed the issue, but it wasn't enough. He and a handful of scientists couldn't save the Earth, not without more citizens on board. See you tomorrow, she added.

Looking forward to it.

Paige woke with a start and glanced at her phone. It was only seven. No need to panic. She could even go back to sleep for a while. Instead she unplugged her phone and returned to the news to check on the wildfires.

They were out of control. She turned off her phone. She wished she hadn't checked.

Paige dragged herself from bed, started the coffee, and looked at her luggage sitting by the door, ready to go. They were supposed to meet at school at one, with their departure from school scheduled for one twenty, which would allow for traffic and still give them three hours at the airport. Jack had planned a session for everyone so it wasn't wasted time.

Ashley emerged from the guest bedroom, dressed, hair styled, and in full makeup. "How did you sleep, Mom?"

"Not great. I think I'm too keyed up." She wanted to ask if Ashley had an audition but didn't want to open a can of worms. "You look nice."

"Thank you."

Paige filled her coffee cup, waited for her daughter to say more. She didn't. "You're sure you're going to be okay here while I'm gone?"

"I'll survive. And don't worry, I'll water your plants on the patio. Nothing will die."

"That's reassuring."

"You'll be gone how long? Sixteen days?"

Paige nodded. "Three or four of them are travel days."

"That's a long trip."

"I know."

"Can't believe you're flying coach the whole way. That's going to be miserable."

Paige stepped back to give Ashley access to the coffee pot. "As a family, we always fly coach."

Ashley reached into the cupboard for the big pink mug that read *Mom loves me best* and poured herself coffee. "Yeah, but you'd think the university could have upgraded you. You're a professor. There should be some perks for being a grown-up."

"Apparently not." Paige suppressed a smile. She didn't know where the mug came from, but it was all the girls' favorite. Whenever all three girls were visiting, Paige would hide the mug to keep them from fighting over it. "Are we still going to breakfast?"

"Can we make it brunch? We're not in a hurry to head out, are we?"

"We have plenty of time before I need to be at school."

"Good, because there's this online film class I've signed up for and it begins soon. Oliver is actually giving it—"

"Oliver . . . as in Oliver King?"

"Yes, Mom, Oliver King," Ashley answered impatiently, adding the tiniest bit of sugar-free creamer to her coffee. "I'll mute myself as much as I can, but in case I have to unmute, don't be doing anything crazy. That would just embarrass all of us."

Paige watched her daughter return to the guest bedroom rather amazed, as well as a little worried. It was good to see Ashley in high spirits, but why was she taking a class from Oliver? What was the class about?

Paige sat down on the couch in the living room and turned on the TV, making sure the volume was low, even as she felt little ripples of nervous energy. She was heading to Arusha today. Once she left for Orange, she wouldn't be back home for weeks. Paige couldn't remember the last time she was gone for a week, much less two weeks. It wasn't going to be like a trip to a fancy Cancún resort, either. Everything was going to be really different. It'd be a fascinating experience. She'd have a real adventure. Now, if only the adventure was a little less petrifying.

Not quite three hours later they were heading to breakfast. It was foggy again, the gray fog low and thick, much like it had been on Thanksgiving. Ashley wanted to eat somewhere inside, somewhere warm, and they ended up in San Clemente at a little French restaurant known for their espresso drinks and omelets. Paige would have been more comfortable eating closer to home, but her luggage was in the car so if time was tight, they could go straight to Orange from the restaurant.

The waiter was slow to take their order and Paige tried not to glance at her watch. She didn't want to be the last person to arrive on campus but at the same time, she didn't want to stress Ashley, either. "Are you going to look for a job while I'm gone?" Paige asked, relieved that the waiter had finally made an appearance.

Ashley shrugged.

"I'm sure a lot of places are hiring for Christmas," Paige added lightly.

"I don't want to work retail. I could make a lot more money waitressing."

"Then apply at a bunch of restaurants."

"I don't know of any good ones hiring right now."

Paige bit her tongue, counted to five. "What will you do while I'm gone, then?"

"I don't know." She shrugged again. "I'm not really stressing about it. Something will come up eventually."

Paige struggled with herself. She knew she was a worrier, she knew she tended to crave control, but money was tight, and the girls were all paying back student loans, making car payments, as well as dealing with balances on credit cards. Paige detested debt, particularly credit card debt. Ashley carried high balances on her credit cards and even though she didn't ask for financial help, it troubled Paige that Ashley's solution to limited financial means was to open a new credit card.

"So," Paige said casually. "How was the film class this morning?"

"Good. Interesting."

"How did you find out about the class?"

"I did some online sleuthing, and it popped up."

"Was Oliver surprised to see you?"

Ashley shrugged. "I didn't ask him."

Paige swallowed her exasperation. Ashley could be maddening, and right before her trip wasn't the time to create a rift.

Exactly at one, Ashley dropped off Paige and her luggage on the Orange campus, right next to the large bus. "I'll be home late on the thirteenth," Paige said, giving her youngest a fierce hug. "Don't worry about getting me. It might be late—"

"I'll get you, Mom. I'll be so excited to see you."

Paige smiled, smoothed Ashley's long hair back from her face. "Be careful. Be smart. Always lock the door—"

"I do, Mom. Don't worry. I lived in New York for two years. I can handle Dana Point."

"Still," Paige said, stifling a rush of anxiety. "I'm going to be so far away."

"Nothing will happen. Not to me, or to you."

"You're right." Paige hugged her once more, and then watched Ashley return to the car and drive away. But as Ashley disappeared, Paige felt a wave of panic. She had a nagging sensation that she'd forgotten something, only she couldn't remember what she'd forgotten. Mentally, she went through it all again. She'd packed, and repacked, chargers, converters, phone, laptop, clothes, medicine—lots of medicine—books, binders, notebooks. Passport. Wallet. Credit cards, ATM card. She should be fine.

She really should be.

So why wasn't she calmer?

Jack wasn't there when she joined the students, but the students greeted her with smiles and hellos. Each student had a backpack, and there near the bus was a mound of duffel bags.

Jack suddenly appeared, carrying a small duffel and wearing a modest backpack. He was dressed in a T-shirt and jeans. The short sleeves revealed thick biceps, and his gaze was warm as it met hers, making her feel funny, fizzy things. The energy shifted the moment Jack joined them, students now joking and laughing. Jack was like the master of ceremonies, making everything appear easy, effortless.

She loved that about him.

She might just love him.

One more terrifying thought.

Jack had the students board the bus, and then he went down the aisle, collecting passports. Back at the front of the bus, he paired the passports with visas. He went through the stack a second time, double-checking, before counting heads.

"We're one short," he said, standing at the front of the bus, arms crossed over his chest. In the snug T-shirt that lovingly outlined his muscular chest he reminded Paige more of a football coach than a famous science professor.

"Who are we missing?" she asked.

The students looked around, several shaking heads. Paige immediately checked her faculty email. There it was. "Molly Bellamy," she said, rising and crossing to Jack, showing him the email. She dropped her voice. "There's been a family emergency and she can't make it."

Jack's brow creased. "That's too bad. She really looked forward to this trip. Can you email her back? Let her know if the situation changes once we head to the airport, have her call me, and I'll come out and get her checked in and walked through security."

Alarmed, Paige hesitated. Her gaze searched Jack's. "I don't want you to miss the flight, too. I can't do this without you."

"You won't have to. Just give her my number. Tell her we want her to come, and we can make this work. She's got plenty of time to get to LAX."

Paige loved his commitment to his students, appreciated that he would bend rules to make things work for those in need. She quickly typed the information, adding her phone number, too. She hoped Molly would make it, but she had no idea what the emergency was, and if it was even feasible for Molly to come.

The bus ride north to Los Angeles was downright jubilant. Students joked and sang songs as if they were heading to summer camp. Paige glanced at Jack, who'd taken the seat next to her and was reading a sheaf of papers. "Is it always like this?" she asked.

He glanced up, looking at her over his reading glasses, looking every inch the scholarly professor. "My students are several years older. But there are usually high spirits. It feels like we're going on holiday."

"But we're not," she said, reading between the lines.

"Let's just put it this way, they won't be singing on the trip home. They're going to be exhausted." He reached for her hand, his fingers curling around hers. "Are you going to be okay, getting everyone home on your own? I feel guilty that I'm staying, leaving you to—"

"I'm not worried." Her gaze met his, held. "I'm a professional."

He laughed quietly, a warm husky rumble of sound that made her smile.

"It will be a little stressful, but that's to be expected." She hesitated. "Now, if it were anyone else, I wouldn't be okay. But for you . . . I'm afraid you've wrapped me around your little finger."

"Have I?" He looked pleased by that. "Good to know."

AN HOUR BEFORE BOARDING, JACK GATHERED THE STU-dents, having them form a circle at an empty gate to tell them about some of the different customs they'd encounter, and how important it was to be respectful of the different values and culture of Tanzanians.

"I know some of you have been doing reading of your own, preparing for our trip," Jack said. "Let's see what you all know before I bore you. What are some of the customs we need to be aware of so that we don't offend during our stay?"

One of the girls raised her hand. "Ask before you snap," she said crisply. "It's rude in Tanzania to take a photo of someone without their permission."

"Don't smell your food. Sniffing it is considered disre-spectful," another student said, "as it implies there is some-thing wrong with it."

Jack checked his smile. "Greetings are important as well. They take time. Every person must be acknowledged, starting with the elderly or most senior. Tanzanians deeply respect their seniors and always show deference to the elderly." His gaze skimmed the ring of students, lingering for a moment on Paige. For a split second he forgot what they were discussing and then he forced himself to focus. "There's another big cultural differ-ence we haven't discussed. Anyone remember? Know it?"

"Your left hand," one of the boys said. "It's considered unclean."

"This is true in many countries. You never shake with your left hand, you never take food with your left hand, as the left hand is reserved for bathroom activities, the right hand for eating and greeting."

The students laughed. Paige grinned, too.

Jack paused a moment just to take in her smile. He loved

the shape of her lips, and the way her eyes crinkled. "We'll have some more specific food discussions in Arusha at the Center, but in case any of you develop an attachment to another in our class, be aware that due to Tanzanian's modesty, all displays of affection are problematic. No hand-holding, hugging, kissing. In your own room, you can wear whatever you want, but the moment you step outside, you're to keep thighs, midriffs, and so forth covered. Please don't make me, or Dr. Newsome, police you. That's not why we're here."

Jack continued to check for messages from Molly, but she never did make it to LAX for the flight. He wondered again about the family emergency, but there was nothing he could do. In the meantime, the students were loading up on snacks at the airport shops and milling about, excitement tangible.

He looked for Paige, who stood off to the side on the phone. She joined him a few minutes later, her expression not as bright.

"What's wrong?"

She drew a deep breath, shrugged. "Nothing's wrong. I'm just a worrier."

"Who is worrying you?"

"Ashley." Her brows pulled, lips pursed. "She's decided to look for an agent and is going to get new headshots next week. That's always expensive."

"She's an adult."

"I know."

"Let her try."

Paige sighed. "I'm trying."

"Let her fail."

"That . . . that's even harder."

He hugged her, not caring who saw. "You got this, champ," he said, voice low. "Relax. Let it go."

PAIGE WAS ONE OF THE LAST TO BOARD THE ISTANBUL flight. As she headed to her seat, she scanned the back of the plane looking for her students. She wasn't sitting near Jack, but there were two students in front of her, and another student in a window seat across the aisle from her.

Paige tried to get comfortable, aware that it would be thirteen hours to Turkey, a two hour layover in Istanbul, and then another seven and a half hours to Zanzibar, where they'd overnight before a short flight to Arusha the next day.

Paige had brought books to read, and there were in-flight movies to watch, but after their meal, she decided to try to sleep, but it was impossible with so many people around her. At one point in the middle of the night, she left her seat, moving quietly through the dark cabin to use the restroom. After, she made a loop through the economy section to stretch her legs. Jack was asleep on the far side of the plane. He had a middle seat, and he was sound asleep, an inflatable neck pillow bracing his head, the airplane blanket over his chest. She watched him a moment, feeling protective. Asleep, he looked mortal, and not the larger-than-life Jack King.

Back at her seat, she read for a half hour before trying a movie. The two students seated in front of her were doing the same. There were going to be some very tired people tomorrow, Paige included.

The lights came on two hours before landing so the flight crew could serve a simple continental breakfast. The coffee was strong but bitter, and Paige needed an extra packet of sugar to make it palatable, and then they were making their final descent. Off the plane, Jack counted heads and made sure everyone was together as they went through customs—the line was very long—before heading to the next gate.

Jack told everyone they had forty-five minutes before boarding, and everyone was welcome to buy food, shop, explore but to be back on time because he wouldn't go looking for missing bodies, and he wasn't going to miss the flight. "You'll be on your own," he said. "You're an adult, and you'll have to figure out how to get back home because you won't be able to join us in Tanzania."

Paige noticed that some students didn't move from the gate area, while others went off to buy juice and breakfast rolls. Every student was back with at least fifteen minutes to spare. No one wanted to be left behind.

"You're good at this," Paige said to Jack. They were sitting side by side in the waiting area. She'd sat down first and then he took the open seat next to her.

"I've had a lot of experience."

"You trust them to do what needs to be done."

"Set high standards, have clear expectations, and hold them accountable. It's the only way these programs work."

"Have you ever had a student miss a connection?"

"Yes."

"And?"

"He had to pay a hefty change fee and use his return ticket to head home."

She studied the hard planes of Jack's face, the light in his eyes, the firm mouth she so enjoyed kissing. He glanced at her, eyebrow lifting. She just smiled. "I like you, Jack King."

He laughed and reached for her hand, his fingers slipping through hers. "I like you, too, Paige Newsome."

She loved the feel of his hand around hers, loved the warmth and comfort. "I wouldn't have come on this trip with anyone else." She looked into his eyes, thinking they were gorgeous with all the gold and green flecks. "But I'm excited to be doing this. Thank you for nudging—um, shoving—me out of my comfort zone."

"You're welcome. And if we didn't have twenty-three students watching, I'd kiss you right now."

"Probably not a good idea, then." She looked down at their hands. "We probably shouldn't be doing this, either."

"Once we're in Tanzania we won't."

"That's right. It's considered PDA."

"By the way, did I ever tell you how much Oliver liked you?"

She smiled, pleased. "No. But I'm glad he did."

"He thinks you're a keeper and I need to hang on to you."

Paige felt her face warm. She thought of Ashley's feedback, that Jack was nice, but Paige's life was perfect the way it was . . . single. She hadn't objected when Ashley had said it, but Paige should have. She should have at least let Ashley know how much she cared for Jack, and how badly she wanted him to stick around. "I really liked him, too. You did a good job raising him."

"That's all Oliver. He was a great kid, and he's become a man I very much admire."

"I like your relationship with him. It's based on respect."

"I love Oliver, and he knows it. He knows I'll always have his back."

"You wouldn't leave him behind at an airport?"

"If he headed to the bar to drink, I would."

Paige's eyes widened. "Is that what happened with your student?"

He nodded. "Amsterdam. A few years back. A student headed to the bar for some drinks and forgot why he was there in the first place."

"Oh no."

"Oh, yes. And I'm fine with alcohol as long as it's in moderation, but drinking to excess? I've no patience with it."

"I've noticed you don't drink a lot," she said.

"My parents both drank. Australians like their drink, and it's fine if you can hold your liquor, but if you can't, if you're getting into trouble, forgetting your responsibilities, it needs to stop."

His tone was flinty, his expression hard. She knew there was a story behind his words but didn't want to probe. "Ted drank," she said after a moment.

Jack's expression darkened. "I know. Just one more reason I don't like the guy."

"You don't like him?"

"How could I? He treated you badly. Makes me livid just thinking about it."

She didn't know what to say, and yet her heart was full,

and her eyes gritty. Jack made her feel secure and beautiful. Desirable. It was a heady sensation, but it also made her realize how much she'd missed being wanted.

The gate agents interrupted, announcing that boarding was commencing for the Turkish Air flight to Zanzibar, starting with premiere passengers and those in first class. It would be awhile before the group from Orange University would board, but Paige stood and did a quick count of their students, making sure no one had slipped away while she and Jack were talking. Fortunately, everyone was present and accounted for. Good. One flight down, two to go.

Eight and a half hours later the jet taxied down the runway in Zanzibar. It was not quite four in the morning in Tanzania and all was dark, with just the runway lights showing them the way.

Sleepy students gathered their belongings. Paige hid her yawn, exhausted. Again she'd tried to sleep, but couldn't. She'd already adjusted her watch, but after doing the math realized it was six o'clock in LA. Dinner time.

It was a slow file off the plane, and Jack herded them all to one customs agent, greeting the agent in a language Paige wasn't familiar with. The agent replied, and Jack said something else that made the customs agent laugh.

The students all had their passports and visas out, and with a gesture from the agent, the students lined up and filed through one at a time.

"What language were you speaking?" she asked Jack as he dropped back to wait with her. They'd go through at the end, once the students had been processed.

"Swahili."

"Are you fluent?"

"I know just enough to get me into trouble, and not enough to keep me out of jail."

She laughed softly, amused. Despite two long consecutive flights, Jack looked rested, even if beautifully rumpled. She loved that he looked as handsome in a T-shirt as he did in a linen shirt. She didn't like to think of herself as shallow, but Jack was incredibly easy on the eyes.

When it was her turn to speak to the customs agent, it was all very matter-of-fact, and then she was cleared, her passport stamped in two places, and Jack came through last. She smiled at him as he joined on the other side. "I feel a little like Mom and Dad," she said.

He looked down into her eyes, expression warm, intimate. "Funny," he answered, voice husky. "I don't think of you as Mom at all."

Despite her fatigue, and the fact that her mouth tasted of cotton and her eyes felt dry as sand, she felt buoyant. Happy.

Jack led the way to baggage claim, where they waited for the bags to appear. Paige's bright lime duffel was one of the first and Jack scooped it up, placing it at his feet. The rest of the bags came spilling out, and it appeared that every bag had made it.

"One more flight," he said. "This is the fast one."

She looked up at him. "I thought we were staying here for one night and flying in the morning."

"We were supposed to, but the airline gave us a much better deal if we went early this morning. It saved us considerably."

"In that case, onward."

Jack directed students from baggage claim to the far end of the terminal, where a uniformed woman was waiting for them along with two young men in matching uniforms.

Paige listened as Jack greeted the young woman in Swahili.

The woman turned to their group and switched to English to greet them. "Good afternoon, my friends from America. My name is Lakeisha, and I'm going to help you on your way to Arusha. The good news is that we will have very nice flying weather. The sun is coming up soon, the airplanes are here, the pilots are ready, and we will get you aboard in a half hour. Leave your bags here with me and do not worry, I promise you'll see them again in Arusha."

Thirty minutes later, Jack raised his hand. "I need twelve of you. The rest will board with Dr. Newsome."

Boarding took place quickly, with Jack and twelve students boarding one of the small aircraft on the tarmac, while Lakeisha led Paige and the remaining students to the second.

Lakeisha gestured for Paige to take one of the front seats, and then told the students to fill in and take any open seat. Once all small bags had been stowed, Lakeisha stepped off the plane, and the flight attendant walked them through the safety briefing. Life jackets. Oxygen masks. Proper position to brace for a crash landing.

Paige listened attentively, hoping, praying, none of those precautions would be needed. Fortunately, they weren't, and they landed in an hour, with a hop on the runway. The planes turned and slowly made their way back to the small terminal.

Once they'd disembarked and collected their duffels, they followed Jack outside to the curb where three minibuses awaited them. Jack greeted one of the drivers with hugs and high fives. There was a lot of laughter and then the students were stowing their suitcases in the cargo hold of each minibus, and then they all boarded the buses.

It was a thirty-minute drive from the airport to the Center on the outskirts of Arusha. The landscape was lushly green, with striking trees and rich red soil. Mount Meru formed a majestic backdrop as the sun continued to rise.

The white minibuses pulled through tall iron gates, then carried on down the dirt lane until they parked in front of a large four-story glass-and-stone building. Staff immediately appeared and Jack climbed from his van to warmly greet the man and woman, a married couple who'd taken over managing the Center, a move Jack apparently approved of. Jack introduced the couple to the students. "This is Nyah and Jabari Mkapa," he said. "Old friends and wonderful managers of the Center. I've worked with them for many years, and we couldn't be in better hands. Now let's get you checked in."

Jack had already worked out the rooming lists, and as students received their keys and maps from reception, he sent them off in pairs to settle in, letting them know they'd meet for brunch in just over an hour. "Brunch will be served on the ground floor in the restaurant, as will most of our meals. Workshops, meetings, and speakers will all take place on the second level in the conference space. Rooms are on the third and fourth floors. Dr. Newsome is on floor three; I am on floor four. The pool is behind the building in the garden. You have your maps, don't get lost, and see you at ten thirty. Oh, and do set your watch. It's just nine twenty right now."

Paige clutched her map and key and dragged her luggage to the elevator. Only a few students were taking the elevator; many had given up waiting for it and had climbed the stairs. Next time, she'd take the stairs, too.

Her room was clean, with crisp linens, a welcoming bed, and drapes she closed against the sun. After using the bathroom, she dropped onto her bed, and the next thing she knew there was an awful banging on her door.

Paige sat up, groggy, and stumbled to the door. She opened it with a yawn. Jack. She should have known it was him. "You can stop knocking now."

"You were out," he said.

"I was sleeping."

"Everyone's eating. I figured I'd better get you." He reached out and lifted a long blond strand of hair from her lashes, smoothing it off to the side. "I know how grumpy you can be without regular feedings."

"Humph." She glared at him, her body heavy, her head aching. "It's one in the morning at home. We should be sleeping."

"No, it's eleven here, and if you don't come now, you'll be really hungry later."

"I hurt all over."

"That's the jet lag. It'll get easier every day." He flashed a very white smile. "And then we'll go home, and it'll start all over."

"I hate you."

"You are adorable. Get your key. You're coming with me."

"Give me a second. I need a scrunchie for my hair." In her small bathroom she dug through her cosmetics bag and added a swipe of pink color to her cheeks and lips and then smoothed her hair into a simple ponytail. Phone tucked into her back pocket, she locked the door and walked with Jack to the lodge.

"Am I really the only one who overslept?" she asked as they approached the restaurant, which had huge sliding doors open to a patio. The outdoor patio was filled with tables. It's where most of the students had chosen to sit.

"Everyone else had roommates to get them here on time." His put his hand on her elbow, steering her through tables. "The buffet is against the wall. Sit wherever you want."

Paige spooned yogurt into a bowl, topped it with granola, added some fruit, and was looking for an open spot when a student waved her over. "Sit with us, Dr. Newsome," the student said.

"Thank you." Paige sat down, smothered another yawn. She felt like she couldn't wake up. She was just about to look for coffee when Jack appeared and placed a cup of coffee in front of her. It already had milk in it. She looked up at him, her gaze meeting his. "Thank you."

He nodded and left. She watched him walk away. Jack brought her coffee. It was such a little thing, and yet it made her feel loved.

She felt a pinch in her chest. Her heart gave a painful beat. She'd fallen for him.

Overnight she'd gone from safe and secure to embracing danger. She could hardly recognize herself these days. Where was cautious Paige? How had she become this impulsive, adventurous, risk-taking woman?

As if aware of her thoughts, Jack lifted his head and looked across the tables, his eyes locking with hers. The intensity in his eyes made her chest tighten again.

She did love him. She loved him. How had it happened?

Chapter 18

WHEN EVERYONE HAD FINISHED EATING, JACK STOOD UP and talked about the schedule for the rest of the day. "I know we've been traveling a long time, but we're here to see as much as we can, and learn about the environment as well as the community. Jabari has very graciously arranged for us to visit his family's coffee plantation on the lower slopes of Mount Meru. We are going to leave right after breakfast; you'll have fifteen minutes to get your cameras and notebooks, and then be on the bus. Jabari is accompanying us, and once we reach his home, his older brother will give us the tour of their town and the farm, and if we're lucky, we'll be able to have a cup of coffee before we go."

The students quickly dispersed and regrouped soon after. At one point during the tour, Jack's fingers brushed hers. It was a secret touch, brief, but it was exactly what she craved. Warmth, connection. The rest of the day passed in a blur of motion and activity. Jack walked with her to her room after the evening activities ended. She was so tired she swayed on her feet as she unlocked the door. "Want to come in?" she asked.

"I'll keep you awake, and you need sleep."

She yawned, covered her mouth, and nodded.

He kissed her forehead, then the tip of her nose, and finally a lingering kiss on the lips. "Sleep well."

"I will."

She fell into bed, certain she'd sleep for days. Instead she woke up in the middle of the night, wide awake.

She stared into the dark. Her stomach growled. She turned on the light, reached for a book, and began to read. She was not a fan of jet lag.

THE STUDENTS SETTLED INTO THE PROGRAM IN ARUSHA immediately, excited, curious, passionate to learn. Speakers from the Nelson Mandela Institute came to them the first few days, and then they were out later in the week, traveling by large jeeps to visit specific locations in the park where scientists were working, collecting data to be used in future studies. Every day Jack found ways to let her know he was thinking of her. He'd give her a smile, a brush of his hand over hers, or pull her aside for a stolen kiss in a dark corridor. The stolen kisses were exciting. Every touch, every glance made her long for more. It didn't help that time was passing quickly, too quickly, with the first week over and the second week progressing with the same breakneck speed.

Students didn't want to leave. Paige felt the same. When still at home, two weeks had sounded so long, but now that she was here, immersed in the field program, housed under the same roof as Jack, Paige didn't want the experience to end. She wasn't ready to say goodbye to the mountains, the big sky, the brilliant Tanzanian lecturers who were becoming friends. Her world felt large and new. Jack made her feel new and exciting. She was only realizing now how much she'd missed by staying in one place, doing one thing. Travel was important. Learning new things was necessary. Meeting others essential.

As was love.

Sunday night after the students had disappeared to their rooms, or to hang out by the pool, Paige went in search of Jack. She knew he was working on a paper. Whenever he was writing a lot, he was polite but distracted. He'd been distracted for two days.

She knocked on his door and he opened it, standing in the doorway in cargo shorts and a white T-shirt that was molded to the planes of his chest.

"You must have read my mind," he said. "I was just about to come look for you."

"Were you, now?"

"I finally finished the paper and it's off."

"That must feel good."

"A little brain-dead, but that's okay." He smiled at her. "If it's okay with you."

She stepped into his room, closed the door behind her, and moved into his arms. "I didn't come for your mind."

"Don't tell me you're only interested in my body."

She squeezed his arms, feeling his ribs, his waist, his body, so hard and strong. "I miss you."

His arms wrapped around her, and he held her close, closer. "I've missed you like mad."

"I leave in a week."

"You can come back."

She tipped her head up to see his face. Jack looked handsome but tired. How many late nights had he been working, writing . . . planning . . . putting together notes for his show? "I think you work too much."

He kissed her. "I do, too."

"Can I stay with you tonight?" she whispered against his mouth. "I'll be gone before anyone wakes."

"Yes."

"We shouldn't, I know the rules—"

"Yes, we should." His hands cupped her face, and he drank her in, a deep, intoxicating kiss that made her feel beautiful and loved.

He locked the door, turned out the lights, and then, kissing her again, he walked her back to the bed and continued kissing her as he undressed her. It wasn't completely dark. The curtains hadn't been drawn and moonlight poured through the window.

She pulled back the covers and slid between the sheets. He looked down at her, a question in his eyes. "Are we sleeping?" he asked.

"Naked?" She sat up, the sheet covering her chest. "We probably should have left our clothes on for that."

He hesitated, looking almost uncertain for the first time. "What are you thinking?"

"I'm thinking we should use protection. Do you have something?"

Jack's eyebrow lifted a fraction and then he went to his duffel and returned with a foil packet. There might have been two.

He set them down then joined her in bed, stretching out over her.

"What about the condom?" she asked.

"We won't need that for a bit. I just want to touch you. Love you."

Paige's eyes burned and her chest filled with emotion. She wanted that, too.

Jack's body was made for loving. She gloried in the shape and feel of him, caressing his taut, broad shoulders, the lean length of his torso, the firm muscles in his hips, his rounded butt.

She felt like a girl discovering the world for the first time. Jack kissed her until she couldn't think, and then he worked his way down her body, waking every place he kissed.

When he finally entered her, it was what she'd waited so long for. He'd been right: this, being together, was right. She remembered how she'd wanted him in Paris but had become nervous and shut down. She wasn't nervous anymore. She loved him and needed him, and as he made love to her, she couldn't believe they'd come full circle. Finally.

There was no faking this orgasm. Or the one two hours

later. After the second orgasm, she fell asleep in his arms, draped across his chest, his hand stroking her hair. She was warm, still breathless. Tonight, being together, had been the best, most intense, most sensual experience of her life.

She couldn't wait for it to happen again.

It was back to teaching the next day, and field research Tuesday, and then there were guest speakers Wednesday, ending with Jack's friend, Dr. Kevin Kanumba, a Tanzanian professor who spoke passionately, eloquently, about the human impact on ecosystem dynamics, particularly in the Tanzanian national parks. At Jack's request, Dr. Kanumba stayed for dinner, and his wife, Salma, a professor of education, joined them.

Salma sat next to Paige during dinner. Paige was fascinated by Salma's work in education, and asked dozens of questions about Tanzania's educational system. They were deep in conversation when a woman entered the room.

"Ah, Dr. Ormond," Salma said, nodding. "I'd heard she was coming early."

Paige glanced at Salma. "Camille Ormond?"

Salma nodded. "You know her?"

"Not yet." Paige's voice faltered. She forced a smile, even as she felt baffled and confused. What was Camille doing here? How did Salma Kanumba know? That must mean Jack knew. . . .

She watched as Jack rose and greeted Camille with a kiss on each cheek. If Jack was surprised to see her, he didn't show it. Camille spoke to him in French, slipping her hand into his, and he answered in French, still holding her hand. Paige, who barely remembered her high school Spanish, felt her heart clench with envy and fear.

Camille wasn't anything like Paige pictured. For some reason she'd pictured the French Canadian professor as a beautiful brunette, someone like Andi McDermott in Orange University's math department, with thick dark hair, high cheekbones, fine features. But no, Camille was a redhead, with long straight hair and wide green eyes. She was tall, too, slim like a Victoria's Secret model, with endless legs and a wide, generous mouth.

Watching Jack and Camille together, the ache in Paige's chest deepened. They were close, very close. Camille still loved him. It was evident in the way she smiled up into his face, her gaze locking with his, her expression so hopeful. Wistful.

Paige swallowed around the lump filling her throat, and for the first time, she wondered why Jack had never married Camille. Why did he not want to commit to her?

The answer came to her, hard, with a vengeance. Jack didn't commit. Jack didn't do forever. Jack loved his freedom and the idea of possibility. The idea of what could be was more appealing than what was.

Paige didn't want to marry, but at the same time, if she loved someone, she wanted that person to love her back. She wanted that person to want her, and fight for her. She wanted to be protected and cherished, she wanted the love she hadn't had in years.

Jack suddenly broke off and, switching to English, introduced Paige to Camille. Paige rose and forced a smile, hiding her chaotic emotions. She crossed to Camille, offering the Canadian scientist her hand. "I've heard so much about you," Paige said. "It's so nice to meet you at last."

Camille shook Paige's hand. "I'm not sure what Jack has said, but I hope it is good."

"Very good," Paige reassured her, stepping back.

A chair was brought out for Camille, and she sat down next to Jack and Kevin, and, feeling dismissed, Paige returned to her seat. She sipped her tea, aware that her hands shook. She hoped no one noticed. She didn't want to appear jealous or petty, but she was shocked. Beyond shocked.

Why hadn't Jack told her? Why hadn't he mentioned Camille? His secrecy baffled her. What did he think would happen? That Camille would show up while Paige was on the trip with the students and then slip away, be gone before Paige and the students returned?

If he'd just told her, just prepared her, at least she wouldn't have been so shaken.

As it was, she was heartsick. Who was this Jack? He'd become someone else, a stranger full of secrets.

Paige tried to focus on Salma but couldn't. She excused herself to use the restroom, and when she emerged, Jack was waiting for her in the hall.

"It's not what it looks like," he said, catching her arm to stop her from returning.

Her eyes searched his face. "No. What does it look like?"

"I didn't invite her. She's not meant to be here. She came on her own. This was her idea."

"Coming to dinner, or coming to Arusha?" Paige asked sharply, stomach knotting, cramping. She felt sick. Betrayed.

"She's part of the conference this weekend."

"This isn't a surprise to you. You knew she'd be here."

He swallowed. "In Arusha, yes. But not tonight, not here."

"But you knew she'd be attending your conference at the convention center, while I go with the students on their three-day safari?"

"Yes." A small muscle pulled in his jaw. "I know it looks bad—"

"Yes, Jack," she interrupted tightly, "it does indeed." She tugged her arm from his grasp and returned to the table, grateful for Salma, the arrival of dessert, and conversation.

In between bites of a caramelized banana custard, Salma shared about a program she'd developed, one focused on creating teachers, especially teachers for girls. "Despite government efforts, there are incongruities between education of our boys and girls. Girls still lag behind the boys academically. They have significantly lower attendance rates, higher drop-out rates, and poorer performance. My goal is to change that."

"I'm a mother of three daughters. I believe in the potential of our girls," Paige said.

"I have two daughters, and they will be some of the lucky ones, because we live in Arusha and there are good schools close by. But for girls in the villages, there are often no schools close, and then there is the issue of marrying young. It's said that two out of five girls marry before they are eighteen, and once a girl is pregnant, it is forbidden for her to return to school. So marriage is a problem, as is pregnancy. I want to see more teachers in the villages, teachers dedicated to educating girls."

"I admire your dedication. I support your efforts—"

"Do you? Then maybe you should come teach here," Salma said, smiling. "We have many students who would love to learn math, to learn how to teach it, so our girls love math like you do. It's a special thing when a woman finds math comfortable."

Page was flattered. Moved. "I would hate to take an opportunity away from someone already here, hungry for work and opportunity."

Salma shook her head. "There are not enough women teaching math and science here. Not enough female engineers. Not enough scientists. Not enough women who can do complex equations. Too often, our very brightest young women go overseas, and then stay. The pay is higher in the US, New Zealand, and the UK. The working conditions are better, and I don't blame these young women who want to be able to provide for their families, but it means we are often losing our best talent, and we always look for great minds, and great hearts, to come here and work with our young people."

"I'll make you a deal; if you ever need me, I'll arrange my schedule so I can come." Paige couldn't quite believe she'd said those words, but it was true. She needed to be needed. She wanted to be someplace where she could contribute in a significant, meaningful way. Even though this past semester had been an emotional roller coaster, it had opened her eyes to what she loved best, which was teaching.

"Do you mean that?" Salma asked. "Because if you do, I will remember."

"I give you my word."

PAIGE HAD ALREADY CHANGED FOR THE NIGHT, WASHED her face, and brushed her teeth, when a knock sounded at her door. She knew from the knock who it was. She didn't want to answer. She had nothing to say to him, and she didn't want excuses. Right now, she wasn't even as angry with him as she was with herself for letting down her guard, allowing herself to dream. She'd been foolish. Naive.

She could still see Camille's expression as she looked up at Jack. Paige wondered if she had the same expression when she looked at him.

There was another firm, insistent rap on her door. Jack wasn't going away.

She checked the buttons on her pajama top and opened the door, holding it close to her side so he wouldn't think he was invited in. "Yes, Jack?"

"I'd like to explain."

"I'm not interested."

"I think you owe me a chance—"

"I don't *owe* you anything." Her voice was sharp, hard. Paige paused, regrouped. "There's nothing you can say now, Jack. You should have talked to me weeks ago, let me know in Yellowstone, or on the way home from Yellowstone when you proposed coming here for the field work, that Camille would be here. After what Sheila said to me, you knew I was concerned, sensitive. We had that whole discussion on my cabin's front porch."

"I wanted to tell you—"

"But what? You couldn't? Because I'm scary? Hard to talk to? Emotional?" They were all things Ted had said, reasons why he had to drink. She'd been hurt then and she was hurt now, pain welling up, heightening the disappointment and grief. He wasn't who she'd thought he was. He wasn't her hero after all.

"Can I please come in?"

"No." She stared into his face, her gaze searching his. She saw remorse in his eyes. She saw sadness. But it didn't matter. It was too little, too late. She'd vowed years ago to pay attention, look for signs, face the truth. She was facing the truth now. Jack had many, many gorgeous qualities, but he was also a man who played the field, and she wasn't playing, not anymore. "We have one day until the students leave on their safari and you head to the convention center. Let's just get through tomorrow. I'll see our students off on the safari, and you head to your conference. We'll meet back here Sunday night as planned."

Jack drew a breath, expression pained. "I don't have a relationship with Camille."

"Maybe not," Paige answered, trying to stay calm, controlled. "But you do have a problem with the truth."

AT NINE A.M. FRIDAY MORNING, PAIGE STOOD IN FRONT of the hotel and did a quick head count as her Orange students climbed into three different open-air jeeps, each vehicle with four rows of seats. Paige had their itinerary memorized—today they'd explore Arusha National Park and stay in a campground there, tomorrow they'd visit Ngorongoro Crater, overnighting at a small budget-friendly lodge, and then Sunday would be a visit to Lake Manyara National Park, returning to the hotel in time for dinner. On Monday, everyone—except for Jack—would begin the long flights home.

One of the girls asked Paige why she wasn't coming. "This is your trip," she said. "You've earned a break from me." Paige smiled at her. "Go enjoy yourselves. Just please follow the rules, and stay safe."

Paige watched the jeeps pull out. She felt rather lost as the cars disappeared. Part of her wanted to go, but she wasn't doing well, and she wasn't sleeping, either. She didn't think she'd slept four hours a night since Camille had appeared.

Paige returned to the lobby, and spotting Jabari at the front reception, she crossed to him, asking if there was anything he'd recommend she do, as she had a few days to herself.

He frowned. "You don't want a safari?"

"I don't know. I just didn't feel right camping with the kids."

"They will have a good time, but you should do a grown-up safari. No camping. Quiet and nature."

That sounded rather heavenly. She could use quiet and nature. "It's last-minute, though, not sure where I could go."

"Let me make a few calls." His frown had turned to a smile. "I know people."

Two hours later the phone in her room rang. It was Jabari. He'd booked her on a short safari in southern Tanzania. A car would be coming soon to take her to the airport.

"I have to fly?"

"Yes, Dr. Newsome. It is a short flight. Fifty minutes, maybe. It depends on how heavy the plane is, and how many stops you make."

"And the cost?"

"A good price for you."

She wanted to ask the price. She was notoriously frugal but at this point she wanted to get away more than she wanted to conserve money. "That's wonderful. Thank you. And you know this camp?"

"Very well. My brother used to work there. Shani, the River Camp's director, has all the details: when your plane is landing, when you must return, as I know it's on Sunday. It's all been handled."

"Thank you, Jabari. I'm grateful."

"I'll call you when your car is here."

Paige packed lightly for the two nights she'd be away,

and then wrote a note for Jack, sliding it under his door for him to find on Sunday when he returned from his conference.

J—

I'm slipping away for a few days while the students are on their tour but will be back in time to escort them home.

Paige

She was downstairs when her car arrived, and then spent an hour at the airport, as her plane had a delay. She was relieved when she was escorted with four others to the tarmac. The aircraft was light and small, an eight seater. The pilot, Pierre, took her duffel, stowing it in the cargo hold. Boarding the plane, Paige glanced around. There was an American couple on board. Two women—sisters, it sounded like—from Australia. And then Paige.

She briefly studied the brochure provided by the airline, scanning the safety information, and then picked up the booklet on the history of the airline. The booklet listed each of the company's fourteen pilots: two women, twelve men. Both of the female pilots were young and Black, native Tanzanians. Paige read their bios and then the bio of the pilot flying today. Pierre wasn't from Tanzania. He'd been born and raised in France and had been flying in Tanzania for five years now. It crossed Paige's mind that a few weeks ago she would have asked Pierre how he'd ended up here, flying a small charter plane between African bush camps, but now she didn't care, maybe because Pierre ended up here the way Paige did—maybe he also ran away.

She hadn't meant to sleep, but her exhaustion caught up with her, and the plane was warm. She closed her eyes for just a moment, and before she knew it, the wheels hit the ground hard, bumping the Cessna up, down, even as they hurtled down the runway.

She rubbed her eyes and looked out the small window just in time to see a herd of elephants moving away from the runway. Beyond them a giraffe nibbled on the leaves of a tree, unconcerned by the plane's arrival. The American couple in front of Paige took photo after photo, and she wondered if she should do that. The husband had a camera with an impressive telephoto lens. But she didn't have a fancy camera, nor did she feel like a tourist. To be honest, she didn't feel anything.

Paige only learned she was the only one getting out here when Pierre removed her lime duffel from the cargo hold and said goodbye. He pointed her to the jeep parked off the runway, and then climbed back into the plane.

The plane was taxiing down the runway before she'd even introduced herself to her driver.

"Welcome," her driver said, closing the distance and taking her duffel and small backpack from her. "I am Baraka and it's my pleasure to drive you to our River Camp. Did you see the elephants?" he asked, stowing her bags.

"I did."

He helped her into the jeep. She took a seat behind him, but where she could still see him easily.

"Sometimes we must chase the animals off the runway. Once there was a rhino, and he did not want to move."

"What happened?"

"The plane had to circle until the rhino decided to move."

As they drove away from the airstrip, Baraka asked questions. His English was superb, but with just enough of an accent that she had to lean in and listen closely to make sure she understood what he was asking her. It was noisy in the open jeep, and after a while her answers became shorter and shorter.

Yes, she just flew in from Arusha.

No, she didn't live there, she was working with one of the universities there.

Yes, she was a teacher.

No, she'd never been to the Selous Game Reserve before.

No, she'd never been on a safari before.

They drove and drove, and she wasn't sure what she'd expected, but certainly not this, not an hour of traveling deeply rutted roads into the bush while her driver pointed out animals. Impala. A lone male giraffe. A warthog scrambling through a scrubby plant. They stopped at one point and her driver lifted his binoculars, scanning the horizon. "There was a cheetah earlier," he said.

Paige tried to appear excited, but on the inside, she felt bereft. It struck her that this was a mistake, traveling to southern Tanzania just to be on her own. She liked wildlife as much as the next person, but her heart wasn't in it. She wasn't one of those people who had ever pored over brochures showing beautiful people dining on a deck overlooking a hippo pool, their meal lit by heavy candelabra. She'd never wanted to sleep in a tent and listen to lions roar outside. She'd come here because she couldn't bear that Jack and Camille would be together all weekend. It didn't matter that they were both attending a conference. They were still together. Working together. Speaking together. Taking meals together.

Hopefully not sleeping together.

But who knew?

The fact that Jack hadn't told her about Camille coming, the fact that he'd planned on Paige being away with the students on their excursion, spoke volumes. He hadn't wanted her to know. He'd intentionally kept Camille's visit a secret. The subterfuge sickened her, reminding her of Ted and how he drank before he came home, and would stay out late, sometimes even checking into a hotel because he'd already had too much to drink and couldn't come home. He'd spent years hiding himself from her. Years acting like one thing when he was behaving differently away from her.

Eyes gritty, a lump in her throat, Paige leaned forward and asked where the camp was. The driver answered that they were almost there.

Paige asked if he'd taken the scenic route.

Baraka laughed. "No, this was the shortcut. But you are in luck, we should hit the camp with just enough time for you to freshen up and go out on the night drive."

Stunned into silence, Paige eyed the back of his head. There was going to be a *night drive*?

"What about dinner?" she asked, her stomach growling. She hadn't eaten much last night, and then she'd skipped breakfast. She was starving now. The last thing she wanted to do was climb back into a four-wheel-drive vehicle and hurtle over dried potholes.

"Dinner is after night drive. Usually at half eight, sometimes nine. It depends on the animals, and if we're far from camp."

She'd decided to come because she'd wanted some quiet, and nature. Her idea of quiet and nature had been resting, lying in a hammock, or maybe in a lounge chair by the pool, reading. Wasn't there a pool?

"What if I don't want to go on the night drive?" she asked tentatively.

Baraka shot her a look as if she'd lost her mind. "But you've come on safari. You've come to see the animals. We have the Big Five, we have it all." They rounded a bend and he stretched his arm out, pointing to a large body of water, a shimmer of silver against the lavender and rose sky. "The Rufiji River," he said with pride. "Our river camp isn't far now. We don't have many guests. I think there are just two other couples, which will make it a very nice stay for you."

No wonder she had gotten such a good rate.

The River Camp director came out to the jeep to meet Paige. Shani was tall, slim, and impossibly beautiful. She thanked Paige for choosing River Camp, and thanked Jabari

Mkapa for sending her. "Mr. Mkapa's brother was a ranger here," Shani said. "He was very popular. We miss him."

"Where is he now?" Paige asked, feeling grimy next to Shani.

"He is at another camp. He is a manager now. He is a rival now." But Shani smiled as she said it. She gestured and Paige's bags were whisked away. Shani presented her with a hot, lavender-scented hand towel. Paige signed paperwork, was given a tall aluminum water bottle that was icy cold and already sweating, and was led back outside to a larger jeep, this one with three rows of staggered seats, rather like theatre seating.

Shani introduced Paige to her guide, Kafil, who was also the driver for the night safari. Kafil was very polite and happy she was joining him and the other couples for the evening. The couples hadn't appeared yet, and she asked if it was possible to get a small snack to take with her. Kafil left and returned almost immediately with two scones as well as cheese and an apple. "I am sorry this isn't more," he said, handing the food to her. "But chef assures me there is a very good dinner tonight and he doesn't want to spoil your appetite."

Paige tried not to be offended, but she was bone weary, starving, and in desperate need of a shower and sleep. Instead, she waited next to the jeep to be introduced to her traveling companions, who were just now making their appearance. The first couple was an older man with a much younger woman. They were European. He was heavyset and balding, while she was blond, tan, curvy, and fit. The second couple was from England, and they were both in their late twenties. They'd gotten married a week ago and were one week into a three-week honeymoon.

Paige kept her introduction brief. She was a professor in California, in Tazania for work.

They welcomed her and since they were couples, she let them choose their seats. The Germans took the high back seat. The British couple took the middle row. She sat in the row right behind Kafil.

They drove for hours looking for wild dogs Kafil had seen earlier, only slowing when they approached a herd of elephants. One of the elephants stood off to the side, near bones on the ground. The elephant's trunk lifted, touched the bones, almost a caress.

"She is paying her respects," Kafil said. "We don't know if the elephant that died was part of this herd, or another, but as elephants pass these bones, there is always interest, and you see the matriarchs stop and stand there, exploring the bones with their trunk."

Paige felt a wave of intense emotion, almost grief, at the idea of an elephant possibly mourning the death of another elephant. She held her breath, worn out, fighting tears.

They stopped for cocktails along the edge of the river. Kafil told everyone to stay close to the jeep, just in case there was a hippo close. Paige chose to sip her wine in the jeep, wanting to play it safe. Kafil passed her some crackers and salted nuts. She thanked him and finished her wine. The wine gave her a pleasant buzz. She liked feeling relaxed, almost numb. Better to be numb than overwhelmed with emotions.

Back at camp, a long table had been set on the deck overlooking the river. Torches were burning, illuminating the space. The tablecloth was white. There were candles flickering down the middle of the table. She heard the roar of lions in the distance.

"I wonder if they're going to walk through camp tonight," she heard the European man say to the young British man. "That was something, eh?"

Paige suppressed a shudder. She couldn't imagine a pride of lions walking through the camp, but then, she didn't want to see a hippo, either, and she'd heard that there was a hippo who did just that. Not every night, or even every week, but he liked to poke around, look for something to eat.

Paige envied the couples who got to walk to their cottages as a pair. Baraka kindly offered to accompany her, and then return in ten minutes so she'd have time to freshen up.

She thanked him profusely.

It was one thing to see big cats, hippos, and elephants at the zoo, and another roaming outside her door.

Dinner was wonderful—a starter, a salad, a main course with many sides. Everyone ate a great deal, and drank even more, but the moment dessert was served, Paige excused herself. She ached everywhere, her head throbbed, she was desperate for a proper shower, her pajamas, and sleep.

Once again Baraka walked her to her cottage, his flashlight on, making the path visible. Her cottage seemed quite far from everyone else. He told her there would be a six a.m. wake-up call, then breakfast. The morning drive would begin at seven sharp. "Animals are most active early in the morning," he said.

She smiled weakly. The morning Yellowstone drive with Jack came to mind. Her smile faded. She did not want to think of him. She did not want to remember anything with him.

Baraka waited while she let herself into her cottage. She said goodnight and then secured her door. After a fast shower, Paige brushed her teeth and put on her pajamas. She turned off the overhead light and was just about to slip between the mosquito nets when she heard a knock on her door.

Paige peeked out the window overlooking the front porch. What?

Jack?

Chapter 19

HAND TREMBLING, PAIGE UNLOCKED THE DOOR. "WHAT are you doing here?" she spluttered, incredulous.

"I came to find you." Jack's jaw was hard, his handsome features set. "I don't suppose you could have picked a camp closer to Arusha."

"I got a good deal here."

"Strange. I didn't. But that's neither here nor there."

For some reason his dark mood made her want to smile. It wasn't the most comfortable trip to the camp, and it probably had been expensive. She didn't consider herself bloodthirsty, but she was glad he found it challenging. She'd found the past forty-eight hours challenging. Make that excruciating. "How did you know where I went?"

"You asked Jabari for recommendations. He told me he'd put in a call to Shani. He put in a call to Shani for me, and here I am."

She lifted her chin. "If you'd wanted to talk to me, you could have just phoned."

"I tried. You didn't answer."

"Must be the poor reception."

"Must be," he said, but from his tone she knew he didn't believe her.

To be honest, she hadn't even turned her phone on. It was still in airplane mode from her flight. "You could have waited until I returned Sunday—"

"I wasn't going to wait."

"You're supposed to be at your conference."

"I've bailed. I came to find you."

He was on her doorstep, so that much was true. "You can go back now," she said primly. "As you can see, I'm fine, and happy here at the Selous Game Reserve."

"Too late. I've withdrawn from the conference."

"That wasn't necessary. We could have spoken when I returned."

"It *was* necessary. I've been worried sick about you."

She arched a brow. "Worried about what?"

"The crazy thoughts going on in your head."

"Crazy thoughts in *my* head? What about the crazy thoughts in *your* head? You knew all along that Camille was coming, you knew she would be showing up in the same place I was, and you didn't think to tell me? You didn't think that I would feel uncomfortable, uneasy, with her being with you while you packed me off on a walking safari with our students? Come on. Surely you understand women . . . *me* . . . better than that?"

He stiffened. "I made a mistake not telling you, but I thought you'd panic, assume the worst—"

"Which I did. But you made me think the worst by not telling me. I don't get it. I genuinely don't understand, Jack." Her gaze lifted, met his, searching for God knows what in his eyes. "I would have much rather heard it from you that Camille was going to be there, while we were still in California, instead of seeing her stroll through our Center as if she owned the place." Paige swallowed hard. "This was my first time coming to Africa. I was excited, so happy to be with you, but then she shows up . . . she's like a nightmare. I can't escape her."

"We do similar work. It's natural for us to move in the same scientific circles."

"Which wouldn't be an issue if you didn't used to sleep together. For years!"

"It was years ago. We don't have a relationship. We haven't had one in years."

"Are you even aware of how she looks at you? She still loves you." Paige snapped her fingers, chest on fire. The problem with being fifty is you knew how these things went. You knew how one could hang on, hoping for something wonderful to happen. She'd hung on to her marriage, hoping Ted would wake up, change, deal with his alcoholism. She'd hung on, hoping they could salvage their marriage. And Camille, a beautiful French Canadian professor, was hoping Jack would choose her again. "Tell me this, is she involved with anyone right now? Does she have a significant other?"

Jack shifted uncomfortably. "I . . . don't know."

"I think you know."

"But I'm not there, Paige. I'm here. With you. I left the conference, I walked away, so I could be with *you*."

They were the right words, at the wrong time. She held herself still, trying to contain the emotions rolling through her, overwhelmed by the riot of love and pain, need and heartbreak. He was everything she'd thought she wanted, but that was before.

Now she saw the truth, and it had been there before her, all this time, only she hadn't wanted to see it.

"Go back to the conference. You can be there in the morning. It's where you belong. Not here—"

"You're wrong," he interrupted curtly. His jaw was hard, lines etched at his mouth and eyes. "If you're here, then I belong here. I belong with you—"

"No."

"Yes. It's why I chased after you when you ran away. I

let you go the first time, but that was a mistake and I vowed I'd never make that mistake again, not with you. Paige, I'm not losing you this time. I won't."

"But I don't want you." Her voice cracked. Tears burned the back of her eyes. She pressed her fists to her sides, trying to keep control. "It's over—"

"Bullshit. You don't get to decide." He ground the words out.

"I can, and I have."

"Paige, I know I hurt you, and you're disappointed, but you can't run away every time there's a misunderstanding. Stand and fight, just the way I'm fighting for you."

"Misunderstanding? Jack, you deceived me. Intentionally." She blinked hard, clearing her eyes. Her chest burned. Her stomach burned. She felt like she was on fire from head to toe, and it wasn't the good kind of fire, it was the kind that destroyed emotion, incinerated love. "I can't trust you. I can't do this with you."

"You can. You're not that fragile."

"You should have told me Camille was coming to Arusha! You should have prepared me."

"You're right. I was wrong. I am wrong. I couldn't be more sorry. Forgive me."

She crossed her arms over her chest, trying to ignore the trembling in her legs and her hands. She felt as if she'd come undone.

"Please," he added. "I screwed up. And I'm sorry, very sorry. Now, can I come in, so we can talk about this in private—"

"No."

"Babe, be reasonable."

"No." Fresh tears filled her eyes. Her throat ached with suppressed emotion. "I can't do this with you, Jack."

"I love you, Paige."

Paige looked away and sank her teeth into the inside of her lip to keep from making a sound.

"I don't love Camille." His voice was rough, low. "I'm completely in love with you. You're meant to be with me. You're my person. My family."

She closed her eyes, stunned by his words. Did he really just say that?

"I know I'm jumping ahead a bit here," he said, "but I fell for you in Paris. It was one of those strange things you hear about. How could one fall in love at first sight? I decided it was a crush, infatuation, and when you returned to California, I told myself okay, she doesn't feel the same way, man up, get over her. But we've always had something, I don't even know what this something is, but I've never felt this with anyone else. Not with Mara, or Camille. Only with you. With you, I feel like me, only better. More complete. Give me a chance, Paige. Don't walk away again. Please."

Every word was perfect. But it was too perfect. None of this could be real. She didn't trust him, or the things he was saying.

"I'm tired, Jack. I don't feel well. I need to go to bed, and you need to return to Arusha. What you do there is your business. All I ask is that you give me space. We're done. I'm sorry. I don't want to hurt you, but it's over. This isn't working for me." Her gaze swept over him, pain splintering in her heart as she saw the shadows in his eyes, the fatigue in his face. "Goodbye, Jack. I'll see you in Arusha Sunday."

She stepped into her cottage on the Rufiji River, locking the door behind her. On her bed, inside the elegant, romantic netting, beneath the high thatched roof, Paige cried her eyes out. Her heart felt broken, just shattered. She'd come so close to having the happy ever after she longed for, the happy ever after she'd wanted so desperately, wanted so badly that she couldn't even let herself admit it.

She loved him.

She loved Jack.

But Jack wasn't the right man for her, not if he didn't understand that honesty was everything, and he hadn't been honest. He hadn't given her the truth she needed.

But oh, his face. The look in his eyes as she said goodbye. It killed her to hurt Jack. She cared so much for him she didn't want to add to his pain, and she could see he was exhausted, could feel his anxiety and concern. She'd always thought Jack was so calm and relaxed, but he'd been anything but calm tonight.

Maybe that was what upset her so much. She knew he cared. Deeply. He hadn't chased her here out of obligation, or guilt. He was here because he loved her, and to hurt someone she loved was incomprehensible. But better to suffer disappointment now, before they were even more attached.

He'd get over her.

She'd get over him.

It would take time, but they'd survive this. They were adults. Mature. Familiar with the game of life. Eventually they'd forget, move on.

HE COULDN'T SLEEP. HE COULDN'T LAY STILL. JACK paced his room most of the night. He tried to lie down but his chest hurt every time he did that, the air trapped inside, making it hard to breathe. It was better to keep moving, better to walk when drowning in shock. Loss.

Jack remembered the last time he'd felt this kind of pain. It'd been the night Mara was dying. That last week she'd been sleeping more and more, her pain only partially eased by morphine, but she'd woken in the middle of the night, looked at him with startling clarity, and told him to love Oliver with all his heart.

It was the easiest promise he'd ever made. He'd kept it, too. He was proud of his son, proud of his strength, proud of his courage and creativity. He was a man with a strong sense of justice, a man who nearly always chose the right thing.

But Oliver had taken a page from Jack's book. He didn't fall in love easily.

He wasn't about to compromise, not in life, not in love.

Relationships were secondary; life's passions came first. His world was the camera and film, and the images he captured for others to enjoy.

But life shouldn't be all work. Life shouldn't just be about accomplishments. There should be love. Companionship. Family. Jack believed in family, and for the past twenty years, Oliver had been his family, but Oliver was grown, and gone, and living his dreams.

Jack wasn't afraid of growing older or being alone. He liked his own company, was comfortable. But Paige had changed everything.

Paige had changed him.

As content as he'd been in his world, with his work and friends, she'd shown him that there was more he'd wanted. More he needed. He needed her. He craved her . . . her company, her smile, her laugh. The little furrow of displeasure she'd get between her brows.

Her uncertainty at his suggestions.

Her love of teaching.

Her absolute devotion to her family.

Her warmth, her kindness, her joy, her curiosity.

He wanted it all. He'd spent most of his life single. He wanted this next chapter of life to include her. He loved her.

He loved her with his whole heart. The good, the bad, the beautiful, the ugly.

Jack finally forced himself to stretch out on the leather sofa facing the sliding French doors. Dawn was close. The dark sky was lightening. The sun would soon rise, and Jack needed to be prepared for the fight of his life.

HE WAS THERE AT BREAKFAST THE NEXT MORNING. Paige couldn't believe it. She didn't know what she thought he'd do—Hide in a room? Take the jeep back to the airstrip and hop on a plane? But no, Jack was at breakfast, freshly shaven, hair combed, dressed in an army-green T-shirt and khaki trousers that hung from his lean hips, making his torso longer, his shoulders broader. The man looked like something out of a movie. He was gorgeous. Masculine. Hers.

No, not hers.

Not, not, not hers. Not anymore.

And yet she couldn't help stealing a glance in his direction as he poured himself a coffee and grabbed a roll and sat down at the far end of the table. How did he look so good after everything that happened last night?

Paige had started with coffee, not sure she could handle much more, but seeing that he was eating, she went to the buffet of fruits, yogurts, eggs, and breads, and took a little of this and that before returning to her chair at the long table where everyone ate family style. Paige ate lightly, trying to pretend she couldn't hear Jack talking to one of the men at the far end of the table. It sounded as if they were speaking German. Or was it Dutch? Either way, she was surprised. How many languages did he speak? Four? Five? More?

The young couple opposite her were blissfully happy. They were the ones on their honeymoon, a British couple, very much in love.

She concentrated on her breakfast—a bite of melon, a bite of mango, a bite of eggs—but it was much harder to eat now that Jack was present. She wished he'd left the camp last night. She wished he'd disappeared so that she could begin moving forward . . . without him. Maybe he was flying out after breakfast. She could only hope.

Kafil appeared in the breakfast room to announce they'd be going on the morning drive soon. "Bring your water bottles," he said. "We will fill them before we go. Fifteen minutes to departure. We've heard there are lions hunting today. We will be going to find them."

Paige glanced at Jack, discovered he was looking at her. She couldn't make out his expression as his lashes lowered over his eyes and the distance between them made her throat ache. She hated that they weren't on the same team anymore, hated that what had seemed so wonderful was anything but.

She turned away, forcing herself to smile at the young British couple who were collecting their cameras and hats, excited by the mention of lions, and were making sure she'd be joining them for this morning's drive.

"Wouldn't miss it," she said, fighting the hot, gritty sensation at the back of her eyes. "Can't wait to see those big cats."

Jack was there with everyone fifteen minutes later when it was time to board the open-air jeep, his icy water bottle in hand. The British honeymooners took the back row. The German couple took the row behind the driver. Paige took the open seat in the middle, certain Jack would take the passenger seat up front. But no, he slid past the others to sit down next to her.

"What are you doing?" she said under her breath, refusing to look at him directly.

"Going on the game drive. What are you doing?" he asked.

She looked at him now, seeing the high forehead, straight nose, square jaw. She ground her teeth together, gave him a death look, intentionally fierce. "I'd prefer you to take the open seat up front."

"And I'd prefer to sit here. With my girlfriend."

She gave him an incredulous look. "*Ex*-girlfriend."

He shrugged. "Semantics."

"If you're not going to move, I will."

"Don't make a scene now. It would just ruin everyone's honeymoon."

She dropped her voice. "I don't make scenes. But I also know when I'm not wanted. Sadly . . ." She gave him a meaningful look before averting her head, her voice drifting off.

Jack laughed.

Paige's jaw dropped, and then she snapped it shut, unable to believe he'd actually had the audacity to laugh now. In the middle of their breakup. "You're cruel," she gritted through clenched teeth.

"You're being dramatic."

Without another word Paige rose, conscious that the young Brits behind her were watching. She gracefully stepped over Jack's long legs and climbed down from the jeep.

Kafil was just about to get behind the wheel and looked at her, concerned.

"Could I sit up front this morning?" she asked. "I sometimes get carsick. I was thinking the fresh air might help me today."

Kafil moved his bag and binoculars off the seat. She thanked him warmly, sat down, and buckled her seat belt. The German couple passed her camp water bottle to her. She knew who had passed it to them, but she thanked them profusely, even as she hoped Jack would forget his seat belt and maybe tumble out when they hit a big rut. It was petty, but it made her feel immeasurably better.

As they left their camp behind, Kafil began talking to them about cats. Lions stalk and chase, but after two hundred yards will give up. The cheetah is more strategic. It's a cunning cat. Leopards chase and pounce. They like to climb trees and lie in wait. Predators have forward-facing eyes. Just like humans.

Like last night, there was a "comfort stop" after the second hour. Everyone spilled out of the jeep. Kafil set up a folding table, covered it with a small checked cloth, placed an ice chest on the ground. There were nuts, muffins, and juices. He poured hot tea for those who wanted it.

Jack took a hot tea. Paige stood at a distance. Suddenly, baboons ran across the field, tearing through a herd of impala, ignoring the big male at the back.

Paige could overhear the German couple speaking to Kafil now, asking about the birds. Last night they'd asked about the birds, too. Apparently, this was their first safari in Tanzania. They'd gone to Botswana last year and raved about the Lilac Breasted Roller. It was common but beautiful. They asked Kafil about his favorite bird. What should they be looking for?

Paige finished her cup of juice and threw the cup in the

waste basket. She could see Jack over her shoulder, studying the landscape.

Kafil began breaking down the table. Everyone started to return to the jeep. The German couple took the second row so that Jack and Paige could be closer. Jack leaned toward her, asking solicitously, "Are you feeling better, dear?"

She turned her head, looked at him, his eyes now hidden by sunglasses. "Much, thank you, dear."

He patted her gently. "Just let me know what I could do to help."

Kafil glanced at her, smiled. "Your fiancé, he's a good man, yes?"

Her fiancé? Is that what he'd told everyone? Paige turned and gave Jack another look, this time arching a brow. She still couldn't see Jack's eyes, but it was impossible to ignore his blinding white smile.

After four and a half hours they made it back to camp. There would be a half hour to freshen up before lunch. Jack headed off to his cottage and Paige watched him go, wanting to chase after him and give him a piece of her mind. Why was he sticking around? Why did he have to torment her? Couldn't he just go? Let her enjoy her safari in peace?

She didn't know how it happened, but the long table from breakfast had been broken into smaller tables, three smaller tables, specifically, one for each couple. The Brits were at theirs. The Germans—an older man and the much younger blonde—at theirs. And then Jack . . . at hers.

She glanced around, thinking there must be some other place she could sit, but there were only the three square tables, each with two place settings.

Baraka appeared from the shadows, walked her to her table, and drew the chair for her. "Good afternoon, Paige," he said cheerfully. "How are you enjoying our river camp?"

"I love it," she said, forcing a smile. "Everyone is so warm and wonderful."

"Did you like the surprise I brought you last night?" he added, gesturing to Jack.

"Quite the surprise," she answered, taking the chair, trying to look anywhere but at Jack.

Baraka went to bring water. Paige drew her napkin off the table and unfolded it over her lap.

"Are we still not talking?" Jack asked evenly.

She jerked her head up, stared at him. "This isn't a game, Jack."

"You're angry."

"Yes, I am."

"Hurt."

"You're very good. A gold star to you. I am angry and hurt. Sad, too. This isn't how I wanted things to go. This isn't what I thought would happen—"

"Then accept my apology. Give me a second chance."

She opened her mouth, closed it. It was a struggle to find her voice. "It's not that simple."

"But it is," he answered. "It's called forgiveness. Forgive me, so we can make this work. There's no reason it can't work. You care for me. I care for you—"

"This will happen again. We'll disappoint each other again."

"Yes. We're human. People make mistakes. Hopefully we can learn from our mistakes and do better."

He wasn't wearing sunglasses now. She could see the shadows beneath his eyes. He looked tired. Troubled. She'd never seen him without that light in his eyes, the teasing glint. It wasn't there now. There was no brightness in him.

"I don't know how to do this," she said quietly, not wanting to inflict more pain but determined to be honest. "I'm scared. Scared at the power you have over me."

"You have the same power over me. My heart—my happiness—rests in your hands. I was planning a future with you. I want you in it." He hesitated. "I need you in it."

Words, she thought. They were just words. But they were also good words, hopeful words.

If only she could believe him.

If only she could forgive him.

Paige wasn't good at forgiving those who hurt her.

She closed her eyes, tried to let go of some of the tightness knotting her stomach. "You know what happens after lunch?" she whispered, not wanting anyone to overhear.

"What?"

"Another game drive." She opened her eyes, looked at him. "Another four hours in the jeep."

He gazed back at her, a long searching look, before nodding once. "There's a lot of jeep time on these safaris."

"I had no idea." She glanced at the other couples. "How do they find it romantic?"

The corner of his mouth twitched. "I have no idea."

Paige cracked a shadow of a smile. "I'm still mad at you," she said after a moment. "We're still in a fight."

"I understand," he said gravely.

"We're not back together," she added for good measure.

He reached across the table and took her hand. "No, we're not." He wrapped both hands around hers, holding it securely between his. "You're angry."

She knew what he was doing now. He was repeating her words back to her. She fought the impulse to melt, or smile. She absolutely, most definitely wasn't going to give him the satisfaction of a smile. Or melting. There would be no melting today. "I'm angry," she agreed.

"You're hurt."

Dammit. He was doing it. Her lower lip quivered. He was breaking her down. He was making her feel. "Yes."

His eyes met hers and held, the gold-brown depths warm, sympathetic. "You're sad."

And Paige's eyes burned, hot, scalding hot, and tears started. She couldn't hold back the tears or the snort of inelegant laughter. "So sad," she repeated, between gasps of laughter. She laughed so hard she cried.

Jack rose, drew her to her feet, signaled to Baraka that

they'd be back, and led her from the lodge to the lounge chairs close to the water. He sat down on one, pulled her onto his lap. She wrapped her arms around his neck and held tight. The tears fell in earnest, real tears, tears because she felt as if she'd lost everything but suddenly hope returned. Possibility was back. She could almost see the future again.

"Jack, I love you so much it scares me," she whispered against his neck. "I can't lose you."

He rubbed her back. "You're not going to."

"I almost did," she sniffed.

"You didn't."

"No, I did," she said firmly.

He laughed softly. "Okay, but it was only in your head. I didn't go anywhere, and I wasn't going to go anywhere. I came prepared to fight for you. I wasn't going to return to Arusha without you, without us being us."

"You should have had a backup plan."

He laughed again, kissed her cheek. "There is you, and only you. And I think that's how it's always been. From the beginning."

She lifted her head, looked into his beautiful face. His smile had faded; his expression was somber, determined. She kissed his forehead, his skin warm against her lips. "Don't break my heart."

"That's the last thing I want to do. It's my job to protect your heart. To protect you." He cupped her face in his big hands, the palms calloused. "Paige, marry me."

She hadn't heard him right. She frowned, stared at him, confused.

"I'm sure you understood me," he said. "My accent isn't that strong anymore."

"But . . ."

He lifted a brow. "Mmm?"

"You don't marry."

"Oh, but I do. If it's the right person." He brushed delicate strands of hair from her brow. "If it's you."

"I didn't want to marry again."

"That's what you've said. I'm not trying to fire you up, but I'm not sure I believe you." He kissed her before she could protest. It was a long, hot, bone-melting kiss that had her leaning against his chest, weak. Dazed.

"You never married Camille," she whispered.

"I never loved Camille, not the way I love you." His expression shifted, lips flattening. "Can we not talk about her, though? I like her. I respect her. But she's not part of this equation. She never has been."

She pressed her lips to his, breathing him in. "What is the equation?"

"For someone so very good at math, it's stunning to discover how you struggle with single digits."

She kissed him again. "Humor me, Dr. King."

He kissed her, another long, scorching kiss, one that wasn't as tender, one that felt demanding, hungry, possessive. "It goes like this, Dr. Newsome. One plus one equals we, which in essence, is one. Together we're one, and strong, far stronger than when we're just . . . one."

"I'm amazed you can even teach statistics. That was terrible."

He grinned. She smiled back at him, loving him, so very much. "Are you really proposing?" She looked into his eyes; the green and gold flecks were ever so bright. "Or is this a spur-of-the-moment desperado thing?"

He reached into his deep trouser pocket, his hand sliding beneath her bottom, and retrieved a handkerchief. Inside the white linen was a ring with diamonds and a large, intensely blue stone. "It's not a sapphire," he said. "It's tanzanite. I bought the ring for you last week—"

"Why?"

His forehead creased. He gave her a look of infinite patience. "Because I planned on proposing before you returned home with the students."

"This wasn't a spur-of-the-moment thing."

"No. Well, today, yes, but I knew I couldn't let you return to California without letting you know how I felt. You're part of my heart, Paige, and I want you to be part of my life. Forever."

"Until we grow old?" she asked, blinking hard, wanting to remember every word because he was saying such nice words.

The corner of his mouth tugged. "I think that's what forever means."

Emotion thickened her throat, and she bit into her lower lip to keep it from trembling. Her gaze dropped to the stunning ring in the platinum setting. "Can I try it on?"

"Is that a 'yes, Jack, I'd love to marry you' response?"

She dashed away the tears. Her smile was watery, but happy. "Yes. I think we've gone mad, and we're breaking all our rules, but I'd love to be with you even when we're old and gray."

He started to slide the ring onto her finger. She stopped him, her hand curling into a fist. "Jack."

"Yes, babe?"

She searched his eyes. "Do we have to get married? Or could this be a ring that says I'm yours, and I'll always be yours?"

"Marriage scares you."

She nodded. "I'm not afraid to love you. I want to be with you. I'm just not sure marriage is the right thing . . . for us." She swallowed hard. "At least right now."

He was silent a moment. "I don't need a wedding. I just need you."

"I need you, too." She hugged him hard, and then whispered, "But can I wear the ring? Can we be engaged?"

"To not marry?"

"Engaged to be together," she corrected. "Forever."

He slipped the ring onto her ring finger. The gorgeous blue stone shimmered in the sunlight. She looked down at the beautiful tanzanite, and then up at him. "I love you, Jack King."

"And I love you, Paige, my queen."

She wrinkled her nose, laughed. "I know what you did there."

"I figured you would." He rose with her, set her on her feet. "Let's go get lunch or we're going to be famished on the next drive."

"I dread these drives."

"We should have a nice break between the afternoon drive and evening one." He took her hand in his, kissed it. "Some people nap. Some do other things."

"I think we need to nap," she said. "It's been an exhausting day."

"I agree with you. Let's nap so tonight—"

"—after our evening drive—"

"—we can do other things."

She kissed him. "Deal."

Epilogue

A LOT CAN HAPPEN IN A YEAR.

Hearts change, lives change, careers change.

Paige spent winter break the following year teaching in Arusha, working with Salma, concentrating on educating teachers who wanted to reach the girls in the communities that didn't have access to the larger, better funded schools.

While she spent January teaching teachers, Jack was in Arusha as well, finishing a course with his Princeton grad students, this being Jack's final year at Princeton. In the Fall, he'd put the word out he was looking for a position in California and immediately the job offers poured in— Stanford, USC, UC Berkley, UC San Diego, and San Diego State, among a half dozen others. In the end, he took the offer from UC Irvine because he respected their environmental science program and it was the school closest to Paige and Orange.

They were going to look for a home together in May, after Jack permanently moved to California. They wanted something near the water, but were open to the foothills, too, possibly property with orange trees overlooking the mission in San Juan Capistrano.

Paige had been able to go on two trips with Jack in the past year: one to his native Australia, and the other to Buenos Aires and then down to Patagonia. It was in Buenos Aires that he proposed again, just in case she'd changed her mind about marriage, or at least, marrying him.

She had.

Oh, she had.

And now they were marrying today, a ceremony organized by their friends Jabari and Nyah Mkapa, because as Jabari said, he knew everyone. And he did.

The wedding was going to be on the other side of the pool beneath the dappled shade of a sculptural acacia tree. Paige had bought a new dress before her trip to Arusha. It was the palest blue, elegant, pretty, with long dramatic sleeves, the lovely fabric fitted but not clingy. Jack looked dashing—impossibly handsome—in a black suit with a crisp white shirt, open at the collar, setting off his face and tan. He'd shaved for the wedding and looked every inch a movie star.

She felt like they were in Paris again, and it was just the two of them. She felt hopeful, joyful, content. They'd decided not to invite their children, or other family members, for the wedding. The wedding would be a surprise, but that was okay, and the ceremony, brief as it would be, was about them, and their vows. They were marrying for good days and bad, knowing full well they weren't ever going to be young again, but in no hurry to be old, either. Age was just a state of the mind, and they were both too happy together to be afraid. Life was short. Time was precious. They'd grown.

Paige only had eyes for Jack as the minister pronounced them husband and wife, but as they turned to smile at their friends, she saw in her mind's eye their children, for they were never far from her thoughts.

In August, Michelle had married her boyfriend, Garrett, at a lovely winery in Woodinville. Paige had been there, holding in her concerns, proud of her beautiful, brave daughter who loved so deeply and couldn't wait to be a mom.

Nichole had had another promotion. She and her boyfriend, Andreas, had broken up again. It was too hard on him to see her advancing so quickly.

Ashley had a place of her own in LA and was auditioning, taking acting classes, and waitressing to make ends meet. When Oliver was in town, they'd get together for a drink.

Oliver was always kind, always encouraging, remarkable considering he'd just earned his first Oscar nomination for Best Documentary. Paige was sure it would be the first of many.

And soon she'd return to California, back to work.

Paige's eyes watered as she looked at her person, her Jack. One more semester apart before they'd be together forever. Spring semester was just ten days away. He'd return to Princeton and she to Orange County, but first, the honeymoon.

The Mkapas and the Kanumbas saw them to the car that would take them to the airport, and then they were flying back to the River Camp in the Selous Game Reserve where Shani had booked them the honeymoon suite for the next week.

As they checked in and signed the paperwork, Paige wrote her name, and then she shyly crossed it out, writing *Dr. Paige King* instead.

She studied the new signature. Dr. Paige King. She loved the way it looked, loved the way it sounded. Glancing up at Jack, she smiled, her heart full.

Fairy tales did come true.

ACKNOWLEDGMENTS

I love my brilliant family of engineers and scientists; my cousins motivate me with their work, their passion, and their desire to leave the world a better place than they found it.

The character of Dr. Jack King was inspired by my cousin's husband, an epidemiologist who works with students and colleagues all around the world.

I must also thank my brother, Dr. Thom Porter, a business professor at UNC Wilmington. I asked Thom endless questions about academia and university policy to make sure I had the details right. Obviously, every university is different, but thank you, Thom, for always taking my call!

This book wouldn't have happened without my good friend and entertainment lawyer Maggie Marr's hard push, and it definitely wouldn't have sold without my agent Holly Root's vision and enthusiastic support.

Thank you to Berkley Senior Editor Cindy Hwang for believing in me. Thank you to Angela Kim for your endless help, and thank you to Hope Ellis for my favorite copyediting experience ever! I appreciate everyone at Berkley who has worked to make *Flirting with Fifty* successful.

Thank you to Barbara Ankrum for your story expertise, and my friends and first readers for being so generous with your thoughts and feedback.

Thank you to Cyndi Johnson for inspiration, encouragement, and forty-three years of friendship. This story wouldn't exist without you!

Lastly, this story is for readers of all ages—we just get better as we get older. Embrace life and love and remember you are valuable, and wonderful, just the way you are.

RAIN SPLATTERED THE KITCHEN WINDOW, WHILE INSIDE the house smelled of roast turkey and mulled wine. Andi McDermott peeked into the second oven where the stuffing, potatoes, and various side dishes were keeping warm. It was December twenty-second and Andi was celebrating Christmas early, hosting her stepson, Luke, and his fiancée for dinner. She'd spent days cooking, decorating the house, even putting up a big tree—a first since her husband, Kevin, died five years ago.

It was the first Christmas since Kevin had died that she felt festive. Maybe it was the cooking and baking that put her in a good mood. Or maybe she'd finally accepted that Christmas would be different, and she couldn't compare the holiday now to what it had been when Kevin was alive.

She'd even begun dating again this year, not that that was going so well, but she was trying, reminding herself that she needed to be open to new experiences, and actively create new memories. Not everything could be about Kevin, and how it used to be. She was too young to live trapped in the past.

But it'd be lovely to see Luke, to have him here. Her stepson was a busy doctor living in Virginia and when he returned to Southern California, there were so many people for him to see that it was hard for him to squeeze her in, but this year he'd accepted her Christmas invitation, and he and Kelsey would arrive any moment.

Andi glanced from the rain-streaked window to the small TV. The local evening news was wrapping up with a feel-good story set at Lake Arrowhead's Santa's Village. It was snowing in the mountains and the pretty reporter kept batting away fluffy flakes as she laughingly asked Mr. and Mrs. Claus if the snow would hamper the delivery of gifts. Santa Claus gave a jolly chuckle, saying that the reindeer were experts, and Rudolph always led the way. The cameraman panned over the charming snow-dusted village and the reporter concluded with the reminder that Santa's Village would be open through five o'clock on Christmas Eve, inviting all to come enjoy the live entertainment, the scheduled light shows, and of course, meet Sant Nick himself.

Andi smiled wryly, remembering the year she and Kevin had taken Luke to Santa's Village. It hadn't been a successful trip. California had been in the middle of a drought. There was no snow and the trees looked brown and parched. The park hadn't yet been refurbished and nine-year-old Luke wasn't impressed, announcing to a line of children that Santa wasn't real, even babies knew that. Kevin and Andi apologized to the other parents, marched Kevin to the car, and returned to their cabin in Blue Jay, where Luke promptly disappeared into his bedroom with his computer, preferring his own company over being with either of them.

Andi brushed a crumb from the counter, turned off the double ovens, and tried to remember the last time she'd been to the cabin in Blue Jay.

It had been years, two or three, at least, and she'd only driven up because she'd been notified by her intimidating neighbor, Wolf Enders, that one of the big sugar pines on her lot had fallen. While it had missed her cabin, he told her tersely, it had crushed the old shed, and was blocking her driveway (and some of his).

She hadn't been able to make the drive to the cabin immediately due to work, but she'd drove up that Saturday morning to meet the tree removal service, paying them a fortune to cut up the huge tree and carry away the massive logs. At any moment she'd expected Wolf Enders and his huge German shepherd to appear, but thankfully, neither did. She'd escaped back to San Juan Capistrano without any uncomfortable scenes. To be fair, she'd never quarreled with Wolf, but Kevin had, and once Kevin sued Wolf for defamation of character, the animosity between Kevin and Wolf made trips to the cabin unbearable.

Andi had hated being caught in the middle, hated how Kevin obsessed about their "trashy neighbor," hated how prickly and uncomfortable she felt whenever Wolf Enders looked at her. Wolf made her feel naked and she didn't like it. She wouldn't call him trashy—she wouldn't call anyone trashy—but they definitely moved in different social circles.

The evening news ended. Andi glanced at her watch. Six thirty.

Luke said he and Kelsey should arrive sometime between five thirty and six, depending on traffic. They were coming from Newport Beach, where Luke's mom and grandparents lived, and traffic could be a bear, especially this time of year. The drizzle of rain just made it worse.

Andi drew a short breath, anxious, excited. The house looked wonderful. The brandied cranberries and green salad were already on the table. Bottles of red and white wine had both been opened just in case Luke and Kelsey didn't want the mulled wine.

Muting the TV, Andi wandered into the formal living room to fluff a couch pillow. The tree glowed with lights and shimmering ornaments. It had taken two days to get the house decorated but it was worth it. She'd forgotten how pretty everything looked decorated for the holidays.

Back in the kitchen she adjusted the cake stand on the marble island, then smoothed her dark green beaded sweater over her hips. She felt a little too solid, and thick in the middle, but the beaded sweater had been one of her last gifts from Kevin and she'd never had a chance to wear it before he died, so she was wearing it tonight. Tonight was a celebration. Luke would be here, and they'd be a family, and being ten or fifteen pounds overweight wasn't the end of the world. Being twenty pounds overweight wasn't the end of the world. Her weight wasn't important.

Family was.

Christmas.

Miracles.

Suddenly Andi's phone rang. It was Luke. She quickly picked up. "Hi," she said breathlessly, leaning against the island. "Where are you? Have you hit some traffic?"

"We haven't left Mom's yet." Luke's deep voice was so very much like his dad's that it gave her a pang. "We got to talking and the time slipped away from us."

She pushed a loose tendril from her warm cheek. "That's okay. I've got everything in the oven. Just give me a buzz when you're a few minutes from the house and I'll dish up. We'll sit down straight away—"

"Something has come up," he said in a rush. "We're not going to be able to make it. I'm sorry. I know it's last minute to cancel."

Her heart fell. For a moment she couldn't speak. "Kelsey's not sick, is she?" Andi asked, grateful her voice didn't quaver.

"No, she's good. We're all good. Mom surprised us with tickets to Segerstrom for the Holiday Organ Spectacular tonight. She forgot we were supposed to be going to your house for dinner, and Kelsey is an organist, she played all through school, music being her minor at Johns Hopkins, and . . ." He stopped talking, waited a split second before adding, "You don't mind, do you?"

Andi blinked hard. Her throat thickened with emotion. She minded. Oh, how she minded.

But she'd never tell him. She was his stepmom, not his mom. She couldn't afford to make a misstep.

Luke filled the silence. "I hate doing this last minute. It's hard keeping everyone happy—"

She wasn't going to cry. She wouldn't be difficult. "I understand."

"Kelsey does want to meet you."

"Drop by tomorrow." She glanced to her double ovens, filled with turkey and casseroles. "I'll have plenty of food."

"Maybe. That could work," he said.

Her heart fell again. A maybe from Luke was never a positive thing.

He cleared his throat. "Next time we're home, we'll get together. I promise. You'll meet Kelsey before the wedding. Maybe at the bridal shower in February?"

Andi heard the maybe again. Maybe meant nada. Nothing. She hated the ridiculous pain making her chest burn. She'd always been the stepmother, never mother, never mom, never needed or wanted, at least, not by him, and that was all she'd ever wanted, to be a mother. To have a big family. But it wasn't to be. Fate had a different path for her. "Maybe," she echoed, brushing a tear from her lashes before it could fall. "Give your family my best."

"I will. Merry Christmas, Andi."

"Merry Christmas, Luke."

Hanging up, Andi set the phone down on the island and rested her hand on the cold marble, throat aching, chest tight. *Don't think, don't feel, don't get emotional. Things happen. Life happens. Roll with the punches. You're good at that.*

But her chest was on fire and she wished she were anywhere but here, in this big empty house, with a big tree that no one but her would see.

This wasn't how Christmas was supposed to be.

This wasn't how she wanted to spend the holidays anymore.

The house was too big for her. She'd been widowed too young. The memories were hard. She missed Kevin and knew he wasn't coming back. She'd even begun dating, but if she was brutally honest with herself, it wasn't going well.

Friends had invited her to join them for Christmas, but being a plus-one at Thanksgiving was a different thing than being a plus-one at Christmas. Christmas was about family, intimacy. It wasn't a party like Halloween or New Year's Eve. It was quiet, personal, *sacred*.

Heart aching, Andi turned and looked at the three-layer Christmas White Cake on the pale pink cake stand—an heirloom in the McDermott family. The Christmas White Cake could have been plucked from Santa's Village with its dusting of sparkling sugar and miniature forest of edible pine trees. It was an old *Southern Living* recipe, something Andi's mother had made when Andi was growing up, and when Andi made it the first time as a newlywed, Kevin asked that she make it every Christmas, and she did. The three-layer cake was a labor of love, and she regretted the afternoon spent making all the delicate sugar decorations.

Why had she gone to so much trouble? Why didn't she learn? Why hadn't she just bought a cake? Why had she thought Luke would show?

Luke had tolerated her, but never loved her.

He was the only child she'd ever have, and she'd tried and tried, not because she had to, but because she wanted to. And now she was fifty-seven, almost fifty-eight, with no children of her own, no husband, and another Christmas alone.

She couldn't do it. Not here. Not like this.

But the cake wouldn't be wasted. Knocking away tears, Andi reached into a drawer for a knife, cut a huge slice from the cake, and fed herself a humongous bite. The cream cheese frosting clung to her lip. The cake was moist. She cried stupid tears as she chewed.

The cake was perfect.

The house looked perfect.

Dinner would have been perfect.

The tears fell harder. Andi threw away the rest of the slice, tore off a strip of paper towel, wiped her mouth, dried her eyes, blew her nose. She couldn't do this. Couldn't fall apart just because Luke had bailed on her.

She needed to rethink the holiday, come up with a new plan, one that didn't require her rattling around this huge house on her own.

Maybe she should drive up to Lake Arrowhead and open the cabin, have Christmas there. With all the fresh snow, it'd be a white Christmas. She'd always loved the cabin. It'd be magical once she was there.

Of course there was Wolf Enders, but maybe he wasn't there. And even if he was, so what? She wouldn't be intimidated. She was tired of being stepped on. Tired of accommodating everyone else.

She was going to create new memories. Start new traditions. She'd drive to Lake Arrowhead early in the morning and have a magical Christmas all on her own.

THE DISTANT, RHYTHMIC THUDDING SOUND WOULDN'T stop, the dull thudding irritating, interrupting Wolf's focus.

Wolf set his drafting pencil down and listened. There was a pause and then the thudding resumed. Someone was chopping something, and very close by.

But there were no neighbors close to him. He lived high on the mountain in a gated community. He was one of the few people who lived here year-round. Wolf had a small house in San Juan Capistrano in the historic Los Rios district, but rented it on VRBO, and due to the proximity to the mission, the ocean, and Disneyland, it was booked most of the time, providing steady income.

When Wolf had bought the cabin ten years ago, it was a

wreck, having been on the market for over a year, the asking price—as well as the condition—discouraging other offers. But Wolf wasn't discouraged, and he'd made a low offer, aware of all the work he'd need to do, and was ready to do, as he'd just retired from contracting work after a career in the Marine Corps, and had time on his hands and a burning need to stay busy.

The owner rejected Wolf's offer, but when five months passed, and no other offers came in, he reached out to Wolf's real estate agent and indicated he was open to a decent offer. Wolf followed up with an offer even lower than his initial one. The owner countered. Wolf countered again, and this time his offer was reluctantly accepted. The bank wouldn't approve the loan after the home inspection report came in. Between termites and wood rot, the inspector said the 1927 cabin should just be scrapped. Tear it down, clear the lot, build again. But Wolf liked the big old logs, the vaulted, beamed ceiling, the scarred hardwood floor, and he was able to get a VA loan, allowing him to purchase the place and do the work himself. Over the next three years he fixed the foundation, replaced logs, reroofed, scraped peeling paint from original windows, put in a new furnace and water heater, replaced the chinking, and restained the interior and exterior. His cabin might be rustic on the outside, but it was comfortable inside. It was Wolf's haven, and with his dog, Jax, for company, he was rarely lonely.

The chopping sound stopped but Wolf was now curious. He rose from his drafting table and stepped outside. Jax followed, always close to his side. Wolf had only two real neighbors—the McDermotts and the Olsens—and neither had been up to Blue Jay for years. The Olsens were in their eighties and lived in a retirement community in Palos Verdes, and after self-righteous Kevin McDermott died five years ago from a heart attack, his widow didn't visit anymore. So who would be cutting what? And where?

Jax whined and Wolf touched the top of Jax's head. "Should we go check it out?" he asked.

The dog nudged his hand.

Wolf went inside, put his heavy boots on, and grabbed his winter coat from the hook by the door before heading back out. The chopping sound echoed through the trees. Wolf crossed the shoveled walkway to stand at the top of his property. He could see a light glowing from one of the McDermott cabin's upstairs rooms. So someone was there.

The slope between his place and the McDermotts' was fairly steep and thickly wooded. Wolf had been adding cedars and dogwoods each autumn for the past several years, wanting more privacy, enjoying his seclusion.

Jax took off, bounding in front of him. Wolf followed, boots crunching snow. It was a cold, clear morning. The sun was shining brightly in the blue sky, casting long gold rays through the tall trees. There would be no more snow for days, maybe weeks, but this high on the mountain, beneath the shade of the big trees, the white stuff would linger.

Wolf heard a shriek and, quickening his pace, reached a clearing where Jax was staring down Andi McDermott. He snapped his fingers and Jax sat, his German shepherd's intent gold gaze locked on the neighbor's face.

He didn't blame his dog. Andi McDermott had a very pretty face.

Her head jerked up, long dark curls falling over her shoulders, wide brown eyes meeting his. "So Axel is still terrorizing the neighborhood," she said tautly, heat blazing in her eyes.

Wolf's dog Axel had been the source of complaints, which led to the lawsuit. "Axel died," Wolf said bluntly. "This is Jax. He's just eighteen months. Still a pup."

She glanced down at the black and gold dog and then up at him, expression incredulous. "A pup?"

"He is a big shepherd," Wolf agreed. He snapped his fingers again and Jax retreated, coming to stand at Wolf's side.

"He shouldn't be off leash," she said, shifting the hatchet

from one hand to the other. Her gloves lay at her feet. Her hands were dark pink with cold.

"He's on my property," Wolf answered. "And so are you," he added, looking past her to the tree she'd savaged. "What are you doing?"

Her chin lifted. She arched an imperious brow. "Cutting down a Christmas tree."

He matched her arched eyebrow with one of his. "You don't have any trees of your own? You had to take one of mine?"

"One of yours? What do you mean?"

He pointed to a yard stake with pink tape over in the distant corner, and then to another stake on the opposite side. "That is your property, south of the stake. Everything north, including where we are standing, is mine."

"I don't know where those sticks came from, but you have it wrong. This is the McDermott property. It's always been our backyard. It's where we used to have a treehouse for Luke. This is where he always played."

"Yes, on *my* property. I never pushed it with your husband, as it seemed pointless with all the other garbage going on, but after your husband died, I had a surveyor come, put up boundaries. Just in case you chose to sell your place."

"Sell? Why would we sell? This property has belonged to the McDermotts for generations. *Generations*," she repeated. "You bought your cabin just a few years ago—"

"Ten," he corrected. "I've been here for ten years now, and I wanted to make sure we were both clear on our property lines." Wolf gestured to the stakes again. "This is all mine. That," he said, pointing to a narrow strip of land below the stakes, "is yours, plus whatever land is in front of your cabin."

"Why am I only learning about this now?"

"You haven't been here in years." Wolf caressed Jax's head. "But now that you're here, you can see the stakes, and let the rest of your family know. My land versus your land."

"And this tree?" she said, two splotches of color in her cheeks, a fiery contrast to the paleness of her skin.

"Mine," he answered.

"Yes, but what do we do now? Do I leave it? Can I have it?"

"You can buy it from me."

She swallowed. "How much?"

"Two hundred dollars."

"What?"

"These are not seedlings that sprang up in this corner. I planted each of these trees over the past few years. They came in twenty-five-gallon containers; the five in this corner alone were over twelve hundred dollars."

"You're bluffing."

"You want to see a receipt?"

"Yes. No." Andi McDermott reached up and touched a line of red on her jawbone. She'd either scratched or cut herself. She turned away from him, staring at the little thicket of trees and then the snow-covered slope. "There are so many trees here already. Why plant more?"

"For privacy. I don't want to see your cabin from my place."

She gave him a quick look before glancing away. "I would have never taken one of your trees if I'd known."

He said nothing.

"Nor would I have trespassed," she added fiercely. "You should have sent a letter, or called me, told me about the survey. You were able to let me know about the tree on the shed. Not sure why you couldn't let me know about the property lines."

"It's not a big deal."

"But it is. I've just killed one of your trees and spent money I didn't intend to spend—" She broke off, pressed her lips together. "Will you accept a check? I don't have that much cash on me right now."

"You can pay me before you head back down the mountain."

"Thank you," she said stiffly.

He held his hand out for the hatchet. She frowned, not understanding. "I'll finish the job for you," he said. "Might as well take advantage of me since I'm here."

Wordlessly she handed him the hatchet. It took him just two whacks to fell the tree. He then made a few more cuts, cleaning up the base, making it more level and removing a few of the lower branches so she'd be able to get it in the stand.

He returned the hatchet to her and lifted the tree, swinging it easily onto his shoulder. "Lead the way."

"You make it look so easy." She picked up her gloves and started walking. "I've been out here forever."

"It would have been easier to just buy a tree already in a stand," he answered, following her. "The tree lots are full of them."

"I thought this would be more fun. Kind of like *Little House in the Big Woods.*"

She sounded a little forlorn and looked like a marshmallow in her big white puffy coat, the tail of her red flannel shirt sticking out beneath. "Next time use an ax," he said. "It's bigger. Even a handsaw would have been better."

"Isn't this an ax?" she asked, lifting the tool.

"It's a hatchet. Axes are bigger. They usually need two hands."

"There aren't many tools anymore, not after the shed came down."

"You never replaced it," he said.

"I didn't see the point. It was mostly storage for summer months, and no one was coming here anymore."

But she was here now, he thought, climbing the stairs to her porch and placing the tree upright against the cabin.

"Thank you for the help," Andi said, facing him, her breath clouding on the air. She looked at the tree, and then reached out to touch one green springy branch.

From this angle, the tree was big. Eight feet, at least. "Do you need help getting it into the stand?"

"I'm fine. I can manage."

"If something goes wrong . . ." He didn't finish the thought. She did. "I know where to find you, but I won't."

Because they weren't friends, and her husband had hated

him. Wolf nearly smiled. It was time he left, but there was something he needed to say. He hesitated. "If I hadn't said so before, I'm sorry about your husband."

"You sent a card after he died."

"Did I?"

She nodded. "It was kind of you, considering . . . the friction."

He admired the way she glossed over a five-year feud. "I'm sure it hasn't been easy, though."

"No," she agreed. "But I'm learning to stand on my own two feet, and it's been good for me. I never had to be independent before." And then, as if she'd said too much, she reached for the tree. "I promise to get you the money before I leave."

"Don't worry about it."

"No, I will. I don't want to owe you anything. It's better this way."

"Fine, then. Merry Christmas, Mrs. McDermott."

Color flooded her cheeks. Her head jerked up and her eyes, brown with those flecks of gold, locked with his, her jaw jutting before she looked away. "Merry Christmas."

Wolf headed down the steps with Jax, crossed her driveway, and walked to the street toward his driveway.

He'd never seen Andi McDermott in jeans before. Or hiking boots. Or in a puffy coat with a flannel shirt hanging out.

He'd never seen her with her dark curls down, or without her pearls, because Andi McDermott always wore pearls—pearls with cardigan sweaters, pearls with tailored blouses, pearls with a perfectly done face, even in the mountains. She dressed like the women who had been his mother's friends in New Orleans. Polished. Sophisticated. Sinless.

He liked women who sinned. Women who loved sex, and he doubted proper Mrs. McDermott loved sex, much less hot, dirty sex. He imagined everything was pretty tame in the McDermott bedroom, and if Kevin wanted something non-vanilla, he went elsewhere.

Although beautiful, the married Andi McDermott

hadn't been his type, but the widowed Andi struggling to chop down one of his trees intrigued him.

It wasn't just the jeans and flannel shirt beneath the jacket. It wasn't just her dark hair falling down her back in long ringlets. It was the emotion in her eyes, the red flush of exertion, the cut across her jawbone, the press of her full lips. She had the most extraordinary mouth. A mouth made for kissing. And other things.

As she'd talked, he'd let her words slide past and he focused on her lips, and the gold speckles in her eyes.

He imagined his hands on her waist and sliding them down to cup her butt. She'd be warm, soft. He hadn't been with anyone in a number of months, too busy with project deadlines, but suddenly he felt the ache of desire.

Of need.

But they weren't friends. They weren't even neighborly. When Kevin died, they'd been in the middle of a lawsuit. Wolf had laughed when he'd read that Kevin McDermott was suing him for defamation of character, but the cost of hiring an attorney to handle the lawsuit hadn't been funny.

Andi withdrew the lawsuit three months after her husband's funeral.

Wolf had received a letter in the mail from his lawyer, letting him know it was over, done. Mrs. McDermott had paid the legal fees for his attorney, too, and after two years of bitterness, everyone was free to move on. Let bygones be bygones.

He should have thanked her today for dismissing the suit. He should have said something about it, but she'd caught him by surprise, chopping down one of his trees with a ridiculously small hatchet.

At his door, he knocked the snow off the soles of his boots and then eased them off once inside. Closing the door behind Jax, Wolf hung up his coat, straightened the boots so they were neatly lined up, and after pouring a fresh cup of coffee returned to his drafting table. He was way behind on his deadlines. He had accepted too many projects, but when you worked for yourself, you couldn't afford to turn work away.

But back at his drafting table, Wolf found it hard to focus on the plans in front of him. He liked the addition he'd been commissioned to do. He was invested in the remodel, historic cottages being his specialty, but he kept thinking of Andi McDermott dragging that tree into her cabin and getting it into a stand. It wasn't going to be easy for her.

But she hadn't asked for his help. She'd made it clear she could handle it.

And to be honest, he didn't want to put up her tree. He wanted to handle her.

ANDI WATCHED WOLF AND HIS DOG WALK AWAY.

She hadn't seen Wolf in years, and she'd forgotten just how big he was. The man was huge, broad-shouldered, long legs, six four, if not taller. He looked like a mountain man, barely civilized, with his wild salt-and-pepper hair and matching beard.

She'd forgotten other things about him, too.

She'd forgotten he had high hard cheekbones, a strong brow, a firm mouth, and light gray eyes that reminded her of mist. He had very straight, white teeth, which you rarely saw as he wasn't inclined to smile, or speak very often.

She'd heard that he used to be part of the military and did lots of dangerous secret operations. She'd always wanted to know more, but Kevin hadn't liked her questions, unhappy that his wife was curious about someone so completely opposite himself.

Kevin had hated Wolf with a passion. Everything about Wolf—the attitude, the motorcycles, the beard, the tattoos—set him off. Andi had been caught in the middle. She'd never thought Wolf was as bad as Kevin made him out to be, but marriage was about loyalty, and the lines were drawn. She knew she had to have Kevin's back. It wasn't an option.

Taking a deep breath, Andi lifted the tree and half carried, half dragged it through the front door, into the living room. The tree was tall, but slender, and after some wrestling, she got it into the stand, determined that she wouldn't need more help. It took a few minutes, but once the tree was in an upright position, secure in the old metal stand, she gave a little cheer, some of her battered self-esteem restored.

She did it.

Everything suddenly seemed a bit brighter.